WIVES
HUSBANDS *and* LOVERS

A COLLECTION OF NINE SEX STORIES

BEN E. DORM

WARNING

Please feel free to send me an email. Just know that these emails are filtered by my publisher. Good news is always welcome.

Ben E. Dorm - **ben_e_dorm@awesomeauthors.org**

About the Publisher

4Fun Publishing, a member of **BLVNP Incorporated**, 340 S. Lemon #6200, Walnut CA 91789, info@blvnp.com / legal@blvnp.com

NOTE: Due to the highly emotional reaction of some people to works of erotic fiction, any email sent to the above address that contains foul language or religious references is automatically deleted by our anti-spam software and will not be seen. All other communications are welcome.

DISCLAIMER

Please don't be stupid and kill yourself. This book is a work of FICTION. Do not try any new sexual practice that you find in this book. It is fiction and not to be confused with reality. Neither the author nor the publisher or its associates assume any responsibility for any loss, injury, death or legal consequences resulting from acting on the contents in this book. Every character in this book is over 18 years of age. The author's opinions are not to be construed as the opinions of the publisher. The material in this book is for entertainment purposes ONLY. Enjoy.

Wives, Husbands And Lovers

A Collection of Nine Sex Stories

By: Ben E. Dorm

© **Ben E. Dorm 2015**

ISBN: 978-1-68030-349-0

Stories Inside!

CORRUPTING BARBARA

BEN E. DORM

Chapter One

The audacity of the question caught Barbara by surprise. She blinks and gulps at her drink, then eventually splutters because she forgot it was wine in the glass. Swigging the stuff down like water was a mistake.

Struggling, Barbara stammers, "I… uh… I mean to say, Tuh-Tanya…" The heat rises in her face and she falls silent. Barbara doesn't have the words to respond. Her mouth hangs open while thoughts collide in a discordant jumble of conflicting impressions.

Everything is all furred up by the afternoon wine. *Dear God*, she thought, *it must be a bottle each by now!*

Barbara eyes, an offending article, a bottle of Sauvignon Blanc sat on the low table in front of her. Rather blurry, Barbara shifts on the very large, very comfortable three-seater sofa. She realizes that it's the third bottle, but it registers vaguely.

Slack-faced she lifts her face towards her host when Tanya cajoles her with, "Come on, Babs. Don't be shy. It's just a laugh."

Looking at the younger woman – who seems unaffected by so much drink – Barbara sees mischievous eyes twinkling in Tanya's elfin face. She takes in the detail of Tanya's platinum-blonde bobbed hair, dark roots visible in a central parting which, she believes, are the season's *de-rigueur*. She thinks dark roots are a particularly trampy look, but acknowledges Tanya carries it off well. In Barbara's estimation her host is a very pretty girl, but the understanding is slowly dawning and Barbara is coming to realize the innocence the young woman projects are rather misleading.

Barbara thinks the tramp style might be appropriate as she lowers her appraisal to Tanya's generous bosom beneath the tight, button-fronted blouse and smart, waist-length fawn jacket. A high-hemmed skirt rides up to Tanya's thighs, exposing a lot of bare, gym-toned and pleasantly tanned leg and Barbara is suddenly even more self-conscious when confronted with Tanya's physical appeal.

"Oh, Tanya, I don't know if that's entirely appropriate…" says Barbara, her tone stiff and pompous. She gulps more wine and wonders how the Liverpudlian girl can be so confident and self-assured, envy at Tanya's effervescence mixing in with what she perceives as her own repressed and strait-laced character.

Tanya's eyes roll as she says, "You won't shock me, Babs. I could tell you things I've done..." Then Tanya's glance flicks to Barbara's empty glass. "A top up?" she asks, reaching for the bottle.

"Oh, God, Tanya, I shouldn't. It's only three o'clock..."

But Barbara soon finds herself holding yet another brimming glass while Tanya grins at her.

"So, come on, Barbara," the blonde insists. "Tell me – what's the dirtiest thing you've ever done? Ever been to an orgy?"

Enough is enough, Barbara decides. "Of course not!" she gasps, bristling with indignation. "How absurd!"

Unfazed, Tanya laughs and continues with, "A threeway, then? Ever had two blokes at the same time?" Her expression turns vulpine, pale-blue eyes narrowing to match the sly grin Tanya fixes on Barbara. "A man and another woman?" Tanya adds, sipping wine, attention rapt and fixed on Barbara's face.

Barbara gasps again. "Tanya, please!" Her mouth opens and closes as she struggles with the disconcerting effects of afternoon drinking and the shocking interview. The wine combined with a totally unexpected line of questioning has her struggling for composure. This *isn't* what she's used to at all. "Why do you insist on embarrassing me?" she breathes.

Tanya laughs again before smiling at Barbara, her look contrite.

Holding up a conciliatory hand, Tanya says, "Okay, Babs, I'm sorry. I didn't mean any offense. I'm just a gobby cow. Always have been. I'm only teasin' ya."

It's the girl's accent, her blonde hair, the confidence and her youth that goads Barbara into revealing more than she knows is wise. Despite Tanya being at least fifteen years her junior, Barbara, at just over forty, feels so staid and unworldly – so bloody middle-class and *suburban*. She knows it's unwise but, fuddled with drink and confronted with Tanya's supposed contrition, Barbara feels obliged to blurt her innermost and very intimate fantasies.

"Well," she says, voice low as she avoids Tanya's eyes, "if you must know..."

***

It's a glorious evening, balmy in the gloaming, a warm breeze sighing through the branches of the three pear trees behind her. Barbara sits with her back to the open doors that lead onto the patio from the house. There's a pint glass of water on the ornate wrought iron table at her side, remedial action against the volume of alcohol imbibed in Tanya's company. She smokes, with her eyes on the middle distance. She has no concept of what she's actually looking at, her thoughts turning over the disturbing and, if she's completely honest with herself, rather arousing events of the afternoon.

Although at that moment Barbara is still in denial with regard to her body's response. She's shocked by her feelings, what she sees as her body's betrayal. Barbara is appalled at where the afternoon visit with her neighbors almost went.

Taking a last drag on her cigarette, she blows a viper's breath towards the darkening sky. She quashes her troubles, refusing to acknowledge the tingling between her legs as she stubs the remnant of her cigarette into the ashtray.

He husband's voice comes at her from inside the house. "No thanks," she replies to his question of a drink. "Not for me."

Barbara stands and walks inside to find Tim in the kitchen. "You're late," she says – a statement as opposed to accuse.

Tim pours a glass of Rioja, sips and then nods, his tie loose, top button of his shirt unfastened. He has the look and tone of someone who's had a busy day at work. "Orders coming in from that Chinese contract," he informs his wife.

Barbara offers her husband a sympathetic look. "That's good," she replies, a sudden and unexpected surge of desire for Tim rippling through her. She looks at him and thinks he's more handsome now than he was two decades earlier. "You get better looking as you get older," she adds.

The comment raises Tim's eyebrows. He grins. "Well, thanks, Barbara, you're not so shabby yourself."

Barbara rolls her eyes in response. "That's kind of you, Tim, but I'm not a young girl anymore."

Tim sips the wine and eyes his wife, one hand resting on the marble counter near the double-sink unit.

He sighs, moving towards her. "But you're gorgeous," he says, a hand going to his wife's cheek, fingers caressing her before sliding to the nape of her neck. Barbara's wavy hair cascades over his wrist. "Why the comment about age?"

"I was next door today. The new woman came round and invited me for a drink." Her cheeks balloon as she blows out a lungful of air, with Barbara wondering how much to reveal. "We knocked off the best part of three bottles."

"Of what?" Tim asks as he leans in to kiss Barbara's mouth.

"Mmm, that's nice," Barbara purrs when the languid slide of tongues ceases. "Wine," she adds, moving in closer.

Tim moves until he's square-on to his wife, her pubis against his thigh. His cock stirs at the pressure of Barbara's body against his leg and he places the Rioja carefully on the counter so he can slide his hands over the curve of her back, fingers kneading Barbara's buttocks.

Heat floods south. "Don't stop," Barbara sighs, squirming.

The couple kiss again, passion igniting.

"Tanya, the girl next door," Barbara moans. "She's stunning, Tim. Slim and fit. Gorgeous legs. She's so pretty…"

"But you're beautiful, Barbara," Tim growls before moving in to kiss her again. His ardour is obvious in the intensity of his kiss and the ridge in front of his trousers.

"Do I excite you, Tim?" Barbara asks, angled at the waist so she can look into her husband's face.

Tim's reply is a growl and a lunge, hands grabbing at Barbara's buttocks. "What do you think?"

Despite her own snarling libido, Barbara twists away. "No, Tim," she insists, shaking her head. "I want to know what you think about me."

Tim grins and makes another grab at his wife. "I think you've gotten me hard. I think you better do something about it." His smile vanishes at a sharp, frustrated retort from Barbara. "You okay?" he asks, frowning. "What brought all this on?"

Tim reaches for the wine and sips while Barbara heaves a sigh and shrugs.

A tumult of emotions and thoughts make Barbara wince. "I don't really know, Tim," she says. "Maybe it's all the wine I had this afternoon. I think it must have muddled me up a bit." Shrugging, she adds, "I'm sorry, baby. I'm not making much sense."

Tim pouts, bottom lip jutting. He nods and kindly says, "You want to talk about it?"

Affection for her husband's consideration swells in Barbara's chest. Her eyes moisten as she pushes her concerns away.

Barbara focusses on the warmth suffusing her vulva. "Later, perhaps," she replies. "When I've sorted out what it is I'm feeling." Then Barbara takes a pace towards Tim and lifts the glass from his fingers. Smiling, head canting to one side, she breathes a seductive, "How about you kiss me again?"

A few minutes later, at his wife's vehement insistence, a surprised Tim is on his knees with Barbara sprawled on the settee.

He can't think of the last time the sex was so spontaneous, so heated, with Barbara so desperate she couldn't wait. They were in the big room at the front of the house, the huge television dark and silent for a change. Barbara's long skirt is bunched around her waist, her underwear discarded. She's wide-legged and hot-eyed, vulva sluiced with desire, bottom lip between her teeth as she gazes at her husband and squirms with anticipation.

The legitimacy of her husband's mouth on her sex goes some way to reconciling the guilty feelings harbored inside her.

Recollections of the afternoon's conversation came back.

"God, Tim," Barbara moans, legs going wider, her need urgent. She holds herself open, splaying labia she's usually shy to reveal, her glistening core exposed. "Lick me, darling. Lick my pussy. I'm so fucking hot."

The obscenity is as uncharacteristic as the lewd display, but Tim isn't complaining. He's caught up in the heat of it, his own ardour steaming. Desire for his wife is hotter than it has been for a long time. Years of marriage and pressures of work – and, yes, perhaps complacency as well have seen love-making diminish. But his wife's vehemence, her lewd mutterings and the way she's flaunting herself at him take Tim to the boil.

"Barbara," he mutters. "Jesus, darling... What--?"

"Shut up and do it," Barbara squeals. She doesn't need his tardiness and she's too hot for questions and answers. Barbara craves action, she's desperate for the physical act of love. "Please, Tim," she adds on a groan. "Lick it. Suck my clit."

So while Tim laps and licks and probes at her with a finger, Barbara bucks and writhes, her imaginings turning to Tanya and what she sensed might have happened that afternoon.

If she had only been bold enough to act on the signals the blonde girl seemed to be putting out there.

"Go on, baby," Barbara groans. "Lick my pussy."

She might be speaking the words to her husband, but it's Tanya she sees in her mind's eye.

***

She's tingling. Every nerve is alive and jangling. Pleasure pulses. Barbara heaves in a great draught of air, heart bouncing. Groaning, she has to satisfy herself by massaging the skin an inch or two above the cleft of her sex, her clit is too sensitive. Electric shocks jab at her every time she attempts to rub the swollen bud.

Mauling at one breast, Barbara turns her head on the pillow. "Tim," she gasps, "that was so bloody good." Beaming at her husband, she heaves over onto her side, hands working on her flesh. "I thought you'd never stop pouring all that love into me."

Flat on his back, Tim's face swivels towards his wife, his expression registering his continuing astonishment. "Whatever was in that wine, Barbara," he gasps, "it worked for you." The man gulps and wipes a hand across his forehead. "That was like it used to be. Back when you lived in that flat with your mum and we had nowhere to go. It was so frustrating not being able to do it, and when we managed to get together, you were mad for it."

Apprehension at Tim's response ripples through Barbara. She has a sense the time is right to tell him about her afternoon, but is scared to do so. Barbara thinks she knows her husband, reckons he'll listen to what she has to say and won't go all weird on her. But there's always the chance she might not know the workings of his mind as well as she assumes. Anxious yet determined she settles on her side, an elbow on the bed, head resting on one fist. Her fingers splay across her husband's chest, idly caressing Tim's skin.

Sucking in a deep breath, Barbara begins with, "It was Tanya's fault, Tim."

"Oh yeah," Tim responds. "What's she like? I've only seen her getting into that Porsche. Good-looking lady."

Barbara's insides curdle with an odd mix of desire and jealousy. "She's absolutely gorgeous," she says. "Really pretty. A lovely figure. I told you before..."

"Is she nice?" Tim interjects.

Barbara pauses to formulate her reply. Nice, isn't the word she'd use in relation to Tanya. She waters down the truth by saying, "She's a bit wilder than we're used to around here, but there's no malice in her." Barbara added the last to temper any negative connotation her words might imply.

Tim frowns. "Wild?"

Barbara sighs and grimaces, struggling to paint an accurate picture of their sexy, desirable neighbour.

"She's adventurous, Tim. Sexually, I mean. You should have heard the things she asked me about. Talk about intimate!"

Tim pauses before replying, soaking it up. He knows his wife well enough to realise there's something on her mind. The robust sex and this pussy-footing around the subject of the new arrival next door indicate Barbara has *something* on her mind.

Interested, Tim probes with, "Tell me more, Barbara. Just what have you been up to today?"

He'd purposely delivered the question as a joke, but Tim saw the blush bloom on Barbara's chest. The rosy glow spreads, suffusing his wife's throat and setting her cheeks aflame, his wife's blushes arousing his curiosity.

"I didn't *do* anything," Barbara is quick to say. "I haven't been unfaithful, Tim. I've never cheated."

There's some concern at Barbara's agitation and the direction she's going in, but Tim's reply is a gentle, "I didn't suggest it for a second, darling." He heaves up and plants a kiss against his wife's lips before settling again. "But something's got you all worked up, Barbara – are you going to tell me what?"

Barbara gulps and rolls her eyes, cheeks flaring. "We talked about sex. About fantasies. I thought…" She pauses and grimaces, realising she's committed in telling her husband and there was no point in holding back. "I told her about this *thing* I've had for years. It doesn't affect us, Tim," Barbara hastily adds. "It's just something that comes into my head from time-to-time. I'm perfectly happy with you darling."

Tim's hand reaches for his wife's. "Barbara," he murmurs, concerns surfacing. However, despite the rising anxiety he calmly continues with, "Just get on with it. Don't over-analyse or feel guilty for having fantasies. It's all right. I get it."

Blinking as love for Tim swells her throat, Barbara croaks, "God, Tim, I do love you."

"And I love you," Tim replies. Then he puts on a mock-stern voice and says, "But, for fuck's sake, Barbara, just tell me what happened today. It's driving me mad. Won't you just tell me?"

Barbara is still reluctant. She opens her mouth to begin, but then stalls. After a pause, she gathers herself enough to say, "Tanya asked if I'd ever had a threesome and I said something silly about having a thing about two or three men at me at the same time."

"A gang bang?" Tim blurts, unable to stop the outburst.

Barbara closes her eyes and nods. "Yes," she bleats, "if you want to put a label on it. But," she continues quickly, "it's more about how they want me. About how the men – and they're anonymous, Tim, it's not anyone we know – it's about how much they *desire* me. I know they want to use me for sex, I don't mean anything to them as a person, and I don't care, it's just sex and fucking."

Barbara is on a roll and can't help letting it pour out.

"But I'm the one who can say yes or no," she goes on. "I have the power of veto. If I don't want them to touch me, I can say no.

"But I *want* them to use me, Tim. I want them in my mouth, in my… in my pussy." It goes quiet when Barbara stops talking. She wonders if she hasn't gone too far. She debates whether to continue. Barbara sucks in air through her nose, a long hiss before, with her eyes still closed, she says, "And in my arse, too, Tim."

Barbara's eyes open. She sees her husband gaping at her, jaw slack.

Eventually, Tim says, "Fucking hell, Barbara."

"Oh, God," Barbara whines. "I've said too much, haven't I? I'm sorry. It's just something silly inside my head."

Tim's response is an instant shake of his own head. He squeezes his wife's hand and eases her onto her back.

"No, Barbara, you haven't," he growls, eyes gleaming. "I understand it, Barbara. You don't have to feel bad. It doesn't mean you're out dogging with strangers every weekend in real-life." He leans in and kisses Barbara with rekindled ardour. "It turns me on to hear you say it," Tim adds. "Look," he says, twisting to reveal a cock at half-mast.

A wide-eyed yet relieved Barbara boggles. "Look at that!" she cries, a smile splitting her face.

"I never knew you fantasised about anal sex, Barbara?" Tim leers at his wife, and adds, "So what else happened?" His hand slides over Barbara's stomach to where he can delve between her legs.

Barbara moans and spreads her legs.

"Not my clit, babe," she breathes, back arching with the anticipation of more pleasure. "It's too zapped to be rubbed. Her hand shows Tim the best place. "There," Barbara moans. She's on fire, lewd, in her need, her words reflecting Barbara's surge of dark desires. "And suck my tits, Tim. Treat my boobs rough. Be one of those men who just want me for sex."

A few moments later Barbara is on her hands and knees, her husband's length squelching into his earlier deposit. Tim crouches low over Barbara's back, fingers mauling her breasts.

"I thought Tanya was going to jump me," Barbara gasps, thrusting back to meet Tim on the instroke. "I really thought she was going to try and kiss me, Tim."

"And if she had?" Tim grunts as he fucks into his wife.

Barbara moans and twists in an attempt to look back at the man embedded in her pussy.

"I can't cheat, Tim. I wouldn't."

Tim's reply is a low growl. "But you wanted her to snog you, didn't you?"

Barbara hears her husband's voice curdled with lust. The tone excites her. "Yes," she squeaks. "I wanted her to make a move. God, it was so horny. I was shaking so much. My pussy was itching for something – her tongue, a dildo, a cock--"

"You should have gone for it," Tim says, the tempo and force of his thrusts increasing. He uncurls and holds Barbara's hips with both hands, his eyes on rippling buttocks as she slams into her. "You could tell me all about it, Barbara. You could have some fun with her and tell me about it when I get home."

"Tim, stop it," Barbara groans, arousal a tempest in the pit of her stomach. "I couldn't do that." Barbara gasps and groans, eyes closing as her head lolls. She gulps and claws at the bed. "Don't talk like that," she finishes, wanting Tim to say more.

"It would be nasty to hear what you got up to with her," Tim says in a low, dark voice. He's behind his wife, easing in and out with very long, very slow strokes. He wants Barbara to feel every inch gliding in. Then, when his balls were deep he pauses, squeezing the muscles to make his cock throb. "Tell me about this Tanya and what you wanted to do."

"I… I can't, Tim," gasps Barbara. "Please, darling, don't--"

"Tell me," Tim snarls, grabbing a handful of hair and hauling his wife upright.

Barbara yelps, more in surprise than pain, although her scalp does sting a bit.

Tim slaps one buttock and reaches round to hold Barbara to him, his arm curled around her brisket just below her heavy breasts.

"Go on, Barbara," the man growls, thrusting, his mouth close to his wife's ear. "I want you to tell me all about what goes on in your head."

He eases Barbara's face around until she's swivelled enough for him to lean in and kiss her mouth. "I still love you," he murmurs in an oddly tender moment.

Despite the harsh treatment, or perhaps because of it, Barbara returns the kiss with passion, her tongue sliding and dancing with Tim's.

The kiss breaks and Barbara moans and falls forward into her hands when Tim releases her.

"Okay," she says. "But fuck me, Tim. I want to feel you really going at me. Do it hard."

It descends into a robust burst of frenetic activity. Tim complies with his wife's wishes, their flesh slapping with metronomic regularity, a slap-slap-slap of meaty thwacks mixed with gasps and groans and muttered obscenities.

"I wanted her to kiss me," Barbara moans. "I wanted her to start off with lovely soft kisses before it got really hot. I wanted Tanya to feel my boobs, to undress me and then lick me right on my clit."

The intensity of their frantic coupling increases. Tim babbles on about how he loves Barbara, how good she feels around his cock. "Keep going, babe," he grunts, the words strained through gritted teeth. "Fuck, it's so fucking dirty to hear you say it."

Leaning in low, resting on her elbows, nipples brushing the bed while her big tits swing and sway, with Tim's fingers digging into her hips, Barbara swivels and snarls, "Don't just *tickle* me with your cock, Tim. Fuck me, you bastard. Come on," she urges, angling her pelvis. "Batter my cunt."

Tim gulps at the wildest use of profanity he's ever heard from his wife. He realises Tanya has really affected Barbara. His wife has never been so wanton, so crudely sewer-mouthed, so completely bound up in the pleasure of simply succumbing to her innermost urges.

"Oh, Barbara," Tim groans, the surge a distinct tingling threat through the core of his cock. "Tell me."

"I wanted it to be me and her and a room full of men. I wanted cocks all angry for me. I'd suck and fuck them all. I want to feel them coming at me. All that spunk all over me: in my hair, sliding over my breasts, my face plastered with cum...

"I'd let them come inside me. Like you just did, Tim." Barbara twists and glares back at her husband, eyes spitting fire. "Listen to it squelching there, Tim," she whines, nose crinkling, eyes heavy-lidded for several seconds. "That's your spunk you're fucking into," Barbara mumbles. "Listen to my pussy..."

Tim can't hold it back. It's too much. The filth pouring from his wife's lips, the torrent of obscenity sends him over the edge. It's doubly exciting because it's a side of Barbara, Tim has never seen before. She's had her moments, in the past, especially in those days they were first courting, but this is something he never suspected her capable of.

And it has him grunting and moaning and grabbing flesh, what semen he has left in him squirting into the mix.

"Barbara," Tim whines. "Darling... I'm coming."

***

It's dark. He's on the cusp of sleep. Tim is drifting in hazy time-lessness.

He hears: "Tim?"

"Uhm?"

"You still do fancy me, don't you? I mean me, Barbara, your wife, the woman I was this morning and yesterday and who I'll be to-morrow. Do I still turn you on when I take my clothes off?"

Tim sighs, fully awake. He blinks into the dark. *Now what? What more does she have in mind?*

Out loud, he says, "Absolutely. I still fancy you when you take your clothes off. Yes, you turn me on.

"What is it? Does that Tanya makes you feel old or something?"

Tim senses his wife's head moves on her pillow.

"A bit," comes the hesitant reply. "You should see her, Tim. She's so lovely. So fit. And she's so confident... a really sassy girl. I like her, I really do, but she intimidates me with the way she just grabs life. I hardly know her, I *don't* know her, but she really impressed me with her zest. And the things she's done. She told me some filthy stuff, Tim. She's not shy. I don't think there's much that scares her."

"What about her husband?" Tim asks. "I'm assuming they're married...?"

"They are. His name's Clive. Tanya said he's ten years older than her. She likes older men, apparently." There's a chuckle in the dark and then Tim hears, "I'd better keep an eye on her around you, don't I? Anyway," Barbara continues, "they won the lottery, you know; that's how they bought the place next door. Clive buys and sells motorbikes, but now he has his own shop. Before the money, Tanya worked in a clothes boutique."

"What has this got to do with you feeling old an unattractive, Barbara?"

There's a pause before Barbara says, "Nothing, I was just telling you about Tanya and Clive."

"Okay, Barbara," Tim sighs. "Listen. You're lovely. You've got a great figure. I mean it." Tim cuts off the protest, he knows is coming.

"You're not a skinny mannequin, darling," he adds. "You're a real flesh and blood woman. You're absolutely ravishing, Barbara. I've seen young blokes looking at you. You said all that stuff about wanting men to lust after you? Well, I can tell you, I've seen them looking.

"So I don't want to hear anything else about you doubting yourself. This Tanya comes from a different generation. She's had X-Factor and Facebook and Ibiza in her diet, and that isn't you, Barbara. We didn't have all of that. We didn't have the internet or mobile phones when we were growing up. Attitudes and perceptions are different now. The youngsters are exposed to a lot more adult stuff than we ever were.

"Okay, she might be a good-looking, sexy, confident girl with a lot of sexual experience – but you're a bit of a goer yourself, babe." Tim chuckles and smiles a rueful smile his wife can't see. "You knocked me for six tonight, darling. And I liked it. We've opened a door to something exciting." He hauls himself up and moves in blindly until he finds Barbara's mouth with his lips. Tim kisses his wife and then finishes with, "Now, can I get some sleep? We can discuss everything tomorrow night. I'll cook us a meal and we can crack a bottle. We can have a real good chat and then end up going at it again."

She's thrilled by her husband's words. "I'd like that, Tim," Barbara sighs.

She murmurs words of love when her husband spoons against her back. Barbara feels loved and secure; an equal to the vivacious blonde in the house next door.

However, as she drifts away Barbara feels a ripple of arousal inside her. Barbara's last thought before sleep takes her is to wonder if she'll see Tanya the next day.

Chapter Two

Barbara denies it to herself in the cold light of day. All morning she's adamant she won't go and knock on the door. The internal to-and-fro has been going on for some time, with part of Barbara's brain flat-out refusing to accept she had a plan all along.

It goes on while she scoops yoghurt straight from the pot. It's there while she sips black coffee on the patio, the sun warming her face, the first rationed cigarette of the day burning in the ashtray.

Barbara bathes and tries to convince herself she's shaving her legs and delicate vulva for her husband's benefit. She chooses her outfit carefully, discarding a whole wardrobe's worth of clothes before opting for a light cotton dress suited to the promise of the blue sky above. She admires the drop of the asymmetrical skirt that shows off her legs, a blush warming Barbara's face when she sees the plunging décolletage and the inner flanks of her big boobs squeezed together.

It's daring and Bohemian, an eye-catching array of bright colours. Barbara experiences a flutter of arousal between her legs, nipples tightening to thick, elongated points when she considers foregoing underwear, a little chuckle coming from some dark place inside her head.

She tries to convince herself it'll be cooler going commando and her choice has more to do with the weather. She denies the invidious reality she's dressing for Tanya. Barbara won't acknowledge the fact, but she can't ignore the pulses in the taut nub of her clitoris. Nor can she deny the clenching of her pussy when her libido cranks up a few gears.

Her high heels peck at the long driveway leading to the scallop-shaped turning circle in the front of Tanya's house. Barbara's pussy is sipping with yearning when she steps up onto the long porch and advances towards the door. She approaches the door, but abruptly halts. Then she turns, nerve failing.

Barbara has taken three steps in retreat when the door opens and Tanya trills, "Hiya, Babs. I was just coming to see ya."

With no alternative, Barbara looks over one shoulder. She sees the blonde eyeing her, a smirk on Tanya's pretty face.

When Barbara turns around, it's obvious Tanya has divined the situation clearly. She casts appreciative eyes over the elder woman and says, "Wow, Babs, you look *gorgeous*. Really, really great, babe."

The blonde pauses and something in her expression sends a shiver of anticipation through Barbara.

"I'm glad you've come over," Tanya continues, eyes gleaming with devilment. "I was gonna ask if you'd wanna come in the hot-tub? We could do another bottle of wine and have a natter."

"Oh," blinks Barbara, taken aback. "I… I'd have to get my costume, she blurts."

Tanya's grin broadens and she waves a dismissive hand. "You don't need to worry about that. We can just get in in the nuddy. It's what I always do."

***

Barbara's eyes are on stalks when Tanya lifts herself from the tub and perches on the edge. There's a swirl of arousal, guilt, and myriad other emotions in the pit of her stomach when Tanya's legs go wide.

"I can't help it, Babs," Tanya mewls, eyes slits, lips pouting as one hand goes to her sex. "I'm so fuckin' turned on, babe. I just gotta play with my pussy."

Barbara stays in the water, agog, jaw slack. She can't believe what she's seeing. It can't be happening in front of her. The lovely blonde girl simply *cannot* be fingering herself.

But by then Barbara's need is also huge. It's been a tense morning, the clock spring tightening as she stripped bare in front of Tanya, the tales of debauched sex spilling from the blonde as they sat immersed in bubbling water. The urge is there, an intense and a near irresistible desire to just let herself go and rub her pussy to a climax. Barbara watches Tanya's fingers describing urgent circles, the blonde's face slack with whatever delicious sensations she's experiencing. Barbara's clitoris clamours for attention, with the only barrier to Barbara's complete capitulation being the sight of the girl's wedding band glinting in the sunlight coming through the open door.

In her mind, it's bad enough being nude with the girl in the hot-tub, watching Tanya rub herself is a step too far without crossing the line completely and doing it as well. Barbara wonders how she ever got into such a situation. She knows she should leave. but can't seem to find the will to stand – she's mesmerised by Tanya's hand, the blonde's fingers busy at her own body.

Seeing the wedding ring breaks the spell. The sight of it reminds Barbara of her vows to Tim.

"I… I have to go, Tanya," Barbara gasps, rising from the water. "I can't do this to Tim. I love my husband. This is wrong."

"I love my husband, too," Tanya groans. "And he loves me enough to let me enjoy myself. Clive wouldn't mind if he could see us."

There's some wincing and moaning from the blonde. Her thighs shiver and her breasts sway when a jolt of pleasure wracks her.

"He'd wanna get in with us, Babs," Tanya adds, her eyes going wide before one lid drops against her cheek in a lascivious wink. "And you should see his cock, babe. My husband is fuckin' *huge*."

The lewd image flashes across Barbara's mind's eye. It's her and Tanya and the as yet unseen Clive. They're all naked, the three of them cavorting in the warm water. Clive is erect, his length in Tanya's fist.

In her head Barbara hears: *You wanna hold this, Babs? You wanna feel how big my hubby's cock is? Try it for yourself. Go ahead, babe. Have a nice little fuck with my husband...*

She's out of the tub and grabbing for the towel. Barbara covers her body and snatches up her clothes, her shoes, and her bag.

Then, thankful for living in such an exclusive area, their lane deserted, "Millionaires' Row" as it's known locally, her barefoot retreat unseen by any neighbour, Barbara passes through her own front gate, grateful for the high wall and dense hedge hiding her from view.

Regardless of the tempest inside her, despite the raging confusion of her own feelings she slumps onto the sofa, opens her legs and then begins to finger the ungainly folds of her meaty labia. She winces and groans when the tip of her forefinger slides over her super-aroused clit, the middle and third fingers then going into her opening.

"Oh, God… Oh, shit… Oh, fuck…" Barbara grunts, working on herself, her climax coming in like an express train.

She gets there quick, the express apparently some way down the track, visible in the very far distance until it's suddenly on her. Barbara writhes and squirms, her body convulsing in a paroxysm of absolute delight. Her pleasure is agony, sobs bursting from her, bottom lip between her teeth as she rocks with the intensity of it.

***

Tim returns home at a little after five in the afternoon. He pulls up to the front of the house after checking the gates are closing behind the Range Rover. Climbing out of the big car he wonders what he's going to find when he walks in. Barbara's mood the day before got him thinking and he's a little concerned.

He opens the front door with his key, steps into the high-ceilinged hall, places the laptop bag on the floor and then calls out, "Barbara? I'm home, darling!"

He hears a voice from the floor above: "Up here."

Tim walks to the stairs, loosening his tie as he goes.

"What are you doing?" he calls, hand on the curved bannister as he ascends.

He's unsure about what he'll find. It could be good or it could be Barbara is hiding out, with the answer hitting him full force when he walks into the master bedroom to find his wife on the bed, naked, a vibrator pressed against her sex.

"God, Tim," Barbara groans, her eyes heavy-lidded with what she's feeling. "I'm glad you're home." Barbara extends her free hand, fingers waggling. "Come to bed," she mewls. "I'm so worked up."

Tim blinks, agog, his jaw slack and his mouth gaping. He stares, gormless. "Buh-Barbara…" he stammers.

"Hurry, Tim," his wife whines, hips bucking. "Take your bloody clothes off, will you! Can't you see I'm dying for you to fuck me?"

A minute later, following a flurry of frantic activity, Tim finds himself on his back, Barbara on top of him, his erection deep inside his wife's body.

"I'm going to come," Barbara moans, eyes closed, a beatific smile on her face. "Squeeze my tits, Tim," she sighs, buttocks rippling as she rides up and down.

Tim massages Barbara's weighty breasts, the flesh firm yet yielding under his fingers. He watches the rapture on her face, sees a gamut of emotions there as his wife's climax rolls over her. With surprise overcome by flaring ardour, Tim moves his hands so he can hold Barbara's hips so he can hold on and fuck up into her.

"What have you been doing all day?" Tim grunts. "What's got you so horny? Have you been next door again?"

Barbara's eyes open, her gaze misty at first. "Yes," she mumbles, attention focussing on her husband for a moment before she drifts out again. Her hips move, buttocks and thighs tensing while she rolls in time with her husband and a low moan comes out of her. Then Barbara's eyes clear and she sighs the blonde's name. "I went round there again. We were in the hot-tub...

"Oh God, Tim. I'm coming. I'm coming..."

Barbara soars with the delight of her orgasm, the waves rolling on and on. She cries out in ecstasy, body convulsing. Her chest heaves when Barbara sucks in air, blurts of pleasure coming out in wracking sobs, her head lolling, eyes squeezed tight.

It goes on, with Tim clinging to his wife, his length inside her, Barbara's body clenching his shaft.

Finally, she cools when the climax tapers.

A few gasps and moans further on and then Barbara continues. "We were in her hot tub," she sighs. "We were naked. She told me about some of the sexy things she's done..."

Barbara groans, head lolling forward again, pelvis moving back and forth, her husband held tight.

"She sat on the side of the tub and... and..."

It's an effort, but Barbara forces herself to be still. Her eyes are open and clear. "Oh, Tim," she mutters. "She just played with herself. Right in front of me. She opened her legs and masturbated."

"Jesus," Tim murmurs.

"I wanted to do it, too, Tim. It was so sexy seeing her do it to herself I wanted to wank as well – just like Tanya was doing right in front of me.

"But I couldn't bring myself to do it. I thought about you and about how wrong it would be."

With his head full of questions and images of Barbara and Tanya naked together, Tim blurts, "So *what* did you do?"

"I ran," Barbara says. "I got out and wrapped a towel around myself. I didn't get dressed, Tim. I just grabbed my stuff and legged it."

"And came home and wanked?" suggested Tim, reaching up to pull his wife down to him for a kiss.

"Yes," mutters Barbara in the second before Tim's tongue invades her mouth.

And then the couple are rutting again, with Tim bucketing towards his climax, squirting his seed deep into his wife while Barbara's mind is filled with thoughts of Clive's big cock.

As Tim pours semen into her, Barbara is imagining herself with the lovely blonde's husband, Tanya alongside, the woman kissing them both in turn, her lovely face going from Clive to her neighbour, eyes shining with mischief.

***

"So you wanted to do it with her?" asks Tim. He sits at the kitchen table, red wine in a long-stemmed glass in front of him. He wears a towel around his waist as a nod towards modesty.

Barbara feels like the accused sitting in a courtroom dock. She's opposite her husband and also wearing nothing but a towel. She studies the grain on the smooth table-top while her thoughts swirl.

How can she tell him how she feels? It's overwhelming: all these urges...

Part of her is mortified, part excited to a fever pitch. Barbara wants more sex. Even having just been royally fucked and with Tim's semen seeping from her, she craves more of the physical side of love.

She sips wine and avoids Tim's eyes. Barbara can't deny the truth outright. Tim is no fool, he sharp enough to divine his wife's true feelings. In response to his question Barbara's chest and throat turn a rosy pink, the heat infusing her cheeks.

"I said I did, didn't I?" Barbara pouts, petulant as a teenager.

Softly, her husband replies with, "I'm not condemning you, darling. You don't have to be so defensive. I'm not angry, I'm not judging you."

Contrite, Barbara murmurs, "Sorry. I'm just embarrassed by it, Tim." She wriggles and keeps the rest of it to herself.

"Don't be embarrassed, Barbara," Tim sighs. He sips wine and considers his next line of inquiry. "But you didn't...?" Tim pauses and fingers the glass. "You didn't touch her, did you? You didn't masturbate like she asked. In fact," he continues, "you ran away."

"Yes," says Barbara, flicking a glance towards her husband.

Her eyes fix on him when Tim says, "You didn't have to, Barbara. If you'd stayed and... and done those things with her...

"I wouldn't have minded."

Barbara gapes at him. "But, Tim, I've never been unfaithful."

Tim nods. "Thank you, darling," he says, voice breaking with emotion. "Neither have I, but..."

Again, he pauses. It's important to get it right.

Sucking in a deep breath, Tim then says, "I suppose it's typically male, but thinking of you with another woman isn't the same as going behind my back with a man."

"Tim--" croaks Barbara.

Holding up a hand and closing his eyes, Tim insists, "No, Barbara. Let me speak first. I need to get this out there for you."

Barbara's throat works, but she remains silent. She lifts her glass and sips.

Tim pauses, mind working carefully on his phrasing. "After what you said last night... And after seeing how aroused you got after talking to Tanya about... about other men, gangbangs and everything--"

Tim breaks off, deciding the image of his wife involved in a scene with multiple men necessitates another drink. Tim glugs the wine in his glass and then stands up. He goes to the bottle and pours, offering it to his wife. "More?"

Barbara stares at the bottle with a vacant expression before rousing herself. "I'd better," she replies.

Tim pours for her, returns to his seat, and continues with, "I've been thinking a lot today, Barbara. And when I got home and--" he gives Barbara a rueful grin. "Well, you know."

Tim's eyes go to the ceiling while Barbara says nothing. She just blushes and squirms and closes her eyes.

"I suppose, what I'm saying, is that I don't mind if you want to experiment, Barbara."

The woman's eyes snap open.

"With Tanya," Tim adds. "Just as long as you tell me about it."

Barbara can't decide which impression affects her more, hearing her husband say it sets a flurry of wings aflutter inside her. She's suddenly elated, euphoric, love for Tim threatening to burst out of her. Lust flares in that indefinable place inside her, way down deep, desire for Tanya and the things she's now free to enjoy warm her like a dense sun low down in her belly. There's heat between her legs and her clit pulses.

But there's anxiety in there, too. Like ink in water, the elements combine, mixing together, the desire tinged with fear. Barbara is elated yet feels a ripple of uncertainty at the same time.

The apprehension balloons into alarm. Succumbing to the base emotions would rock Barbara's world. She had always viewed cheating on a spouse as a weakness. To her, marriage is a serious commitment, a partnership between equals. If Tim were to confess to an affair, she would be devastated, inconsolable, bereft.

Hadn't her fantasies already caused her guilt? And what about being naked in the hot-tub with Tanya? Could that little adventure be viewed as infidelity?

No, Barbara decides, the hot-tub incident wasn't being unfaithful to Tim. Despite their nakedness there had been no intent on Barbara's side. But it could so easily have led to an indiscretion, a besmirching of her vows. If she'd stayed there much longer and watched Tanya masturbating things would have definitely gone crazy.

Guilt wracks her. "I don't think I'd be able to actually *do* it," Barbara murmurs, mostly to herself. She blinks at the table and then looks at Tim. "I… I'd be too scared to be that wanton, Tim." The woman shrugs and shakes her head. She gulps wine. "You setting me free has made me realise I'm too much of a scaredy-cat in real-life. Fantasy is one thing, but..."

"But all that stuff about--" Tim begins and then changes tack. "You were so horny, Barbara." He chuckles, head going side-to-side incredulous at the memory, a lopsided grin on his face. "Sex these last two evenings has been amazing, darling." He spreads his hands and gives his wife a sympathetic look. "But, if you don't think you can actually get physical with Tanya, that's okay, just don't stop doing what you're doing with me." He winks at Barbara. "Just keep on getting yourself all worked up. Although," he finishes, making a joke out of it. "If it does get hot with her, be sure you phone me straight away."

"Oh, *you*," Barbara says, shooing a hand at Tim.

Then, in an abrupt change of mood towards domestic needs she asks, "Now, what about that meal you were going to cook?"

While Tim prepares the food Barbara takes a long soak in the bath. It was Tim's insistence that took her there.

"Leave this all to me," he says, smiling at his wife.

In the bath, with the almost-too-hot water enveloping her in its gentle embrace, she drifts on the edge of dozing.

There's a residual tingle of arousal in her body. Places pulse with yearning as dark urges well once more. Her mind, inevitably, turns to her blonde neighbour. Barbara touches herself between the legs and fingers the folds of her labia while wondering about what might happen if she just let herself go.

"Nothing," murmurs Barbara. "I'm sorry, Tanya, but I'm just too frightened about where it will end."

Then she remembers the towel she took when she ran. It has to go back.

Chapter Three

She holds the towel in both hands like an offering. There's a brief moment of utter panic while Barbara wonders just what the hell she's letting herself in for. She suspects her own reasoning for being there.

Then the door opens and Tanya appears, the blonde smirking as she props herself against the doorframe, arms folding beneath her breasts.

"You ran off in a hurry yesterday," she says, her amused expression turning an accusation into a humorous statement of fact. Mischief twinkles in her eyes as she continues with, "You just brought that back?" Tanya nudges her chin in the direction of the towel before she springs away from the doorframe. "You want to come in?"

Barbara dangles, uncertain, anxious, terrified.

There's an urgent pressure in her bladder. "Oh, God, I need the loo!" she squeaks.

Tanya grins. "You'd better come in. I don't want you peeing in the bushes, **Babs**." She scoops the towel from Barbara's hands when the desperate woman hurries past her.

"Second door along the hall!" Tanya calls when Barbara's pauses and turns an anguished face to her. When Barbara scuttles on, Tanya shouts out, "I'll break the wine open."

***

They're outside, in the garden where it's cool in the shade. Barbara sits on a director's chair, the aluminium frame squeaking whenever she moves – which is often since she's so fidgety.

From another director's style chair Tanya looks at Barbara, her perennial grin twisting her lips. "You want one, Babs?" she asks.

After staring at the packet of cigarettes as though it's some new thing just dropped in from outer space, Barbara leans forward. "Thanks," she says, fingers trembling when she takes one from the packet.

"You're just a bundle of nerves, aren't you?" says Tanya, her tone sympathetic. "Haven't I been awful – mucking about with you like I have been?" She lights her own cigarette and hands the lighter to Barbara. Taking a drag, with her eyes on her neighbour, appraising the older woman, Tanya then blows smoke towards the sky. She holds her gaze steady on Barbara's face, cigarette held daintily aloft, an elbow resting on a canvas chair arm.

Barbara smokes with quick, agitated puffs, eyes darting everywhere.

"Do I make you nervous, Babs?" Tanya asks, predatory snake-eyes fixed on her neighbour.

Barbara nods quickly and admits it. "A bit. Yes."

Tanya grimaces and says, "Do you want me to stop with all the mucky stuff? I got a bit carried away yesterday." Her eyes roll as she chuckles and adds a rueful, "Sorry about that. I don't know when to stop. I've always been the same. Always have to be the centre of attention. I'm always showing off, Babs. I can't help meself, luv. If I've given you any reason to be offended... Well, I'm sorry, Barbara."

Canvas squeaks when Barbara shifts in her seat. She smokes and says, "I'm not offended, Tanya. I was just shocked. It isn't what I'm used to. I..." Barbara blinks and shuts up, unable to formulate any more coherent sentences.

"Did ya like it?" asks Tanya, expression sly.

The look on the girl's face causes a pulse of excitement inside Barbara. Flesh tightens, her insides clench. *Oh, God, She's going to start again!*

"It... I... You..." Barbara begins, voice quavering. She sucks in a deep breath and her jaw sets. "Bugger it," Barbara spits, determination stiffening her spine and hardening her expression. "Of course I liked it, Tanya. Hearing about those men and what you let them do..." Barbara's eyes roll as the heat blooms between her legs. "Seeing you masturbate. Oh, God," she gasps, "I so wanted to do it as well."

Tanya's eyes hold Barbara's. Her voice is barely a whisper: "Why did you run, then? Why didn't you stay and do it too?"

"I'm married," murmurs Barbara. She shakes her head. "I couldn't do it behind my husband's back."

"But you're here now," says Tanya, her voice low and narcotic. "Why? Changed your mind?"

Gulping at the intensity of pale-blue eyes in the elfin face, struck by the near overwhelming desire to kiss the Cupid's-bow lips, Barbara croaks, "Not exactly." She pauses, tension bowstring taut. "I talked to Tim last night. He said he didn't see it as infidelity – me with another woman. He said as long as I told him about it…"

"Do you wanna do something now, Babs?" Tanya breathes. She rises slowly from the chair and stubs out her cigarette. Gently, her tone hypnotic, she adds, "Do you, babe? Do you wanna come indoors with me? We could have a little fun right now."

"Oh, God, Tanya, I don't know." Barbara stares up at the blonde. "I… I think so. I'm turned on but I'm so nervous."

Tanya extends an arm, fingers inviting Barbara's hand. "Come with me," she murmurs. "Let's go inside."

After staring at Tanya's fingers for some time, Barbara reaches out. "Oh," she whines. "Oh, God, what am I doing?"

"Coming inside for a little girly-fuck," the blonde replies.

The obscenity and the image exploding into her mind send an arterial burst of desire through Barbara. "Yes, please," she squeaks, vulva flooding with heat and moisture.

Then she's following after Tanya, the blonde virtually dragging her across the patio.

***

Tim's phone rings. He isn't busy and picks the instrument up off his desk, recognising the ringtone as Barbara's.

"Hiya, Barbara," he says, smiling his wife's name. "Missing me? Want me to come home early?"

"I think she might," an unknown voice says.

Tim recognises a Liverpudlian accent, but doesn't have a clue who the female caller might be.

His first question is: *Why is this woman using Barbara's phone?.* Out loud he asks, "Who is this?" Then the obvious hits him. "Shit," Tim gasps. "Uh-Ii Barbara with you? You're Tanya, yes?" He knows he's babbling but can't stop. "Oh God. Tanya… Barbara… What?"

The woman chuckles. "Calm down," she says. "Barbara's fine." There's a couple of seconds of silence before she purrs, "In fact, your wife is better than fine. I thought I might just let you know that I've just licked her pussy. She's come and come. Babs watched me fucking myself with my big dildo, too. We've had a lovely morning together."

There's some commotion from the other end of the line. Tim hears his wife's voice. Numb at the information he's just been presented with, unable to soak it up in the moment, Tim gasps, "What? I..."

"It took some doing, Tim, but I persuaded Babs to let me make the call. She told me about what you said to her. You know, about telling you if she and I got down and dirty. Well, Tim, we've been down and dirty, and now you know. We've been such mucky tarts together, Tim." There's a pause for a few accelerated heartbeats before the woman finally murmurs, "What do you think about it?"

That was a question! Just how does he feel?

"Shit," Tim hisses, eyes wide, fingers running through his thick hair. "I don't believe it. It's a wind-up, right?"

There's a place in Tim that hopes it is a joke. He can see it: two women tipsy on wine, Tanya gets the idea because she sounds like the kind of woman who'd enjoy a joke like this. Barbara is reluctant, but after some cajoling, allows herself to be talked into it.

His mind works in a rush. Confusion reigns for a few seconds. Tim latches onto the certainty it's a joke. He refuses to believe his Barbara would go for it.

However, after the last two evenings, following Barbara's apparent sexual epiphany and the pleasure, Tim experienced as a result, he isn't so sure.

Then, in the depths of his psyche, something dark uncurls: his wife with another woman? The dim question comes to him through a mist of emotions – would they let him join in?

With murky desire blooming, a thrill of illicit sex curdling inside him, Tim hears a low chuckle coming through the phone.

The sound elicits a shiver of arousal and he's half hard after Tanya tells him, "No, Tim, this is no wind-up. Absolutely not. I can tell you, babe, we've been kissing and licking and touching..."

"Your gorgeous wife is here with me now. We're both naked, Tim. I'm touching her boobs, babe. She's got lovely breasts. Your missus got great tits. You know what, Tim," Tanya purrs, "I reckon you should try to knock off work early. If you get home soon, I think we could talk Babs into letting me watch the two of you fuck."

It hits him with a sledgehammer blow. It's impossible, the woman can't mean it. People just don't behave this way.

"Twenty minutes," Tim croaks after several seconds of staring at the office wall.

***

If anyone were to ask Tim about the drive home, if there were any questions about the specifics of the journey, he couldn't have answered.

It takes him a little more than twenty minutes. Road repairs hold him up and by the time he arrives home, he's thrumming with nervous anticipation. He's hard, has been since the phone call. Tim's cock is a steel rod, desire a cauldron bubbling away inside him. He waits for the gates to swing open, muttering under his breath at their sedate pace. Tim bores up the drive, the Range Rover at an acute angle to the front of the house when he abandons the vehicle.

There's no sign of Barbara inside. Tim searches each of the six bedrooms on the upper floor. He checks the en-suites and the two bathrooms on the same level. Nothing. There's no sign of Barbara and their neighbour.

They're not in the living room, the kitchen or even the garden.

Frustrated and anxious, desperate and jittery, Tim pulls his mobile from his suit jacket and calls her.

"We're at mine," Tanya informs him. "Where are you?"

"At home," Tim says.

There's a laugh and, "You coming round? We're still naked. I've been keeping your wife on the boil. You should see her, Tim," the woman purrs. "She looks *gorgeous* with that just-fucked look on her face."

It's a mad dash down the drive and out of the gate. Tim follows the reverse course of his wife's dash of the previous day and then rushes up the long driveway to Tanya's house. He bounds up the steps and is about to hammer on the door when it opens.

Then he boggles. Barbara hadn't been exaggerating: the blonde is stunning.

"You must be Tim?" she says, so casually naked, apparently unconcerned at presenting herself nude to a total stranger. "I hope you are," the woman giggles, "otherwise it could get complicated if you're delivering a parcel." Tanya steps out and reaches out a hand to stroke Tim's cheek. "And I'd be disappointed if you're not her husband, she purrs." Tanya steps back a pace and eyes the gobsmacked man from shoes to crown. "You coming in?" she asks, her tone teasing.

A band of steel tightens across Tim's chest. It isn't a heart attack; the pain is just his lungs, letting him know he hasn't let out any air for some time. He's been standing there gaping at Tanya, his eyes taking all of her in, his brain soaking up the detail of the blonde hair and blue eyes, her dimpled smile and amused expression. The woman is slim, toned, and tanned – sunbed colour rather than the real thing, Tim notes vaguely. He ogles the big round breasts and the coins of the areolae, the fullness and pleasing shape of Tanya's boobs sending a tickle of deep arousal through him. There's a deep-rooted and primeval urge to lunge at her, to grab that lush body and pull her in so he can feel the texture of her skin, his hands on her breasts and buttocks as he forces his tongue into her mouth.

"Fucking hell,' Tim breathes, his gaze lingering on a tight waist, jewelled navel, and the depilated smoothness between Tanya's legs.

Then she turns and hip-sways away, pelvis rolling in that feminine way that never fails to flick Tim's switch.

He could moan when he sees the sweep of those curves: the cheeks of Tanya's bottom; the hips; her waist and the track of her spine.

Desire comes out of Tim on a whimper.

Tanya halts and swivels at the waist, regarding Tim over one shoulder as she invites him in.

"Don't be shy," she breathes, like a Hollywood icon from the 50s. "Come on in. I wanna watch you fucking your wife. I love watching people fuck."

***

In days to come Barbara will look back and consider what she started when she allowed Tanya to use her phone. In certain moments, when the 'old' Barbara visits, she's appalled at how easily she caved, amazed at actually allowing Tanya to hijack her mobile to call Tim.

What she finds even more difficult to believe is what happened afterwards.

She was ready to bolt again, fearful that they'd gone too far. Receiving a phone call like that must have hit Tim like a bolt of lightning. She'd panicked when Tanya began speaking, her desire cooling to a bellyful of winter slush.

"No," Barbara murmurs to herself. She thinks about going for the phone, making a grab for it so she can wrest it from Tanya's hands.

But by the time she makes her decision and attempts a feeble lunge it's too late; Tanya was talking, already dripping lewd suggestions into the phone.

"He said he's on his way," Tanya tells a somewhat shell-shocked Barbara when the call ends.

"God, no... Really?" Barbara is aghast, horrified that things have gone so far so fast.

Then Tanya is with her on the bed, the blonde's voice soothing. "It'll be fine," Tanya says, easing Barbara backwards.

The older woman blinks up at her, uncertainty plain to see.

"It'll be fun," says Tanya. "I promise, babe, it'll be such a turn on. Think about it, Babs: you said you wanted to get fucked by a load of guys at once... Well, this is just gonna be me, you, and your hubby. The two of us will look after you. We'll both make sure you have a good time.

"Just think about it. Imagine it – your husband's cock fucking you while I rub my pussy. If you like, Babs," Tanya adds, smirking. "I could kiss you while your Tim shags you. What do you reckon to that?"

Barbara's reality slews. It cannot be real. "I... I don't know, Tanya," she quavers. "My husband...? You? In the same room...?"

Tanya is draped across Barbara, a hand going between the other woman's thighs. "Wait and see," she sighs. Her fingers come away from Barbara glistening. She holds the digits up. "Look at how fuckin' wet you are, Babs," she grins, winking before slipping the index and middle fingers into her mouth. "I love the taste of your pussy. Come on," she urges, "let me give you another lick."

Barbara orgasms again, her body convulsing with it, back arched, pelvis thrust up, thighs shivering with nerveless spasms. She gasps and sobs and groans, fingers clawing at the bed, at Tanya, anything.

It barely cools when the woman is at her again, this time with the length of molded rubber. Barbara gasps and watches open-mouthed, her back propped against two pillows, torso angled so she can see Tanya easing the improbable girth of the dildo into her body.

"You wanna fuck yourself with this?" asks Tanya, her expression avid, almost feral with her own arousal. "Or are shall I do it, babe? What do you fancy, Babs?"

"You do it," Barbara groans. "Please," she implores, with her stare all hot-eyed, jaws clenched and a hand on Tanya's wrist.

Barbara's reasoning is somewhat vague, but if it's Tanya using the dildo on her body, she can absolve herself of any responsibility. In her mind, with carnal urges rippling through her, Barbara recall her husband's words about how he wouldn't mind Barbara and another woman. He's already set her free, released her from the matrimonial shackles under the caveat it's Tanya she plays with.

Barbara is suddenly euphoric, wild with reckless abandon. She mauls her breasts with her free hand while maintaining her grip on Tanya's wrist. "Fuck me with it," she grunts.

Tanya chuckles and says, "Looks like you're in the mood now, babe." She settles on her knees alongside Barbara, splaying the woman's ungainly flaps with her fingers before she screws the dildo into Barbara's opening.

"Shit," hisses Barbara. "How *big* is that thing!"

"You should see Clive's cock," Tanya says, leaning in to suck a thick and elongated nipple. She teases the flesh with her lips and teeth, swinging over to kiss Barbara's lips, one hand controlling the dildo, the other sliding over the older woman's skin wherever it can get to. "He's about as thick and as long as this," she adds, the rubber cock slipping from Barbara's opening. "It's a fucker trying to give him a fucking blowjob, babe."

Then Tanya attempts to demonstrate, her lips stretching tight over the big domed tip.

"I'd love to taste your pussy on my husband's cock," Tanya breathes, shivering at the thought.

"Oh, God, put it back in," Barbara wails, her fingers working at her clitoris. "Put it in and kiss me again, Tanya. It's so bloody good!"

The blonde laughs and complies.

She's still using the dildo on Barbara when the mobile rings.

***

She feels the ridiculous urge to cover herself up when her husband walks in. It's mental, but Barbara is suddenly so self-conscious about being naked in front of two people. She reaches for the duvet on the carpet next to the bed.

"Look who I found on the front step!" Tanya cries, clambering onto the bed to yank the cover off Barbara. "What are you doing?" she asks.

"I… I…" answers Barbara, her eyes on her husband. She gulps and gives up, releasing her grip on the quilt. "Tim…" she murmurs, waiting for some response.

Tim's eyes go from his wife to Tanya and back again. "Jesus, Barbara," he gasps, arms flapping once, then resting at his sides.

"Are you mad at me?" the woman asks, face tight with concern, her jubilation of earlier evaporating in her husband's presence.

It takes Tim a moment or two to realise his wife is worried he'll be angered by what she's done. He sees the anxious face and hears the apprehension in her voice.

"Mad at you?" he replies. "God, no, Barbara, why would you think that? I told you--""

He would go on but Tanya comes off the bed and interrupts with, "You gonna get your kit off then, Tim?"

Barbara sits there agog, legs tucked beneath her as the scene unfolds. She sees Tim's attention focus on Tanya. She recognises the look he gives the blonde – it's the same hungry gaze, she longs for from the men in her fantasies.

"Fuck," Barbara mutters, her pussy clenching when she realises the enormity of the situation.

She's actually present in that room with her husband and another woman. All three of them are going to be nude together as soon as Tim finishes taking his clothes off. Then she's going to take her husband's erection into her body. Barbara can't quite believe she's actually going to do it with Tanya looking.

"Your hubby's lovely," Tanya drawls, her comment interrupting Barbara's thoughts. "I love the distinguished look of a man in a suit. He looks like a bloke who can take charge." The blonde's eyes sparkle as she extols Tim's virtues. "He's pretty fit too. *Gorgeous* shoulders and arms. You didn't tell me he was so good-looking, Babs," admonishes Tanya with a smile at the other woman. "Nice cock, too."

The sight of Tanya standing there square on to Tim has Barbara gaping wide-mouthed while some corrosive emotion curdles her insides. Jealousy bites her hard when the blonde moves in close and takes hold of Tim's erection, her other hand going to his shoulder.

"You gonna fuck your wife with this?" Tanya purrs, her fist working the length with a forehand grip on like she's holding a tennis racquet.

Tim doesn't reply, he's just gazing down at the hand jacking his dick.

"I want to see it," Tanya whispers, teasing Tim with her innocent little girl look, the tip of her pink tongue poking from her mouth. She winks at him and adds a breathy, "Come on," while turning to lead Tim to the bed with his cock. "There she is. There's your lovely wife."

It takes some urging from Tanya, but finally, Barbara lies back and opens her legs. She's trembling, terrified as she looks from Tanya to Tim. "Are we really--?" she asks her husband.

There's a quick glance at Tanya before Tim answers with an enthusiastic, "Fuck yes, Barbara."

He jacks his cock and climbs onto the bed, then shuffles on his knees towards his wife, continually fisting his length as he goes.

Tanya gets on there too. She climbs onto the bed and moves to Barbara's side.

Swivelling her face to Tim, the blonde grins and says, "Watch me kiss her. Watch us and then let me see you slide it in."

There's a gasp and an oath from Tim when he sees the two women together. He stares at their tongues writhing and squirming. He gapes at Tanya's fingers sloshing at Barbara's sodden vulva, her digits squelching into his wife's opening.

Tim is struck by the differences between the two. He takes in Tanya's lithe body, her athletic proportions so different to Barbara's voluptuous curves. In that moment, for the life of him, Tim can't decide which he prefers. Both women are beautiful. He knows some men would be drawn by Tanya's more obvious down-to-earth and slutty appeal, but there would also be a good percentage who would find Barbara more attractive of the two.

Not that it matters to Tim, he loves his wife. That she could countenance participating in this little scene is something he'd never thought her capable of. If he wasn't there witnessing it, he wouldn't believe it. But there she is, his Barbara, his lovely wife of so many years is wide-legged, her core exposed and vulnerable as she lies supine, her pussy awash with desire.

"I love you, darling," Tim coos as he holds himself over Barbara on one straight arm, his other hand holding his dick aimed at her body.

"Oh, God, Tim," his wife sighs as Barbara shuffles her rump, eyes fixed on his face. "You're going to do it with her watching, aren't you?"

And then she's gulping, blinking as he penetrates her.

"Yes," he groans.

***

"I just love watching," Tanya squeaks, her eyes set on Barbara's body where the flesh is tight around Tim's girth. The blonde rubs at herself. She's kneeling there next to Barbara, chewing her bottom lip, eyes glazed with lust. "I wish he was fucking me like that," she whines, chest hitching. "Oh, Babs," Tanya continues. "Your Tim's a handsome bugger, isn't he? You're a lucky girl."

When she hears Tanya's gasping praise for Tim, Barbara comes up from the depths. She blinks and, with her hips working against her husband's downstroke, looks into the blonde's face and mumbles, "I don't believe I'm doing this."

Tanya laughs and places one hand on Tim's shoulder while her other hand squeezes Barbara's rolling breasts. "Oh, you're doing it, Babs; and your gorgeous hubby is doing *you*."

Tim breathes an oath when he sees Tanya duck in to kiss Barbara's mouth. "Fuck," he growls, redoubling his efforts against his wife's pussy. "Look at that. Seeing you two kiss..."

"You kiss me, Tim," Barbara whines when Tanya rises upright. "Fuck me, darling. Kiss me."

"Yeah, Tim," interjects the blonde. "Kiss her."

Tim does it, he kisses his wife with burning ardour. When he comes up from doing so, he sees Tanya sitting on her bottom, legs splayed, two fingers in her opening while she rubs the nub of her clit with her middle finger.

The look he witnesses, the scrunched up agony of Tanya's ecstasy twisting the blonde's face pulls the surge through his core. He glances down at his wife, sees her delight, her big breasts shivering, her pussy accommodating his length.

"I'm going to come," Tim mewls, gulping.

"Not yet, Tim!" Barbara cries. "Please, darling, try to hold it in. I..." She gasps, blinking, her mouth open. "I need to come first."

"Take it out," suggests Tanya, her hands falling away from her sex. "Let me at her." She rises up and pulls at Tim's shoulder. "Cool down a little," she says. "Watch."

It's with great reluctance that Tim complies. He withdraws, cock waggling, Barbara's desire glistening on the shaft while Barbara writhes and shifts her rump against the bed.

She rubs at herself, wincing. "Please..." she squeals.

Flabbergasted, Tim looks on, eyes wide with disbelief as Tanya settles between Barbara's legs. Then it happens; he sees it for the first time. The blonde looks at him and winks with lascivious delight, knowing the effect she's having. Tanya forces Barbara's thighs wider and ducks in to slide her tongue along the older woman's pussy from anus to clit.

"Jesus!" Barbara yelps. "Oh God, oh fuck..."

She writhes and groans when Tanya's fingers and tongue get to work.

Tim watches it all with a slack face while slowly cranking his cock. His brain struggles to keep up with what his eyes tell him is happening. He gapes at them – his beautiful wife and the stunning blonde. It occurs to Tim to wonder at how he got so lucky, and he's only dimly aware of wondering if he'll get a crack at Tanya.

Wouldn't it be sweet to poke his dick into her!

The blonde lays out flat on her stomach, taut rump moving from side to side as she laps at Barbara's sex. Tim can hear his wife groaning and gabbling on about how good it all is. He can also hear the occasional moan coming from Tanya and realises the woman is lying atop of one arm, her fingers busy at her own clit.

"Shit-shit-shit," Barbara gasps, the urgent explosions grabbing Tim's attention, drawing his eyes away from where Tanya's fingers diddle at her plump vulva. "I'm there," the older woman grunts, teeth clenched, cords in her neck tight hawsers as she cranes to look at where Tanya is working her magic. Barbara groans and falls back against the bed, succumbing to the rise of her orgasm. "I'm… Fucking… Coming…" she spits.

With her fingers rubbing at Barbara's insides Tanya rolls onto her hip, staring at Tim through eyes all heavy-lidded with desire.

"Fuck her again," the blonde gurgles, the words thick and clotted. "I wanna watch it some more. Go on, Tim," she urges, clambering away while Barbara continues to writhe and moan. "Give it to her."

"Are you going to play with yourself?" asks Tim.

A mischievous smile curls the corners of Tanya's mouth. "If you want me to," she purrs. "You like watchin' me wank, Tim?"

Tim gulps and nods, mouth slack as he tugs hard at his cock. "God yes," he sighs.

Tension crackles between the pair. Tanya knows Tim would love to have her on her hands and knees, his cock inside her from behind. She throws him a look, a conspiratorial exchange between her and Barbara's husband.

Running a tongue over her lips, Tanya winks. Her expression sends out the unspoken message: *You so want to fuck me, don't you?*

The blonde cups her breasts in her palms. She squeezes her own flesh, teasing the man with them, mocking him with her eyes.

"I'll fuck myself with my fave dildo," Tanya breathes. "Watch me do that while I watch you fucking her." The younger woman nods at Barbara, whose climax is finally tapering. "From behind," Tanya adds. "I want to see her big boobs swing as you fuck her."

A few minutes later, with Tim thrusting hard, Barbara's hips rippling, breasts swinging, while Tanya grunts and mutters obscenities, one hand shoving a moulded rubber cock into her body, a man's voice startles them all.

"Well, well," Clive says. "What the *fuck* is going on here, Tan?"

Chapter Four

Her stomach feels watery. There's the nervous need to pee. Barbara raises her eyes and catches Tim's enquiring gaze.

"What am I doing?" she asks.

Her husband regards Barbara for a long moment, before he shrugs and says, "Don't you want to? It isn't too late to say no."

There's a flutter in her tummy. Arousal sipes into her underwear – satin knickers she won't be wearing for very long.

She considers her feelings and then shakes her head. Barbara answers with a determined, "No... I want to do it, Tim." She offers the man a wan smile. "I'm just so bloody nervous."

Also unsure of his own feelings, Tim nods. "Okay," he says. "As long as you're sure..."

Sensing her husband's uncertainty, Barbara asks, "Don't you want to any more, Tim?"

Tim's thoughts go to their blonde neighbour. There's a flash of desire, a primeval yearning tugging on a visceral level. In his mind's-eye, he sees Tanya naked, her impish smirk teasing him, high cheekbones defined. He pictures the pleasing roundness of her full breasts, those orbs splattered with semen; just as they had been the afternoon it all began, when Clive had walked in on them and later on sprayed a heavy rain of ejaculate over Tanya's boobs.

He goes back to when Tanya was on her knees, the terrible girth of her husband's cock huge in her little fist as the thing spat a long gobbet of jizm right between the blonde's eyes.

Tim can still hear the high-pitched squeak exhorting Clive to do it, spunk sliding over the bridge of Tanya's nose.

"Come with me," Tanya had yelped, her tongue coming out to catch the semen slipping down her face. "On my tits," she added, shuffling on her knees and straightening her back so she could aim the eye of the cock at the target. "Cover my tits, babe. Show Babs how much cum you can make."

Clive's appearance had been a shocking surprise, but how things had changed in the three weeks since.

Tim has mixed feelings as he eyes his wife's reflection. He knows what's going to happen. He's already shared her with Clive, a reciprocal deal since he also got to know Tanya very intimately. But the plan for the evening is a bit beyond same room sex and partner swapping, and it hits him like a hammer blow: this is Barbara in the corset and stockings; it's his wife dressed for sex with multiple men – his *wife* for God's sake!

Love for Barbara squeezes tight fingers around Tim's chest. All of a sudden he doesn't want it to go ahead. The thought of her doing it repels him.

Tim's mouth opens then closes. He gazes at Barbara for long seconds. Half a minute passes while jealousy drags at his guts. Then, when it comes out Tim can't quite believe what he's said. He was certain he was going to say no, that he didn't want to do it.

Instead, what came out was a croaking, "Yes."

When Tim looks into his wife's face, he knows it was the right thing to say. It was what Barbara wanted to hear.

"Oh, God, thank you," Barbara sighs, breasts bubbling over the corset cups. "I'm so nervous, Tim," she quavers. "But I'm so bloody turned on, too." She swivels in her seat, make-up subtle, light-brown hair streaked with blonde teased about her face. Blinking and smiling softly at her husband, she says, "I didn't imagine how hot it would make me to see you with another woman. I thought I'd be jealous, but seeing you fuck Tanya…"

Tim's throat jumps at the reminder and the curdled jealousy evaporates. His mood lifts. He's going to fuck that gorgeous blonde again! Tim's cock thickens when Tanya's face all screwed up with pleasure comes to mind. There's a spike of deep arousal when he thinks about her looking at him, her legs wide, her insides clenching around his girth.

Tim is fully erect with anticipation of the young woman's potty-mouthed exhortations he knows are coming. He savours the swelling ache of anticipation, lust for the blonde ballooning inside him. During sex Tanya puts it out there in no uncertain terms. She tells it exactly as she's feeling it. Tim finds her lewd and crude and totally shocking and he's mad for it.

"We talked about all this, Barbara," Tim says, suddenly determined he wanted all the night has to offer. "If it's what you want to do…"

Barbara nods. "How long have we got?"

"We should go now, darling," Tim answers.

There's a flutter in her stomach when Barbara hears it's time to go. "I love you, Tim," she breathes. It's all she can think of to say. It's important he hears it. They both need the reassurance their marriage is solid.

The couple clasp hands when Barbara rises to her feet.

"I love you, too, Barbara," Tim replies. "You look so beautiful."

***

They drive, taking the Range Rover on the extremely short journey from their home to the next door. Barbara in a corset, stockings and heels might raise a few eyebrows if she attempted the journey on foot. Their lane might be quiet but sod's law decrees *someone* would see.

Tanya, wearing nothing but a pair of black hold-ups and shoes meets them at the door.

"Don't you look amazing," she says, eyeing Barbara from top to toe. She turns her attention to Tim. "You ready for me, babe?"

Tim blinks and feels the heat rise in his cheeks. He's suddenly absurdly shy given his maturity and experiences with the blonde already. Arousal is a deep, aching void in the pit of his stomach as he looks at the woman and sees her impish smile.

He glances at his wife as though gauging her response, then says, "Yes, Tanya. I am."

"Good," the woman coos. "I'm looking forward to a nice dirty fuck." She grins at Barbara. "What about you, Babs? You look forward to it, too?"

"God, Tanya," Barbara sighs. Barely contained in the corset cups, Barbara's big breasts swell as she sighs, "God, Tanya, I don't know what to think. Is it really happening? I'm so scared."

Tanya pouts. "Don't worry, babe. It'll fine once we get started. It's just me and Clive at the moment. Thought we'd get a couple down us first." She mimes a drinking action and then indicates her neighbours should step inside with a jerk of her head.

The three of them move into the house, Tanya leads them to what she refers to as the sitting room, a place of solid wood flooring, contemporary furnishings and a huge window looking out over the vast and very private lawn at the back of the house.

Clive turns to greet them. He's naked, the elephant's trunk between his legs swinging. "Hi there," he says, unconcerned by his nudity, his leering gaze lingering on Barbara's chest.

When Barbara sees the look her insides melt. Heat floods her vulva. It was what she wanted: a man to look at her with hungry desire in his eyes.

"Wow, Barbara," Clive continues as he walks towards her. He nods and grins, over-emphasising his appraisal, a hand cupping his chin.

"You're not buying a car," Tanya interjects, rolling her eyes at her husband's obvious enthusiasm. "Forgive my husband, Babs," she says, adding a sharp, "Stop fuckin' gapin', Clive."

Unabashed, Clive winks at his wife. "Yeah-yeah," he says.

"Dirty sod," Tanya mutters as she approaches Tim. "You gonna get undressed, babe?" she asks while throwing a faux-disgusted look towards her own husband. To Tim she lewdly purrs, "I thought we could start off with me sucking your cock?"

"Let him have a drink first, eh, Tan," Clive remarks with a laugh.

Tanya pouts and then pokes her tongue out at her husband. "I can suck his cock while he's having a drink, can't I?"

Five minutes later and Barbara is staring at Tanya bouncing up and down on Tim's erection. The sight of her husband's rod embedded inside the blonde causes a huge flare of yearning in Barbara. She drags her attention away from the Tanya's derrière, the younger woman's pelvis angled in such a way that Tim's cock is clearly visible while Tanya's flesh stretches and bulges on the outstroke. Barbara can clearly see Tanya's desire glistening on Tim's shaft when the blonde rises.

She chews her bottom lip and eyes Clive while mumbling, "My husband and your wife."

The clotted words coming through slack lips bring a smirk to Clive's face. "And me and you," he replies, the smile predatory as he strokes his impressive length. He nods at the other couple as Tanya squeaks and grunts and blurts sharp obscenities. "Would you like to have a go on this, Barbara?" he asks. "Before--"

"Please!" Barbara groans, squirming on the sofa, legs automatically going wide.

"Take those knickers off," Clive instructs. He's standing in front of Barbara with his huge dick so close she could lean in and lick the end. "Kneel," the man barks. "Lift that lovely arse in the air. Shove it out. Really stick it at me so I can fuck you."

"Like this?" Barbara sighs while leaning in low, elbows on the arm of the settee, rump thrust high.

There's a movement behind her and Barbara feels his touch on her buttocks. Then, knowing Clive can see all of her, she groans. "You dirty bugger. That's my arsehole."

Clive dabs at the dark roundel with the tip of his tongue while working his fingers at Barbara's sex. "I know," he says, dipping in to wriggle deeper, invading the woman's anus before tickling her clit and probing her gooey opening.

"Jesus," Barbara sobs as she scoops her breasts free of the corset. "Lick my arse, you mucky bastard."

Clive chuckles. "In the mood are you, Barbara?"

The woman's head goes back. Her mouth falls open while she squeezes her eyes closed tight. "I have been all day," Barbara groans, squirming, She opens her eyes and looks back at Clive, breasts swinging as she lifts herself up on straight arms. "God, please just lick me, Clive."

Tanya sees what's happening and slips off Tim's cock.

"Go on, Clive," the blonde says, walking to the sofa, elegant in her heels. She stands alongside for a moment, eyes gleaming with carnal delight, both hands massaging her breasts.

Clive grins at his wife. "You want a taste?" he asks.

Smirking, Tanya replies with, "I've been licking her pussy most days, babe. While you boys are out at work, we've been practicing."

Clive rolls his eyes and then he's back to business behind Barbara.

"You enjoying that?" Tanya asks, squatting so she can look right into Barbara's face.

The elder woman's head comes up, her eyes clearing when she focuses on Tanya.

With her throat working, Barbara nods. "Mm-hmm..." she squeaks.

"Kiss me, Babs," the blonde insists, reaching for Barbara's face.

Their tongues slide, with Barbara merely opening her mouth while Tanya does it all, the elder woman's cheeks sandwiched between her hands.

When they break, when Tanya pulls away, Tim is standing there cranking his dick.

"Here's your hubby," Tanya murmurs, a hand on Barbara's shoulder to attract her attention. "Suck him," she orders.

Tanya grabs Tim's cock and tugs at his length for several robust strokes. She smirks up at the man's face, her tongue sliding over the knob-head, pre-cum leaking out of its eye.

"Two women sucking your cock, Tim," mutters Tanya, a hand between her legs. "Come on, Babs," she adds, "suck him with me. Let's share."

Tim's girth stretches his wife's lips and Tanya watches for a time. She fingers her own sex and then takes hold of the cock, pulling it from Barbara's mouth so she can take a turn.

Tim groans and blinks while the women swap him back and forth. "That's my pussy on your hubby's cock," he hears Tanya murmur to Barbara. You want my hubby to fuck you with his big fucking dick, Babs?"

"Oh, fuck, yes," Barbara mumbles, her throat clogged with desire. "Please..."

Nodding, Tanya rises to her feet. "You heard her, Clive," she says, looking at her husband. "Fuck her, babe."

Clive stands and guides Barbara onto her back. The woman blinks up at him, face soft, not really getting what's going on at first.

"I was going to come," Barbara complains. Then her eyes go wide when she realises what's about to happen.

Barbara shunts her buttocks over the chair she's arranged over the precipice. She's all scrunched up, bent with her chin on her chest, pelvis angled with her pussy presented to Clive while he arranges her legs to suit his needs.

Barbara gawps at the terrible bludgeon and mewls, "That big fucker is going to split my pussy."

Then the huge dome nudges her.

"Oh, fuck," she squeaks, hands against the settee as she struggles to lift herself up.

Clive's tongue is poking out. He's concentrating hard, brow furrowed like there's a difficult mathematical question to be solved.

"Shit," hisses Barbara when the mushroom-head pops her open. Clive moves forward. "F*uuu*ck," she drawls, with the vowel stretching, her mouth gaping like a landed fish. Barbara claws at the sofa, lips stretched across her teeth in a rictus of agonised delight, stomach tensing with the effort. "Oh God," she squeaks, spluttering and moaning as inch by relentless inch has eased into her.

She takes the whole thing, the entire length of it slipping in.

Tim gapes at it, he sees his wife tight around that cock, her flesh bloodless while Clive's balls hang there all nestled in against the cease between Barbara's buttocks.

"Shit," Tim mumbles when he sees the skin, distort, Barbara's body bulging when Clive begins the slow withdrawal.

The man senses a presence next to him and turns to find Tanya has moved alongside.

"Fucking fantastic isn't it?" she purrs, an arm going around Tim's shoulder. The blonde's body presses against Tim's flank, a breast squashed between them. She takes his erection in hand, slowly stroking while they both gaze, transfixed.

On the sofa, Barbara wails.

Clive is balls deep again.

It goes on for a minute and more, with Clive speeding up after each stroke. Soon he's holding Barbara's legs wide, feet fighting for purchase against the carpet as he ploughs her.

"That's it, Clive," Tanya breathes. "Smash her. Smash that pussy." She turns to kiss Tim, eyes blazing. "I wanna fuck, babe," the blonde mewls, dancing on tiptoe as though she needs to pee. "I'm so fucking horny seeing them at it."

Tim looks back, risking being turned into a pillar of salt as Tanya drags him away. He can't stop from watching, he can't help himself. It's compelling – his lovely Barbara being *taken* like that!

"Fuck me, Tim," the woman urges, desperate as an alcoholic at pub opening time.

Tim turns to see the very pleasing shape of Tanya's rump offered to him. The woman is kneeling on one of the chairs that match the sofa. Her spine is curved in such a way her buttocks are a delightfully pleasing invitation.

"Oh shit," Tim whines, the mollusc of Tanya's sex peeping at him from the concavity at the top of her thighs. Her labia are slick and gaping, her arousal a beacon.

Tanya rests her elbows on the back of the chair and turns to face Tim. Her tiny waist is creased, her shape emphasised while the blonde offers herself. "Just put it in and fuck me," she purrs. "Hard," she urges, expression snarling. "Fuck my tight little pussy," the blonde growls, biting off each word, a jungle carnivore on a carcass.

Tanya's body tightens around Tim's cock when he slides into her molten embrace. "Ah, that's good," he grunts, his sole focus centered on his dick.

Tanya pushes back, her flesh slapping against Tim. "Harder!" she cries, with her fingers tight against the chair. The woman implores Tim with her eyes, her nose is all crinkled as she grits her teeth and spits her need. "I want you to bang me. Really punish me with it. Your cock's perfect for hard fucking, Tim. Use it on me, babe."

The realisation percolates through to Tim. Vague though it is, he understands her husband is simply too big for them to really get carried away. If Clive hammers at Tanya the way she urging Tim to she'd probably not walk properly for a week. Either that or his cock would come through the top of her head.

It dawns on him that he's just what Tanya needs. His size is just right for the robust fucking she wants.

Tim's groans, his hands full of taut flesh. Tanya is tight, gym-wired, young and toned. She's a delight to feel beneath wandering fingers. He reads the young woman's body like braille. It isn't that the blonde is any more exciting than his wife, she's just different: a Porsche and a Jaguar.

He wonders if it's the same for the women. Tim has a moment to ponder the differences between his size and Clive's tremendous offering, thinking about how his wife might feel being stuffed full of meat.

Then Tim gets caught up with the immediate. Tanya is squirming and gasping and pouring forth a litany of sewer-mouthed exhortations. Her accent is harsh, almost grating, the eroticism of the filth she's muttering heightened, in Tim's opinion, because of it. Tanya isn't an angel with a dirty face, she an angel with a dirty mouth, and Tim loves to hear the crude obscenities pouring forth.

That room resonates with groans and grunts, gasps and sighs and obscenities, meaty thwacks and liquid squelching.

Barbara feels stuffed full of male gristle while Clive's hands maul her breasts and his breath gusts warm on the nape of her neck. Tanya squeals and shrieks, vocal in her enjoyment, revelling in the debauchery.

It's only going to get better for Tanya. In a few minutes – when the other men arrive, that's when the party really gets started.

The blonde cranes round, throws a heavy-lidded glance at Tim and then takes in the scene of Barbara's body accommodating Clive's cock.

"I fuckin' love it," she hisses, her hot-eyed stare fixed back on her friend's husband.

The man nods, face loose with his own pleasure. "You're sensational, Tanya," he mumbles.

Tanya winces and sucks in a breath. She reaches round and splays her buttocks, opening herself, inviting Tim to do his worst. "Damage me," she groans. "Smash my little pussy."

It's close to the crescendo. It can't go on. The four of them groan and moan, muscles tensing. Heads loll, breath comes in short spurts, precious oxygen is sucked in while each one strives towards the pinnacle.

"Oh fuck," Barbara wails. "That's so fucking big…"

And, while the older woman revs up for a noisy climax, with Clive probing deep, his own surge threatening, the doorbell chimes.

***

Paul Baxter's head bobs up and down in appreciation. "Tanya," he says, affecting a nonchalant air, as as though naked beauties open their doors to him every day of the week.

"Hello, lads," Tanya says, beaming a smile at the new arrivals. She eyes Paul and then studies the man standing next to him.

They're both in their twenties, gym-twins with boy-band faces. They're typical of their ilk, cocky, confident of their appeal to the opposite sex. In Tanya's opinion they both possess just the right dose of cheekiness to make it work. Paul has dark hair, gelled and spiked while the other is a suede-head, his scalp bristly with blond stubble.

"Glad you could make it," Tanya adds. She gives them her trademark smirk and rolls her eyes. "We started without you." A jerk of her head indicates the interior of the house. "Barbara's just enjoying herself on my hubby's cock. That's her making all the fuss."

"What's the score with tonight?" Paul asks as the moans and squeals reach him. "Sounds like she's having a good time," he remarks.

He's been chosen for his good looks and relative youth, while his stamina and propensity to squirt like an erupting volcano are also a consideration.

Tanya takes a moment to appraise their muscular bodies before replying. "It's a friend of ours… and her husband," she says. "She told me about this thing she has about shagging a few blocks at the same time." The blonde's eyes turn to slits. She grins again. "So I thought I'd get a couple of my favourites round here."

Paul smirks and nods, the man next to him – Dave Wilton – doing the same.

The pair exchange a look as Tanya continues with, "You two have a special talent that'd be great tonight."

Dave looks puzzled. "What's that?"

Still smirking, Tanya replies. "You both come like fountains." Then she goes on quickly. "Anyway, let's stop all this gabbing. Do you wanna fuck my friend or not? I promise you, boys, she's bloody sexy."

The two men exchange a look before shrugging at one another.

"Let's go," says Dave.

Whereupon they follow Tanya's swaying rump into the house.

***

It's a surreal moment for Barbara when the two men appear and Tanya makes the introductions.

"Oh my God," Barbara gasps, struggling to catch her breath after her exertions. Sucking in air, she stares at the men.

"Nice," she hears Paul comment. Her skin tingles when she sees him staring at her breasts. It's a thrill to have a hot young man gazing at her just as she'd wanted. "*Very* fucking nice." Paul's look is bestial. Barbara realises he doesn't give a stuff about her or her life. He's there for his own gratification. It's uncomplicated sex he's looking for, purely carnal. The young man doesn't need or indeed want conversation.

Barbara shivers. Goosebumps erupt on her arms. She's tingling, delighted and appalled. *Oh God, this is it. Oh dear God...*

"Here they are," Tanya says, one hip cocked, arms splayed in a *tah-da!* gesture. She grins at Barbara like the cute and smiling dolly-bird on a 70s game show. *And tonight's star prize is...!*

Suddenly it's too much to take. Barbara jerks upright on the sofa. Unreasonably modest given the circumstances, she covers her breasts with an arm and splayed fingers, legs snapping closed.

On the settee next to her, Clive, the veteran of many encounters such as these, throws up a lazy wave. "Hello, lads," he says.

Standing, Tim glances at his wife and appreciates how she feels. He's also self-conscious in his nudity, a fledging actor on the stage during his big break, he's about to fluff his lines. Tim is very aware of his age and the size of his dick compared to the section of fire hose sported by Clive. He's in decent nick but isn't going to delude himself. He can compete with Tanya's husband and the two fit youngsters eyeing his wife.

Then it hits home, their looks send him the message that theory has become fact. The two newcomers are eyeing Barbara with carnal intent, expressions lupine. Tim expects them to throw back their heads and howl at any moment when he sees them ogling Barbara so hungrily. It's a pivotal moment for him, the epiphany when Tim fully appreciates just why they're there.

The two men are going to fuck his wife.

Tim is reeling when a double handclap from Tanya grabs everyone's attention.

"Now, lads," she says to Dave and Paul, fists on her hips while pouting like a disappointed schoolteacher staring down a couple of recalcitrant pupils. "You two should get out of those clothes." Tanya next regards Clive, adding, "Get the boys a drink." Finally she turns her attention to Barbara. "Why are you acting all shy, Babs?" Tanya regards Barbara with something akin to pity. "The boys have come to play with you, show them your *gorgeous* figure. Don't be shy, babe."

Clive is away getting the beers Paul and Dave have asked for, while the men themselves are in early stages of undress.

Barbara looks at Tanya, anxiety obvious. She's frightened, suddenly petrified at what she's unleashed. She's jittery and anxious and a quick glance at her husband tells Barbara Tim isn't going to be much use to her. Then she focuses on the two men. For the first time she really pays attention to the pair of them. Paul is bare-chested, his muscles bunching and flexing as he continues to undress. Then, noticing Barbara's intent examination, Paul and Dave pause to settle their feral gazes on her.

Desire rushes in a hot tide between her legs when Barbara sees their hungry stares coming back at her. Barbara's arm falls away from her front. She gulps when she hears the mutters of appreciation from Dave and Paul. Emboldened by their complimentary remarks she casually reclines. She's cool and confident, legs parting to reveal the dark triangle of her pubic bush crowning her cleft, her vulva depilated.

Barbara's cheeks burn as she flaunts her body. She's thrumming with arousal. Her clit has a pulse of its own; her breasts ache to be touched, fondled and mauled.

"What do you think, Babs?" Tanya asks.

Barbara grins and nods, her eyes fixed on the two young men. "I think I'm going to enjoy this," she replies, squirming and daring to slide a finger through her labia. When her finger slides over her clit, Barbara groans and winces.

Then the boys are naked, cocks waggling as they move towards her. The older woman levers forward, hands reaching for two erections.

The next thing Barbara is conscious of is cranking away at both of them. She has two substantial cocks in her fists, two hard dicks attached to two gorgeous hunks.

"Suck them," Tanya breathes before she leans in to kiss Barbara's mouth. "You suck these two while I give Tim something to smile about. He's looking a bit lost there."

Clive returns with two beers and is confronted by a scene of debauchery. "Let's get the party started!" he cries.

***

The scene is different things to different participants: six alternate impressions.

Paul and Dave are of a similar mindset and attitude. For them, it's a matter of a good time, of poking it into a gorgeous woman.

For Clive the situation isn't too unusual. He's used to the group thing. The new twist is involving their neighbours.

Tim, however, is out of his depth. He feels awkward and intimidated by so many Alpha dogs. He'd be lost, floundering on the rough seas of his emotions if it wasn't for Tanya being down on her knees sucking and cranking at his cock, her attention going from his hard-on to the scene as it develops. Tim struggles, torn between the desire to save his wife from what's going to happen and savouring the experience of Tanya's mouth and pussy. It's gut-wrenching, knowing his wife is going to be used as a sex toy – he's her husband for God's sake, he shouldn't be letting it happen. But Tim can't tear himself away when he sees Tanya grinning at him, her lips and face distorted around a mouthful of cock.

Tanya? Well, she loves it all. She adores the fact she's been instrumental in seducing Barbara, *corrupting* her. The preceding days and weeks have been fun. Easing her neighbour along the path, taking it slowly, introducing each new thrill and seeing the older woman's response has given the blonde so much delight. Now it's about to culminate, Tanya hopes, in Barbara fulfilling her fantasy. She feels good, proud to have taken a handful of clay and gently moulded the formless lump into a work of libidinous art.

The final barrier falls when Barbara glances at Tanya and sees the blonde with Tim's cock in her mouth. She stares at the scene for a few seconds, unable to register fully it's her husband she's seeing fucking Tanya's face.

She moans when the reality of her situation hits her. Barbara's body thrums with desire. She gulps and drags her attention away from Tanya and Tim, her focus returning to the feral intensity in the young men's eyes. Their look gives Barbara the spur to carry on. Her anxiety evaporates. She feels beautiful, wanted, desired. The two boys are hungry for her, they *want* her.

Lust flares even brighter. Molten desire floods her sex. She's on fire, suddenly desperate for it all. Barbara recalls the times with Tanya: the dildo, the lube, the blonde's gentle cajoling.

"Oh my God," Barbara sighs. She catches Tanya's eye, sees the other woman cranking Tim's dick. *That's my husband.* The shock of it makes her gulp; her tummy flips with excitement. "I'm going to do it," she says out loud.

Tanya grins and nods, gaze fixed on Barbara, holding the older woman's attention while she licks Tim's bell-end.

Then there are two men with her, one either side. Her breasts are in their hands and they're fondling her, squeezing tit-flesh. Paul ducks in and sucks one thick, elongated nipple.

Barbara groans while Tanya calls, "Yes, babe, you're gonna do it."

The next thing Barbara knows she's on her back, spread like a picnic for the men to devour.

Paul drops to his knees. He's between Barbara's legs, his thumbs splaying the ungainly folds.

"You're fucking ace," the man says, enthusiastically.

"Oh!" Barbara yelps, the shock of it catching her by surprise. Even though she knows it's coming, the reality of what's happening is a cold water shock. "He's licking me," Barbara squeaks to Tanya as though it's news. Her face, gape-mouthed and stunned, swivels to Tim. "Oh my God," she breathes.

"Barbara," Tim gulps.

Tanya is quick to distract Barbara's husband. She senses he might be on the point of stepping in to call it off. Tim was always going to be difficult when it came to it. The men usually were. The fantasy appeals to them, but the reality, well, that's completely different. Sometimes, in Tanya's experience, the men got all territorial, sometimes aggressive when they realise their wife is actually going to fuck another man. They especially don't like it when the woman seems only too keen to climb aboard a stranger's cock.

Barbara has been always malleable, easy to manipulate and open to suggestion, whereas Tim was the one likely to balk when it came to it.

There was no way to gauge male ego and territorial instinct. No way to determine how a husband might react. The only way for Tanya to ensure Tim's compliance was to keep him distracted.

The blonde rises to her feet with supple, liquid grace. She jacks at Tim's root, maintaining the pressure, keeping him interested.

"You should fuck me again," she, her voice dragging Tim's eyes from his wife.. Tanya sees Tim focus on her breasts. She takes a pace back, stepping to one side as she guides Tim around so Barbara and her paramours are behind him. "You want to put it in again, babe?" she asks, cocking one hip, head tilting. Throwing her most mischievous smirk at him, eyes flashing, cheeks dimpling, cranking up the heat, Tanya hefts her round breasts with both hands. "Come on, Tim," she murmurs. "I want you to fuck my tight little pussy again. We got interrupted before. Let's have some real fun."

The combination of false innocence and the reminder what it was like to be inside her works on Tim. He looks at Tanya for some time, taking in the exquisite shape of her, soaking up the angelic features. The contradiction between Tanya's beatific smile and her true nature sends a surge of desire through him. He's suddenly eager to get at her again.

Tim decides he can live with it. Seeing his wife enjoying other men isn't such a big deal. They love each other, their hearts are linked. This is just sex. It's nothing but lust and heat and physical satisfaction. Let Barbara have what she wants. She'll only love him all the more for letting it all happen.

And a one-on-one with the blonde isn't something he's going to turn down. He's inflamed by her looks, her body and her attitude.

Moments later, Tim is sitting in the chair with Tanya astride him. She's sliding up and down on his dick, she moans in his ear, swaying breasts brushing his face.

Tim grabs taut buttocks and splays the globes with his fingers. He feels for their conjunction, for where Tanya's body accepts him. His cock is slippery with them both. He can feel Tanya's lust sipping from her, the woman's own need sliding over his balls.

"Fuck," Tim splutters, head tilting back. He looks up to see Tanya wincing down at him, her lovely face creased with the pleasure of it.

"Fuck me," the woman moans as she ducks in for a long kiss. "Give it to me, Tim. Fuck me and let it go when you want. Come inside me. Let's make a cream pie, babe."

***

There are hands on her. Barbara doesn't know which pair belongs to which man – and it doesn't matter anyway. She's lost, out there, at their mercy. Barbara has capitulated. She's given up and surrendered herself to their whims. There's a basic plan about what's to happen, a map of sorts. The destination is clear, just the road to it hasn't yet been decided upon. There are several routes and Barbara has left it up to the men to decide which one they'll take. It isn't that Barbara is a passenger, more like she's the vehicle.

There are three of them at her: Clive, Paul and Dave. She thinks it's Paul still down there between her legs, his tongue busy, breath hot on her vulva. Barbara knows Clive is on her right; she's got him in one hand, the size of him instantly recognisable.

A mouth covers hers, a tongue slides between her lips. Barbara returns the kiss with avid enthusiasm, groaning and gasping at the wrongness of it all.

I'm a slut. I'm going to get gang-fucked. I don't know who's at me...

Barbara sees it's Dave when the man pulls away from the kiss. He gazes down at her for a long moment before presenting his cock for her to suck. She lies there, helpless, her body all curled up like a question mark with Dave's hand on her shoulder while Paul holds her thighs and laps at her sex.

A fledgling begging for food, Barbara opens her mouth and squeals at Dave to give her his meat.

"Closer," she urges, craning forward as far as she can. "I can't get it."

Clive hears the woman's entreaty and moves in as, pressing in alongside Dave, his big dick waggling and waving.

"Two cocks," Barbara gurgles before her tongue flicks over Dave's knob-end. "Three cocks," she corrects herself, grabbing for Clive so she can pull him in closer. "I'm going to get all three at once." Barbara slurps at Clive's, her tongue swirling like she's licking a toffee-apple.

Movement between her thighs takes Barbara's focus from what's in front of her face. She looks down, peering around naked skin. What she sees and then feels brings an excited squeak from her. It's Paul, kneeling upright, cock in his fist as he rubs the head of the thing through her vulva.

"You're going to put it in?" she gurgles, her voice like a blocked drain. *Bareback*, Barbara has time to think. *It isn't supposed to be like this.*

Her mouth opens, she's going to object, they'd agreed on condoms.

But then Paul's inside her. His cock is splitting her open. It feels so good: *so fucking lovely.*

Barbara can't bring herself to order Paul to withdraw. "Fuck me," she hisses, grabbing at Clive's cock and slurping at it, one hand holding the awful bludgeon in an underhand grip. She pulls at Clive, tugging his length, smearing gooey pre-cum over her cheeks and chin, eyes sparking while she gazes at Paul's face as he fucks into her. "All of you boys," squeals Barbara. "Fuck me."

It gets crazy. First, it's Paul down there while Barbara writhes and moans, male meat in her mouth, Clive stuffing between her lips until she gags and coughs and spits thick ropes of silvery drool. Hawsers of the stuff shiver from her chin. The upper slopes of her breasts glisten.

Barbara is manhandled around until she's on her hands and knees so Dave can get at her. He's behind Barbara, his cock replacing Paul's.

Dave slides in and Barbara tastes herself on Paul's length, swapping him for Clive who once more stretches her lips so much she thinks her skin will tear. It's either that or her jaw will pop.

Dave ruts at Barbara's body, fucking into her, fingers digging into her hips. He's frantic, grunting and moaning, his tight washboard stomach colliding with Barbara's buttocks, their coupling a staccato rhythm.

While that goes on, Tim is doing his best to hold it in. He's close to pouring all he has into Tanya. The blonde is divine, so lovely to look at, exquisite around his cock. Tim feels Tanya's body clenching around his girth. Her skin is velvety smooth under his hands as they slide over every available inch of her body.

"I'm gonna come," Tim hears the woman mumble, her hot breath right in his ear, the words coming out thick and clotted. "You gonna fill me, babe?" she whines, pelvis moving with brisk urgency as she grinds her pubis down on him. "You gonna squirt?"

They're kissing, tongues sliding until Tanya lets out a bestial grunt and corkscrews her hips.

"I'm there," she sighs, eye closed, head lolling back. "I'm fucking *there...*" The woman rocks back and forth. She embraces Tim, pulling him close so they can kiss again while Tanya gasps and grunts into Tim's mouth. When she pulls away, she's exultant. Tanya's eyes shine, her grin as wide as a crocodile's. "Thank you, Tim," she purrs, easing off his cock. "Oh!" the blonde cries. "Tim, look at your wife. Look at Barbara, she's suckin' and fuckin'..."

Tim gasps when he sees it, that odd mix of jealousy and arousal swimming inside him again.

"Barbara," he breathes, boggling. "Jesus..."

"She sounds like she's enjoying herself," Tanya says, her words directed at Tim while she stares at what's going on. "The dirty mare," she adds with a wistful sigh.

Tim catches sight of the blonde's smirk and recognises the devilishness in her. It's obvious by the twist to her mouth and slits for eyes. It's a lascivious expression, debauched and full of mischievous intent.

Tim's desire flares again. He's suddenly euphoric. *I'm going to fuck the arse off you again. There's going to be more of this.*

Tanya interrupts Tim's licentious thoughts by saying, "Let's go and watch. This is what I've been getting her ready for." She leans down and kisses Tim's mouth, the kiss full of energy, Tanya's own dark desire in that press of her lips and the sweep of her tongue. "I want you to fuck me while your wife gets made airtight."

Tim has no clue what Tanya means by "airtight". It's an expression new to him and he doesn't grasp the meaning at first. But, hand-in-hand with Tanya, as he approaches the scene of his wife's depravity, the penny drops.

There's that slide again, the greasy I'm-going-to-be-sick feeling in the pit of his stomach. "Oh God no," Tim mumbles.

Clive is sitting on the sofa, his eyes on Barbara as he cranks his cock. The woman stands and adjusts the cups of the corset to suit her. She tugs at it until her big breasts are presented to her satisfaction and comfort.

"Go on, Babs," Tanya urges, eyes aflame when she looks at Tim to gauge his mood. "I'm going to help," she grins, showing two rows of white teeth in her enthusiasm to get involved. "You get behind me. You can fuck while I sort Barbara out. Then," she adds, eyes rolling with the anticipation of the fun to follow, "we can really get going." Before she moves to the side of the settee Tanya kisses Tim and adds, "I'm gonna come on your cock while your wife takes on those three."

Tim wonders if he really wants to see it. "Barbara," he murmurs.

The sound of her name reaches Barbara. She faces her husband just as she's in the act of throwing a leg across Clive's thighs. Her hand goes down to take hold of Clive's huge lump of meat. She's rubbing the cock-head across her sex when she says, "I love you for this, Tim." Barbara closes her eyes, wincing when the slippery dome slides over her clit. "I honestly, truly love you, darling."

Tim stands there and watches his wife's body accepting Clive's dick. Barbara grunts and gasps and whines until a great sob of delight bubbles out of her.

"Let me ride it," Barbara sighs, hips rising and falling slowly. "Let me get used to it before…" She throws a look behind her and sees Paul and Dave jacking their cocks. "Which one is going in my arse?" she mumbles with a heavy-lidded look of pleasure and expectation.

For Barbara the dam has burst: her anxieties, the concern about the effect of her realising her fantasy on her marriage, the reticence, all of it has gone. She's away on the flood, kept afloat by the hunger she's seen from the men, their desire for her overwhelming every other consideration.

If Tim's bothered – and there have been snatches of it in the way he's looked at her and the things he's said – they can talk it out later, tomorrow, whenever. All Barbara wants as of the moment is Clive in her pussy, his lovely cock stuffed inside her while one of those gorgeous boys break in using the back door. Then, when she's sandwiched between the two men, both of them moving, their hands on her body, Barbara will invite the other into her mouth.

There's no thought for anything beyond. Barbara has no care about taking their semen. They can squirt inside her or cover her in the stuff.

None of it matters.

She's in the here and now.

When Clive's fingers squeeze her buttocks, Barbara groans and squirms, the cock inside her probing just that bit deeper.

The woman looks down and offers her breasts to him. "Suck my tits, Clive," she hisses, her teeth clenched, lewd in throes of her ardour.

"Yeah, Clive," Tanya interjects. "You keep going on about Babs's tits. There they are."

Clive grins at his wife, holding her attention fast with his eyes as he sucks one nipple, his eyes telling Tanya exactly how it is.

"Time for me to grease you up," Tanya says to Barbara.

She reaches for an insignificant and the hitherto unnoticed tube on the small table a pace or two away from the settee. A twist of the cap and a squeeze and Tanya is smearing gunk over the puckered smudge of Barbara's sphincter.

"That's it, Clive," Tanya says. "Hold her open for me. Jesus," she adds, gasping. "Look at your cock stretching her. Fuck, babe, it looks so fucking good."

Tanya turns to Tim and, breathless and squirming, says, "Bend me over the settee, Tim." She's already halfway there before Tim can respond. "Put it in," she squeaks, splaying her buttocks with one hand. "Fuck me."

So once again, Tim finds himself inside Tanya, the molten embrace gripping his shaft. He leans low over her back, crouching so he can hold her breasts and rut into her like he wants to. *You want fucking? Here it is. I'm going to fuck you 'til you fart...*

Tanya moans. Her head lolls loose for a moment before she looks up, her expression an atavistic snarl. "Fuck her in her dirty hole," the blonde shrieks as she claws at the sofa fabric. "Go on. Get to it."

Then Tanya is gone too. She sobs and moans, head rolling while she thrusts back against Tim's length.

After that outburst, when Paul and Dave exchange a look, with a shrug passing between them, after Paul has clambered onto the sofa and arranged himself between the limbs already present, it descends into a free-for-all.

***

The training helps. All those times Tanya gently teased Barbara's sphincter with the end of the dildo have made it possible. But It's odd having a man back there. No matter how careful he's being, regardless of the lube and the arousal that has her enthusiastic to take a cock in her anus, it's still a very odd sensation and a matter of complete trust.

Her pussy is packed full of Clive. Barbara is astride Tanya's husband and feels stuffed with dick already, never mind another man butting the head of his cock against a ring of muscle designed as an exit. Paul shouldn't be there, Barbara's sphincter is telling her as much and the puckered ring resists the invasion.

Paul mutters a curse and wriggles around a little. Then he pushes again.

Pressure builds. Barbara gulps and tries to hold herself still. She's concerned that she'll be hurt if she moves as Paul's cock-head presses against her. But having Clive in her pussy feels so good and her instinct is to fuck against that huge cock. Barbara wants to grind down on it, to force Clive deeper. She wants him where no man has ever touched before. He's so fucking *thick*. Her pussy is stretched so tight.

"It isn't going to go in," Barbara gasps. She struggles to turn and face the man nudging at her anus. "Clive's too big. I'm too small for both of you at the same time. The pair of you will rip me apart."

Watching it all, with Tim thrusting robustly behind her as she forces herself back to take his dick, Tanya's jaw clenches. "Get in there, Paul," she says, the words strained between gritted teeth. "I wanna see her take both of you. Go on, babe," the blonde urges. "Go on…"

Paul swipes at his forehead with a forearm and rises up on tip-toes, his height angled steeply, legs straight, thighs and calves tense while he eases slowly back at the waist. He's got his cock in one hand while straight-armed against the sofa back with the other, friction between his toes and the floor all that's stopping him from slipping away.

The trio on the sofa tussle. It's a gasping, grunting time with Paul struggling to penetrate Barbara's sphincter. Not that Clive is having much to do with it. He's mostly resisting the urge to fuck up into Barbara. It's there, the tickle in his core, the need to use the woman for his own ends. If this goes on much longer he's going to snap. Clive will force Barbara onto her back and, using a phrase that passes so often from his wife's lips, smash her pussy with his big cock.

Simultaneous cries from Barbara and Paul interrupt Clive's vague planning.

"Oh God!" yelps Barbara when the cock-head pops the tight ring.

Paul feels the sudden yielding, the tight muscle surrendering and, as he slides in, half his length slipping into the taboo of Barbara's anus, he lets out a cry of triumph. "Fuck!" he calls. "It's in! I'm there."

"Steady," Barbara replies, gulping and blinking as she cranes around. "Just keep still," she gasps, a hand going to Paul's chest. "Let me get--"

She swallows again, wall-eyed while swivelling back to face Clive, her breasts squashing against him when she slumps forward.

"He's in my arse," Barbara mutters, all glazed of eye when she looks at Clive from beneath heavy lids. "He's in my arse," she gurgles. "Oh God, Clive, he's got his cock in my backside."

Clive grins and attempts a shrug. "That's what you wanted, Barbara," he reminds her.

Tanya leans in with Tim working inside her. She stares at Barbara, face slack, her fingers on her clit. "Get used to it, babe," mumbles the blonde, wincing and moaning before she whines, "How does it feel? Two cocks at once, Babs, isn't it just the sluttiest..." Her head lolls and she hisses, the hand between her legs moving quickly. "Give us a kiss, Babs," Tanya gasps. "I wanna kiss you while your hubby fucks me. I think I'm gonna come."

The women kiss, with Tanya doing most of it. She's mad with yearning, desperate for her climax. Tanya's tongue invades Barbara's mouth, the blonde snuffling and groaning, the pleasure overwhelming her reality.

"I'm full of cock," Barbara says, her expression and tone still surprised. It's as though none of this was planned. Barbara acts like she didn't know *what* was going to happen. "I'm stuffed with them, Tanya."

Tanya rises, turning her attention to Paul as she reaches for him. "More," she insists, pulling him in to kiss his mouth. "Get into her balls deep," Tanya snarls, face twisted with desire. "Fuck her arse. Give it to her."

Paul moves, easing in, brow furrowed in concentration. His urge is to simply drive it home, to sink into Barbara in one deep lunge. But he realises that doing so would probably bring the evening to an abrupt and dramatic halt. Rampaging at her virgin rectum would more than likely have Barbara screaming hysterically and making all kinds of fuss. So, with the woman's sphincter a tight collar around his dick, Paul sets his hands on her waist. His thumbs are on the rack of Barbara's ribs, at the back, fingers curled around her. Leaning in, he nuzzles Barbara's neck, holding himself still, cock pulsing.

"Are you ready, Barbara?" the man murmurs. "More?"

Grateful for Paul's consideration Barbara gulps and nods. "Slow," she breathes. "Nice and slow."

Paul grits his teeth. He's an athlete preparing for the crack of the starter pistol, a meditation guru settling his breathing. Fighting the instinct, calming the beast within that snaps and snarls at him to rut into the woman's delicate sphincter, Paul gently pushes.

Another inch slides in, his shaft greasy with the gloop smeared across the dark smudge of Barbara's muddy hole.

Clive holds still while Barbara gasps and nods encouragement at Paul. "A little more," she gurgles.

Paul moves again, pressing home until his body comes to rest against Barbara's buttocks. "I'm in all the way, babe," he mutters.

"Oh God," groans Barbara. She swivels as best she can, not easy since she's sandwiched between two lovers, but she's desperate to kiss the man whose cock is stuffed into her anus. Barbara feels an overwhelming urge for his mouth against hers during their shared intimacy.

All three remain immobile for a time, with Barbara kissing Paul before she then offers her lips to Clive.

"Two men," Barbara sighs, her pelvis jerking. "Together. At the same time … Two cocks." And then she's working at them, hips going back and forth, the mechanics of three-way fucking synchronising naturally.

As Barbara squeaks and moans one cock is on the inside while the other eases out, the tempo increasing in direct proportion to Barbara's rising confidence.

"It feels so good!" the woman cries, fixing Tanya with an exultant gaze. "It burns in my arse but I like it," she whimpers. "I fucking LOVE it," adds an over-excited Barbara, hands on the sofa back as she forces her body down onto Clive's root.

"One more," Tanya responds when she breaks away from a heated kiss she's been sharing with Paul. "In your mouth, Babs. Just one more cock and you're there."

The next one is easy.

Barbara looks at Dave. "You going to give me that?" she asks, breasts swinging against Clive's face as he hangs on beneath her. "Let me taste it," the woman says while Dave stands there cranking at himself. "Now!" she squeals.

Dave gapes for a few more seconds, face slack and moronic until the request filters through. "Unh?" he says, blinking.

"In her mouth, for fuck's sake," Tanya growls, fucking back onto Tim. "Come on, you dozy bugger."

So Dave slots himself into the puzzle. There's an arrangement of limbs, bodies entwined, a heaving mass as Paul pumps into Barbara's anus – the fiend set free.

Clive is doing his best to time his upward thrust, synching with Paul's urgency while Barbara grunts and gurgles around a mouthful of Dave's cock.

While this goes on, Tim is going at Tanya. He understands what Tanya meant by airtight. He knows it's his wife in amongst the melee, every hole filled with cock. Tim can hear her gagging and spitting and urging those three men to give it their all. He still isn't sure how he feels about it, but forces all that down for the time being, deciding to concentrate on taking it out on Tanya. He slams into the blonde, what little spare flesh she has on her hips rippling – which is exactly what Tanya wants.

Tanya groans and gasps and reaches for Dave's cock, Barbara's husband pounding at her. She takes hold of a shaft smeared in saliva, gooey strands of drool dangling from the bulging bell-end. She tugs at it with one hand before sucking on the big dome, tongue tickling the banjo string at the frenulum.

"Here," Tanya gasps, a whine following when Tim goes deep and hard. "Have it back, Babs. Suck it. Suck him again."

Barbara has no choice, Dave is wild with lust. He holds Barbara's face with one hand and forces his cock into her face.

"Oh, fuck, I'm gonna come," Tanya moans. "I'm... I'm..." The blonde goes into it sobbing and rubbing between her legs, hand sawing at her body while Tim hangs on.

Tanya's orgasm rolls on and on while, on the sofa in front of her, four people work their own agendas.

The men probe and poke and thrust, each intent on fucking into Barbara, their own needs paramount. None of them is particularly concerned with the woman at that point, not that Barbara is bothered by the lack of finesse and tenderness – for her it's a revelation: she can handle all they have to offer.

Barbara is jubilant, positively euphoric. "More," she grunts, saliva shivering in thick ropes from her chin. She jacks at Dave's cock, sucking at it, frantic, her climax coming at her. The cock-head plops from between her lips once again. "More I said, you bastards!" screeches Barbara, hips moving in desperation. "Fuck my pussy," she yelps at Clive. "My arse," she adds, her entreaty no less strident as she squirms to look at the man behind her. "Fuck that dirty-hole. Go on, shag my arse." Then she's jacking at Dave again, a maniac with one aim in mind as she gulps at the length dangling in front of her face.

"I'm gonna come," Paul gasps. "Fuck," he groans. "I'm—"

"All over her back!" Tanya calls out, her orgasm cooling. "Shower the bitch in the hot stuff."

Semen pours over Barbara's back when Paul pulls out and tugs his dick. Gouts of jizm flick from the eye of his cock, the first splatting over the woman's skin at the nape of her neck.

Barbara yelps when she feels the outpouring rain down onto her. She cranes round as far as she can manage, pivoting on Clive's erection, the whole length of him buried deep. Barbara is totally impaled and loving it, and now there's all this spunk spitting out of Paul, squirt after squirt of cum spattering over her.

Barbara is liberally coated in the stuff and the sight of all that cum pumping from Paul gets her there.

This is what she wanted, men lusting after her, their cocks spitting out of control.

"Look at it all!" Barbara squeals, rubbing good into her buttocks. Her hand comes up smeared. "Oh, fuck," she moans in response to all she's seeing and hearing and doing. "I'm coming too."

While Paul grunts and squeezes the last drops from his cock, Clive growls that he wants to get into Barbara while she's on her back.

"I can really go at you that way," he says, pushing her up and off his penis.

"The fucking settee!" Tanya cries in protest. She's lived in penury most of her life, the money is still a novelty, her concern for the furniture an automatic response.

"Fuck the settee," Clive snarls, hunger in his eyes as he quickly arranges Barbara to his preference.

"I'll buy you another fucking suite," Clive snaps at his wife. "But I want her on her back so I can get at her properly."

During the ill-timed domestic exchange, Barbara is mindless to it all. She's still writhing and groaning through her orgasm, limbs writhing, thighs juddering in nerveless spasm.

"Oh God!" cries Barbara, eyes wide when Clive sinks into her up to his balls. Her legs go wider, folding at the knees. "Fuck me with that thing," she squeaks.

Paul staggers away, spent for the time being. He collapses into a chair and sees Tanya has Dave in her mouth, the blonde sucking at him while Tim keeps on at her pussy.

"Fucking hell," Paul breathes, eyes set on what's going on.

He watches Clive hover over Barbara on straight arms. Clive is looking down at where his girth is packed into the woman's pussy as he eases back, most of him coming out of her, just the head remaining inside. Then Clive slams back in, the robust lunge causing Barbara's breasts to shiver and roll. After that, Clive is in her, fucking with an intensity that has Barbara grunting and moaning, their robust rutting leaving Paul agog as his desire flares again.

Then Paul's focus returns to Tanya. He sees her on one long roll of pleasure, the blonde's orgasms seemingly melding into a single prolonged ride. She gasps and groans, head lolling, body slack until everything tenses and she's as tight as an overwound spring.

For Tanya the moment is all about witnessing another woman taking Clive's big cock. Seeing the expressions on their faces is always a thrill. She's always been the same: sex always has to be on the edge. Tanya has never subscribed to normality. Swinging with her husband, group sex and corrupting her neighbour gets her there. It's what she needs.

"I fucking love this," Tanya moans. "Fuck, Clive, look at you, babe. Slam that bitch." Tanya disengages from Tim, moving forward to leave him with his cock waggling in the air.

She collapses onto the sofa and inserts herself into the tiny space available. Once there, Tanya takes control, grabbing for Dave's cock so she can suck at it for a few seconds before heaving her body around until she's in a position to kiss Barbara.

It goes on for a short time, with Dave alternating between the two women, his erection going from one mouth to the other while Tim gapes, lost and unsure.

Then Tanya spots his look and curls an arm at him in invitation. "Come here, Tim," the blonde cries. "Get over here and join in."

It's a moment of irony for Tim. *How generous*, he thinks – after all, just whose wife is it in the midst of all that heaving flesh?

He looks on for a second or two longer before muttering, "Fuck it."

Tim moves in to have his dick sucked by Tanya, the woman slurping her own desire from the shaft.

***

It ends with Barbara impaled on her husband's cock. Tim is sitting on the sofa with his wife on his lap, his erection packed into her anus. Tanya made the suggestion, husband and wife staring at one another before Barbara gurgled she would love to feel Tim back there.

There's a quick flurry of activity before Barbara slides down onto Tim, his hands coming round to squeeze her breasts as she opens her legs for Clive to return to her pussy.

Tanya watches, rubbing herself to that sustained pleasure-state while Barbara goes airtight again. It's Tim in Barbara's anus, Clive in her pussy, and Dave in the older woman's mouth. The blonde fingers her sex, her vulva sodden, labia smeared and sticky, clit a pulsing nub of tender flesh.

She goes at herself, gazing in rapt delight at the heaving mass of rutting, groaning people. Then there's a huge bellow from Clive. He's all gritted teeth, wall-eyed, and agonised in a mask of ecstasy.

"Fuck," Tanya's husband grunts a second before he probes deep. The jackhammer fucking ceases and the only movements from Clive are those tensing buttocks and his Adam's apple bobbing up and down, the big muscle at the base of his cock pumping cum.

Ejaculate spurts into Barbara and she yelps with delight, eyes wide, mouth falling open while Clive floods her pussy with semen.

"He's coming!" she squeals. "Oh God... Clive... Come, babe. Do it."

"Me too," Dave snarls, his fist working his dick. "Ah... Shit... I'm--" Jizm spits from him, a long ribbon of the stuff flicking across Barbara's shoulder, another vehement burst splatting right on her cheek.

The sight of spitting cum galvanises Tanya. She's up and on Dave in a flash, moving in quickly so she can control the outpouring and hopefully save her furniture from too much staining. Her method is to wrap her lips around the spitting knob-end, jizm splashing against her palette while she swallows like a baby bird at feeding time.

During it all Dave is gasping and moaning, spurt after spurt of cum bursting out of him. When it ends, there's Jizm sliding over Tanya's chin, the blonde holding a mouthful of the stuff she then shares with Barbara by forcing her goo-coated tongue into the older woman's mouth.

The two men, cocks seeping spunk, move away. They leave Tanya, Tim, and Barbara alone, semen dribbling from Barbara's scarlet, gaping core.

Dave goes across to Paul. He perches on the arm of the chair, while his friend occupies.

"It's going to be a mad night, isn't it?" Paul says, looking up at Dave.

Dave pulls a face, a pout of agreement. "Tanya," he replies, shrugging.

Paul grins and nods. The mention of the blonde's name says it all.

Meanwhile, Tanya is still kissing Barbara, a hand smearing cum across the other woman's breasts as Tim struggles to reconcile the fact he's wedged deep in his wife's rectum.

Tanya sucks on Barbara's nipples, hefting both heavy breasts in her palms, tit-flesh spilling while she goes from one teat to the other, her tongue scooping cum from Barbara's shoulder before she homes in for another lengthy twist and slide of tongues.

"All those men," Tanya whispers, shining eyes fixed on her neighbour's face. "What do you think, Babs?"

Barbara gulps and stares. She swivels at the waist, twisting to look at her husband. "I don't know what to think, Tanya," she mumbles. "Not yet." The woman's eyes roll as she winces at the pleasure of it. It isn't so much the physical sensation of her sphincter stretched around the invading girth, although being filled with meat in such an intimate place is odd, but Barbara experiences a sudden rush of emotion for what she's sharing with her husband. To her, it's as though a whole new life has opened up in front of them. "We're going to have so much fun," Barbara mutters to Tim. "I love you, darling," she breathes.

Then she adjusts her limbs so she can use her arms and legs to control her movement on her husband's dick.

"You're in my arse, Tim." The words come out thick and clotted. Barbara's face falls slack. "Oh, fuck," she moans. "I never want this to stop…"

She's sliding up and down on Tim's greasy cock while Tanya' hands are all over her. Barbara's anus itches, the burn is relentless, the only way to find relief is to fuck on the length of male gristle invading her.

Barbara comes with Tanya's fingers rubbing her insides. The young woman works at her, those digits moving on *the* most sensitive place.

It's divine, a sensory overload that has Barbara squealing and squeaking. She writhes and sobs that she's coming… again.

All the noise and friction are too much for Tim. His wife's excited cries and the sewer-mouthed torrent of obscenities spewing from Tanya get him there. He's been fucking Barbara's arsehole. It's unbelievable – his staid, timid wife in a corset and stockings and heels just letting herself go.

Tim saw Barbara taking three men at once. He witnessed the depravity, all of the degenerate nastiness of Barbara being used and fucked. Tim saw his wife's mouth stretched around Clive's cock; he saw her coughing and gagging and spitting drool, her pussy tight around Clive's girth while Paul plugged her rectum with his erection. Tim has seen semen splashing over Barbara's skin and witnessed her wanton delight at having three men at her simultaneously, and there, amongst it all, the orchestrator looked on. Barbara's corruption is all down to one person. The filth and depravity of it is due to Tanya, that gorgeous blonde with the kinkiest mind Tim has ever encountered.

And there she is, licking semen off Barbara's body, the two of them kissing…

"Shit, Barbara…" Tim moans as he falls into the abyss. Then he's squirting into the dark cavern. Tim gasps and grunts and floods his wife's rectum with cum.

End of the 1ˢᵗ Story

THE
TRADESMAN

BEN E. DORM

His attitude stinks. It's an ongoing tussle. Kate is about sick of it.

"Why do I have to be the one?" she asks. Kate is standing beside the hob island in the centre of the vast kitchen. A cardboard tray with half-a-dozen eggs is within arm's reach. It crosses Kate's mind that she could easily launch the lot. She could just pick it up and lob a tray of eggs at him, the result being three hundred and fifty pounds worth of tailored suit in need of dry cleaning. In her head she sees it all: the eggs arcing in a slow parabola, a direct hit, egg yolk and snotty whites dribbling while his self-satisfied, conceited smirk gets replaced by gape-mouthed shock, her husband boggling at her in slack-jawed surprise.

She allows herself the fantasy, even though she knows what the outcome of the latest power struggle will be.

"Well, Kate…" Mark begins.

Here it comes.

"I've got a busy day. People coming in from everywhere. It isn't just me, I'm thinking about. If I don't get in, ten or fifteen other people will have wasted a day." Mark shrugs and gives his wife a what-can-I-do-about-it look. "I did say when I booked the man; I *told* you I'd be busy today."

So, it's all my fault? Typical-bloody-Mark.

Kate snorts and somehow resists the resurgent urge to smash the eggs into his face. Frustration rises inside her. She knew it would come to this.

"I'm busy too," she protests. "I run a business, Mark. I bring money into the house, too. I know you reckon it's easier for me to drop things, but, now and then, just bloody ONCE, don't you think *you* could take the time to help with the house? Why do you always leave it to me? Why do you assume your work is more valuable, more important--"

"Because I bring in three times what you do." He slurps tea and checks his watch. "Sorry, Kate; got to go."

Incredulous at the slight, Mark's words like a slap across the face, Kate explodes. "Shit… What?!" she cries. "You wanker. You absolute fucking arsehole!"

But she's ranting at the closing door. Mark has gone.

Kate gasps, absolutely livid. Her fists are clenched and tears of rage and frustration prick her eyes. She feels humiliated and, worse still, helpless.

Still in a rage, the heat of it boils inside her, jaw tense, fingers clenching into fists, Kate storms into the hallway. She goes for the illicit packet of Marlboro Lights in her bag. Her hands tremble as she sparks up and she sucks the smoke in deep. She knows Mark hates her smoking. He thinks it makes her look common or cheap and that it reflects badly on him.

Defiant, she takes the cigarette and her mobile phone through the kitchen to the back garden. There, with the fence at a skewed angle, the root cause of the argument, Kate calls Rebecca.

"It's me," she says. "Can you manage on your own until two-ish?" Kate nods in response to the question that comes down the phone. "The man's coming to fix the fence. Yes," she sighs, "Mark's left me to deal with it. I've got to stay here to let the bloke in and to make sure he's getting on with the job." There's more chatter from Rebecca before Kate says, "I'll make it up to you, Becca." A pause while she smokes. "Yes, I know, he's a pig... I told him he was a wanker, but he's still left me here to get on with it.

"You'll be okay...?

"Thanks, babe... I'm really sorry... Yes, yes, all right... Bye."

Kate smokes and plots, thinking up ways of doing her husband in and living it up as the merry widow. It's an indulgence she has no intention of seeing through to actuality –of course she isn't going to murder Mark, but the fantasy makes her feel so much better.

The doorbell rings.

"Pig," Kate snorts at her absent husband when she drops the stub-end of her cigarette down the drain near the back door. She's still cursing him when she opens the front door.

"Oh," Kate blurts when she sees the man standing on the door-step.

Oh my God... he's gorgeous.

Kate blinks some more and then settles into gaping at him some more. He's young, mid-twenties, she vaguely estimates. He's rough in that unshaven Jason Statham mould she finds so attractive.

"'Hello," the man says husky-voiced cockney.

Kate gets a hint of Ray Winstone when she hears the young man talk. He smiles at her with a grin that speaks volumes. He's got that easy, confident charm to match his looks and voice. Kate can see he knows he's got it and doesn't care about being thought cocky or arrogant. She sums him up in an instant, albeit in a distracted, wet-knickers kind of way. He's like a character from a Guy Ritchie film: the looks, the manner, the attitude.

And isn't she just bowled over by how sexy he is!

"Fence?" the man says, smirking while Kate continues to gape.

"Oh," Kate says again, dropping back to earth. She clamps her mouth closed when she suddenly notices the weight of her dangling jaw. Her face warms with embarrassment, she feels an idiot, just gazing at the man as though she's a teenager in front of her favourite boy-band. "Yes, right," Kate adds, flustered, stunned by her juvenile reaction. "Uhm, sorry, yes, round the back…"

Kate turns, hyper-aware of the state she's in. She's a mess, or so she thinks: hair pulled back and tied in a ponytail; no make-up; baggy tee-shirt and pyjama bottoms.

"If I'd known you were going to be so early I'd have dressed," she babbles.

The man behind her chuckles. "Don't worry about that on my account," he says. "I don't mind at all."

He's a cheeky sod, Kate thinks, but something slithers in her stomach. It's a dark, illicit urge that surprises Kate with its intensity. She's also taken aback by the tiny pulse between her legs.

Jesus. Stop it…

"Any chance of a cuppa?" the man asks as they enter the kitchen.

Kate faces him and the mischievous glint in his eyes sparks another physical response inside her. The lub-lub in her clit quickens and her pussy clenches, nipples tightening. Then, when she sees him looking at the twin points outlined beneath her tee-shirt, Kate feels a sudden and very urgent need to masturbate. The power of the unexpected urge almost has her gasping. She's flustered, uncharacteristically rattled by her body's response.

What the hell is wrong *with you? Get a grip…*

"What?" replies Kate. She's confused, flustered by his blatant appraisal of her nipples. Part of her feels she should be offended, but she isn't, not really.

"A cup of tea," the man growls as his eyes move up from Kate's chest.

His blue-eyed stare fixed on her face rattles Kate even more.

"Before you... uh... get dressed," he adds, smirking.

It takes a few seconds for it to filter through to Kate that he's teasing her.

Kate feels her body thrumming in response to the flirting. She looks at him, takes in the wide shoulders, the muscled arms and the definition of those well-developed slabs of pectoral muscle beneath his tee-shirt. He's showing off white teeth in a cheeky grin.

Why not? There's no harm. It's just a bit of fun. Only banter...

"You're one of those naughty boys, aren't you," Kate says, finally recovering her composure. She flicks her ponytail with her fingers, cocking one hip as she rests an elbow in the palm of one hand, forefinger at her chin while she pretends to study him. "I'll have to keep an eye on you, won't I?" She's smiling as she says it, letting him know she up for some to-and-fro, a little verbal cut-and-thrust.

He's all full of false affront as he grins back. "Me?" he says. "Naughty?" The man pouts and shakes his head, the impish glint never leaving his eyes. "I don't know what you mean, missis."

Kate rolls her eyes. "Oh yeah?" she answers, worldly wise. She lets him know she's heard it before. "I just bet you don't." Then she gives him a smirk of her own, just a little encouragement.

There's a few seconds of deep and meaningful as they weigh one another up, their eyes locked.

"You on your own?" he asks, breaking the tension.

Kate chuckles. "You mean, 'where's your husband?' – that's what you're asking, isn't it?"

He's still grinning when he replies with, "If you say so, missis." The man pauses and adds, "Anyway, what *is* your name? I can't keep on calling you missis..."

"I'm Kate," Kate says. "And...?"

She half expects him to say Jason, as in Jason Statham, there really is a striking similarity.

"Adam," he says, and Kate can't help but feel a little disappointed.

He sees her look and asks what's wrong.

"Oh, nothing," Kate replies, "you just remind me of that actor bloke."

She can tell he's intrigued and, as Kate expected, he asks, "Which one?"

Feigning nonchalance, as though it's just something that struck her, Kate says, "Jason somebody-or-other..." She pauses, eyes cast towards the ceiling as though the name is right there but she just can't get it. "Jason... Jason... Jason--" Kate says, with snaps of her fingers punctuating each repetition.

"Statham?" Adam puts in.

Kate is full of false enthusiasm when she cries, "That's it! That's him. Jason *Statham*."

Adam's chest swells. He's pleased with himself. "You reckon I look like him?"

Kate knows he's fishing, Adam knows very well who he resembles.

He's fishing, but Kate takes the bait anyway. "Oh yes," she breathes, nodding. She pauses, hesitating on purpose before adding a murmured, "I quite fancy a bit of Jason Statham."

"Really?" Adam says, the grin almost splitting his face.

"God, yes," Kate responds, wistful. Her cheeks balloon as she fans herself with her fingers. "Just a bit," she says with an appreciative roll of her eyes. "The things I'd let that lovely hunk do to me."

Kate deftly changes the subject. Let him ponder it for a while.

"So, you fancy a cup of tea before you start, eh?"

***

"My husband's at work," Kate says. She sips coffee and eyes her Jason look-a-like over the rim of the cup. A fresh wave of tingling and clenching rushes over her: *What a gorgeous man he is.* "We had a bit of a barney about who should stay at home to let you in. I lost, but now I'm beginning to think I won."

They're in the garden, Kate with her coffee, Adam with tea in a huge mug he's collected from his van.

Inside Kate's head, on a parallel track to the part of her brain running her mouth, she's astounded at the way she's behaving. Okay, yes, he's a good-looking bloke. Sure, his mere physical presence gets every nerve end vibrating. Kate can picture herself ripping her pyjama bottoms off and straddling him, her tongue in his mouth as she gasps and groans and grinds down onto him...

This really is ridiculous. Stop it... For fuck's sake. What's got into you?

There's a dark snicker from a deep, dark and very seldom visited part of her mind. A tiny voice murmurs: *What you want is for your Jason lookee-likey to get into* you, *you randy old tart.*

Adam grips his mug with the web of his hand hard up against the side, fingers and thumb encircling the circumference. He looks at Kate. "I'm glad it's you and not him."

Kate's face warms as she blinks and glances away. Her eyes go to the sagging fence and her throat works. "Sorry," she murmurs, "I don't know why I'm behaving like this. I..." She's flustered again, feeling foolish and middle-aged. She's a woman making a show of herself with the tradesman – how ridiculously pre-menopausal and desperate. Kate sighs and fixes her attention on her feet. "You must think I'm a silly bint," she says in a voice little more than a whisper. "I bet it happens to you all the time. Ladies of a certain age must get all giddy and stupid – just like I am."

Adam shrugs and pouts. He's picked up on Kate's sudden switch in mood and blames himself.

"It doesn't happen all the time," he tells Kate. "I know some ladies like the look of me," he adds.

It occurs to Kate he's totally sincere. Adam has dropped the cheeky lad façade for the time being.

"And it makes me feel good," he continues, "'course it does." Adam offers a conciliatory smile and tilts his head. "To be honest, and I mean it, Kate, I don't reckon you're silly at all. I was enjoying myself just then. There's nothing in it, eh? Just a bit of flirting. No harm done."

He fixes Kate with an intense gaze, the blue of his eyes making her shiver as goosebumps break out over her arms.

"As for you fancying a bit of Jason Statham," he goes on, the grin returning. "I reckon Jase wouldn't mind a crack at you, either."

That does it, the blue-eyed sincerity works on Kate. Her confidence soars. She's thrilled, ebullient. Then, with lust surging inside her, Kate says, "Flirting can be fun, can't it?"

Adam nods, his gaze roving over her body. "Oh yeah. Absolutely," he agrees.

The young man's appraisal feels like twin lasers. Kate swallows heavily, body responding. She notices the tremor in her hands as she raises the teacup to her lips. She's sure her nipples are about to rent holes in her tee-shirt. Kate is absolutely certain the air is redolent of her desire: *Oh, God... I can smell my pussy!*

She squirms in her seat in an effort to repress the itch between her legs. When she speaks next, her voice breaks with the tension building inside her. "Have you got a girlfriend?"

Adam pouts again. "Nobody steady," he replies.

Kate laughs and clears her throat. In an attempt at jocularity she says, "So, more than one, eh?"

Adam's grin tells her she's on the money.

"No comment," he says, continuing with, "So what do you do all day? You got a job? You said something about you and the hubby arguing about who stayed to let me in…" Adam's head tilts as he looks at her, expectant of an answer.

Kate can't rid herself of that damnable itch. It's very distracting, as is Jason's – *Adam's* – proximity. She sucks in a deep breath in an attempt to calm her snarling libido. "I run a boutique, well, I *own* it actually. We sell high-end lingerie. You should pop in sometime." Kate gives him a sly grin, lips twitching as she suggests, "Bring one of your girlfriends. I'll dress her up and make your eyes pop out."

She laid it out for him perfectly. All Adam had to do was scoop it up.

He's wide-eyed when he blurts an incredulous, "What? Like Ann Summers?"

Kate snorts and shakes her head. "N*ooo*," she says, drawing out the vowel, "we're a few rungs above. No crotchless knickers or peephole bras. We deal with tasteful lingerie. I've got corsets and stockings, baby-doll nighties. We do shoes and even some specialist clothing for Goth societies. Our stuff is sexy as well as tasteful."

Kate lets it hang. There's a momentary silence and then, Adam, albeit several seconds later than Kate anticipated, says, "Do you ever... uh... model the lingerie yourself?"

There's an upsurge of heat from Kate's vulva when desire floods her. She's suddenly reckless with yearning, bold because of the way her body vibrates, her insides clenching.

She looks at Adam, eyes glazed and heavy-lidded.

Squirming again, her voice throaty, the need clotted in her throat, Kate says, "I might... If I had someone to model for."

Apparently at random, Adam informs Kate his mate will be at the house in an hour. "I'm meant to be making a start on ripping the old panels out." Adam tilts his head towards the fence. "He's picking up the new ones as soon as the supplier opens."

Kate blinks, puzzled for a second or two before the penny drops. Her throat works when she realises what it is Adam is trying to tell her.

"Oh, right, well... I suppose I'd better leave you to get on with it." She throws a look at Adam and, her voice laden with meaning, adds, "I'll just go up and have a shower. I'll come down in half an hour or so to see how you're doing."

***

She masturbates in the shower. Kate gasps and sobs while crouching bent-kneed and slack-jawed while water cascades over her. She's dimly aware of her attempts to keep her hair dry, a difficult task since she's writhing and squirming, the middle and third fingers of one hand inserted into her opening. Those digits feel so bloody good inside her. At last she can scratch the insistent itch.

In her mind's eye, there's Adam. She pictures him shirtless, the man exhibiting his superb physique. "You lovely bastard," Kate mumbles. She winces and takes her lower lip between her teeth, fingers working her insides. "No," she gasps, her imagination taking her to where Adam is stroking his cock, a full-blooded erection that he wants to fuck into her. "I'm not on the pill... My husband, he's had the snip. Yuh-you can't put that thing inside me. If you come..."

The thought of it, imagining a lovely length of manhood flooding her with semen appalls and thrills her in equal measure. Unspeakable as it would be in real-life, toying with the idea of unprotected sex gets Kate hot.

She masturbates, so close to orgasm she's grunting and bug-eyed. It's as though she can *feel* Adam's cock inside her, the thing pulsing as it spits ejaculate into her vulnerable pussy. In her mind, she's a whimpering mess while, powerless to stop him, Adam pumps squirt after fertile squirt of jizm into her unprotected womb.

Her climax hits her like an explosion. Kate groans and grunts and curses. She's sobbing, knees threatening to give way completely, water pouring over her breasts and stomach, fingers still wedged inside her body.

Kate's teeth are clenched, the words strained through an enamelled portcullis when she hisses, "Oh, Jesus. Oh, fuck… Fill me up with all that spunk. Come on, you horny bastard. Flood my pussy with it."

Kate staggers from the cubicle. She's trembling as she wraps the towel around her body. When she catches a glimpse of herself in the mirror she can hardly recognise the shell-shocked victim looking back at her.

Somehow she manages to dry herself and then moves into the bedroom from the ensuite. Before she realises it, Kate finds herself in another room. Not that she's completely surprised she's in there, after all, there's been an inevitability about it all along.

In what she pretentiously calls her dressing room, a spare bedroom at the top of the house, Kate chooses carefully. A fist of anxious dread gripes in her guts, she knows what she's doing, knows she really shouldn't but can't stop herself all the same.

Once the ensemble is laid out she sits in front of the dressing table, combing out her hair before piling it on top of her head. Kate uses a long, tapered clip like a tropical bird's bill to hold her blonde tresses in place. She purposely loosens a few strands, the stray tendrils wispy at her temples. Satisfied with the look and realising time is against her Kate then quickly applies the minimum of make-up. A quick dab around the eyes, a smidge of lip-gloss and she's done.

Kate hooks the suspender belt around her waist, clipping the dangling straps to the tops of the sheerest, most insubstantial stockings. Then there's the black and white Axford waspie. It takes a bit of doing, but Kate eventually manages to fasten the thing tight enough around her torso, blushing at her audacity when she sees her generous breasts cantilevered over the corset cups.

"You mucky tart," she whispers to the woman smirking back at her from the mirror.

Kate knows she's sodden. She can feel her vulva tacky with lust, her labia gooey even after her recent shower.

There's a brief moment of hesitation. Kate thinks about what she's doing, the danger she's courting. She can't quite believe it of herself. It's madness, a form of insanity brought about by a great hormonal surge.

Looking at herself in the mirror, Kate balks. No, she can't do it. No way. But a sound from outside draws her attention and when she goes to the window and looks down at the garden at the rear of the house she sees Adam shirtless.

He's better than she imagined him to be. Adam works at warped fence panel free of its moorings. He wrenches the board away from the concrete post, muscles rippling.

Kate boggles, moaning. "Sweet Jesus," she blasphemes.

With a rush of desire so great it has Kate whining and squeaking, the woman rushes to her dressing room for her shoes. To complete the ensemble she goes for the patent black Louboutins, the uppers as dark as her intentions, heels as lethal as an assassin's blade.

Thus attired, breasts and depilated mons exposed, Kate ventures forth, the thrill of it coursing through her.

***

Her heels peck at the floor when Kate crosses the kitchen. The sound brings Adam's head up. He turns and then boggles.

"Fucking hell," the man mutters. "Fuck... Kate..."

From the doorway, Kate lifts a forefinger to her lips. She shakes her head. Next, after crooking the same finger at Adam, she turns and presents her derriere.

The sharp hiss of his breath tells Kate he appreciates the view. There's a short and silent prayer of thanks to a vigorous gym regime, yoga, and abstinence from alcohol – Saturday nights excepted. Kate is confident of her physical appeal. She hopes the packaging of corset, stockings and shoes enhances the aesthetics. Kate knows she's probably competing with tight-bodied twenty-somethings. A hottie like the tradesman, she can hear following behind her would have to beat them off with a shitty stick. Especially since the girls all seem so *forward* these days.

Kate pauses by the hob island, the self-same spot she occupied during the frustrating altercation with Mark. It's a bit of a shock to Kate to recall that spat can only have occurred an hour previously.

She wonders at how quickly life can turn, swivelling to confront the tradesman looming in her kitchen.

All thoughts of Mark and their silly, petty disagreement evaporate. She can see the hunger in Adam's expression: *Jesus, he looks bloody dangerous!*

Surprising herself with how calm she sounds, insides in turmoil, pussy sipping desire, Kate says, "So, what do you think?"

Adam stands a few feet away. He's gaping at Kate, eyes constantly moving while his face conveys stunned disbelief. While he stares, mouth opening as though he's going to comment, Adam's hands twitch while he blinks, no sound coming out of him.

He just stands there and gapes, mouth closing again.

"I reckon Jason Statham might go for an older bird," says Kate, lips pursing into a moue as she pretends to muse on the actor's preferences. "What do you reckon, Adam? An older lady with big tits…?" Kate pauses and smirks, fists on her hips. "Is that the sort of thing *you* might like?"

"You're fucking kidding me, right?" the man breathes. He swallows heavily, eyes bulging before his tongue slides over his lips. Adam chuckles, the delight showing on his face and the tone of his voice when he adds, "Just look at you. Look at those *tits!*"

His eyes come up to meet Kate's. Her stomach lurches when she sees his feral expression, a leaden sinker of some dark and indefinable emotion plummeting into the pit of her stomach.

"You're exactly the sort of thing I might like." Adam nods, enthusiastic in his praise as he continues with, "The sort of thing I fuckin' *love.*"

"Show me," Kate responds with a challenge in her tone. She nudges her chin at the man. "Let me see your cock."

Smirking, his stare remained fixed on Kate's face. He dares her to look away as he unbuttons and unzips.

Now it's Kate's turn to gape.

"Shit," she breathes, gape-mouthed at the sight of the gnarled and veiny lump of male gristle dangling there like a threat.

"Yeah," Adam says, shrugging, "thought you'd like it."

Kate's throat works as she drags her attention from the impressive jib. "We... That is I..."

She closes her eyes and shakes her head to dispel the image of herself bent over the hob island, Adam behind her, his length splitting her open.

"We can't fuck," Kate eventually manages to gurgle. "I'm not taking any contraception. My husband has had a vasectomy."

Adam spits an obscenity that he follows up with, "I've got some johnnies in the van."

Kate is tempted, so very fucking tempted to sling caution to the wind. She glances at Adam's cock, pussy growling for it.

"Oh, shit," she whines, licking her lips. "I want to. Oh, fuck, do I want to. But..."

Then Jason goads a long groan out of her. He jacks at his cock, deliberately flaunting its size. "I really wanna fuck you, Kate," he growls, eyes gleaming with animal lust. At that moment, Adam doesn't care a jot about his sperm finding Kate's vulnerable core. As far as he's concerned he's the Alpha male, fully erect, rampant with need. In that moment of yearning, Adam doesn't care about his potency, he's filled with the primeval instinct to take the female.

Kate wavers, almost losing the internal struggle. *One fuck. He could pull out before letting go inside me. What were the chances...?*
"Oh, God," she whines, a hand moving between her legs. She moves towards Adam, her heels click-clack-clicking against the tiles. "Wank it," she breathes, wincing and gasping when her fingertip slides over her clit. Kate mauls at one breast, eyes fixed on Adam's fist jacking his length.

Adam's face is slack as he cranks his cock. He licks his lips and mutters, "Watch me do it."

Kate sighs and rolls her eyes. "Oh, I'm watching, you horny bastard. Keep doing it. Show me."

It's important for her to know she can affect a younger man. Kate needs the positive assurance, which Adam gives to her in spades. He lets the woman know in no uncertain terms. He stares at her, his demeanour feral. Adam caresses himself with both hands, hips jerking. The swollen cock-head peeps and disappears, peeps and disappears, the action bringing another moan from Kate.

"How would you like me to fuck you with this?" Adam grunts. He repeats the lewd gesture, twice, thrice and yet a fourth time, fucking into his fist while Kate gazes. "I bet you're dripping for it," he growls. Adam's cheeks balloon and his eyes go from the heavy, swaying breasts to Kate's face. He sees her look, the expression of absolute delight on her face. Then he spots the woman's fingers massaging her vulva, the obscene squelching of her desire reaching him. "Fuck, Kate... you're one sexy lady." He gasps and then whines, "Can't I just put it in, babe? Go on, Kate, just a few strokes of it. I'll take it out before I come."

Kate's head moves side-to-side. "God, Adam, I want to. Really, I so want to do it right now." She gasps, eyes closing, another climax rushing at her. "I bet it's lovely... Fucking that big cock... Oh, shit, I'd love to let you do it."

"Please," Adam grunts, tugging hard. "You're so gorgeous, Kate. I'm gonna go fuckin' mental if I can't shag you."

But, despite the near overwhelming desire to let the rogue scoop her up and hold her aloft, his girth filling her, Kate is adamant. It's a close run thing, but the consequences are too terrible to contemplate.

Kate's fear wins in the end. "We can't," she groans, her jaw clenched with effort. "I'm sorry," Kate sobs. "Oh, God..."

It hits her, Kate's orgasm slams into her. Her stomach tenses, her heels skid across the tiles. The only way she manages to stay upright is by a desperate one-handed grab at the hob island behind her.

Leaning back, breasts shivering while her body trembles, bestial grunts bursting from her, Kate comes and comes.

Adam takes it all in. He watches agog, awed by the display of raw ecstasy. He's had some cuties in his time, seen some lovelies with their pretty faces all twisted up with pleasure. Adam has taken a few to the same place Kate is in at the moment, but never before has the sight and sound of a woman in full cry had such an effect.

He looks on, with Kate all wall-eyed and gasping, Adam's own surge catching him by surprise.

"Ah, no, shit..." he yelps. But all he can do is keep yanking at his dick. He's driven by a primordial need to experience the rush. It's exquisite, those seconds of pure bliss as it all pumps out of him. Adam groans and mutters obscenities, his heavy-lidded gaze set on Kate's breasts and contorted features, semen spurting from the eye in his cock, ejaculate flicking through the air in viscous ribbons that spatter down onto the kitchen tiles.

"You filthy fucker," Kate mumbles when she sees cum dolloped on her kitchen floor. "What a mess... And you wanted to put that thing inside me!" The woman looks up, her own orgasm cooling, expression incredulous. "Fucking hell, Adam, I'd have ended up with a belly full of arms and legs for sure. How much of that stuff has come out? Jesus..."

"Shit," Adam grunts, jaws clamped tight. "I'm coming..."

A snort from Kate. "You don't bloody say! I can see you're coming, you mucky bastard. Look at the state of that floor."

It ends with Kate's chest heaving as she sucks in air, her legs still watery. Adam moans and gasps, squeezing his cock until the final ooze drips off him.

Then, in the aftermath, with some sensibility creeping back, Kate is embarrassed by how far she went. She's mortified as the madness slips from her. "I don't believe I did that," Kate mumbles, the reality of her situation hitting home. "I... I must have been mad."

She's keenly aware of her dishabille. Her breasts and smooth vulva are right there out in the open for the young man to see. Her cheeks burn with shame, glowing hotter, her chest suffusing pink as she recalls the potty-mouthed torrent of obscene language that passed between her and the tradesman.

"Shit... Oh, God, Adam. Please, you won't tell anyone..." Kate's fingers go to her mouth. She's horrified at being so compromised.

He's still dangling when he wipes a hand across his face. That big cock is right there in accusation, evidence of her culpability.

"Kate," Adam gasps. "Don't worry. There's no way I'm gonna tell anyone about this. I don't kiss and tell, babe."

Relief floods the woman. "Oh, thank *God*," she sighs. "My husband..." Kate pauses, the impact of her close call smashing into her. "Jesus," she breathes, aghast. "If you'd fucked me ... If you'd let go with all that spunk..."

Adam grimaces, chagrined. "Yeah," he says. "Sorry about getting all wound up and asking you to do it. I suppose I was just..." He shrugs and offers Kate a wan smile. "Well, you know. I suppose I went a little mental there too." His eyes appraise Kate. She feels vulnerable under his scrutiny. "It's just you're so fucking lovely, Kate. I have to tell you."

Kate gulps. "Thanks," she replies, suddenly keen to be away so she can shed the ridiculous ensemble – the waspie, the stockings and the shoes are abruptly inappropriate.

She's in her kitchen, it's not even half-nine, there's spunk everywhere and a virtual stranger is eyeing her breasts and bare pudenda. "But I'd better go and... Well, I should make myself decent before your colleague arrives," Kate finishes.

It stays with her as she leaves the kitchen. When she pauses and removes her shoes in the hall, Adam's enthusiasm lingers in her mind. She climbs the stairs, mind working. At the top of the house, extricating herself from the restrictive confines of the corset, welts left on her skin from its embrace, Kate thinks about that impressive appendage, wondering just how divine it would have been to accommodate the mass of it inside her body.

"You could have sucked it," Kate chides her reflection. "Wanked it a bit."

The waspie goes back on its hanger. Kate unfastens the tops of the stockings from the suspender belt, removing the apparel of a bordello whore and replacing the lingerie with suburban chic after sponging her vulva. Dressed in tight jeans, canvas shoes and an outsized shirt, cuffs rolled up to the crook of her arms, Kate then unpins her hair, combing it through before pulling it tight and looping the elastic to make a ponytail. The make-up she leaves as it is.

When Kate returns to the kitchen, she sees Adam has given the scene of the crime a cursory going over. There's a patch of wet near the hob island to show where he's given the area a quick wipe with the mop.

Better than leaving dollops of spunk all over the place, Kate surmises, shrugging.

She's sheepish when she steps out into the garden. "Another tea?" Kate offers, placing the mug down on the table.

She's relieved to see Adam is once again wearing his tee-shirt as she lights up a second illicit cigarette.

Adam avoids her eyes when he ambles across to collect the brew, but the sound of Kate's voice gets his attention.

"You know," the woman begins, tentative and unsure. "If... say in a month's time..." She has no proper clue how long the contraceptive pill takes to kick in, but a month sounds reasonable. "If something got broke and I got my husband to give you a call..."

At first Adam is puzzled; then his frown clears. He nods, grinning. "Yeah, Kate – what if it did and you did? What if he calls me?"

"Well, I was wondering." She's smiling broadly now. "If I ended up being the one who waited at home for you to arrive...?"

"I'd make it my first job of the day," Adam replies.

Which is just what Kate wants to hear.

End of the 2nd Story

A MONOLOGUE
in BLUE
A Wife's Confession

BEN E. DORM

It was close to 2 a.m. when she came home. I was awake and out of bed. I can't sleep when she's out, my mind works constantly, I imagine lewd scenes where my wife is the centre of attention. All I can see is her involved in all manner of debauchery. The longer she stays out, the worse it gets. The later she is returning home, the worse her conduct becomes in those torrid imaginings in my head.

It was the old familiar slide in the pit of my stomach when I saw her before she left. Stuff curdles in there when I see her all dolled up, looking gorgeous, a magnet for every hound-dog lothario I know will be out there on the prowl. Jealousy and anxiety and a heavy splash of arousal mix together. It's a potent cocktail that makes me want to grab my wife's wrist and pull her back into the house so I can rip the bodice of that dress away.

If I did it her big breasts would swing and sway, unfettered by any bra beneath the dress. I could squeeze her tits and suck on those thick, elongated nipples, my cock pulsing with lust.

I could lift the hem of her dress and soak in the sight of her thick-lipped vulva, the pubic bush sculpted to a thin landing strip. She'd yelp and protest, complaining about me ruining her hair when I push her onto the sofa, limbs sprawling, pretty face twisted into a pout of disdain.

I'd lick my wife's pussy and suck her clit between my teeth. I'd finger her opening and find her already wet with desire.

But she wouldn't be dripping with lust because I'm at her. No, her arousal would be as a result of her anticipation of the night ahead, an evening of teasing men until one, perhaps two if she's in that kind of mood, takes her fancy.

Then, if, or more accurately, *when* she chooses, I can only imagine what she'll let him do to her.

At the door, with my wife in her blue dress, acres of décolletage on display through the keyhole design, those full breasts presented for maximum effect, hair piled up on top of her head, pearl-drop earrings dangling, a triple strand of the same pearls nestled in the deep crease of her cleavage, my wife smirked and told me not to wait up.

I wanted to tell her not to go. It was Thursday evening and I wanted to ask her if she'd be home by the morning. Or would she be out until Saturday… or Sunday?

The only reply I received was a look of pity followed by arched eyebrows and a waggle of her fingers.

Her last words were, "Don't wait up."

Then she sniggered as the door closed behind her.

***

Hearing the low murmur of a car engine at the end of the drive might just be my imagination. It happens a lot when I'm waiting for her to come home. It's a thrill of anticipation, my stomach flips, and I hope, for once, she's come home without that smell on her.

Quite often it's a false alarm. My mind might be playing tricks, especially when it gets late and I'm tired and prone to dozing. I'll hear the sound of a taxi pulling up and I'll get that jolt in the guts, a visceral tug while the cuprous jealousy corrodes my innards. Sometimes it might be a car passing or a neighbour pulling up, but mostly it's in my head. The hope will flare, burn brightly for a second or two, the flame extinguished by a wave of disappointment.

Whenever that happens, I check the time and wonder where she is, with whom, and then I'll dwell on what she might be doing.

But, that time, as I scan the screen on my mobile phone – the one she never calls or sends a text to, even though I keep it with me constantly – I heard the definite clunk of a car door. My stomach flipped and I held my breath, counting the seconds until--

Then I heard the peck-peck-peck of high heels across the flagstones of the drive. Her key then snicked into the lock. My throat worked when she dropped her bag onto the table just inside the front door. I heard her keys clatter down.

She walked into the sitting room to find me nursing a whiskey.

"Oh," she said, studying me, expression inscrutable.

I was sitting in the same leather arm chair I always occupied during these vigils, gazing back at her as I examined my wife for signs.

Her head tilted to one side, her fists went to her hips. "You're still up," she said, feigning surprise. Then she moved to the other chair and, after shrugging out of the full-length leather coat and allowing it to fall to the parquet flooring, lifted the hem of her dress. She arranged the dress to her liking as she sat down, leaning forward to rest her elbows on her thighs, hands dangling between her knees like a labourer on a smoke break.

"You'll never guess who I saw in town tonight." Her eyes gleamed as she taunted me with it. My wife paused and then said, "Your boss."

She smirked when she saw my throat work.

"He bought me a few drinks. Paid me a *lot* of attention. You know he's always had a thing for me, right?

"I was going to get a taxi home, but he insisted on driving me. He's got a lovely big car. A Jaguar he told me. Plenty of room in it, I can tell you.

"Especially in the back..."

She smirked again and eased back in the chair, legs going wide. Then she lifted the dress higher, bunching it around her waist to expose her sex.

Forcing her thighs wide, my wife looked at me, her belligerent stare a challenge.

I swallowed heavily, my eyes going from her cold gaze to the full, round breasts threatening to burst free, the bodice only just restraining my wife's generous bosom. The dress is so designed, so daring that the outer flanks of my wife's tits were visible to anyone who cared to look.

Of course, with her sex so blatantly exposed I couldn't resist glancing at her vulva. When I looked between her legs I saw the labia tacky with God-knew-what, the sight of her so obviously used dragging at my guts.

Those meaty, sticky folds were a deliberate taunt: she was mocking me.

Then her voice dragged my attention back to her face, my wife's features set in a cruel, glittery-eyed appraisal as she continued to pour the humiliation over me.

"We parked up in a lay-by out on the ring road. It was quiet in there, a few cars going past every now and then.

"I made out like I didn't know what he was up to. I played it all shocked that he thought I'd be up for it.

"'I'm a married lady'," I said. "I showed him my wedding ring and told him I couldn't...

"But he was *very* persuasive."

My wife shrugged in a gesture of complete indifference to how this talk would affect me.

"Of course, in the end, I gave in. I sucked him…

"He's got a *very* big cock.

"Then he wanted to fuck me. I told him I didn't think I could do that."

My wife's fingers went down to her pussy. She split the sticky folds and something slithered in my guts when I saw those fleshy flaps shivering as she touched herself. I gaped at her when she winced and hissed, the tip of a forefinger sliding over her clit.

Groaning, her voice clotted with whatever pleasure she was experiencing, my wife went on.

"I told him you wouldn't like it. I said you wouldn't appreciate me being in that car with him, the two of us alone.

"I said I couldn't fuck him… Not without a condom."

My wife giggled at that, her eyes shining while she watched me for a reaction.

My insides curdled when she continued with, "He laughed and asked if I was on the pill. Then he shrugged when I told him I wasn't."

Oh God, my wife then probed her opening, her finger sliding into the second joint. When it slid out again a dribble of some viscous ooze slid out of her.

I gaped at the three glistening blobs on the floor between her shoes.

She looked at those damning globules and turned her face to me. "Oops," she murmured, a feline grin fixed to her face. "Sorry."

With that taunting glint in her eyes, she shrugged again and, absolutely remorseless, said, "I told you he had a big cock and was very persuasive, so I got in the back of his car and he fucked me from behind.

"He kept going on about my big tits and how he'd always fancied me. He told me I had a great body. He said he couldn't believe I was in my fifties; he kept telling me how gorgeous I was; and all the time he was fucking into me with this huge fucking cock.

"I could tell he was going to come. I told him to take it out, but he just wouldn't listen. He just held me tighter and grunted and swore. Then I felt him push really deep…"

My wife blinked and rolled her eyes.

"And he went so fucking deep," she breathed, nodding. "He must have pumped at me for a minute. All that cum just flooded me. Can you see?" She held herself wide open, fingertips splaying her flaps like a specimen butterfly pinned to a display. "His cum's been leaking out of me for ages."

My wife looked up at me again, the tip of her tongue pink and shiny between her teeth while she examined me for some kind of response.

"You know," she murmured, fiddling with her labia. "I'm still horny." She winked at me and grinned. "How about we go to bed? You can stir up his spunk with your cock.

"Are you hard?" she whispered, knowing the answer.

My wife stood and reached back to slip the strap of the dress over her head. She shimmied and then posed to flaunt her body.

I stared at her, my eyes going from her face to her breasts. In my mind's eye I saw her in the back of his car, her rump presented so he could fuck into her from behind, my wife's big tits in his hands.

Emotions surged. I could hear her encouraging him with her potty-mouthed talk. I could hear her pretending to be all reluctant about him coming inside her when she really wanted him to flood her with semen.

My wife smirked and, with loose tendrils of blonde hair whispering at her temples, held out her hand.

I noticed it was her left hand she offered, the jewels in her engagement ring sparking, her wedding band gleaming.

"Come on, let's go to bed. I'll let you fuck me, tonight, too. You can stir up the mess those men left inside me. Oh," my wife added as though it had completely slipped her mind. "I didn't tell you about the other lovely man I met tonight. The one I fucked in the toilets in the club before your boss drove me home…"

End of the 3ʳᵈ Story

AN
INTERVIEW

BEN E. DORM

I'm surprised by the innocuous front door. It seems so innocent; so benign; so *normal*. I don't know what I expected, but I'd imagined a pornstar's home to be a little more... well... obvious, I suppose. But there it is: tidy lawn and double fronted garage, a smart two-storey new-build in a quiet cul-de-sac in middle England. It's benign; quiet; genteel. I find myself checking the address with the one written in my notebook, but everything corresponds: the postcode matches the one plumbed into the SatNav, the number on the door fits the one written down.

There can be little room left for doubt – I've arrived at Wendy Gilcrest's house.

A leaden sinker of apprehension plummets, coming to rest in the pit of my stomach when I switch off the ignition and reach for my bag. It's a strange mix of apprehension and arousal. I'm anxious about meeting her face-to-face and keen to create a good impression. It helps the interview if there's a rapport.

The doorbell chimes inside the house. I stand and wait, feeling self-conscious until I spy a brief flit of movement through the opaque glass squares set at eye-level in the door.

Then the door swings open and it's Wendy herself smiling at me. "Hello," she says. "Thanks for coming." She says it like *I'm* doing *her* a favour.

So, there she is, completely normal: a well-presented, attractive lady I know to be somewhere around the mark of mid-forties. Subtle make-up, nothing garish; hair neatly styled, a dark burgundy shade familiar to me from hours of viewing her work. She's wearing a light summer dress, the hem at a flattering point above her knees, bodice scooped to show an appealing décolletage. In a café, a supermarket, walking past in the street, she'd be worthy of a second glance. There's something about her that appeals, tugs on a primal level, stirs a man to carnal thoughts – or perhaps that's just because I know what I know? I know what this lady with the dimpled smile and twinkling eyes does for a living.

The door opens wider. "Come in," she says, stepping aside. When I hesitate, she adds, "Don't worry about your shoes." Wendy points down the corridor. "Along the hall. First door on the right. Can I get you something? A cup of tea, coffee... or a beer?"

I'm struck by her accent. There's no regional inflection, Wendy's diction is quintessentially English. Not quite BBC but bordering on it. Whenever I hear her speak in her films I'm reminded of all-girls' schools and hockey, which seems to add to her wide appeal. She's an almost posh girl with earthy appetites.

While she's busy in the kitchen preparing tea and coffee, hers and mine respectively, it occurs to me that it's her 'normalness' that makes her so popular in the adult film industry. Wendy Gilcrest is attainable, or at least that's the perception. She isn't false, all molded plastic and Botox. Our Wendy could be the woman walking past in the High Street. There's more to her charm, of course there is. Wendy up close oozes promise. It's on her face and the way she moves. Just being in close proximity to her gets things moving around the body. There's a definite glint in her eyes, a twist to her lips that sends a sure signal that she's a minx. Hearing Wendy mutter obscenities in her films, seeing her face contorted into a mask of delight, which appears completely genuine, her elocution at odds with the profanity...

Well, it stirs men up. Makes them want her. Or at least it does it for me.

And I don't know how anyone can fake a squirting orgasm. I truly believe Wendy loves what she does. Being paid is simply a bonus.

Five minutes later and we're cozy in the living room. I'm in an armchair; she's on the sofa, knees primly together.

"Okay," she says, reaching for a delicate china cup. "I'm all yours."

I can't help but notice her smirk and wonder if that wasn't a deliberate double entendre.

"If only you were," I reply, the remark earning me a beaming smile as Wendy's eyebrows arch. "Maybe later," she responds.

I'm speechless: touché, point to Wendy.

She laughs at my hanging jaw. "Come on, let's get on with it. What do you want to know?"

Interview with Wendy Gilcrest:

Me: All right, I know it's history and out there already, but could you confirm how you got started? These days, you're a well-known...

well, *face* in the industry, but is it correct that it was Rob, your husband, who made the suggestion you'd be good in adult films?

Wendy settles back in her seat. Making herself comfortable, she's in the corner of the sofa, reclining with her legs crossed. To my eye, she is very desirable in that pose.

Wendy: Actually, yes, it was. Do you want me to give you some detail?

Me: *Nodding.* Yes Please, Wendy; as much as you like.

Wendy: Okay, right. To go back a bit, Rob and I were a fairly typical couple: married, kids, job, car, mortgage...

We've always been quite open about sex, relaxed about it. There were as a time on holiday abroad where we'd had a few drinks, years ago this was, and we met a couple who were a bit older than us. It turns out, as the conversation moved along, that they were swingers and, well, one thing led to another and we had same room sex – me with Rob, the two of them together. No swapping partners or anything.

Then, predictably, I suppose-- *There's a roll of Wendy's eyes and a wry chuckle* --the next night, when we met them in the bar and had a couple of drinks it escalated to a full on swap.

We were both sort of appalled the next day – Rob and I, that is. You know, neither one knew what to say? We were both too embarrassed to discuss it. But, as the day went on and we had more drinks and loosened up we both ended up saying how exciting it was. We had another encounter with the same couple that night, too. Actually, it went on for the rest of the holiday – about four nights I think.

Me: This was before the children came along?

Wendy: *Shaking her head.* No, both the kids were born; they just weren't on that holiday. *Wendy waves a hand in a casual, airy manner.* Rob and I had some time alone. It was a busy time for him at work. Stressful. The kids stayed at my mum's.

Me: Ah, okay...

Wendy: Anyway, we got home and put the adventure aside. It wasn't part of our "real life".

Then, as time went on and the sparkle faded in the marriage – as happens with everyone it seems – we started to look at ways to liven it up. We did the usual: role-play, pretending to be strangers in a pub, me dressing up...

And all of it was fun, it worked. Then Rob mentioned the holiday and tentatively suggested we visit a swingers' club.

I was kind of excited at the idea, scared but it turned me on – you know?

Me: N*odding but say nothing.*

Wendy: *Wendy sighs wistfully; then continues.* Right, so, off we went... And I loved it. I was popular. I couldn't believe the attention. Women as well as men!

Okay, yes, I've always known I'm attractive. I've always had looks from blokes and that. But I don't want to sound vain or conceited, I didn't think I was "all that", and it was a real surprise to suddenly be this woman people wanted to... well, that they wanted to fuck. It was weird at first, quite intimidating, too. I had quite a following at the club. Whenever we visited more and more people chatted me up.

Me: So what was Rob doing?

Wendy: Having a good time. We were there very much as a couple. People respect boundaries in those clubs. It isn't a melee with blokes barging in, cocks in hand, trying to stuff it in wherever they can. No, Rob and I would make a choice and make it plain he was included. He isn't a bad-looking bloke so it wasn't all one-sided and all about me. But I will say I was one of the most popular ladies there.

Me: Group sex, multiple men, women?

Wendy: At first it was just Rob and one other man, usually the partner of the other lady. I'd take on both boys at once – which is where I came to start to enjoy DP. Sometimes I'd watch the other woman getting fucked while I kissed my husband. It's so *sexy*, it's such a turn-on kissing Rob while he's shagging someone else.

Wendy's eyes are slits, it's a feline look, very calculating and sly as she watches me for a reaction.

I also love kissing women while they're fucking. Sometimes they're so engrossed with what's going on with their pussy that it takes a moment or two to realise I want to snog. It really gets me going when a woman opens her eyes and sees me there. I love it when their eyes clear and they smile and then we kiss.

Me: *Hearing Wendy talk and being so close to her in the flesh has caused a definite swelling in my cock.*

I try to ignore it.

So, from swingers' clubs to adult films…?

Wendy: *Laughter.*

Rob reckoned I should be in porn. We'd been watching one of Simon's films – Ben Dover that is. The lads were supposedly picking up girls off the street and fucking them. It was all designed to look so spontaneous. I liked the style of it and said so.

Rob jokingly said I should write in and ask for an audition.

I got thinking about it. I'd be in a shop or something and drift off into a fantasy about two men chatting me up and convincing me to go with them to get filmed fucking. Sometimes I dreamed about it being a couple of tasty mechanics in the repair place, the old clichéd scene where they ask for payment in kind.

It got to the point where I'd rub myself off in places I might get caught, and one time I masturbated in the car at the supermarket car park while a security guard watched.

In the end, I wrote to Simon and arranged to meet.

Me: *Somewhat hoarse in voice.* Was Rob aware?

Wendy: When I got a reply saying they'd like to audition me, I confessed to him then.

Me: And his reaction at the time?

Wendy: He wasn't too sure. It went on for a week or so, us discussing it. In the end he made this little speech about how much he loved me, but if I wanted to give it a go...

I understood he was feeling vulnerable. Rob had this idea I'd have so much fun fucking other guys that I'd up and leave.

Me: Which hasn't been the case.

Wendy: *Shaking her head again, expression grave.* Absolutely not. This is something a lot of people can't get their head around. I do what I do for the fun, the excitement… and the money, of course.

Wendy chuckles and grins.

I can compartmentalise the sex from emotion. I might really get into a bloke when we're shagging. I can come and come and feel really fucking good. But I'm emotionally attached to my husband. I love Rob.

Wendy shrugs.

The sex is one thing. I really love fucking. I'll suck cock, take one in my arse and one in my pussy; I'll take spunk over my face, my tits… anywhere. If an actor has a medical certificate I'll do him bareback; he can come in my pussy or my anus ... I'll pretty much do anything except animals and kids.

Oh, and shit. There's no way I'm getting involved with poo. *Wendy grimaces and wriggles on the sofa.*

Me: *Grimacing* Yeah, right, I don't blame you.

Wendy: So we had this deep and meaningful. It was very emotional. Then I called Simon and arranged a date.

They all trouped into the old house. I don't know what the neighbours thought. There was Simon and a couple of his boys; a girl for make-up and that; another couple of blokes for the technical stuff...

All this gear – lights, wires, cameras...

Me: How did you feel that day?

Wendy: I was climbing the walls. I needed a vodka at ten in the morning! I was scared witless, but also dripping – literally dripping with anticipation. I was going to get fucked in my own living room with all these people standing around watching.

My husband was going to be there, too.

It was mental, surreal. When it came to the time I was trembling so much.

But when we got started, I went fucking mad for it.

Me: Yes, I've seen it.

Wendy: *Grinning hugely.* Thinking about that morning has me wet right now.

She looks at me, that vulpine gaze fixed on my face. I can't figure out if she's teasing or...?

What about you? Did it get you hard, watching that clip?

Me: *I blink, unable to answer at first. There's a lot of discomfort with my cock caught in my jeans the way it is. I can feel pre-cum seeping out and wonder if I'm going to have a wet patch to embarrass me.*

I always get hard watching you, Wendy.

Wendy: *Another huge grin. She winks at me. Laughter.*

Ooh, you naughty boy.

Anyway, that was my start. Simon puts me out there and it just went crazy. Now I've got a blog, Facebook, Twitter, requests for private photo shoots and videos...

Me: Good stuff, Wendy. I take it you're doing okay financially. *I look around the room, indicating the house with a sweep of an arm.*

Wendy: We're comfortable, yes. Rob still works. There's a tidy income from the videos and other stuff.

Me: Tell me, Wendy, what do you look for in the men you work with? What's your ideal?

Wendy: *Immediately, she's been asked this before, obviously.* My husband!

Laughter.

Actually, there's no "ideal". Young or not so young, fit or a bit flabby, it doesn't matter. As long as we can have some banter and I like the bloke we can usually have some lovely sex. It's the personality of the guy and how hard his cock is. I'm not a girl focussed on a man's looks – up to a point, anyway. The camera is incidental; I'm not shy in front of it. I'm there to fuck. If it's been recorded that only turns me on more.

Me: *Joking.* So if looks don't matter too much, I'm in with a chance, then?

Wendy: *Apparently not joking.*

Absolutely.

Me: *Gobsmacked.*

Wendy: *Laughing.*

What else would you like to know?

Me: *A moment or two of more gaping.*

Uhm… DP, Wendy, I've heard you really enjoy it. Is that true?

Wendy: *A dreamy expression, a wriggle of her bottom against the sofa and a sigh.*

Yes, it's true. I just feel so… full like that. There's also the thrill of two men working on me. I can handle two blokes at the same time.

Wendy laughs again.

Well, I suppose, technically, I can handle five.

She looks at me, waiting for me to catch up.

Mouth, pussy, arse…

Wendy waves both hands, fingers spread.

… One in each fist.

Me: That's a talent, Wendy. Must take some concentration.

A pause.

What about women?

Wendy: What, you mean *me* and other women in one-on-one or in a group thing?

Me: *A shrug.* All of the above.

Wendy: Well, for a scene in front of a camera I'll go along with a girl and me on our own. It's okay, it's fun, but I'm the kind of lady who needs a cock inside her to really enjoy herself. Dildos and whatever are okay, but it's the living, pulsing *thing* inside me that flicks my switch.

Wendy turns on that wicked grin again.

And for best results, like I said, DP will do it every time.

In private, it's been known for me to have some fun with another woman along with Rob. I mean, Rob's got to have some spice too, eh? If I can suck another girl off my husband's cock...

Wendy shrugs once more while I sit there and picture that little scenario.

Me: *Voice croaking.* Rob... Wow, lucky man.

Wendy: Would you like to see my latest? We filmed it last week. It's the uncut version, so there's a lot of scene breaks and chatter and that kind of thing. Real behind the scenes.

Me: Wow, yeah, Wendy. That would be really good.

***

So I'm sitting there with this actual, real-life, no-kidding porn star. I've got the raging horn; I mean it's a visceral tug way down deep, a primeval urge that's pushing me to the point of lunging at Wendy and grabbing for her tits.

On the huge expanse of what passes for a television screen – honestly, this thing wouldn't have looked out of place in one of those drive-in movie places – Wendy is entertaining two men in someone's back garden. She's wearing the stockings and shoes and a lacy suspender belt and has the bodice of her dress down to expose her breasts while the hem is ruched up to show off her vulva.

At the time, as I'm attempting to squirm surreptitiously and untangle my poor cock, the on-screen Wendy is wincing and gape-mouthed, eyes glazed as she's robustly fucked from behind.

I've already seen her come once, rising up from squatting on an erection, viscous squirts jetting out while her thighs shiver in nerveless spasms.

"You know," Wendy says, smirking at me. "If you want to sort yourself out," she nudges her chin at my discomfort. "If you want to have a little wank, I don't mind."

I don't quite believe it. Wendy Gilcrest is inviting me to knock one out in front of her. This is a highly unusual situation and I don't know what to do. Then I analyse the scene, the realisation hitting me – Hey, dickhead, this is *Wendy-fucking-Gilcrest*. She fucks men for a living. Seeing you tug your dick isn't going to faze her.

Next she has me really boggling. Right there in front of me Wendy is lifting her dress. Her rump comes up off the sofa. She's got the dress bunched around her waist.

Wendy notices me staring and says, as casual as you like, as though she's just slipping off a pair of shoes that are pinching her feet, "I think I might have a wank, too. I'm just in the mood." She blinks and asks me, "You don't mind, do you?"

There's no answer to that. Or I suppose there is, it was just I didn't have the wherewithal to formulate a coherent response in the seconds that followed. I gape, open-mouthed and bug-eyed at Wendy Gilcrest getting it all out!

Wendy slumps down on the sofa, scrunching up so her chin is on her chest, backside hovering over the precipice as she spreads her legs – wide. She gives me a heavy-lidded stare and chews her bottom lip, fingers splitting her labia.

"Ooh, fuck," she gasps, wincing, stomach tensing. "That's so nice. My clit…"

I'm still staring when she splays her labia, her pink core exposed, desire glistening. The nub of her clit looks swollen to me, the woman's moan and twisted face testimony to the tenderness when she rubs at it.

"You're… Not… Wanking," Wendy says, spitting the words at me like an accusation. "Come on, let me see. Don't be shy. You know enough about me. You've seen me in action." Wendy moans and slides the middle and third fingers of her left hand into her opening. Light glints off the big jewel set in her engagement ring – one that Rob bought for her when the money came in as a replacement for the original more modest stone. I see more glitter from an eternity ring, the dull gleam of a gold wedding band, too.

Wendy fucks herself with two stiff digits, gasping and baring clenched teeth. It looks like agony, but, having seen Wendy's films, I know she's just expressing what it is she's feeling.

It goes on for thirty or forty seconds, but I'm not clock-watching so I'm not sure. Then there's an explosive grunt from the woman, she jack-knifed forward and, sitting upright, a stunned look on her face, snarls, "Fuck it. This isn't going to get me there." Her feline stare falls on me. Wendy smirks, a hand moving slowly through her vulva. "How about you come here and lick it?" she purrs.

Wendy stands up and pulls the dress up over her head. She poses, fists on her hips while eyeing me, her expression expectant.

I whine when I see her naked. My throat works at the house brick lodged there.

"Oh, Jesus," I groan.

Wendy pouts at me while I stare at her for several seconds longer. I can see she's exasperated and probably a little puzzled as to why I'm just sitting there with my jaw dangling.

I close my eyes and open them again. It's the same sight, the same wondrous image: Wendy Gilcrest, naked.

When I stand I expect the dream to evaporate at any moment. The bubble has to burst. There's no way this is reality. But if it isn't real it certainly feels that way. Especially when Wendy ambles across to me, takes hold of both my wrists and guides my hands to her breasts.

The spongy softness of Wendy's tits springs it. Lust boils inside me. I groan and squeeze, fingers closing over her flesh while Wendy unbuttons my jeans, unzips ma, and then hauls it out.

"Oho!" she cries, a fist closing around my girth. "This is nice. This is a lovely cock."

A few strokes later and I'm gulping and pawing at her. Now I can't get enough. My hands are all over Wendy as I savour the texture of her skin, test the firmness of her buttocks and then, with another low groan bubbling from me, slide a finger through the cleft of her sex.

"Rub it," Wendy moans, her breath wafting across my cheek. "Finger that pussy. See how wet I am?"

I moan and nod. "So wet, Wendy." Then I gulp, swallowing heavily, her desire slick on my fingers.

"You want to lick me?" Wendy purrs. I'd love it if you did. I'm so fucking horny I could just go for a good licking."

I'm agog. I'm going to lick Wendy Gilcrest!

The question comes out of me in a voice curdled with yearning. "Cuh-can I fuck you?"

She steps back, releasing my cock. Head canted to one side, Wendy chews her bottom lip and formulates her response. "You don't have any certification, do you?"

I gaped at her, blank and gormless.

"Medical," Wendy says. "Free from infection and all that…"

Ah, that kind of certification.

Disappointment slides in my guts. I can feel the dream slipping away as I say, "Uh, no, sorry."

Wendy pulls a face and shrugs and I think it's all over.

I could curse. I could weep with the frustration of it.

So close… so *fucking* close.

Wendy holds up a finger. "Right," she says, decisive. "Two things…"

I'm all ears. All is not lost.

Maybe…

"I'm going to call Rob," Wendy tells me.

Rob? Why is she calling her husband?

"This isn't the way I usually do things," she explains.

I'm still confused, but decide to keep my mouth shut. There seems to be some progression towards me getting to fuck Wendy Gilcrest.

"He knows there's an interview today, but doesn't know about… this."

By "this" I assume Wendy means her nudity and me standing there with my cock hanging out of my jeans.

Wendy confirms as much by adding, "He isn't bothered about me fucking other men, but he likes to know. I'll call Rob and let him know the situation." Wendy grins at me and rolls her eyes. "Yes, I know, strange relationship, but it works."

"And then?" I ask, fearful this is going to stutter to a halt.

"Condom," Wendy tells me, walking away. "I've got loads of condoms."

I'm gazing at that feminine hip-sway as Wendy calls out, "Just getting my mobile." She pauses at the door, swivelling at the waist to look back at me, smiling as she suggests, "Why don't you get undressed. I won't be long." With a nod, Wendy indicates my dick. "Keep that stiff, won't you."

***

I can taste Wendy Gilcrest. I'm lapping at her pussy like a thirsty Labrador at a puddle. I can hear her sighing and moaning. She's murmuring stuff about how good it feels to have me licking her.

Me! I'm giving a porn star a good time!

Her monologue is something to behold. Wendy gives a running commentary, describing what she's feeling as well as what she wants me to do. It's like we're in one of the scenes she features in. Wendy's use of profanity keeps me on the boil, which is totally unnecessary because I'm rampant enough without her potty-mouthed exhortations. As if I need *anything* to keep me hard! I'm so excited I'm more concerned about a spontaneous eruption, I feel like I could explode at any time. But, as dangerous as it is in terms of premature ejaculation, listening to the lady herself is an experience I wouldn't want to miss.

"Lick my clit," she squeals, squirming. "My pussy, yes. Lick it. Fuck, that's good."

Then Wendy levers upright and almost yanks my head off my shoulders as she pulls my face up to hers. She gazes at me, really stares into my eyes, smiling.

"Kiss me," murmurs Wendy. "I want to taste myself on your tongue."

I'm kissing her. Our tongues slip and slide while Wendy cranks my cock and I feel the skin of her back with my palms and fingers.

"What do you think?" she gasps, breaking free, her eyes shining with an almost manic intensity.

I'm not sure exactly what it is I'm meant to be thinking, but I gulp and tell her I don't believe it.

"You're Wendy Gilcrest," I breathe. "I can't be naked with Wendy Gilcrest. This has to be a dream. Am...?" I swallow heavily once again, eyes wide, head going side-to-side. "Am I *really* going to fuck you?"

Wendy nods, the grin widens. "Do you want to fuck me?" she growls, emphasising the f-word, making it sound like there's nothing she wants more.

Wendy slides past me, getting down onto the carpet on all fours before rolling onto her back. She spreads her legs and splays those meaty folds, holding her labia open with the tips of her fingers. She dips a finger into her body, wincing and gasping.

"Lick me some more," the woman demands. "Suck my cunt."

So I'm down there again, slurping and licking, giving it my best while Wendy writhes and begs me to slip two fingers inside.

"Rub it," she snarls, tendons straining in her neck. "Rub me hard… Yes! Right there. Right- On-That-Spot…"

Wendy spits each word, cords in her throat stark, teeth clenched, eyes squeezed shut.

She grunts and gasps, muscles straining. Her stomach tenses with the effort, her breasts shiver. She grabs at me, groping for my wrists. It's like she's in some sort of fit, gabbling and clawing at me, spitting mad.

"Keep going," the crazed bitch wails. "Oh fuck! Oh yes! Keep going. I'm close. Keep going. Don't stop. Oh!" Wendy cries, eyes snapping open. "Oh!" she calls out again, expression all surprised. Wendy looks at me, glazed eyes clearing as she forces a grin through a rictus of bared teeth and tight jaw. "Keep rubbing, you bastard," she snarls. "Keep…

"Oh, fuck… I'm going to…

"I'm going to come!"

And then she's really writhing about. Wendy's limbs thrash as she grunts and then lets out this bestial roar. I'm going at her, three fingers working at the same place inside her. Then there's this squelching sound and a vehement squirt of clear, viscous gloop spurts out of her as her body actively repulses my fingers.

Wendy's insides squeeze the digits I'm working into her. She grunts again and another spurt of hot liquid splashes over my forearm.

"Fuck!" I yelp.

"Keep going," warbles Wendy, muscles in spasm.

Her thighs shiver and jerk. More liquid squelches from her until, still juddering, wall-eyed with whatever ecstasy grips her, Wendy pushes my hand away.

"Oh, God," she gasps, rolling onto her side, knees coming up. "Oh… Oh, fuck."

Wendy slowly eases down to where she's merely gasping for breath, breasts rolling while she lies on her back, a forearm draped over her eyes.

Then she blurts a laugh, eyes on me as she grins in delight.

"That was fucking gorgeous," she informs me. "Truly marvelous," Wendy says. Then she gets that sly look again and, winking at me, asks, "What about our fuck? You ready for it?"

The truth is I'm a little daunted by the vehemence of Wendy's orgasm. I'm not sure I can follow that with my cock. How am I meant to give her a thrill after she's just pissed cum all over my hand and arm, not to mention the parquet flooring in her front room? She's also infinitely more experienced than me, so I'm not feeling too confident.

But lust trumps lack of confidence. There's all that flesh on display, too. All of Wendy Gilcrest, naked. I can fuck her if I want to.

I lay alongside Wendy and stroke her skin. Her breasts are in my hands, their texture firm yet pliant, nipples showing her arousal. My hand slides down over her soft tummy, the triangle of pubic hair Wendy keeps sculpted at the apex of her slit crinkles beneath my palm.

Wendy chuckles with a deep, rich sound that bubbles out of her when my fingers find her sodden core. Then she rolls onto her front and angles her pelvis, buttocks rising.

Desire bursts inside me when I squeeze firm globes.

Wendy purrs, resting on her elbows, derriere raised.

"Smack my arse," the woman murmurs, squirming.

I give her a slap. Her buttocks jiggle. Wendy yelps and hisses at me to do it again.

Another two stinging thwacks and I'm mad for her. My cock pulses; I'm desperate to devour Wendy. It's such an urgent yearning I rose to my knees, tugging at Wendy's hip.

"Get up higher," I snarl. "Shove your arse back."

Wendy complies, looking back at me over her shoulder. "What are you going to do?"

Without replying or giving Wendy time to react, I part her buttocks and gasp when I see the dark smudge of her anus nestled there. Her labia dangle, the meaty folds all gooey.

"Oh!" Wendy squeaks when I lean in. She chuckles again, the next words coming out clotted. "My arse," she croons – and I can hear the delight in her tone. "That feels fucking lovely. Go on," she urges, gasping. "Tongue my muddy hole, you dirty fucking bastard."

Emboldened by the enthusiastic response, I probe at Wendy's sphincter. She grunts and squirms and generally lets me know she loves it. It goes on for a minute or so, with Wendy's fingers slipping over her clit while I dab at her dark stain.

"I'm going to come again," I hear her groan. "Come round here... Kiss me. Squeeze my tits. Handle me.

"Be rough!" the woman snarls.

And she's gasping into my open mouth as we kiss. Wendy bucks and jerks, convulsing, her tongue wild with mine as her climax grips her and she sobs and moans and lets it roll over her.

When it's over she looks at me through heavy-lidded eyes.

Wendy says, "You should join me in the next production. What do you think? You want to be in porn?"

It might be a nothing comment, a throw-away because of the way she's feeling at that moment. Or perhaps she means it? I just don't know. Either way I get no time to analyse her question because Wendy clambers to her feet and, with that very arousing hip-rolling gait, dances away.

"Upstairs," she says, crooking a finger.

***

I'm inside Wendy. She's on top of me, straddling my thighs while her body clenches around me and she rocks back-and-forth, hands on my chest, her eyes closed. She looks like she's enjoying it. Her face is relaxed, expression dreamy. My hands slide over her, moving from her hips up to her breasts.

Wendy's eyes open. She smiles down at me and then rolls forward, leaning in to kiss me. I embrace her, holding her tight, our tongues sliding while I thrust up with my pelvis.

"Nice and slow," Wendy coos, kissing me again. She's gentle, calming me with her words and eyes. She forces me to control the insistent jerking of my hips. "Let's just build into it," she murmurs. "So much of the stuff I do in front of the camera is rough and tumble, it's all about the fucking. You've given me a couple of orgasms and I'm in the mood for slow and easy." Wendy smiles at me and adds, "I promise it'll get wild later. I promise you can fuck me good and hard and deep."

Another languid kiss and we're almost immobile, although Wendy's hips never quite stop their rocking.

She's squeezing me with her insides. "Let me savour this lovely feeling," Wendy breathes. Her eyes gleam. "Let me feel your gorgeous cock."

It's difficult. My instinct is to drive up, to roll her onto her back and plunge deep. The urge is strong to plunder her cunt until I grunt and pump the johnny-bag full of semen.

Wendy shushes me, the backs of her fingers smoothing my cheek as she stares into my eyes. "Steady... Take it easy... It'll last longer and be so good when we come."

I gulp and nod.

"We'll see if we can get there together," Wendy adds. "Let me control it. You just tell me if it's getting too much." She rolls her eyes and grins. "It isn't all about pounding away as deep as you can. Believe me; I can come by doing it this way, too."

So we move together, with Wendy watching my face for any sign I'm about to get carried away or explode.

I try to close my mind to the sensations, tingling away in my root. I concentrate on the texture of Wendy's skin, my hands moving over her contours.

But that rapidly gets to be too much, a sensory overload that, coupled with the constant reminder of just who this is gently massaging my cock, sends the zinging precursor to my orgasm bubbling through my core.

"God, Wendy," I grunt, grimacing through clenched teeth. "I can't believe I'm really here. Like this. With you."

She chuckles and gives me that lopsided smirk. "I decided when I first saw you. I've been watching those scenes all morning and got all turned on. I hoped you'd be cute so I could tease you into submission –

otherwise I'd have been wanking all day. Poor Rob wouldn't get any tea when he got home. I'd have jumped him and demanded a good seeing-to."

"He's so lucky," I moan.

Wendy pulls a face and says, "The poor love can't keep up with me." She throws me a wink. "So the films and the fact he gives me some free rein means I'm not a frustrated girl." Wendy smiles at me as she comes in for another kiss. "And it also means *you* get to fuck me," she mutters.

I offer a silent word of thanks to Rob. I don't know how he can countenance it all – his wife with other men. It occurs to me that I should ask *him* for an interview.

I file the thought away for future consideration, my focus suddenly fixed on Wendy and her increased pelvic activity.

I look at her face and see she seems to be concentrating hard. Her brow is furrowed, her eyes half-closed. Her bottom lip is caught between her teeth.

Then her eyes clear and she smiles at me again. "You okay?"

I nod, hands gripping her hips.

"Good," Wendy says, still smiling. "'Cause I'm going to ride this a little harder. Tell me if you're going to pop."

She lifts up and drops back down, repeating the process, breasts jiggling.

It gets more robust, our skin slap-slap-slapping while moans of appreciation pop from Wendy and I desperately fight to suppress the surge.

"Oh," Wendy whines. "I can feel it. I can feel it coming. It's good," she gasps, nodding, face slack. "Touch me. Touch my tits. Squeeze them. Go on... fucking *squeeze* my tits. Smack my arse."

I comply, my hands full of breast-flesh or taut buttock as Wendy shifts up through the gears. I grab the cheeks of her arse and part those globes and my fingers find our conjunction, my latex-sheathed cock slippery with Wendy's desire. I smear gloop with a forefinger and then probe at the roundel of Wendy's anus, her eyes going wide when the top joint slips into her.

"You dirty bastard," the woman sighs, smirking. "You want my arse?" she asks. "Finger it. Get your finger right in that dirty-hole."

Wendy gasps and squashes her breasts between us, her mouth locked over mine. She grunts and squeals while we're fixed together at the lips, her pelvis corkscrewing so she can grind harder against my finger.

"Later," the woman says, eyes gleaming with the plan. "Can you come back later today? When Rob's home. You can DP me." Wendy fucks onto me, her voice strident. "You can use my arse while my husband's in my pussy." She licks my face, grinning like a maniac. "You want to do that? Eh? Do you?"

"Shit, Wendy," is all I can manage in response.

The episode passes when Wendy sees I'm on the verge of shooting my bolt.

"If you want to," she purrs, vehement movements slowing to that sublime rocking back-and-forth, which is just enough to stem the rush through my cock. "We can do a little threesome tonight. I mean it, Rob in my front while you knock at the back door." She lets that idea take shape in my head, kissing me again, pelvis working more and more quickly until her ardour flares hot one more.

"Are you close?" asks Wendy on a sigh, her head lolling back as she massages her breasts. "Because it won't take much for me to get there. I could come quite easily."

I gulp and grimace, my mind full of what it might be like to take Wendy's anus. The thought of her husband being present is a difficult one for me to reconcile, but if it means more time naked with Wendy I suppose I might get used to Rob being involved.

After all, she's his wife. I'm the interloper.

"Can I really come back later, Wendy?"

She nods quickly. "I'll talk to Rob later... When we've—

"Oh, shit, I'm going to come."

It's a frantic time. Wendy rides me hard, great sobs bursting out of her. Her fingers go to her sex and Wendy rubs at her clit, mewling and gulping and mauling her breasts with her free hand. She grunts and grinds down on me, pleasure twisting her face.

I look up to watch Wendy features while her orgasm boils, my hands all over her skin, her body writhing beneath my touch.

My surge doesn't erupt. It's strange but in the midst of battle I don't climax. Instead, what happens is Wendy gasps and wails through her orgasm before her eyes snap open and, with her body still in spasm, she rolls off me.

"From behind," the woman snarls, lifting up onto her hands and knees. She's positioned with her derriere presented to me, her hot-eyed gaze fixed on me over one shoulder. Wendy parts her buttocks with one hand, her cunt gaping at me. "Fuck me," she growls. "Hurry up. Put it in…"

And I'm there. I'm deep inside Wendy, rutting into her while she drops down onto her elbows and mumbles her delight into the bedcover.

It seems her climax hits boiling point again as she sobs and frantically fingers her clit.

This time, with me leaning low over her back, crouching, arms circling Wendy's brisket, breasts spilling over my hands, I grunt and moan and pour it all into the prophylactic sheath. Jizm pumps out of me; squirt after squirt of cum, the teat in the end of the condom dangling and heavy with the volume of goo it's captured when I eventually withdraw.

Wendy turns, scrambling a one-eighty to then tug the condom off my cock.

"Shit," I blurt when she gets down on her front and grabs for my oozing dick.

Then she's busy with her lips around my cock, cheeks concave while she cranks me at the root. "Oh, that's bad," I say, chuckling when Wendy gives it her dirty pornstar best, painting her cheeks and chin with the gloop oozing out of me.

"Thought you might like that," she grins, rising up on her knees to wrap her arms around my neck.

Then we're kissing again, her breasts pressed against me, my hands around her waist, my dick never dipping below the horizontal.

"I'll call Rob now," Wendy says. She glances at my penis and adds, "Maybe you should stay here this afternoon? Then, when Rob gets in…?"

I'm wide-eyed and speechless, thinking this is the best interview I've ever conducted.

End of the 4th Story

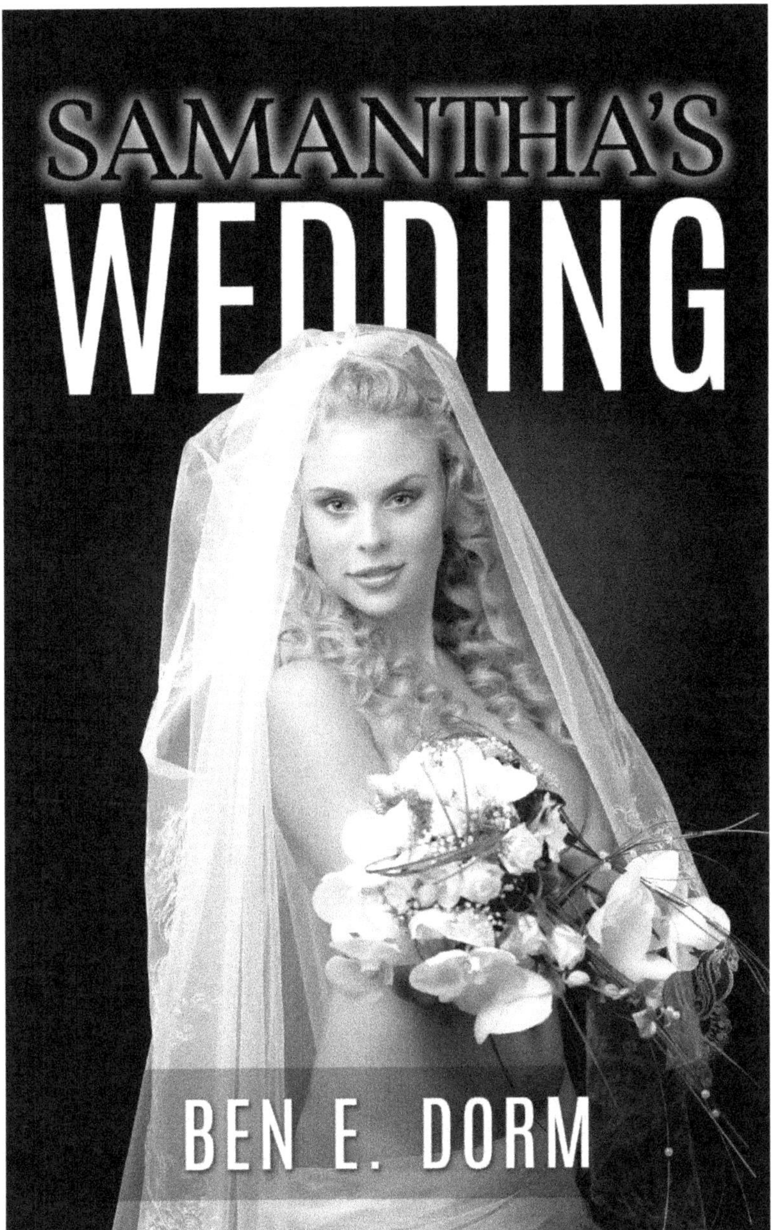
SAMANTHA'S
WEDDING
BEN E. DORM

Samantha is damp between her legs, her delicate underwear soiled by jizm.

The organ music shifts in tempo and volume, going from a benign background hum into the instantly recognisable *Bridal March*. The assembled stand, all faces swivelling towards Samantha as her father escorts her down the aisle.

There's a murmur of appreciation from both sides of the church.

The sound thrills Samantha. She feels beautiful when the rise of voices reaches her. It's her big day, and so far it's been perfect. Looking forward, her eyes go to the altar where her intended waits. Beneath the veil Samantha's cheeks warm when she sees him looking back at her.

Semen trickles from her opening.

They arrive at the altar and her father, somewhat reluctantly, moves away to take his place on the pew next to his wife.

Samantha leans in to take the groom's fingers with her own.

Philip smiles when Samantha squeezes his hand, his eyes flicking from his bride's face to the vicar when the ceremony begins.

"Did you do it?" asks Philip, murmuring at his fiancé.

Samantha nods quickly, insides flipping. "Yes," she whispers, "his cum is leaking out of me right now." She sees Philip's throat work as he swallows heavily. Samantha watches him close his eyes, wondering what it is he's thinking and feeling. "Thank you," she adds, squeezing Philip's hand again. Emotion swells in her chest. "I love you," she says.

***

The knot inside Philip loosens when he hears her say it. The ache of uncertainty that's been sitting there for days melts. He decides it was the right thing to do. Releasing his fiancé from the shackles of convention had been the right decision.

It had bothered him, of course it had. At first, when he'd overheard that to-and-fro between Samantha and her personal trainer he'd been appalled. Listening to it had been a torment.

He'd phoned her mobile when she was meant to be working out in the gym, with Samantha failing to disconnect the call properly, the result being Philip had overheard a conversation between two people who were obviously very intimate at the time.

Jealousy and rage had fused in a fiery ball in the pit of his stomach. The infidelity had staggered him.

With the connection still live, Philip had eavesdropped and overheard Samantha uttering filthy exhortations to a lover. Horrified, he held the mobile to his ear and heard all about his fiancé taking another man's cock.

A few weeks after that momentous event and Philip can recall every word. In his head, he can replay the scene over and over, every groan and gasp and sigh.

"It's just so hot seeing you do that to me. I won't be able to stop. When I'm married, I won't be able to stop myself cheating. I'll keep coming to see you. Even on my wedding day. In the morning I'll come here and we can fuck. I want to walk down the aisle and feel my pussy all tender from being battered by your lovely cock."

"You're a bad bitch," Philip had heard the trainer mutter in reply. *"That's so bad it's getting me close."*

Numb with shock, too stunned to fully appreciate just what was happening, Philip had held the phone to his ear, gape-mouthed, wide-eyed, and listened to while Samantha snarled, *"Then fuck me. Really slam me. Rip my cunt apart. Punish me, you lovely bastard. I'm a dirty, cheating slut. I deserve to be punished."*

Outrage had welled inside Philip, a hot tide of something so powerful the urge to visit violence on everything and anything – everyone – was almost overwhelming. The emotion engulfing Philip was so primal, so utterly all-consuming that he could have wrung the life from Samantha. In his mind, he pictured himself with his hands around her slender neck, that beautiful face all twisted and purple while he squeezed and squeezed.

Then, as the shock wore off and a second wave of rabid anger raged inside him, Philip had grabbed for his car keys and stormed from his flat.

He knew where she was.

It was a drive fraught with recklessness and, looking back, Philip is amazed at how he didn't wreck the BMW on the way to the gym. By some miracle Philip arrived without causing harm to himself or anyone else. Then he had scoured the car park for Samantha's Porsche, the distinctive electric-blue Targa 4 taunting him when he saw the car in the yard.

Spitting curses Philip barged into the building, intent on retribution: the faithless bitch needed a lesson.

But, confronted by muscles and testosterone in the foyer a sense of hopelessness filled Philip and his anger evaporated. Seeing muscular men in their physical prime overwhelmed him. Tears welled and threatened to embarrass him. He hated himself for his weakness and inability to exact revenge, cowed by the physical superiority he saw all around him.

Returning to the BMW he'd let it come. Philip sat in the car and sobbed. It was over, done, finished. The engagement was off. But, after a full ten minutes of anguish the thought occurred to him: he was more upset about losing his beloved Samantha than he was by her infidelity. Philip reached across to the passenger seat to retrieve his mobile..

He called her, but it went straight to voicemail. Hanging up immediately, he couldn't leave some garbled voice message, Philip sucked in a deep breath through his nose and cuffed at his eyes, struggling to think.

In the end he decided he needed time to analyse his feelings. He had to get his head straight before making any kind of approach.

***

The ceremony closes. The groom kisses the bride and it's time to leave the church. There are the inevitable photographs. Outside the summer afternoon smiles on the newlyweds, Samantha beams before the happy couple and the entourage convoys to the former manor house for a lavish Wedding Breakfast.

Being the focus of attention, Samantha and Philip don't have much opportunity for any unguarded conversation. It's all nods and smiles and handshakes, congratulations and kisses from everyone.

The time for intimacy will come later. Philip can't wait. He's anxious to be at his bride despite knowing another man has fucked her already that day.

"How are you?" Philip manages to murmur when they're all seated.

"Overwhelmed," Samantha replies.

Dark arousal slides deep inside Philip. He croaks a question: "Was it good? This morning? With him?"

The upper slopes of Samantha's breasts bubble over the bodice of her wedding gown as she sucks in a deep draught of air. Desire dribbles from her, insides clenching at the reminder of the big cock that had split her open. She suppresses a low moan when a vivid image of his muscular body and an erection stiff enough to hammer nails arcing up from those dangling balls comes to mind. She gulps at the memory of semen spurting into her.

She feels the near irresistible urge to rub herself and squirms her rump against her chair, the itch in her pussy suddenly so demanding. In her mind's eye she sees herself hike the skirt of her gown up around her hips, plant the heels of her shoes against the table, haul her sodden knickers aside, and just finger herself to orgasm. It's an impossible desire – it's her wedding, she can't succumb and rub her cunt. It's unthinkable. All those people... her parents...

"He fucked me and filled me with cum," she whispers to her husband. "I want you to stir it up with your cock as soon as we can."

"Jesus, Sam..." Philip mutters.

But that's all he can manage before he's interrupted by Samantha's mother.

For a second Philip is mortified his new mother-in-law may have overheard the exchange. A flash of anxiety hits him, his sphincter loosening at the thought of anyone knowing his and Samantha's unusual arrangement especially her mother!

Although, once it's apparent his mother-in-law is only commenting on how lovely her daughter looks and how handsome Philip is as a groom – for the umpteenth time in the last hour – Philip concedes he wouldn't mind a crack at the old girl. She might be touching fifty, but she had it all going on in a tight-bodied, cougar style.

The imagining grows more lewd: Philip and his wife's mother rolling around on the nuptial bed in the suite upstairs. In his head, Philip sees the woman divested of her dress, big breasts cantilevered over her bra, long legs encased in dark stockings. In the fantasy his mother-in-law keeps her shoes on, gazing at Philip's hard-on as she sits on the end of the bed, legs crossed, her fingers reaching for the ardent tumescence.

Philip gulps, his cock pulsing while he imagines those red-painted lips puckering over his knob-end.

The question comes from his wife and interrupts his sordid reverie. "What are you thinking?" Samantha asks. "Your face…"

Philip smirks and says, "I'll tell you later."

… *Maybe.*

***

She's going to go mad with it. Of course she's ecstatic that her day is going so well: the ceremony was magical, her dress and hair and make-up works of art. Her father had been generous, splashing out tens of thousands on her wedding, the banquet alone cost more than a family car. But, if she doesn't get fucked soon, if she doesn't cool the heat between her legs, she's going to go insane.

Then, finally, the speeches are done, glasses are raised. There's a lull, time between the reception and the party to follow. There are games and other entertainments for the guests, a scaled-down version of a fun-fair set up in the grounds.

"Do you think we'll be missed if we--?"

Samantha doesn't finish the sentence before her husband has her hand and is leading her away. She's giggling as they hurry up the stairs, dancing from one foot to the other with anticipation while Philip attempts to slip the key into the lock.

"Oh, Jesus," Samantha blasphemes. "Oh, fuck… Come on, Phil. Come on…"

The key snicks into the lock and the door opens. They bundle inside, hands urgent, mouths locked.

"Don't mess my hair or the dress," Samantha gasps. She's bright-eyed with devilment as she hauls up the skirt of her wedding dress. Samantha turns and presents her rounded derriere, her hips swaying side-to-side, her pussy hot and impatient. "Pull my fucking knickers off," she snarls, looking back to a gape-mouthed Philip. "I'm so fucking horny. Fuck me, Philip. Come on, fuck your wife."

***

He sees her with her dress up around her hips, white stocking tops attached to an elaborate six-drop suspender belt. Samantha's legs look superb, lean and taut at her thighs – proof that the gym time wasn't wasted, that Samantha had worked more than the trainer's cock.

Philip experiences a momentary stab of residual jealousy when he thinks about Samantha's transgression. But, he decides as he peels his wife's underwear away from her body, he's beyond that now. He's going into the marriage with his eyes open, their understanding freeing them both in his opinion.

"God, Sam," Philip breathes as his wife kneels on the end of the bed and invites him into her opening. "You're so bloody gorgeous." Then Philip is sliding in, his cock displacing the other man's deposit.

Semen squelches and farts around Philip's girth as he thrusts, a long and low groan of appreciation coming from Samantha.

"I love you, Philip," the blonde sighs. "Thank you, thank you for everything. We're going to have a good life together, aren't' we?"

"I love you, too," Philip grunts at his wife, wondering what her mother's breasts are like in the flesh. "Of course we'll have a good life," he adds, thinking a mother-daughter combo would be incredible.

Then Philip crouches low over his wife's back, probing deep with his cock while he slips the restrictive bodice of the dress down to expose her tits.

Samantha yelps in protest. "I told you not to mess me up," she says.

"I'm going to pump you full of spunk," growls Phil, ignoring Samantha's objection as he mauls breast-flesh. "Another load for you, my darling wife. Two in one day," gasps Philip, his own words causing the irreversible surge. "Ah, Sam," he grunts, "I'm coming."

Samantha's fingers work between her legs. Her husband's grip is tight on her boobs while his cock throbs inside her. She can hear him moaning and muttering, his breath hot against her neck where he nuzzles at her.

"Am I wicked, Phil?" the woman groans, her own climax looming. "I fucked another man this morning. I could feel his cum sliding out of me while we were getting married…"

Then it hits her and, with Samantha's head lolling, a guttural moan of sublime pleasure curdles from her throat. "Phil," she whines. "Oh, fuck, Phil... I'm there... I'm fucking *coming*. Give it to me, babe. Give me all that love."

Philip hears his wife, but is too caught in the ecstasy to respond. At that moment he's overwhelmed. Philip still can't believe such a physically appealing young woman is his. Samantha is a stunner and Philip is amazed she's actually married to him. She's also dripping with money, clever, witty and devastating in bed. Okay, they might be starting out with an unorthodox arrangement, but at least there's honesty involved. He now knows that the woman he loves wouldn't be content to go through life in a monogamous relationship, which was quite an adjustment for him to make in the run-up to the wedding.

Samantha can have her lovers and so can he – Philip is just a little unsure still about seeing his wife with another man. Hearing about it is one thing, witnessing the reality could be something different.

Then, with thoughts of his mother-in-law filling his mind again, it all gets too much and he succumbs to his orgasm, joy filling him as he floods his wife with ejaculate.

***

"That's the difference, isn't it, Sam?"

Samantha looks down at her husband. She's still wearing her veil, the stockings and her suspender belt, but is divested of her wedding dress. She's pleasantly squiffy on the wine she's quaffed and is currently rounding off her perfect day with a slow ride on her husband's dick.

Her breasts sway as she slides up and down on Philip's erection, her fingers splayed across his chest, her weight supported on straight arms.

It's 2 a.m. and Samantha feels she could do it all night.

"Hmm?" she murmurs. "What's the difference, babe?" There's a throaty rasp to her voice, hoarseness brought on by wine and cigarettes and sex.

She feels so alive, so free and in love.

"Well," Philip replies, his hands on Samantha's waist. "What you said this afternoon, when we snuck up for that quick fuck--"

He's interrupted by a deep chuckle from Samantha. "God, I came so *hard*," she breathes, coming down to kiss Philip's mouth.

It goes on for a minute and more, with Samantha's hips never quite still, their tongues sliding in a serpentine swirl while Phil's hands explore bare skin.

"You were saying?" Samantha purrs when, finally, she breaks away.

"When I came, you said to give you all the love." Philip pauses and reaches up to pull the woman down for another kiss. When they parted again, with Samantha's pelvis corckscrewing, her bouncing more urgent, he adds, "That's the difference, isn't it, Sam? When it's me and you, it's love? When you're with someone else... well..."

Recognising Philip's need for some reassurance, and truly meaning it, Samantha says, "God, yes, babe." She strokes his face, easing back with the robust action. "I feel blessed, Phil. I can't tell you how glad I am we got that awful business out of the way."

Shame heats Samantha's face. Her eyes close as she whispers, "I'm so sorry for being that person."

She cries out in surprise and then giggles when Philip, in a quick and very agile roll, turns his wife onto her back.

"Oh, fuck, babe," the blonde purrs as her legs are hooked behind Philip's arms and he goes deep. "Give me the love..."

***

Two days later Phil is blinking at the opulence.

"Your dad has really pulled it out of the bag, Sam – Look at this place!"

Unfazed, Samantha drawls, "He likes to spoil me." She pulls her sunglasses from her hair and slides them onto her face before she steps out of the limousine. "Come on," she says, leaning back into the car to regard her husband. "Let's get changed and have a swim." She winks at Philip, who's still sitting and gaping at the vast frontage of the resort hotel.

Twenty minutes later Philip is laid out on the most comfortable reclining sun-lounger he's ever known. He's sipping a rum and Coke and waiting for his bride to make an appearance in her new bikini.

When a shadow falls across him, he opens his mouth to speak, the words jamming behind his teeth when he sees a paragon of female pulchritude standing at the foot of the sunbed.

"Hello," the woman says, fists on her hips, head canted to one side, her interest very obvious. "Just arrived?" she asks.

Something living jumps inside Philip's chest as he stares at her, taken aback by her forthright manner, intense gaze and the scraps of string and cotton patches that pass for swimwear.

"Uh…" Philip manages to gurgle. He levers himself upright, babbling," Oh, hello, yes, just got here…"

With some enthusiasm, the woman responds with, "You're English! Oh my God, say something to me." She pauses and throws a lascivious wink at Philip before adding a suggestive, "Preferably, something *nasty*."

She's at least fifty if she's a day, Philip muses, one of those well-maintained wealthy women with a libido in the red zone. *Fake tits, but a hell of a good job regardless.*

Recovering from the woman's startling entrance and with thoughts of his mother-in-law in mind, Philip smirks, wondering if this is the time to suggest a threesome to Samantha as he says, "How nasty do you want me to be?"

End of the 5th Story

THE PHOTOGRAPHER'S
Wife

BEN E. DORM

It was a hot afternoon and the client wasn't home: perfect for working shirtless. John Banks worked without thinking, guiding the lawn mower didn't take much brain power after all. It was simply a matter of ensuring the machine kept moving in a straight line. The thing also had an engine so it didn't need much guidance. All-in-all it was a nice easy job to finish off the day.

John had four or five more journeys up and down the long lawn before he could call it a day. He was just walking along behind the mower, thinking of nothing much when the movement caught his eye. It came from his left some twenty feet away, over the fence in the neighbour's back garden. When he looked up John was surprised to see a woman in a bikini strolling along the path, a rolled up towel tucked beneath her arm.

The sight of her almost caused a wobble in the so far precise lines the client insisted upon, but John recovered quickly and regained mastery of the mower, walking on behind the machine, the woman moving beyond his line of sight.

If John wanted to take a longer look at her he'd be forced to look back over one shoulder, a move he was reluctant to make because the mower had to stay on its line. Also, turning to look would be a blatant action, potentially embarrassing for the client's neighbour and, in John's eyes, inappropriate.

Although, in his opinion, from the brief glance he had allowed himself, John thought she was very tasty and deserving of a second look.

Still, he had a job to do. He was a professional and forced himself to maintain a steady pace even though he was tempted to rush it and reach the end of the row so he could turn the mower around for the return journey. Of course he wanted another look at her. John was a young man with hot blood in his veins, he could appreciate a good-looking lady, but it was his job, his livelihood, he couldn't afford to lose his hard won reputation by veering off course – no matter how distracted he was by a sexy, good-looking woman.

He carried on, focussed on the task in hand until duly reaching the turning point. He eased the big mower round and set off on the run back towards the house, diligently ensuring he was working in a straight line before he allowed himself a quick and, he hoped, surreptitious glance over the shoulder-high fence.

"Fucking hell," he muttered, blinking in surprise.

She was on her front, resting on her elbows and forearms wearing nothing but a pair of sunglasses and a sheen of sun lotion.

With the woman apparently engrossed in a paperback book, John boggled and somehow managed to keep moving, his brain not quite able to grasp the reality of what he was looking at in the adjoining garden. His throat worked as he swallowed heavily, heart bouncing inside the rack of his ribs, the necessary forward momentum taking him past the ninety degree angle in relation to the woman's position.

Again, with immense will on his part, John resisted the near overwhelming urge to rush it. "Steady," he murmured to himself while turning the memory of the woman's physical appeal over in his mind.

John assessed her at the middle- to top-end of her forties. An attractive woman with a very appealing figure, she had certainly looked good in the bikini. It hadn't taken much beyond his initial glance for John to appreciate the lady took care of her physical appearance. She looked like a woman who kept to a sensible diet, took a lot of exercise, and very likely abstained from too much booze. John had also managed to register short dark hair before the task of mowing the lawn took her beyond his line of sight.

And she was naked! She was just lying there calm as you like – as though John and the buzzing mower didn't exist.

John's excitement surged as he doggedly maintained course. He badly wanted to get another look at the woman, to soak up each detail during the time it took to move beyond her again. Desire lay like a brick in the pit of his stomach while arousal tugged at his vitals. He could feel the beginnings of an erection swelling in his shorts, awkward since he really needed both hands on the mower. Adjusting himself inside his clothing wasn't an option at that point.

In regard to his burgeoning erection the wooden fence was an ally for which John was grateful. At least she wouldn't be able to see the effect she had on him.

He reached the turning point and maneuvered the lawn mower through its arc, allowing the machine to trundle along with the minimum of attention as he looked over the fence and saw the woman was still on her front.

Looking at the globes of her buttocks, which were as lightly tanned as the rest of her, John deduced – albeit it in a hazy kind of way – that she was no stranger to the naturist style.

He came level with her and let out a low moan as the flanks of her breasts and one nipple in profile came into view.

The woman's head turned as John moved past her again, with John gulping in response when she flashed him a smile.

"Shit," John muttered when the sway of her breasts caught his focus. Arousal flared while hot, but John managed to nod in reply. Then, despite him doing his best to keep his eyes on the dark screens of the woman's sunglasses, John couldn't help but let his attention flick down over her body. When he looked into her face again, his face warmed, her smirk telling John she'd caught him looking.

On the penultimate journey, after turning around again, John muttered, "Ah fuck…" He couldn't believe it, couldn't readily accept the fact that the woman had put down her book and shifted round onto her back. "Look at you," he murmured, no chance at all of being heard above the clatter of the machine. "Just fucking *look* at you."

She had to be doing it on purpose John decided. The woman had to be deliberately provoking him, taunting him with her body. The thought of it irritated John, he didn't like teasers and did his level best to ignore her – Easier said than done.

John tried hard, but when he finally made the turn for the last run, he couldn't resist the lure of taking a quick peep. A wave of intense, gut-dragging yearning rolled over him when he saw her there all bare, that ripe body blatantly displayed,. In his mind's eye John was scrambling over the fence so he could drop onto the towel and push the woman's thighs wider. In his fantasy he went at her, slurping her pussy while she mumbled encouragement.

His cock was hard, stiff with desire as he reared up, kneeling between the woman's widespread legs.

"Ooh, yes, give it to me," the fantasy breathed, eyes gleaming with lust, fingers diddling her clit.

John moaned when the molten embrace claimed his length, her body closing around him.

In reality, during that final journey with the mower he kept the woman in sight, eye balls straining to the corners of his eyes while he endeavoured to keep his face pointing straight ahead. John feigned total concentration on the job as he moved past the ninety degree mark and struggled to exorcise the woman from his thoughts. He planned his evening, thinking about finishing work and meeting the lads in the pub for a beer or two. He could tell them about the naked woman and listen to their incredulous responses. There was no way they would believe him – he almost didn't believe it himself. He pictured himself loading the mower onto the trailer, driving home and then tugging his cock, thereby relieving himself of the churning frustration he was currently suffering. Not much of a deviation from the original plan, but one sorely needed. He could still meet the boys for a beer, but he needs to find some relief first.

John reached the end of the row and lifted the blades so he could turn and wheel the mower towards the path at the side of the huge Victorian house. Instinctively his eyes moved to where he expected the woman to be, but, to his surprise, she wasn't laid on the towel any more. Instead, to John's increasing physical discomfort, with him boggle-eyed and gaping, he saw her looking at him over the fence.

He could see she was trying to say something. The woman's mouth moved, but John couldn't hear above the clatter of the mower. She pushed her sunglasses into her hair and raised a hand to beckon him over.

Gulping, stomach flipping with the possibilities, John killed the engine.

The silence that followed was almost preternatural, the solitude deafening. The houses were set in a road of detached properties on the periphery of town, with the neighbouring property at the end of the row – a fact, John vaguely considered, that probably suited her propensity to saunter around her garden in the buff.

In that few seconds of near total quiet the pair stared at one another, John too surprised to move or speak.

"Could you come here?" she asked.

John hesitated, unsure.

Eventually, he moved, mind in turmoil.

The closer he got, the more of her became visible: bare shoulders and the jut of her collar bones; the upper slopes of her breasts; tapered waist and the swell of her hips – the light fluff at the apex of her sex.

Excitement thrummed inside John. Lust clenched its fingers in some indefinable place way down deep while a primal urge to physically possess the woman uncoiled and tasted the air with a forked tongue.

For a few seconds John entertained the notion she might be about to ask about his availability to work, an idea which the woman quickly dispelled.

"Hello," she said, smirking in a way that did nothing to put John at ease. "I'm Christine... Chrissie, usually." Her eyes moved over John's bare torso before her attention flicked back to his face. "What do I call <i>you</i>?"

It was difficult with his cock clamouring for attention and the band of iron tightening around his chest, but John managed to mumble his name.

"I saw you working, John," Chrissie said. Her head moved in the direction of the big house, she'd appeared from so unexpectedly. "I was inside and heard the mower. When I came out to look...

"I must say," she added, her accent a posh Surrey drawl, "I did appreciate you working without a shirt on." Her eyes moved across John's upper body again and her grin broadened. Chrissie bobbed up on tiptoe and peered over the fence. "I noticed your bottom, too." She paused while gnawing her lower lip, eyes going up to confront the young man. Then, with her grin breaking into a full-on, beaming smile she murmured, "It looks to me as though you don't mind seeing me without any clothes on."

John gulped and shuffled his feet, warmth rising in his face. Speechless in the face of such candour, his mouth opened but nothing came out. He simply didn't know how to respond. The last few minutes had been a little overwhelming for the gardener, layer on layer of astonishment.

"I think you've got a gorgeous body," Chrissie was saying, her voice permeating through the fog that seemed to have enveloped John's capacity for coherent thought. "Lovely deep chest; nice big arms... I love your tummy," she added wistfully, eyes glazing for a few beats. "I wouldn't mind seeing your bare bottom either," giggled Chrissie, the corners of her mouth twitching.

The full impact of her words didn't register immediately. John blinked, mouth hanging open when Chrissie went on with an astounding,

"I don't suppose you'd like to come to my house, would you, John? You could let me see that big hard-on in all its glory. I could give it a tug for you, too. I'll suck it if you want me to, but what I'd really like is for you to fuck me with it."

John gaped at Chrissie as he stammered, "I... uh... it...," his brain struggling to comprehend.

"Do what you have to do here," Chrissie cut in. "Pack up your stuff and then knock at the front door. I'll be waiting for you."

Chrissie turned and sauntered away, the feminine sweep of her waist and hips holding John's attention. He stared at her, slack-jawed and reeling from the encounter. "Fuck," he breathed, eyes slipping to the twitch and jiggle of Chrissie's buttocks. "Fuck," he repeated, adding, "No way," head shaking side-to-side in utter disbelief.

He continued to stare at Chrissie's retreating form, the woman teasing him with the exaggerated roll of her hips until she disappeared through the open back door. He watched her until she was out of sight, attention focussed on Chrissie's rounded rump. He was so focused, so intent he failed to see the figure watching him from behind an upstairs window.

***

It took fifteen minutes for John to secure the mower on the trailer after emptying the hopper of cuttings. He tidied the client's garden and completed the myriad tiny tasks that signalled the end of a working day. All throughout these small but necessary jobs John remained distracted. He worked automatically, hurrying in his eagerness to get finished, keen to get to the house next door.

John's mind turned the event over and over, with Chrissie's nudity clearly fixed in his head. He recalled her words, staggered by the woman's boldness and her invitation. Could she actually mean it or was it a joke? John relived the scene. He examined Chrissie's expression and tone of voice, replayed her words again and again. In the end, he decided that as improbable as it might be, the stuff of fantasy that his friends would not believe, Chrissie really did mean it.

Then the anxiety hit him and his nerve failed. John's confidence slipped, plummeting because he didn't think he would live up to her expectations. Chrissie was obviously so much more experienced, she must have had known a few lovers in her time. Doubts assailed him, arrows zinging in to pierce his ardour: What if he came too soon? What if he couldn't get it up? Not that he truly thought an erection would elude him, but the prospect of stage fright did linger like a dark shadow, lurking in the corner of his mind.

Finally the moment was on him. It was decision time. There was nothing left to do but either get in the Land Rover and drive away or take the walk up the drive.

John prevaricated, hesitating, nervous as a virgin. His body thrummed, blood rushing to swell his cock when he called to mind the moment he'd seen Chrissie naked. Desire surged, lust boiling, libido demanding what it craved.

"Fuck it," he muttered under his breath, feet moving before his brain had informed John the decision was made.

It was an odd thirty seconds between the gate and front door. In an out-of-body moment, as if he'd remained in the street next to his Land Rover John watched himself make the journey. He saw himself from behind, approaching the blue door, his mind coolly detached. He could feel his excitement churning, recognised the deep, urgent physical need of his body's response. At first the impressions only seeped in on a vague level, but this strange sensation was short-lived with John snapping back into the moment when he heard the jingle-jangle of the front door bell inside the house. When the two-tone bing-bong reached him, John was surprised to see his finger coming away from the button fixed to the wall.

Yearning swelled with a visceral ballooning of desire when, still nude, Chrissie opened the door to him.

"I thought you weren't going to show," she said, smiling before opening the door wide with complete disregard for her nudity. Not that was much chance of anyone other than John witnessing Chrissie's exhibitionism; not a vehicle had passed all the while John had been busy in his trailer. No cars or vans or even pedestrians had happened by. "Oh," Chrissie added, pouting in disappointment, "you've put your shirt back on." Her eyes glittered with mischief as she stepped back a pace and moved to one side. "Come in," she invited. Chrissie eyed John's shirt and then drawled a command. "Take it off," she said. "I want to feel your lovely muscles."

John peeled off his tee-shirt while Chrissie closed the door behind him.

"You've got a gorgeous body," the woman breathed, eyes flicking over John's torso. "I love a fit young man."

John gulped when Chrissie's hands pressed against the slabs of pectoral muscle. He almost whined when her palms slid south to his stomach.

Chrissie sighed and grinned happily, smiling into John's face as she murmured a dreamy, "You really are a yummy specimen. I think I'm going to enjoy you."

John gasped and gulped again when Chrissie squeezed his erection through his shorts.

The woman nodded, her attention going to John's biceps. She tested the circumference of John's upper arms with her fingers and thumbs, clasping and squeezing as though testing for quality. Apparently pleased with the size and density of the young man's muscles, Chrissie let out a tiny satisfied moan. "I hope you've got a big cock, too," she murmured.

Before he could react, John found himself unbuttoned and unzipped, shorts and underwear at his knees.

"Oh-ho! Yes!" Chrissie cried, delighted at what she saw. Her grin and wide-eyed expression were an indication of her approval. "Lovely!" she yipped, fingers closing around the generous girth. "Long and thick…"

"Fuck," gasped John when Chrissie's hand began to work on his length.

The woman nodded with some enthusiasm. "Yes indeed," she smirked. "I certainly want this thing *fucking* me." Jacking at the young man, she added, "I want to sit on it, I want it from behind. I want you on top of me so you can fuck hard and deep."

John moaned, wall-eyed at the tingling through his core.

"I'm going to suck it and fuck and wank it," the woman crooned. She leaned in, body pressing against John's, fingers caressing him throughout as she then kissed her promising young lover on the mouth.

John's hands moved up, one arm encircling Chrissie's shoulder, his other hand on one breast. He squeezed the pliant flesh, pulling back from the kiss so he could take one nipple between his lips.

Ardour flared brighter as his confidence bloomed. "You're fucking gorgeous," croaked John, appreciation heartfelt, Chrissie's sewer mouth the crudest he'd experienced.

"So are you," Chrissie returned, moving in for another kiss, her tongue insistent.

It went on for a few minutes, with the pair constantly touching and kissing, moaning and gasping as they explored one another. Finally Chrissie stepped back, her gaze raking John from top to toe and back up again.

She nodded, fists on her hips, breasts jiggling with the movement. "You know," she began, "I also quite like a big cock in my arse."

John's eyebrows shot up to his hairline at the news.

"It's kind of uncomfortable," added Chrissie, "but I feel so… so *full* that way. What do you think, John?" she asked, expression sly as she calculated his response. "Would you like that? Would you like to fuck my dirty-hole?"

Gulping and boggling, John gaped at Chrissie for half-a-minute. "I…" he spluttered. "I've never…"

"We'll see how the mood takes us," Chrissie said. "How's that?"

John pulled a face, mouth twisting with uncertainty, more an expression of surprise than distaste at the offer. "Uh, yeah, why not," he managed eventually.

Chrissie's head tilted to one side as she appraised the young man. "There's just one more thing," she said, stepping in to grab John's erection again.

"What?" groaned John, his cock pulsing. If she didn't stop cranking his dick he would squirt jizm all over the front door mat.

"Well," Chrissie said, quickly jacking the length of male gristle in her fist – she wanted him too wound up to refuse. "We can do all those sexy dirty things together, but…"

"But what?" the young man grunted, really concerned about his rising urge to let it all go.

"My husband," Chrissie replied.

Husband?

Had she really said husband?

"Where is he?" John asked, deeply perturbed, concerns about ejaculation evaporating. His eyes flicked to the front door. "Is he likely to come home soon?"

A nod of Chrissie's head indicated a door along the hall. "Oh no," she said, calm to the point of indifference. "Don't worry," Chrissie added, pressing close to kiss John's mouth again. "He doesn't mind. Trust me."

"What?" John hissed, agitated. He pulled away from Chrissie, his hands going for his jeans and underwear. "He's here? Jesus, he's at home *now*?"

Chrissie's fist tightened around John's cock. She held him tight, her free hand going to his shoulder. "Look at me," the woman insisted, fingers going from his shoulder to his cheek. "*Look* at me," she urged.

John boggled. "Are you crazy?" He gave the doorway a nervous glance and then blinked into Chrissie's face. "Your husband's just along the hall and you expect me to... for us...?"

"That's exactly what I want, John. I want to fuck you." Chrissie pointed to the door. "Don't worry about him. He knows what's going on." Her tone softened when her fingers went to John's face again. "Isn't it obvious that he's okay with us doing it?" Chrissie soothed. "I promise you it's all right. You have nothing to worry about. It's just you and me, darling."

John stared, his mind whirling.

"In fact," Chrissie went on. "He wants it this way. You're fine being here. He doesn't mind if we fuck. He *wants* us to do it."

John calmed a little. He continued to stare at Chrissie for a few more seconds and then blinked quickly. "Does he... uh... join in?" The young man's eyes widened when the thought touched him. "He doesn't want to do anything with me, does he? I don't want his dick near me. I'm not touching it or anything."

Chrissie chuckled at John's babbling. "No-no," she assured John. "There's nothing like that involved." She gently caressed John's length, coaxing a moan coming from him. "It's just you and me. We can kiss and

I'll suck your cock. You can lick my pussy. We can fuck. I don't mind what we do. You can have my mouth, my pussy, and my bottom. Just the two of us, John." Chrissie went up on her toes to force her tongue into John's mouth. She purred when he returned the kiss, his hands going to her breasts.

"He really doesn't mind?" groaned John when the kiss broke.

With her hand jacking John's length, Chrissie replied, "No, he doesn't mind." The woman paused, fingers working their magic. Then she added, "All he wants to do is take photographs."

"Photographs!"

Chrissie was quick to respond. She didn't want him running because of the latest shock. "For his personal use," she replied. Her eyes sparkled when she added, "And mine too... sometimes." She kept up the pressure on John's cock. "He'll do his best to keep your face out of the frame. In fact, he even obscures faces digitally later on. And tattoos, anything to identify you, he'll fix. I promise, John. It's all okay. You won't be compromised. You know where we live. You could come back and do anything to us if you weren't happy. Come on," the woman urged, moving up to kiss John again. "Just go with it, darling." She squeezed him gently. "It'll be fine. And I'm so bloody horny..."

"You've done this before?"

"A few times, yes," Chrissie shrugged. "It's his 'thing'." Pausing for a second or two, she then said, "And I have to admit the exhibitionist in me loves it."

Chrissie released John's member and stepped back, eyeing him with an up-and-under look.

"Don't you want to fuck me?" she sighed. Chrissie ran her hands over her skin, starting at her hips and finishing with breasts cupped in both palms. "You can do anything you want to me, John. You can fuck my pussy with that lovely long cock. You can fuck these tits and you can plunder my arse."

It was the use of "plunder" that worked the most on John. His over-active mind's-eye saw Chrissie on some as yet unseen bed, her rump thrust high as she rested on knees and elbows, the mollusc of her sex pouting and scarlet while she invited him to use her muddy hole.

Chrissie pouted with feigned admonition, breast flesh still spilling over her cupped hands. "*Anything* you want, John," she breathed.

John stared at her, throat working, lips sliding over dry lips. "Oh, God, yes, please," he murmured.

She led him along the corridor by his dick. When they turned into the doorway, John saw a man sitting in a leather armchair, a large, expensive-looking digital camera resting on the chair arm.

"Ignore him," Chrissie instructed. She thrust her chin towards her husband, the man staring back at the pair. "You don't need to speak to him. Just forget he's there. All you need to do, John," Chrissie murmured as she swivelled to face her love head on, "is to ride the fucking arse off me. I want you to touch me; I want you to feel my boobs, my pussy... oh, hell, anything you want." She tugged John's erection again, excitement obvious in her voice, the woman's expression suddenly feral. "We're going to have a good time, aren't we, John? Are you as horny as I am?"

I got hard when I saw you," John replied, watching Chrissie's husband from the corner of one eye. Regardless of Chrissie's assurances he was still wary.

The woman chuckled. "That's good to hear. I went out purposely to seduce you. I saw you next door and *had* to try." With her free hand Chrissie smoothed a palm over John's chest, breath hissing from her nose, eyes closing at the firm texture of him. "Feel how wet I am, John," she crooned before moving in for an ardent kiss.

John heard the first click and whir of the camera during that kiss. He ignored it and, with Chrissie's pussy slick beneath his fingertips, savoured the feel of her arousal. It went on for a full minute, their tongues sliding and writhing, the camera working away in the background, Chrissie moaning into John's open mouth as his fingers worked her body.

Finally, hot-eyed and gasping, Chrissie stepped back. When they parted, she released John's hard-on, the jib of the thing waggling and waving.

"Upstairs," she croaked as she stepped lightly away. "You can have a shower and then I'd like to suck your cock."

Without a glance at Chrissie's husband, the photographer already consigned to the back of John's mind, he followed the naked woman out of the room.

Showered and cleansed of the day's exertions, John found himself standing in front of Chrissie, the woman sitting on the edge of a very large bed. It was a bright room, afternoon sunlight streaming in through big windows. The door was open, Chrissie's husband standing in the frame, camera working.

John took his eyes from the sight of Chrissie's lips stretched around his girth and glanced towards her husband.

A moment of eye contact followed, with the two men staring at each other. During that eyeblink of time John wondered what could possibly motivate a man to stand and watch his own wife sucking another man's dick. Chrissie was an absolute treasure in John's opinion. If he had such a gorgeous wife – not that John was interested in marriage – there was absolutely no way he would countenance sharing her.

No way. Not a chance.

But there he was, watching his wife slurp and slobber and mumble at John's cock, and even taking photos of it.

Pictures? What the hell was that about?

Chrissie's voice pulled John's attention back to her.

"This is a lovely big cock," she muttered, a hand jacking at him while John groaned and sighed. She grinned up at him, eyes flicking towards her husband before, with her hands on John's hips, Chrissie purred, "Fuck my mouth with it. Use my face."

She took the big dome between her lips, holding John still by pressing her hands tightly to his pelvis. Chrissie then tilted her face towards the man with the camera, inviting him with her eyes to take the shot, her features stretched and distorted.

A gasp came from the husband – the first sound John had heard the man utter. The camera clicked and buzzed and John's hips thrust.

Chrissie released her grip on his hips and it went a little fuzzy for John at that point. Later on he could recall Chrissie's eyes fixed on his face, her lips thin and bloodless as his dick probed deeper. The woman sucked gamely, sometimes pulling back so she could hold John's length and slurp at the purple cock-head or lick the shaft, always popping the knob back into her mouth. During those intervals the woman would mutter obscenities, sometimes taunting her husband with references to the length and girth and rigidity of John's erection.

Chrissie was mad for it, slapping her own cheeks with the keel of that heavy cock, her face smeared with gooey pre-cum and saliva. Following one particularly potty-mouthed episode she urged John to fuck her throat, fingers gripping his hips again, her face angled to best accommodate the length of his dick.

A few instinctive hip thrusts had her gagging, with John withdrawing while she coughed and spluttered and spat gloopy drool. The stuff dangled from Chrissie's chin, a viscous thread that shivered when she moved, breasts and thighs awash with saliva.

"Take the fucking pictures," Chrissie urged her husband in a voice cracked with lust. Aroused to fever pitch, Chrissie held John's cock close to its root and gommed at it, grunts and moans of appreciation bursting from her. "You want photos of me sucking dick?" she snarled. "Well, you've got photos of me sucking dick." Waggling John's cock in the direction of the photographer, who was deep in the room by then, Chrissie added, "Take all the pictures you want of me with this lovely cock. I'm going to suck it, it's going to fuck my cunt... I'm going to take this big fucker in my arse, too.

"You take your photos and then wank over them. This is what it looks like when a real man is turned on.

"You see this big thing? It's going to make me scream. It's going to squirt cum into me. I'm going to let him bathe my rectum with his seed."

John heard it all and boggled. "Jesus," he breathed. "I don't believe it."

"Oh, you better believe it," Chrissie replied, her hand working as she grinned at her young lover. "I'm so bloody wound up now, John. I'm so bloody horny..."

He couldn't take much more of it. The way the woman was tugging at him, the way she sucked his cock and mouthed her obscenities had taken John to the brink. If it went on he'd be spraying her face with semen, which, he thought in a moment of clarity, she would probably let him do. The filthy bitch would probably love it.

John considered letting go. He saw himself squirting spunk over Chrissie but chose to prolong the exquisite agony. He pushed Chrissie off his cock, the woman sprawling backwards with a yelp of surprise.

Lust raged inside John as he knelt and spread Chrissie's legs with his hands against her inner thighs.

"Oh, God, are you going to lick me?" Chrissie breathed, legs falling apart, boneless. She scooted her backside across the quilt, sliding closer to her lover so he could get to her sex with his mouth. "Go on," the woman urged, eyes flashing, jaw set, her expression a challenge. "Suck my pussy. Finger me, babe. Lick my clit and get me all worked up. Make me come on your face."

The camera worked away in the background while John went at Chrissie the way she wanted him to. Minutes passed, with Chrissie writhing and gasping and clawing at the bed. She spat instructions at John, urging him to *lick me just there, finger my pussy, suck my clit...*

"Oh, God, yes!" Chrissie yelped, feet coming up, while her legs folded at the knees and she hauled John up to her face for a meeting of tongues. "Keep doing that," the woman grunted, John's face sandwiched between her hands, her eyes locked on his. "I'm so close to coming," she squeaked. "It won't take much more. Lick me to an orgasm, darling. Please, just get me there."

John did just that. He went back to it and, with the shadowy husband flitting here and there, lapped and slurped and probed. The camera captured it all while Chrissie whined and grunted and writhed, her body juddering, orgasm roiling. She squeaked and moaned, rubbing at her clit while jack-knifing forward to force her tongue into John's mouth.

"God... Oh, fuck!" the woman gasped, wincing and shaking her head, a hot-eyed gaze fixed on John's face. "That was gorgeous." Chrissie grinned, eyes shining, delighted, her whole demeanour exultant. "You did it. I came on your face," she sighed. Chrissie snaked in for another lingering kiss, their lips parting with an audible plop when it broke. "I can taste myself on your tongue," she gasped, falling back.

A few seconds later, after sucking in great gulps of air, chest working up and down so her breasts shivered and rolled, Chrissie chuckled and rolled onto her front. Pushing at the bed with her hands, she rose onto her knees, buttocks upthrust.

"Get up here with me, John," she purred, smirking back over one shoulder. Chrissie's hips swayed side-to-side in obvious invitation. "I want to fuck. Take me from behind. Put that big cock in my pussy."

***

John eased into Chrissie, taking his time, savouring the sight of her body slowly accommodating his length. He found her sodden and hot, Chrissie's insides a slick and easy, the sweep and curve of her body, adding to his arousal as he soaked up the detail for future use. He wondered if he could get his hands on a set of the photos Chrissie's husband was busy storing on the camera's memory card. Would they be willing to part with copies?

The idea was so appealing John muttered, "Come closer, mate." He nodded at the place where Chrissie's body accepted his cock, her pussy stretched and scarlet. John held himself still and spread the woman's flesh, splaying the globes of her buttocks to better show off their conjunction. "Get a few pictures of that," he smirked, the other man's expression impassive.

Chrissie's husband complied. He glanced at John quickly and then moved in to capture the scene from several angles, with Chrissie growing impatient in the process.

The delay annoyed Chrissie. "Just fuck me," she grunted, forcing her hips back. Pushing at the bed with both hands she added a whimpered, "Tickle my arse and fuck my cunt at the same time. God, I'm so fucking horny. Please, John…"

Chrissie craned around, waist creasing as she challenged her lover with slits for eyes, imploring John with a tortured expression and a whine.

"Fuck me, darling. Just *use* me." Chrissie pushed back again, desperate to take John's erection deep. "Treat me as your fuck-toy," she gasped, obscene in her need.

In response to the lewd instruction, John groaned, eyes rolling, pelvis working to the primal urge that exploded inside him like petrol doused on a fire. "Shit, Chrissie," he gasped, buttock flesh smooth beneath his palms as he stroked her body. "That's just dirty. You're a real nasty cow, aren't you?"

The woman wrinkled her nose at him, smirking before wincing and chewing on her bottom lip when her pleasure spiked. "Treat me like I deserve," she grunted in reply, reaching a hand back to part the cheeks of her backside. "Fuck my hungry pussy, finger my arsehole. Get me ready back there, John. I want you in my dirty-hole before we're finished."

It was the filthiest thing John had ever heard a woman utter. The scene was also so weird – Chrissie's husband calmly taking pictures, Chrissie herself showing no inhibitions.

What a pair, John thought privately. Twisted – the pair of them.

But who was he to complain? After all, wasn't he the one screwing his cock into Chrissie? Wasn't she just gorgeous? Wasn't Chrissie the archetype of the mature cougar? So what if her kinky husband wanted to take photos? John was happy enough to let the old perv snap away if it meant he got to feel Chrissie's pussy clenching around his cock.

And her arse! That would be a first. John had never given it much thought in the past. Fucking into a woman's anus had never been up there on his list, but if Chrissie wanted it that way he'd give it a go and be glad to.

"Do you think you'd enjoy that, John?" Chrissie grunted, head low, weight forward on her elbows, rump thrust high. She forced herself back to meet John on his instroke, what little spare flesh on her hips rippling with the force of it. "Rogering me up the arse? Does that idea turns you on?"

"*You* turn me on," the young man replied as he buckled at the waist. It was getting dangerous. The urge to let it go and flood Chrissie with semen was nearly irresistible, close to irreversible, the desire growing more urgent with each stroke.

John leaned in, arching low over Chrissie's back, his hands going beneath the woman's body in search of those swinging breasts. He captured them with both hands, squeezing their spongy softness, the texture of Chrissie's pliant flesh thrilling him.

"Ah fuck, Chrissie," John gurgled close to her ear. "I'm gonna come if we keep on fucking like this. You're so sexy, so fucking lovely..." John groaned, pelvis jerking in short spasms, his instinctive need to pour his seed into Chrissie's body overwhelming his senses.

"Not yet," Chrissie mewled, her own desires close to boiling point. "Please, John, don't come yet. Try to hold it back. I'm not ready for it to end. I want to enjoy this. Make it last."

When the idea came to her Chrissie eased forward, John's cock sliding out of her. It was an act performed with great reluctance. She adored being full of youthful ardour and wanted to prolong the pleasure, but knew she would have to slow things down or else the game would be over.

John's meat slipped out and Chrissie collapsed face down onto the bed. She rolled beneath her lover, wriggling onto her back as John also fell to one side.

Chrissie squeaked a near breathless: "Watch me. I'll have a wank and you can cool off."

She scooted to the side of the bed, leaning onto her side while reaching towards the top drawer of the bedside cabinet.

While Chrissie's fingers groped into the drawer space, John couldn't resist giving her vulnerable bottom a smack with the flat of his hand.

"Oh, you bugger!" the woman yelped, rolling back to face her tormentor. "You can spank my bum another time." Chrissie grinned and waggled a dense length of moulded rubber at him. "I'd enjoy squirming around on your lap while you make my bum cheeks burn, but right now I want you to sit there and watch me fuck myself with this. No touching your cock, though," added Chrissie in mock admonishment. She smirked at John. "You cool down while I get myself to a nice little orgasm." Eyeing John's penis meaningfully, Chrissie finished with, "Then we can put your cock to good use again. I'm looking forward to seeing how much I can coax out of you. I want your spunk on my tits." She jutted her chin towards her husband, "He likes pictures of me drenched in cum."

John's eyes flicked to the photographer when Chrissie said it, his mind's eye filled with the image her words had put there: her round, weighty breasts splattered with semen, her face smeared with stray spurts.

"You're fucking filthy," the young man breathed.

On the bed, laid on her back, shoulders propped up by two pillows, Chrissie casually allowed her legs to fall apart. She nodded and grinned, splitting her gooey labia with the blunt dome of the dildo's end.

"Filthy as you'll find," she replied with a wink. She moaned, back arching, her body greedily accepting the rubber cock in one slide.

***

Chrissie used the dildo hard, forcibly fucking it into her opening. She grabbed the shaft of the thing and worked it in and out, her face twisted into a mask of agonised ecstasy. She worked it deep, gripping the shaft to pull it out, her desire squelching and farting under the onslaught when she drove the thing back in again. Chrissie rubbed her clit with her free hand, big breasts sandwiched between her upper arms, those tits shivering like jellies while she pounded herself vigorously.

It didn't take long for her to get there.

Chrissie mewled and grunted and squealed in to a juddering climax while John gaped at her slack-jawed, her husband moving in for close-ups of the dildo stuffed into her cunt.

She regarded the camera, her expression tortured while sobbing, "I'm coming!" Chrissie writhed and squirmed, her proclamation entirely unnecessary. "Oh fuck... I'm coming. It's so bloody lovely."

John groaned and couldn't stop himself from reaching for his dick. Chrissie's gaze bored through him, the look on her face goading him into jacking his length.

Chrissie saw him going at it. "You'll come, won't you?" she gurgled, laid on the bed, legs wide, everything exposed, still twitching as her orgasm tapered. The dildo hung out of her, half its length dangling obscenely, Chrissie's labia clinging to the shaft.

"I can't help it," John replied, kneeling up on the bed. "Seeing you like that..."

He nodded at Chrissie, fist cranking harder, buttery globs of her arousal visible on the dildo's length.

"Give it to me," Chrissie moaned, rolling onto her side to lever herself up onto one elbow as she reached for John. "Let me suck it."

John shuffled in on his knees and offered his erection to Chrissie, who then shifted around and slurped at the cock-head, her tongue then tracing a line from the tip to John's dangling testes.

"Big balls," Chrissie murmured, teasing the heavy sac with her fingers. She cupped the taut scrotum in her palm. "Have you got lots of lovely spunk for me, John?"

She levered upright, awkwardly positioned as she sucked at the domed end of John's cock, her hand going from his nuts to the dildo still hanging out of her.

"You'll soon see," the young man replied, grunting and buckling at the waist. He sucked in air through gritted teeth as he straightened, rising upright while his hand went to his cock, a fist cranking away.

The stuff spurted from him, the first splash catching Chrissie across the face, a second vehement squirt following immediately in a near continuous rush. Jizm arced high before raining down, the goo a thick rope clinging tenaciously to Chrissie's hair.

Chrissie's husband worked hard with the camera, capturing image after image of his wife's ruination while John groaned and grunted and Chrissie yelped with surprise, her cry turning to a deep chuckle as she moved to offer her breasts to the deluge. "On my tits," she squeaked, dollops of viscous spunk spattering against her skin. Chrissie smeared the stuff over her breasts, leaving the orbs glazed while the eruption continued. "That's it, John, cover me in cum. Look at me, darling; look at my tits all wet with it."

The shower of semen abated. The flood became a trickle, John's cock leaking spunk, a long hawser of the stuff shivering as it dangled from him.

Chrissie scooped the trembling strand with her forefinger, sucking the digit like it was a lollipop, lips pursed, cheeks concave before she smirked at the young man.

Winking, Chrissie asked, "How soon until you can go again?"

John shrugged and teased his oozing length. "Now?" he suggested.

***

Semen clung to her hair in a thick, snotty rope. Chrissie had wiped her face with the back of a hand, traces of spunk drying on her skin. She ignored her glazed breasts, simply making a cursory gesture towards tidying herself up by smearing the gloop into her flesh.

Grinning into the camera, she posed for a few seconds while her husband took the pictures. The camera whirred and clicked while its digital drive caught image after sordid image.

Chrissie tilted her head and smirked at her husband. "You'll be wanking yourself blind looking at those pictures, won't you?" she asked.

The man said nothing in reply. He simply took his photos and stepped back, a tacit signal for his wife to continue.

Chrissie shrugged. "Pathetic," she muttered. What sort of man takes photos of his wife plastered with another man's cum?"

John had no answer to that question; he didn't have a clue what motivated the photographer. He did harbour a suspicion that Chrissie's scorn was all part of the act, just another element in the game the twisted pair was playing. And he didn't give a toss – he was having the time of his life.

"You want to take some picture of this gorgeous young stud fucking my arse?" Chrissie called out. "Would that give you a hard-on, you fucking perv?"

She turned her attention to John. "What about you, handsome? Have you ever shagged a lady up the bum before?"

John wondered where the 'lady' was, but kept his mouth shut.

"Do you want to fuck mine?" Chrissie added when John shook his head. The woman threw a contemptuous look at her husband and laid it on thick. "You can pack my muddy-hole with your gorgeous cock, John. I want you to fuck my arse 'til I squeal."

A few moments later John found himself dabbing lube over the roundel of Chrissie's sphincter. The woman was on her side, resting her head on a fist, elbow dug into the bed. In that position, with Chrissie twisted at the waist, she held her buttocks splayed, exposing her anus and the scarlet gape of her cunt simultaneously.

"Just a little squirt," she instructed her lover. "A little goes a long way."

After applying a dollop of the gunk to his cock-head, John settled in to spoon behind Chrissie.

"Uh, Chrissie," John muttered, his cock in his hand, the end aimed at that vulnerable stain. "I… I, uhm, don't want to hurt you."

"Just push it in me," Chrissie replied, nudging her pelvis back. "Just hold it steady. That's it. I can feel it back there nudging me. Hold it steady. Don't lunge at me… It'll go…"

John gulped, swallowing heavily, anxious about not forcing himself in too robustly. "Oh fuck, Chrissie," he breathed. "I don't think it's going to go in."

"It will," grunted the woman through clenched teeth. She eased back further, fingers pulling at her skin. "Just ease it in, lover. A little more. Just press a little harder."

John gulped again, eyes wide as he stared at where the big dome pressed against Chrissie's taboo hole, her sphincter greasy. His cock looked impossibly huge for such a tender place to accommodate. He was about to suggest they try again later, that they fuck in a more conventional style when he felt himself push past the taut ring.

Chrissie's cry of delight and subsequent gurgle of pleasure told him he was there.

"Fuck!" the woman yelped. "You're in my arse, John. Nice and easy, babe. Don't go fucking that big thing into me just yet. Oh God," she added, clawing at the quilt. "It burns. It itches." She felt the man begin to ease out and added a vehement, "But don't you take it out. Push it in slowly. Fill me up nice and slow. Ease all of it into me."

John complied, terrified, but exhilarated at the same time. He slid in deeper using Chrissie's moans and sighs as a barometer to his progress until, finally, a satisfied moan coming out of Chrissie, his cock was fully embedded.

"Let me get used to it, John," the woman whimpered. She craned round, twisting at the middle so she could look back at her lover. "How do you feel?" she murmured. "You've got all of your cock stuffed into my arsehole. I can tell you it feels bloody divine, too. Do you like it, John? Do you like being in my muddy-hole?"

The young man was lost for words. It had been an incredible afternoon.

The answer to Chrissie's question came from John's expression. She looked at him and saw the surprise there, his incredulity at being inside her anus. Chrissie winked at him and began to move, easing forward while a low, curdled groan came out of her.

"A bit faster and a bit harder," hissed Chrissie after a few preliminary strokes. "Ramp it up, John," she urged. "I'm used to it now. You can start to fuck. My arse can take it."

***

"Bugger me, darling," Chrissie gurgled. Her face fell slack as the sensations overwhelmed her.

Then it got very urgent very quickly.

Chrissie thrust back, forcing John to probe deep into her dark tunnel. The flesh on her hips rippled as she squeaked and flung back a torrent of sewer-mouthed obscenity at her lover.

"Fuck me, John," Chrissie snarled, eyes flashing, lip curled. "Bugger me. Fuck my arse. Really fuck it with that big cock. Rip it up, you lovely bastard."

Her husband clicked away with the camera. Chrissie fixed him with a glare of contempt and snarled, "This is a real man. Look at how a proper man fucks me. This is what I want: a gorgeous cock getting fucked into me by a lovely young hunk. It feels good to have him in there. I'm fucking *stuffed* with him. My arse is full of dick. He's fucking me just how I love it."

John experienced a vague and fleeting notion that Chrissie's taunts might cause the photographer to react. He wondered, on that dim and slightly unfocused level, just how the man could put himself through such humiliation. But thoughts of how Chrissie's strange husband might be feeling didn't last. The bubble popped when John suddenly found himself moving with Chrissie as the woman rolled onto her front.

"Keep it inside me," Chrissie squealed as she reached back to press a hand against John's buttock. "Come over with me, darling."

John didn't quite understand her meaning at first, but quickly realised what was going on when Chrissie started to move, rolling with her until he was resting his full weight along her back.

"Up," the woman grunted, bucking up into her lover. "Rest on your elbows and reach under me. Squeeze my tits and push your dick into my arsehole."

Chrissie went up onto her forearms, giving John just enough room to get his hands under her. She angled her hips, tilting her pelvis to allow the man the best slant at which to offer more of his length to her anus.

"Stuff my arse full of meat," Chrissie mewled.

The heat was truly on her; she was wild with desire, the need pouring out of her in an obscene litany.

"I'm full of hard cock," she groaned, her husband capturing her glazed-eyed, slack-faced stare. "A big cock wedged in my arse. I love it, I fucking LOVE it!"

She began to hump up urgently, desperate to take as much of it as she could, the girth stretching her sphincter.

"Fuck me," she spat, craning round to glare at John. "Get up there and slam my arse. Get up on your hands. Rip my poor bottom apart..."

John went up onto straight arms, hands on the bed as he fucked into Chrissie, their bodies smack-smack-thwacking together.

"You're the dirtiest..." John began, unable to finish because of his abrupt desire to squirt what liquid he had left into Chrissie's rectum.

Ignoring the comment, too lost in her own pleasure, Chrissie slumped onto the bed and grunted, "Keep fucking me. Don't stop." She slid a hand between the bed and her body, fingers finding her clit, the nub greasy with lust. "Keep at it," she groaned. I'm going to come. I'm going... To... Fucking... Come..."

Chrissie wailed and groaned, writhing and thrashing beneath John when her climax broke. She spat torment at her husband, the man himself recording every twist of his wife's tortured visage.

"Chrissie," John gasped, probing deep, hips jerking. "I can't help it."

"Yes," the woman hissed, exultant. "Bathe my rectum with cum, babe. It's okay. I've had such a great time. I've come and come. If you need to let it go, just do it."

When it was over, with John slumped across his lover's back, their bodies still joined, the photographer took several final shots and slipped from the room.

John slipped out on a greasy slide, watery jizm dribbling from Chrissie's anus. When the woman rolled onto her side the bed was stained with the evidence of their taboo coupling.

John shifted to face Chrissie. He stared at her, awed and already a little in love. They kissed in an extremely intimate and tender moment following the robustness of their time together.

"I think I need a gardener," whispered Chrissie, her eyes locked on John's, her fingers stroking his face. "What's your hourly rate?"

John grinned and leaned in for another kiss. He moaned with pleasure while their tongues slid and writhed together.

"I think we can come to an arrangement," he smirked.

End of the 6th Story

YOUNG & DANGEROUS

BEN E. DORM

Chapter One

She thinks it's incredible that nobody else has noticed – how can they *not*? It's so *obvious*.

They passed bowls of food to each other; spooned vegetables onto their plates and offered words of thanks, her husband and her son apparently blind and deaf to what was right there in front of them.

Angela had known instantly. When Colin brought his friend home, she'd immediately recognised the danger he presented. It was instinct working; Angela took one look at Carlos and *knew*. Angela saw him looking and felt her insides flutter. She couldn't say how, but she knew the good-looking young man possessed a dark soul.

The understanding hit her full force: despite his age, he saw through her. The knowing was in his eyes and the smirk hovering on his lips. He knew she was all an act.

Taking in the short hair, his dark good looks and muscular torso in a tight, pristine white tee-shirt, Angela had felt the flip of anticipation in the pit of her stomach, her insides clenching with carnal yearning. She managed to keep her expression neutral – pleasant yet benign – when Colin made the introductions.

"Mum, this is Carlos," Colin had said, oblivious to the tension between his mother and his friend. They were in the kitchen where Angela had been supervising dinner arrangements with the cook.

Angela's pussy flooded with heat when the young man took her hand and looked into her eyes. When she heard him speak her insides oiled with desire..

Carlos had held on to Angela's fingers following their perfunctory handshake. "Thank you for letting me stay, Mrs Brodie," he smiled, politeness personified.

But Angela sensed the predator behind the smile. He was the Big Bad Wolf charming Red Riding Hood in the forest.

She was shocked and mortified to hear herself giggle.

Embarrassed further by the quavering she heard in her own voice Angela replied with, "You're welcome, Carlos."

Angela gathered herself, cheeks warming as she glanced first at the cook, then at her son, neither of whom seemed to have a clue.

"Please, call me Angela," she continued, steadier in tone. "Mrs Brodie sounds so, well, so formal. You make me feel old."

If Carlos noticed her discomfort, he gave no outward sign. The young man had clasped her hand and smiled to show off two rows of perfect teeth.

Shark's teeth; wolf's teeth...

His voice was a low murmur, clandestine. It was as though Colin wasn't there when Carlos stared intently into Angela's eyes and said, "I'd prefer Mrs Brodie, Mrs Brodie." Carlos paused and then added, "If you don't mind?"

Angela's stomach twisted, her pussy tightening in keen anticipation. She understood the man's meaning perfectly well.

It was the first of their secrets.

Oblivious, Colin stood by, grinning, ignorant of the nuances passing between his mother and his friend. "Forty-four isn't old, Mum," he blurted, thinking he was being kind. "And you look good." Then, bless him, if Colin didn't go and add, "Tell her, Carlos. Tell her she looks great."

If they'd been alone Angela would have lunged in to kiss Carlos's mouth, her libido roaring when the young man complied with Colin's instruction. "Stunning, Mrs Brodie," he crooned.

Angela felt goose-pimples rise on her skin when his eyes raked her up and down. She felt naked, vulnerable and powerless.

"I mean it. Absolutely gorgeous."

Still unaware of the tension crackling between his mother and Carlos, Colin jokingly nudged is friend with an elbow. "Okay, mate. No need to give the old bird a big head." He smiled at his mother to take any sting out of his words. "Anyway, come on upstairs and I'll show you your room."

With a reluctance that was only plain to Angela, Carlos released her fingers.

"You can unpack," Colin was jabbering, preceding Carlos on the way out of the kitchen. "Then we could nip to the pub for a beer, eh?"

After a lingering look back at her over his shoulder Carlos followed Colin.

Angela fled the kitchen after a hurried excuse to cook. With the young man's smouldering look fixed in her mind's eye, she went to the living room and slumped gasping into a chair.

"Good God!" she gasped on an explosion of exhaled air and pent-up emotion. She lunged forward and dropped her head in her hands, elbows on her knees, body thrumming, mind whirling.

For the sake of her marriage and her family, Angela knew she was going to have to keep her distance from *that* one.

But, as she sat and struggled to calm her boiling emotions she wondered how she was going to manage it.

***

Angela Brodie's family: Colin, her son – twenty years old, student. Andrea, her daughter – Colin's twin, also a student. Andrew, her husband – forty-six, barrister, busy consolidating an empire.

She didn't work, at her husband's insistence. Andrew Brodie was a man with old-fashioned ideas. He preferred it if his wife stayed at home and brought up the children. A task now redundant since Colin and Andrea had both flown the nest.

With a lot of time on her hands, Angela kept busy with a volunteer job in a charity shop two afternoons a week. Another way of filling the newly-acquired spare hours was keeping fit. When her children left home, Angela joined a gym, using the machines and the pool with enthusiasm. She took a Pilates course as well, the benefits visible in a matter of weeks. Angela found herself with more energy and a zest for life, her body toned and shapely, waist tight, muscles firming. Angela took cooking courses and a philosophy class, hosted coffee mornings and kept the house as her husband liked it.

She also kept a stash of pornography on a secret laptop computer in a shoebox in her wardrobe. Andrew would no more think of rummaging in his wife's exclusive domain than he would run naked through the high street. Besides, if for some unfathomable reason he *did* happen across the computer, Angela had a lie all prepared: it was a gift for Colin's birthday she had hidden away. It was either a birthday or Christmas depending on when – likely never – Andrew made the discovery.

However, what Angela would have greater difficulty explaining to a bug-eyed husband was the collection of vibrators and dildos she had tucked away as well. It wouldn't do to suggest the sex toys were a gift for their daughter, so Angela would just have to swallow down the embarrassment and admit to a dalliance with a moulded latex cock now and then.

The problem was, her collection of sex toys was growing – as was her stash of filthy film clips.

It wasn't that Andrew was boring, *per se*, merely… indifferent. He could take it or leave it. For him sex wasn't a strong motivational force.

For his wife it was a different story all together. The older she got, the hornier she became, a torment she could only assuage by frequent masturbation. Angela held it all together for the sake of her marriage, her family, and her reputation. In over twenty years with Andrew she had remained faithful – a semi-drunk hand-job on holiday in Jamaica notwithstanding. Angela had caressed the black length and been sorely tempted to bend over to take it from behind. Not that it was anything huge, just dark and different. The illicit thrill of wanking a stranger's cock had been almost overwhelming. Angela had nearly succumbed to her base urges, but she hadn't succumbed. She'd groaned and chewed on her bottom lip and tugged that length of male gristle until the man grunted and spurted forth gout after gout of jizm.

The episode was her sole transgression, one often called to mind and replayed with a very different outcome. Angela would relive the time while masturbating with a dildo purchased specifically for its colour. In *those* fantasies she not only cranked her lover's dick, but sucked and fucked him as well.

And now, dammit, if Colin's friend didn't have her juicy and squirming at the dinner table, her pussy itchy as she sluiced desire into the gusset of her underwear.

Carlos was aware of the effect; she could see it in his face writ plain. How could Andrew and Colin sit there and not notice?

They were at dinner, arranged around the dining table with Carlos immediately opposite Angela's position.

The chatter from Colin had been driving Angela insane. She loved her son, but dearly wished he'd shut up and eat so she could end the interminable meal and flee.

"So, Carlos," her husband said, fixing the young man with his eyes. "Spanish ancestry?"

Carlos nodded, politely turning his attention to his host. "My mother, Mister Brodie. I kept Carlos even though I'm English by birth. I prefer it to Charles or Charlie."

It came from nowhere. "It suits you," Angela blurted. "Your lovely black hair and Mediterranean colouring…" She blushed, heat suffusing her face. "The Spanish version of the name, I mean," Angela added weakly.

"Absolutely," her husband concurred, brow furrowing as he looked at his wife. "Anyway," he continued, shrugging Angela's outburst off, "I'm prosecuting a case tomorrow. Leeds Crown Court. I wondered if you two lollygagging students might want to come along?"

Colin nodded, his life's course set on following in his father's footsteps. "I'd like that, Dad. The experience would be good for my course." He looked towards his friend. "What do you think, Carlos?"

A tumult of emotions and sensations erupted inside Angela when Carlos politely demurred. Just in time she stifled the gasp that threatened to burst from her while Carlos cited his time might be better utilised in some research of his own. He was on a different degree course to his friend, and while seeing Mister Brodie in action would be very interesting, if it was all right with the gentleman, Carlos would stay at the house and use the internet and fill up his notebook.

"Not at all, dear boy!" Andrew Brodie returned, mindless to the tension winding his wife tightly. "So, Colin," he went on, "just the two of us tomorrow… father and son." Andrew smiled and added a stern, "Ready at six-thirty. A suit would be best. And not too much beer tonight, eh? I know what you students are like!"

Angela's husband guffawed with rare good humour, the conversation moving on to Andrea's trip to South East Asia. While Colin wittered on about his sister and Facebook Angela sat there and restlessly shifted food around her plate. With her dinner nearly untasted she struggled to make sense of her conflicting thoughts, Colin's jabber so much background noise.

The thought of Carlos in the house all day thrilled her. Yet, paradoxically, the prospect also filled her with dread.

Twenty minutes later, when the meal was eaten and Angela was at her wit's end, with Angela in the kitchen loading the dishwasher, Carlos appeared.

The young man wasted no time. He placed the pile of crockery he'd brought through onto the work top, immediately moving to Angela.

"Carlos, what…?" she managed before Carlos grabbed for her. "Jesus, what are you *doing?*" she hissed, casting an anxious glance at the door. She wanted him to touch her and yet, simultaneously, recoiled.

"You know exactly what I'm doing, Mrs Brodie."

Angela gulped in response to his throaty tone. "God, Carlos; are you mad? My husband… Colin - they're right there!"

"The only thing I'm mad for is you, Mrs Brodie." He pulled her close, hands moving to Angela's buttocks. "I want to fuck you," Carlos growled.

He squeezed Angela through her skirt, the action, bringing a low moan from her before, somehow, in an immense effort of will common sense asserted itself. "Yuh-you shouldn't say that to me," she stammered. "For God's sake, I'm married. I'm twice your age. Stop it. Stop it now…"

But she didn't want him to stop. Dear God, what she really wanted was to wrench her knickers off, leap onto the counter, and spread her legs.

His response didn't help to cool Angela's simmering lust. "That makes it so much hotter, Mrs Brodie, you being married. You being older than me only makes me want to fuck you more." Carlos leaned in and kissed Angela's mouth. Before she could react his tongue was in there searching, one hand remaining on one cheek of her bottom while the other came up to maul at her breasts. "You're so fucking sexy," he breathed, nuzzling her neck. "These tits… I want to rip your clothes off right here."

Despite her body's clamouring, regardless of her insides pulsing and siping desire, Angela managed, with another supreme effort of willpower, to push the young man away from her.

"No. Stop it." The refusal came through clenched teeth and Angela's clamped jaw. She flicked another terrified look towards the kitchen door. "My husband…"

Carlos grinned at her, his expression hungry, lupine in its intensity. He pouted and nodded, eyes slits. To Angela it was a sly, calculating look, predatory in intent. "This isn't over, *Mrs* Brodie," he said, his growl low and deep to match his expression.

For a moment, it seemed Carlos was about to lunge. He continued to stare at Angela, bestial with his intent. But, abruptly, he turned and left Angela with her heart jackhammering inside the rack of her ribs, chest heaving as she sought to calm herself and bring her breathing under control.

"Oh God," Angela moaned. "Oh God... Oh *shit*..."

***

She heard the crunch of tires on gravel when the car moved down the drive. Angela lay in bed and wondered how long it would be until Carlos came prowling.

Anticipation surged. She was anxious and aroused, deliciously turned on yet dreading the moment of confrontation. Infidelity was nothing casual for Angela, and this was a day of reckoning.

While she laid there, emotions surging, Angela was certain he would come knocking. However, time passed, with Angela languidly stroking her sex as the day brightened beyond the curtains. Finally, after an hour of waiting and suppressing the desire to rub harder, denying herself a climax, Angela had to accept Carlos wasn't going to appear. His failure to arrive was both a disappointment and a relief. She was torn by her desire for her son's good-looking friend, yearned for his mouth and fingers to explore her intimate places, but also dreaded the consequences their coupling might produce.

Eventually, however, miffed at what she saw as a rejection, Angela flung back the quilt and decided quite determinedly to put the man out from her mind. She showered and critically examined her stubbly pubic bush, kidding herself it was for her own benefit when she next sat on the toilet seat, legs wide while applying a gentle shaving lotion before tidying things up. It took some time, but she kept at it until satisfied her vulva was as smooth as she could manage. Angela showered for a second time to rinse away the foamy residue, drying and powdering herself with talc as a precaution against any unsightly rashes.

Next, again denying the reality of what she was doing, refusing to admit it was for *him*, Angela chose her wardrobe carefully. She searched for suitable attire, her eyes finding the box with the laptop inside lurking at the back of the cupboard. Angela swallowed heavily and steeled herself to resist – she would NOT succumb to the base urges and fuck herself with one of her dildos.

Shutting images of gangbang pornography from her mind – her latest absolutely *filthy* online discovery – Angela applied the slightest hint of make-up: basic lippy and eyeliner. She teased her honey-blonde hair into an attractive halo, scrunching the wavy ringlets with the tips of her fingers to achieve what she hoped was a sexy, tousled, fresh-from-bed look. Next, she chose a bra and panty set in diaphanous pink beneath a white gypsy-style blouse and denim mini skirt, complementing this entirely inappropriate ensemble with precipitous heels and, once again lying to herself she would have chosen the outfit anyway, left her boudoir.

Angela's heart skipped a beat in teenage expectation when she found Carlos in the kitchen, the scene of their thrilling encounter the previous evening. The young man was at the breakfast bank, a laptop on the counter, a cup of coffee close by.

As soon as she set eyes on Carlos her resolution to put lusty thoughts from her mind evaporated. Heat flooded her vulva, desire reigniting as the woman leaned against the door jamb and drawled a husky, "Good morning, Carlos."

He barely glanced up, fingers at the keys while studying the screen, apparently engrossed.

His greeting was a less than enthused, "Hello, Mrs Brodie." There was no hot-eyed stare or intent appraisal, no burning look at her bosom straining at the blouse, of which – of course – the topmost buttons were unfastened. Carlos didn't linger over her legs, toned and shapely from her rigorous workouts, their definition enhanced, with the high heels putting added tension on Angela's calves. He scarcely acknowledged Angela's presence, merely muttered his greeting and focused on the computer again.

His indifference rocked her. The lack of enthusiasm confused Angela, especially after his ardour the previous evening. She stood in the doorway with the heat rising in her cheeks, feeling foolish rather than sexy. Her choice of clothing abruptly seemed a ridiculous choice.

With uncertainty rising, Angela decided to try again. "Sleep well?" she asked in a monotone.

He didn't deign to look at her. "Yes, thanks…"

Ire bubbled, the irritation simmering towards anger. Who the *hell* did he think he was?

Angela folded her arms beneath her breasts and glared at him. "Are you busy?"

If Carlos heard the sarcasm and rising indignation in the question he chose to ignore it.

Anger flared red hot – the cheeky shit couldn't be bothered to articulate a proper response!

Incensed, Angela turned and stalked away.

"Fuck you, Carlos," she muttered when she stormed into her bedroom. Angela kicked off the high heels and padded barefoot to the wardrobe. Still chuntering, she pulled the box from the hiding place, choosing one of her favourites: improbably large with a big domed head and a shaft all crisscrossed by veiny protrusions. Angela loved the way the knob-end of the thing split her open, the gnarled length of it rubbing her in all the right places.

The laptop came out next, with Angela firing the machine up after hauling her skirt to her waist. She was spitting mad and too frustrated to be bothered with removing her clothes. Instead she pulled her underwear down and stepped out of it, climbing onto the bed and settling with the computer next to her.

With the laptop going through its internal processes, Angela eased onto her side and spread her legs. She teased her labia with her fingers, peeling back the slippery prepuce to reveal her clit all taut and shiny.

"Fucking pig," Angela spat, her finger moving over the mouse pad. "Bloody wind-up merchant…" She selected a file and clicked through several options before finding what she wanted. "Oh God," the woman groaned, her attention fixed on the screen. "You lucky bitch… You lucky, *lucky* bitch…"

If Carlos didn't want to give her what she so desperately needed, Angela would sort herself out.

She stared at the screen and watched a woman entertaining a room full of men. Angela couldn't be sure, but estimated there to be twelve of them: men of all shapes and sizes and ages. It seemed that the lady at the centre of all that male attention didn't discriminate on the basis of age or colour or race.

She was good-looking and well-spoken. Judging by the lady's diction she was intelligent and decently educated, with Angela putting her accent at somewhere within the English Home Counties. Angela had done some quick research and discovered the model's name: Wendy Gilcrest, a woman who had actually been persuaded into porn by her own husband.

It was inconceivable to her for a time: Angela had been scandalised to learn people could actually *live* that way. How could the husband bear to watch his wife fucking other men? She could envision a situation where one other man might be possible – swinging perhaps – but a *dozen*? How could their marriage survive? Could they be happy? And what about their wider family - her parents and children for instance? Did anyone else know or was it a secret? Angela couldn't see how Wendy Gilcrest and her husband could keep it clandestine. Surely someone would find out?

Angela set all those thoughts and questions aside when the dildo splits the folds of her labia, her focus shifting back to the scene on the computer.

"Suck them," Angela murmured, face slackening as she gazed at the debauchery. "Fuck them all, Wendy."

Discovering gang-bang porn had been a shock, as had her body's responses. Before the accidental find she'd been of the opinion that a woman who let herself be used and abused – *humiliated*, in fact – was quite simply a slut. However, as deserving the woman might be of that appellation, when Angela analysed the situation further she came to the eventual conclusion that the woman must also be very brave. Wendy Gilcrest obviously had the guts to allow her carnal urges free rein. As far as sex went it seemed the woman had few limits.

How *liberating*, Angela thought. How bloody lovely it must be to just let yourself go like that!

As it went, Angela formed the impression that although the men used the woman for their own gratification, the woman actually owned the power. It was she who opened her legs and invited the men to fuck her; Wendy chose which one to suck when her ardent admirers presented her with an array of cocks. At points in the clip she urged the men to come – over her and inside her, she seemed mad for their semen.

It really did look like Wendy was having a good time as she offered her sex to a man behind her. She angled her pelvis and thrust her buttocks high, inviting him to enter her as she growled and snarled and whined at the assembled crowd to use her, to fuck her, and to plaster her in cum.

Angela gaped at the scene and imagined herself in Wendy's place. They seemed to share a lot of similar attributes: physically, in years, and – following Angela's epiphany – outlook. The difference was Angela wouldn't *dare*. She didn't have the nerve. Angela lived the scene vicariously, with Wendy actually doing it.

"Oh God," Angela groaned again. "Let them at you, Wendy. Oh, you filthy mare... Yes, go on... Take them on..."

Angela's eyes glazed as she used the dildo against her body with some robustness. She was on her way, her climax rolling towards her while she watched a man unload all over the porn star's breasts.

"Suck him" Angela moaned, as though Wendy could hear. Wendy complied, slurping jizm from the man's swollen bell-end, the cockhead huge and purple. "Another," she mumbled, her body sloshing and squelching around the dildo while, on screen, the actress offered her mouth to yet another erection, the man behind Wendy obviously pumping her full of his seed. "Oh God, oh fuck... Oh shit," gurgled Angela. Seeing Wendy casually allowing men to ejaculate inside her never failed to trigger a vehement response.

Angela's orgasm bubbled like a pan of milk on a stove. Any moment and she'd be there. She was so close... So fucking close...

"Well, Mrs Brodie," she heard. "Aren't *you* a bit of a horny bitch?"

Panic seized Angela in a cold water shock which brought a gasp from her chest. She was caught, porn on the computer and her cunt stuffed with rubber cock.

At first she thought it was Andrew who'd walked in. Carlos the visitor being in the house had completely left her mind. She boggled, unable to make sense of what she was seeing. Her mind reeled under the impression her husband had made the indelicate discovery. But, in the next instant she realised, another gasp of surprise coming out of her, it was Carlos walking into the room.

"Got a use for this?" Carlos smirked, cheeks dimpling as he fisted his length. The young man sauntered into the bedroom, beautifully naked, his body magnificent. He offered Angela a predatory grin, the erection in his fist enormous.

Angela gaped at the terrible lump of male appendage. It was simply *gorgeous*. "Oh dear lord," she croaked. "You're bloody lovely."

The man winked and clambered onto the bed. He knelt there, his cock a huge carving of male virility as he lifted the laptop and glanced at the screen.

"You get off on *this*?" he asked, eyebrows up in his hairline. Carlos watched a few seconds of filthy action before snapping the machine closed. "I knew you were a hot-blooded bitch, Mrs Brodie," Carlos hefted the laptop in one hand, "but this? ... Well, this is more than I expected from you. I'd never have guessed."

Carlos leaned over to place the computer carefully down on the carpet while Angela whined, "I'm so horny. I thought you were going to come to me this morning. I waited and waited and--"

He cut her short by leaning over her and moving in for a long kiss.

It went on for some time, with Angela moaning into Carlos's open mouth, his hand exploring the contours of her body.

When they broke apart Carlos eased Angela's thighs wider, the dildo hanging out of her like an obscene tongue.

She blinked up at Carlos as he withdrew the length of moulded latex. "Are you going to fuck me?" Angela squeaked.

"All day," he replied. "I can come and still carry on, Mrs Brodie. I'm going to batter your cunt so hard…"

Angela gulped and squirmed, rubbing at herself with one hand, the other going to his cock.

"That's so filthy," she breathed. "Tell me more. "Tell me all about the dirty things we're going to do. I mean it, Carlos. Shock me. Don't hold back."

Carlos snickered. "I knew it," he said, shuffling along the bed on his knees. "When I first saw you, Mrs Brodie; I *knew* you'd like this."

Angela worked a hand along the length presented to her. *It's so thick. I can barely get my fingers round it... Jesus, he's huge...*

"You knew I'd like what?" she asked.

Carlos said nothing. He took hold of Angela's hand and held it still, fucking his cock into her fist.

Angela gulped and moaned when she felt the gnarled shaft move through her fingers: flesh and blood with a core of steel. "You're magnificent," she breathed, her attention going from the young man's penis to his face. The predatory expression she saw there curdled her insides with yearning. Angela groaned and rubbed her clit and mumbled, "God, Carlos... you're a beautiful young man."

Carlos nodded and grinned. "I wanted to fuck you last night, Mrs Brodie. I didn't care if your husband caught us." Fires of lust burned in Carlos's eyes. He reclaimed control of his erection, tugging at himself while saying, "I would have made him watch. I would have fucked his wife in front of him. I would have fucked you while your husband watched us doing it, *Mrs Brodie*."

The image flashed into her mind. Angela moaned again when she saw the scene inside her head.

Carlos went on, a hand at himself while he went between Angela's legs with the other. He rubbed at her, fingers finding her labia all greasy with yearning.

"You're a slut, aren't you, Mrs Brodie?"

Angela squirmed and whined, cords on her neck stark as knife blades. "Oh God," she mewled, eyes fixed on his face.

"You're all wet for my cock. You dressed for me, didn't you? I saw you downstairs in those shoes and this skirt and your tits bulging out. You were hot for my cock..."

Angela yelped when Carlos reached for the front of her blouse with both hands. Buttons popped and the garment lay gaping, Angela's breasts bubbling over the cups of her bra, chest heaving as she sucked in air.

"Then I find you fucking yourself while looking at porn." Carlos hauled down Angela's bra to free her rolling breasts. He mauled her flesh, bringing more moans and gasps out of her. "You want to be that woman in the film, Mrs Brodie?"

Lost for words, speechless at his perspicacity, Angela gulped and stared up at Carlos. It was all so quick, so abruptly real and so very exciting. "I... It... You..." she said, head shaking side-to-side. "Oh God, I don't know. I just get so turned on. I just get so frustrated."

Carlos grinned. He rose upright and, still kneeling, looked at her, taking all of Angela in from crown to her feet. "Mister Brodie isn't paying you enough attention?" he smirked.

His assertion wasn't quite correct. Angela knew her husband was distracted by work and fretted over his career. They did make love, but Angela needed the physical element more frequently. As she drifted into mid-forties, she seemed perpetually on heat, her mind constantly drifting towards sex. Angela would be out and about and see a good-looking man standing at the pump station next to hers as she filled the car with fuel. Her imagination would ignite, scenarios bursting across her mind's eye where she let herself be picked up, agreeing to meet for a coffee or a drink.

The fantasy always spun out of control towards Angela's latest peccadillo, her current lewd favourite being group-sex and gangbang scenes. During those times her imaginings slewed towards herself in some contrived situation: a pub full of men where she'd met her casual pick-up for a drink where, for some incredibly improbable reason, she would have cocks coming at her from all sides.

Of course Angela would be the sole female present, the gangbang slut, the bukake whore. Through it all she realised it wasn't her husband's fault at all, Andrew was blameless. She was the twisted one.

And so far she'd managed to keep herself under control.

But now she was on the bed – the *marital* bed, Angela realised, shocked by where her carnal urges had led her. She was on the bed with a naked man next to her, his cock iron hard while she lay there panting for him to fuck her.

Suddenly the world slewed. Reality rushed back into her life, water through a breached dam. What she was doing was wrong, so morally corrupt Angela felt nauseous. She was on the verge of cuckolding her husband in the bed they'd shared for years.

God, what am I doing? *Andrew... My husband... I'm married. It's wrong... No!*

Angela hefted herself up onto elbows and forearms. "We can't," she blurted, eyes wide, expression pleading. "We shouldn't be here. Carlos," Angela gasped, appalled. "We can't do this. *I* can't do this. I'm married; you're my son's friend."

Angela moaned at the treachery, the sickening deceit.

"We have to stop – Now!

"Yuh-you have to go. You have to get out of this room." She sat up, pulling the gypsy blouse together, hiding her breasts from the young man's feral gaze.

"I think you should shut up and suck my cock," Carlos replied.

Angela opened her mouth to utter a refusal, determined to get away, to fight her body's craving. It was all wrong. She needed help from a counsellor or psychiatrist or some-bloody-one... *Anyone* who could help her.

Angela's lips parted, the denial was right there just waiting to be spoken...... but his fingers found her again.

He rubbed at Angela's clit and the desire exploded inside her. "Oh God," she sobbed, pleasure zinging along every nerve. "Give it to me," Angela mumbled, succumbing to the inevitable. "Let me suck it, Carlos." The extreme reluctance of only seconds before dissolved. It was instant, a blink of an eye between her intense agitation and wallowing in the depravity. "I wish there were ten of you," she croaked, fingers curling around stiff cockmeat.

Hunger yawed inside her. Angela rolled onto her side and rested on one elbow, blouse gaping open, big breasts swaying free.

"This is wrong," she whispered the moment before the big domed head pushed between her lips.

***

He came in a deluge of sticky fluid, the stuff cascading over Angela.

Carlos caught her by surprise, tugging his cock and aiming the eye right at Angela's face.

"This what you want?" Carlos grunted, snorting air in through his nose.

"Oh!" Angela squealed. "Oh, Carlos! Jesus!"

The woman was on her hands and knees, Carlos upright as he knelt on the bed. For the previous five minutes or so she'd vigorously worked that cock, sucking and slurping and pouring out a litany of potty-mouthed exhortations, a lewd list of her desires.

"You'll stay hard, won't you, darling?" Angela whined, her eyes on his face. She rubbed herself, a hand between her legs, fingers alternating between her clit and her sodden opening. "I'm so close to coming, but I need to fuck. I have to have you inside me. God, please, Carlos, tell me you'll stay big and hard."

"For you, Mrs Brodie, I promise."

And then the first splash of ejaculate flicked across Angela's cheek. She yelped and flinched, a second and third gush catching her in a rush of goo. More of the stuff spattered over her, a silvery rope of jizm glistening in her hair while she stuck out her tongue and tried to take some it in her mouth.

"Fuck," the woman snorted. "Look at all that cum." She turned an exultant and jizm-spattered face towards Carlos. "You should be in porn," Angela squeaked. "God, I'm *plastered*."

By then Carlos was on the move. He went behind Angela, his dick oozing semen as he parted the globes of her buttocks and gazed at the obscene sight of her gaping cunt and puckered sphincter.

"You're a hot lady, aren't you, Mrs Brodie?" he said, with Angela's corrupted countenance regarding him as she craned back to look over one shoulder. "You're all swollen and soaking. I think my cock might fry if I put it in there."

Angela moaned, a glob of cum shivering with fragile delicacy while dangling from her chin.

"I've got to fuck," she mumbled, eyes glazed with lust. Her fingers moved through her vulva as she sought some kind of release. "I need to come. Please, Carlos," she gasped, wincing. "Fuck me. I'm so bloody horny, darling."

When he slid into her, Angela groaned. The sound came out of her long and low, ecstasy evident in its tone.

"Big," the woman croaked. "So fucking big... It's splitting me open. It's filling me." Angela moaned on for a moment or two and then grew vehement. She pushed back, her face twisting as she snarled, "Now fuck me. Smash my cunt. Batter me, you gorgeous fucker." Angela's vocabulary was much broadened after her saturation in porn. She found the thrill of dirty talk exciting, so different to when she was with Andrew. "I'm your slut. Use me…"

And didn't he use her like she wanted him to! It was all Angela hoped it would be. The sex was precisely what she needed. Carlos was a machine, a flesh and blood piston that kept on at her, his cock – his gorgeous big dick – filling her. Her cunt was stuffed full of man-meat while her mind was filled with joy. Carlos was sensational: ardent, virile, bloody lovely to look at and lovely to feel inside her.

His fingers dug into her hips, grabbing at Angela's flesh as he dragged her back onto his length. He crouched over her, arms encircling her brisket so he could hold onto her swinging breasts.

Carlos was deep, his body pressed against Angela's buttocks and her tits in his hands as he murmured obscenities into her ear.

"I should take you out somewhere, Mrs Brodie," he muttered. "Out in your car. I can find somewhere outside where I can have a load of men ready for you." He squeezed her and held himself still, not moving while his cock pulsed inside her pussy.

Nudging forward slightly, Carlos forced a little more of his length into Angela's body to make her gasp and moan.

"What about it, Mrs Brodie? What do you think? Am I going to do some research and find somewhere I can take a slut like you? You want a gang of strangers to fucking you?"

"Oh… Jesus," gasped Angela. "No… Yes… Oh…"

Wouldn't that be so… so… so fucking dirty!

"You could suck and fuck and take their cum all over you, Mrs Brodie. I can make it happen. It's up to you."

Angela came. She climaxed hard, her fingers at her clit while Carlos throbbed inside her, the scene filling her mind just as he described it.

"That's it, Mrs Brodie," the young man whispered, moving again. His length slid out, almost plopping free, just the head of the thing remaining inside Angela while she grunted and moaned and began to squirm. "Come for me," Carlos continued, fucking back into her. "Let it all out. Scream the fucking house down. Let the neighbours know how you feel."

Then he was slamming in hard, pulling out so far he almost fell clear before going back in, the woman's buttocks rippling, her insides clenching.

"More," Angela gasped. "Tell me more. Fuck me harder. Oh, I'm coming, I'm coming, darling. Please, Carlos, keep doing it. I want you to keep...

"On...

"Fucking...

"Me!"

Then she was lost.

Chapter Two

"This isn't real. This isn't me."

Carlos took his eyes from the road and grinned at her. "It's real, Mrs Brodie," he smirked. "It's time to live it like you really want to – like *I* know you want to."

Angela experienced a sudden bloom of emotion when he said it, something hot and indistinct, a yearning so insistent she let out a low keening sound. A primordial force hit her, but what was it she felt? Excitement? Fear? An insane need for the same freedom she saw in Wendy Gilcrest's films?

All of it and more, she decided.

Angela squirmed, delicious anticipation thrilling her. She desperately wanted to rub her pussy, to touch herself between her legs where it was all hot and itchy and wet.

"But I'm married," she mumbled, the comment meaningless. She was set on a course of action and knew, in her heart of hearts, she would see it through to the end. Whatever Carlos had in mind, she would do.

Angela was damned because being married only made it so much filthier. It was wrong, immoral, a betrayal so heinous Andrew would divorce her in an instant. Through the past week, through all the times she spent with Carlos, reckless with lust and her insatiable desires, adoring of the young Adonis and his magnificent cock, Angela had known the risk she was taking. It was foolish, ridiculously irresponsible and yet, despite knowing of her folly on an intellectual level, when it came to denying herself the illicit pleasures, she simply couldn't resist.

Carlos glanced at her again. He was driving Angela's car, her Porsche, chauffeuring her in her own vehicle to what would be a scene of utter debauchery. His grin was terrible to behold when he crooned back a delighted, "Yes, Mrs Brodie, you are. You're a married lady and I'm going to ruin you."

"This isn't me," the woman repeated. "Please, Carlos," she breathed. "Please take me home."

He laughed. Carlos kept his eyes on the road and guided the powerful car towards their destination, his tone derisive. "Oh, come on, Mrs Brodie. You know this is exactly you. This is who you are."

"Oh God," Angela whined. He was right, he was so bloody *right*.

***

It wasn't even night. There was no cover of darkness to conceal them. It would be done in broad daylight on a day when the weather was fortunately benign.

Angela vaguely recognised the route. With her head full of what was to come she spotted landmarks she knew.

Carlos followed the robotic instructions from the sat nav, taking them from Angela's large house in the town out towards the Fens. They ran parallel to the main A1 trunk road towards Huntingdon, veering away from the main artery with the vast, flat wetlands ahead. Carlos took them through quintessentially English villages, the bucolic scene at odds with the perversions in store for Angela as she stared blindly out at cottage pubs and ancient hedgerows, churches and village greens.

Less than ten miles from Angela's house Carlos turned the Porsche into a narrow lane which in less than a mile became little more than a bridle-path. Angela experienced a momentary flash of fear the car would be damaged when the hedgerows squeezed close. How would she explain it to Andrew when he asked what the scratches and dents were about.

For the briefest time she forgot about this devil's errand, concerned for her car and questions from her husband.

Then Carlos spoke and a whole flock of birds took flight in the pit of her stomach.

"We're here," he said, pointing a forefinger at the navigation unit.

Angela blinked and looked around, head swivelling as she took in the press of green next to her. Then, as she looked beyond Carlos and out through the driver's side window, she saw a place where several vehicles could park.

It was a space very occasionally used by repair crews on the main East Coast Main Line railway, workers whose activities were mainly nocturnal. Carlos eased into the gap and cut the engine, the silence suddenly enormous around them.

Adrenaline surged when Angela noticed there were two vehicles already there. Her heart hammered, her breathing quickened and panic rose. "Are they--?" she began.

"For you? Yes, they are."

Angela sat and stared out of the window when Carlos opened the car door and climbed out.

"Come on," he said, crouching to look back in.

Angela shook her head, expression like a frightened rabbit's. "No," she gasped. "I can't."

He took her at face value, shrugging before he climbed back into the driver's seat. "Okay."

Angela's jaw dropped when Carlos fired up the car's heavy motor. "What are you doing?" she gasped.

He aimed his torso and a dark look towards her. "Taking you home."

The casual acceptance confused Angela. She felt oddly deflated, disappointed but also relieved.

Her heart slowed as she calmed. "Really? That's it? You'll take me home?"

Carlos pulled a face, pursing his lips, head canted to one side. "If that's what you want, Mrs Brodie."

A sigh came out of her. "Oh, Carlos, thank--"

"But it's over between us," he snapped, cutting Angela short. "If you're okay with that, if you're happy it's ended I'll take you home and never see you again. I thought this was what you wanted. I arranged it for you. I *thought* you were exciting. The things you've said to me, the things you look at on your laptop..."

Angela gaped at the vehement response. "Over?" she breathed, appalled at the prospect.

Carlos lifted a shoulder in a half-shrug. "Yeah... I suppose I was wrong about you--"

The Porsche's engine purred like a big cat, the soft growl patient, waiting for Carlos to select a gear.

"But, Carlos... I'm just so... so nervous." Angela blinked several times, eyelids fluttering as she added a more strident, "Please don't chuck me, Carlos. Can't we still do it? Can't we be together? Nobody excites me like you, Carlos. With you I can be myself. I can say things to you I could never say to Andrew."

Angela hadn't realised just how hooked she was. She'd had no idea of the strength of her addiction until Carlos threatened to leave her high and dry. He was so lovely, so fucking talented in bed. Suddenly, the thought of doing without his magnificent skill sent Angela into a spin. On a logical level, she knew it would be over soon anyway, Carlos would leave their house, the vacation over. She would have to face it soon enough, but she didn't want it to be today. She wanted a little more time with her lover.

"Please," she moaned, hot tears welling.

Carlos sucked in a deep breath and regarded Angela with disappointment. He stared at her for a full half-a-minute before appearing to relent.

He switched off the ignition.

The car fell silent once more.

"Right here," he growled, the randomness of that statement causing Barbara to ask what he meant. "You and I, Mrs Brodie, get out of the car and you suck my cock... right here."

Angela threw an anxious look through the windscreen. "But what about--?"

"My cock, Mrs Brodie. You suck me and I'll fuck you. If they come to watch--" Carlos shrugged.

He left it unsaid, but the scene filled Angela's mind's eye. She'd be fucking outdoors. She'd be fucking Carlos while men watched. Her body responded with a surge of renewed desire. Angela's pussy clenched, she felt her nipples tighten.

Warmth flooded south. "How many are there?"

Understanding the question, he smirked and said, "Three... perhaps four, one was only tentative. He didn't know if he could escape work."

Angela swallowed, libido revving again. "And they'll just watch? If you tell them there's nothing else on offer?"

At first she thought he was about to refuse. Carlos stared at her for some time before murmuring, "If you say so, Mrs Brodie." Then he opened the car door and got out.

He didn't bother to ask if she was coming.

Angela paused, hesitating, still unsure. She thought about losing her lover and clambered across the cockpit to exit through the driver's door, a necessity since the hedgerow at her side was so close. Angela emerged into daylight, grateful for the cover of the trees and bushes and hedge almost completely surrounding them.

Angela looked up to see Carlos with his jeans down at his knees, a fist working his length as he gazed at her.

The sight of his cock thrilled Angela. It always did, but this was something different. They were outdoors. They were going to have an audience.

Looking at it, Angela marvelled at how long and thick and so fucking *ready* it was. The feral look in her lover's eye brought a moan from her lips, Angela's insides churning at what was about to happen.

It was quite difficult negotiating the half-a-dozen paces required to reach him. The unsuitable high heels he'd insisted she wear made walking demanding and hazardous, but Angela arrived with no mishap, her lover stroking his cock as he growled at her to get onto her knees.

"I thought you put a blanket in the car?" Angela said, complying with the instruction nonetheless. "My knees... My stockings... They'll be ruined."

"So will you, slut," Carlos smirked. "Just wait and see."

***

Carlos refused to allow Angela to cover the car seat with the blanket when it was over. Instead, with Angela thoroughly corrupted, Carlos jumped into the Porsche and reversed onto the track.

"Don't leave me here! Carlos, please. Don't abandon me!" yelped Angela, horrified. She stood there, heart hammering while, for a few terrible seconds, it seemed he was going to drive away.

Carlos manoeuvred the Porsche next to Angela. "Get in," he said – an order, not a request.

"But," she began, "I need to clean up. I have to wipe this muck off, Carlos. I have to get dressed."

"Get in." His eyes were dark, pitiless pools.

Angela gulped, incredulous. "The blanket," she whined. At least let me put the blanket over the seat. Let me wrap it around me. I can't sit there like this. Jesus, Carlos…" Angela gestured towards herself with both hands, "Just *look* at the state of me." She paused and grimaced before adding, "I'm full of cum. The seat--"

He remained implacable with cold snake-eyes fixed on her face. "Get in or I'll leave you here as you are."

Left with no choice, Angela complied, opening the car door and climbing in while doing her utmost to stop the ooze from staining the leather.

Carlos made her sit in it during the journey home. Angela fervently hoped the seat would come clean. Her husband would do his nut if he saw the Porsche seat damaged. It would be bad enough if Angela claimed it was Coke that got spilled, God only knew what his reaction would be if he knew his wife had taken three loads of semen into her body, a heavy volume of which was sliding out of her as the debauched convoy of vehicles made their way along the lane.

"Did you have a good time, Mrs Brodie?" Carlos asked as they passed through Abbots Ripton.

"You bastard," she hissed, the words laced with venom.

He ignored her ire, laughing and saying, "You know you did. You fucking loved it. I saw you. I heard you… When you started sucking them…" Carlos nodded and flashed his pristine grin. "When they fucked you, Mrs Brodie…"

She could have slapped his face in that moment. Carlos had tricked her, lured her out of the car with his big cock and his obscene yet narcotic charm.

Angela had sucked him and worked her fingers through her vulva until she was too wound up to refuse his command to stand and brace herself across the front of the Porsche. Then he'd splayed her apart and slid into her from behind, the length of him, his gorgeous mass of dick filling her.

When the others appeared, and there were four of them, Angela had grabbed for the first cock to present itself.

Her cheeks burned at the memory as Carlos drove her towards the city. It had been an appalling thing to do. Amazed, shocked by her own wanton behaviour, Angela relived the sordid, chaotic scene. She ran through the events on a fast-forward track in her mind. Angela had no real recollection of the men themselves; to her they were amorphous entities, of no real substance other than the physical manifestation of their cocks. Those men were simply the engines powering the erections thrusting into her. Squirming with mortification, Angela recalled taking them orally, her lips tight around them in turn while Carlos fucked his length into her.

Angela cringed internally as she thought about those men, complete strangers using her pussy. Her stomach twisted into knots of anxiety while she wondered what had possessed her to allow them to squirt their semen into her body.

Carlos had been the first. He'd fucked at her with no finesse, no tenderness at all. It was all bestial rutting. He used Angela for his own twisted ends, grunting and pouring ejaculate into her before sliding out on a rush of cum. Jizm plopped onto the grass when Carlos withdrew, dollops of it staining her shoes. Almost immediately, with semen oozing out of her, she felt another man at her gooey opening, his cock squelching into the creamy deposit.

She had another man's dick inside her before she properly understood what was happening. Hands pawed her body. The men mauled her breasts and smacked her buttocks as they made ribald comments and laughed among themselves.

"Go on, mate," Angela heard one of them mutter. "Fuck her. Fuck her good."

"Here," another insisted, his hand pulling at Angela's shoulder while he introduced her to his cock. "Suck this... Come on, bitch, suck me."

"Oh God, Carlos," Angela squeaked, aghast at what she was letting them do to her. "I shouldn't ... Andrew... Oh my God, I'm a married woman! You lot can't fuck me--"

They laughed when Angela fell silent, her cries muffled by the meaty cock pushing between her lips.

Angela grunted and mumbled around her mouthful of male gristle while one man said, "I'm glad she's not my wife. What a slut."

The comment was followed up by a stinging slap against one buttock.

"Where's the hubby, slut?" the man growled. "At work?"

"Poor bastard," another voice muttered.

There was more laughter and Angela wanted to object. She wanted them out of her body. They were rude, coarse and obnoxious. They were using her as fuckmeat. That was all she was to them, nothing, just a slut who deserved to be insulted and humiliated.

And wasn't that exactly what she'd desired? Wasn't the situation precisely what Angela had craved? Those thoughts got Angela most of the way to her climax. It was what she'd fantasised over. She was getting what she'd imagined and secretly yearned for. Lust exploded in an arterial burst of desire that had her thrusting back onto the cock inside her. She gommed and gobbled and cranked at the one in her mouth, tugging the shaft close to the man's heavy balls, sucking her cheeks concave around the cock-head.

"He doesn't know a thing," Angela gasped, one hand on the penis at her face, the other working against her clit. "I'm out here fucking while he works. I'm a slut and he doesn't know."

The man in her pussy went with Angela when she came. He let loose while Angela groaned and sighed and moaned. She grunted obscenities as he poured into her. When the man had finally stopped digging his fingers into her hips and gushing cum, Angela had cried out for more.

"Another!" she squealed, eyes wide, teeth bared. Emulating her porn idol Angela snarled, "More cock. I want more fucking cock. Give me more spunk."

The vehement exhortations set off the one at her face. "She's wild," he moaned, cranking his cock and aiming it between her eyes.

A heavy burst of ejaculate caught Angela across the bridge of her nose and cheek, a second violent burst splashing over her lips. Gout after gout of cum spattered her skin, dollops of the stuff defiling her face, ropes of gloop clinging to her hair.

Crazed with lust, exhilarated by her lewd conduct, Angela painted her face with the oozing cock-end. She smeared cum over herself, licking and slurping at the man as she squealed, "This is what I want! Creamy cocks spunking over my face. This is what I need. Fill my cunt, boys," she gasped, her obscene appeal bringing muttered oaths and comments from the men.

"She's incredible," one man gasped, his words bringing more cries from the cock-mad female.

"Use me," Angela gurgled, her hot-eyed gaze sweeping the assembly. "This is what I love. I fucking LOVE it."

She rode the next one because she thought he was quite good-looking. He was younger than the others, mid-twenties, lovely body and tight buttocks. What made him even more special was his long, thick dick working inside her.

"What are you doing out here fucking me?" she'd asked, the question a rhetorical curdled mumble. "Oh Jesus that's good," Angela added, sighing when she sank down. "What a lovely, lovely cock. Let me fuck this thing. Oh God, I'm going to come again--"

When it was done, she stood on shaking legs. Amazed and appalled Angela stared at the men while sucking in desperate lungful's of air.

She couldn't believe what she'd done and said. Angela wondered just where the slut had come from. From where inside had this crude and rude alter-ego emerged?

Shame and guilt hit her like a train. The men were finished with her and were pulling on items of clothing discarded in the general melee to be at her. Semen leaked from Angela's pussy, she could feel the stuff cooling and drying on her skin. There was cum on her face, in her hair, and smeared across her breasts where the last man had let fly.

Her insides lurched with horror at her situation when she caught Carlos looking at her, his expression inscrutable.

An image popped into her mind: her husband's face.

Angela moaned with despair.

Andrew. Oh my God… My husband… I'm full of cum… I'm married *for God's sake – what have I done?*

She voiced the question to her young lover, the architect of her disgrace. "God, Carlos, what have you brought me to? Why did I do it?"

He didn't reply, just walked to the Porsche, the other men leaving as well.

Then, during that drive home, after the little episode over the blanket, Angela's thoughts whirled: unprotected sex? What had she been *thinking*!? Barebacking strangers? Taking their seed?

She decided she hated Carlos. Angela blamed him and despised the bastard for being the catalyst. He'd taken advantage, used her sordid fantasies and coerced her into it. She hadn't been thinking clearly and he'd had her under some kind of spell.

Fury ignited inside the woman. "I want you gone," she hissed. "Out of my house. I never want to see you again, Carlos. You're a disgusting, degenerate pig. You'll leave. Today. As soon as we get home, I want you packed and gone."

Carlos yanked on the wheel, startling Angela with the sudden movement, the Porsche swerving onto the grass verge. The car came to a standstill. There was nothing but open countryside all around.

"You're the one covered in cum, Mrs Brodie," Carlos sneered, swivelling swivelled to look at her. "What would *Mister* Brodie say if he could see his wife now?"

Angela trembled, every sinew taut as piano wire. She positively thrummed with outrage. "Don't you fucking *dare*," she spat, eyes blazing.

Carlos stared at her for several seconds before, in a flurry of activity, he unsnapped the seat belt and opened the car door, lunged out and moved round to the passenger's side before Angela could react.

"Out," he snapped, reaching in to grab at her arm. "I'll leave, Mrs Brodie…" he snarled when he had her out of the car.

Carlos pushed the woman away with sufficient force that she had stumbled, unsteady on her high heels. Angela only just managed to avoid falling into the ditch at the side of the road.

Mocking her with his expression, Carlos continued with, "I'll pack up and be gone, but you'll fucking walk home." Carlos sniggered and swept Angela up and down with a look of pure contempt. "Or you can get a lift… But I'd like to see you explain it to your husband.

"What will you tell *Mister* Brodie about being found out here dressed like that and covered in spunk?" Carlos slowly shook his head, amused while waiting for some kind of response.

It went through Angela's mind in a flash. In less time than it took to blink, she could see the devastation. Her life would be ruined, smashed, totally irretrievable. Her marriage, the house, her reputation and... oh dear *God*... Colin and Andrea! What effect would this have on her children? Andrew was one consideration – but them?

Given Carlos was meant to be his friend, Colin would be especially affected.

"No," Angela mewled, aghast at the scenario unfolding inside her head.

"Get in the car, Mrs Brodie," said Carlos, the words clipped, precisely delivered through the gate of the young man's teeth.

She had no choice. Angela knew he had her at his mercy. "Wuh-what are you going to do?" she moaned when the Porsche was back on the road.

His grin chilled her. "From now on, Mrs Brodie, you're going to be my slut. If I phone you and tell you to get your arse," Carlos paused and smirked at Angela, "and it's a fucking gorgeous arse, Mrs Brodie. You're fucking hot for an old bird." He grinned and shrugged and finished with, "If I tell you to get your arse to London one weekend, you'll do it."

Angela blinked. "London?" she gasped. "Why?"

Following his look of pity, Carlos said, "Because that's where I go to uni, Mrs Brodie... With Colin. Your son. Remember?"

Confused, Angela stammered, "Cuh-Colin...? What... I...?"

Carlos barked a laugh. "God, no, Mrs Brodie. I don't mean *that*. Not Colin and you together. No, what I mean is you'll come down to London and check into a hotel and I'll bring some of the lads around to give you more of what you've just had."

The enormity of her situation staggered her. She was disgusted, shocked, absolutely revolted by the idea. How could he even *think* she'd be willing to let it happen to her a second time?

But, as the thoughts wormed their way into the darkest recesses of her mind, Angela couldn't deny the tickle of arousal fluttering inside her.

The pair drove along in silence for several minutes, Angela's thoughts turning ever more foul with the illicit thrill of it all. Despite her humiliation and guilt and self-loathing, all of which just made it so much nastier in her mind, Angela fingered her creamy cunt, fingers diddling her clitoris.

"How many?" she groaned.

When he glanced at Angela and saw her face all slack with lust, when he noticed her hand working between her legs, Carlos laughed.

"Fucking lots of them," he said.

"Oh God," Angela breathed, wanting it all. "When…?

End of the 7th Story

BEN E. DORM

Watching

Sarah was pushed for time when the ringing phone caught her. Her immediate thought was to disregard the urgent clangour. If she was going to get to the bus she had to leave immediately – but she couldn't bring herself to ignore a ringing phone.

Inquisitive by nature – nosey, her mother said – Sarah had to answer.

"Hello?" she said, breathless in her rush.

An eerie sound came down the line: white-noise, a hissing mishmash of whispering ghost voices. For a moment Sarah had a notion there was no corporeal entity on the other end. She shivered, goosebumps breaking out along her arms, certain a ghastly gurgling voice from another time or dimension was about to speak. It was the twilight zone. Sarah gulped, swallowing heavily, the sudden need to pee pressing her bladder with some urgency.

"Hello?" Sarah warbled again.

A voice reached her. "Sarah?" she heard, her name coming from a long way away, distant and vaguely tinny. "Is that you? It's Jean, Sarah. I'm calling about the boiler--"

It took a few moments to make sense of it.

Sarah blinked, confused. "Jean?" she said. Then the twilight zone lifted and the need for the toilet evaporated.

"Oh my God, Jean…" Sarah gasped, feeling ridiculous for her silliness.

Her face warmed and she was thankful Ray wasn't at home to see. He'd want to know why she'd gone red and would then winkle the reason out of her. Sarah's husband would tease her mercilessly for days. Ray would make stupid ghost jokes whenever the phone rang.

"Good grief, Jean," Sarah went on. "Where are you? This line is dire. You sound like you're in outer space."

Sarah thought she heard a chuckle, but couldn't be sure. "In a crappy Egyptian hotel, dear. I can't tell you how awful--" Jean paused, disengaging from the conversation with Sarah. "Yes, yes, Rob," she said. "I'm getting to it. Sorry about that, Sarah," Jean continued. "My husband has been a pain in bum--"

The comment precipitated another exchange between the distant Jean and her husband. Irritated, Sarah glanced at her watch and winced. If she didn't leave soon – now – she would miss the bus for sure.

"Jean?" Sarah said, forced to repeat her neighbour's name twice before the other woman responded. "What is it? I'll be late for work and-
-"

"Oh, right, sorry. It's the boiler, Sarah. *Our* boiler next door. Rob's got this *thing* about the bloody timer."

Sarah rolled her eyes and was half tempted to put the phone down when Jean's husband interrupted again. "Jean," she sighed, "my bus--"

The other woman squawked, "Oh, yes, sorry, Sarah. Okay, the thing is, could you go and check the boiler next door? Not now, obviously, but later on today perhaps? You know where the spare key is near the back door. Just check the timer light's flashing green and the code is set to… What was it, Rob?"

Jesus Christ – come on, Jean!

"One-Four-Seven… Is that all right, Sarah, honey?"

"One, four, seven," Sarah repeated, harried and anxious. "Yes, okay, I'll write it down now. I'll do it later, Jean. I have to go. I'll be late." Sarah uttered a quick goodbye and cut her neighbour off halfway through Jean's farewell. She grabbed her bag and left the house, cursing her neighbour's Luddite tendencies – why Jean couldn't handle a text message or email.

After all the rush, Sarah caught the bus. Much relieved, she then spent the morning at work taking minutes of meetings and transcribing notes onto the computer. She ate lunch and worked on until 4:30 p.m., oblivious to the shocking discovery she was about to make.

***

Sarah remembered the phone call as she walked past the neighbours' house. She hesitated, torn between getting home for a surreptitious glass of wine before Ray returned and getting the favour done. Sarah sighed, resigned to her own diligence – she always puts others' needs before her own. With a rueful shake of her head, she pushed open the gate, following the path alongside Jean and Rob's red brick semi.

Sarah turned the corner and immediately moved towards a small patch of greenery bordered by rocks and stones, one of which was nothing more than moulded plastic shaped like a stone. In the hollow set in its base she found the key.

A sense of wrongdoing crept over Sarah when she pushed the door open. A silly notion she told herself – after all, Jean had asked her to go to the house, but Sarah couldn't shake the clandestine feeling, like she shouldn't be there and she was intruding.

"You're not a bloody burglar," Sarah muttered to herself when she crept into the kitchen. "Just get on with it."

However, regardless, she couldn't shake the feeling and continued to move quietly.

The boiler, Sarah knew, was in a cupboard on the second floor landing. To get there she would have to use the stairs, the foot of which was by the front door at the end of a wide hall some distance ahead. The route would take her through the kitchen, along the corridor, and past the living room.

What she saw following a casual glance into the living room froze Sarah in shock.

There was a man in there.

He was sitting in one of the armchairs, his presence so unexpected, Sarah was too surprised to move. Her breath caught in her throat and she couldn't even gasp while her heart bounced in her chest, the organ rubbing frantically: a frightened bird in the cage of her ribs. Sarah heard a strange roaring sound, wind through a tunnel – her own blood surging through her veins, the hot flow spiked with adrenaline. It was a cold water dash of fight or flight.

Then, almost immediately, Sarah realised she recognised him.

It was Jean and Rob's son sitting there – Alan, a student at a university in a different city.

Sarah took everything in a blink of an eye, it just took her brain a little longer to process what her eyes were relaying to her stunned mental faculties.

She was on the point of opening her mouth to call out the young man's name when the images on the television screen solidified and she could make sense of what Alan was staring at so enraptured.

The second shock came hard behind the first when Sarah realised he was looking at porn.

The noises from the speakers reached her, Sarah heard the groans and gasps and excited squeals. A torrent of sewer-mouthed filth poured from the Cupid's-bow lips of a very pretty girl with long black hair. Sarah blinked in response to the stream of invective.

In a vague way, with her brain still catching up, she wondered at the girl with the face of an angel spitting obscenities so freely. She looked to be in her early twenties: and so *pretty*. Did she really have to do these films? Couldn't a lovely young thing like her get a proper job?

Time compressed, condensing to allow several near simultaneous impressions to form in Sarah's mind. Later on, when she would analyse the moments in detail it would strike Sarah that the young woman really did seem to be enjoying the experience. She might be laying it on a bit thick with the obscene comments – exaggerating the lewdness because, well, it was porn after all – but she did appear to actively revel in the act of urging her lover to use her rectum to his fulfilment. She also seemed to *enjoy* having her anus stuffed with a rather large penis while sucking a second cock. The girl grinned with manic enthusiasm while spitting her filthy litany before shrieking with pleasure, wall-eyed and slack-faced as a climax hit her.

Sarah boggled at the screen, unable to take her eyes of the scene of such wanton debauchery. Despite the shocks, Sarah recognised a little flutter of sexual arousal low down in her vitals. The flame ignited and warmth spread south, with Sarah's vulva heating and her clit beginning to tingle.

The noise coming from the television explained why Alan hadn't heard Sarah's arrival. She realised he was so engrossed in the action his entire focus was shifted that way. The fact she had literally tip-toed along the corridor had further masked her presence, leaving Alan oblivious.

Then the third shock of the afternoon hit her like a physical blow. If Sarah's libido had snorted from slumber because of the obscene action on the screen, what she noticed next brought sexual desire fully awake. Lust roared like a snarling, ravenous beast. Carnal longing burst inside her. Sarah's insides clenched and she experienced a near overwhelming urge to rub at her clit.

It hit her like a train: a surging need to let go and wallow in depravity.

She looked at Alan while he carried on stroking his cock – and wasn't it just a bloody lovely-looking thing! What a gorgeous big dick, larger than Sarah had ever encountered.

Despite the terror of being discovered, emboldened by lust, Sarah crept towards the doorway.

She couldn't help herself, recognising the insanity even as she did it. Sarah couldn't believe she was doing it: the risk was huge, the consequences enormous.

Nevertheless, flouting the danger, Sarah slowly eased her skirt to her hips and slid a hand into her knickers.

***

Sarah chewed her bottom lip and resisted the urge to moan. She watched Alan from just outside the room, her position ninety degrees from Alan's chair, in full view if he turned his head in her direction. She watched Alan cranking his long cock while the full danger of her situation asserted itself in Sarah's mind. She thought to leave, but found she couldn't bring herself to step away – the scene was just too compelling, too lewdly hypnotic for her to simply leave Alan to his privacy.

Sarah kept allowing herself a few seconds more, the sheer clandestine nature of her voyeurism as powerful as any drug. Sarah had heard of sex addiction and always scoffed at the absurdity. To her mind addicts of any kind were weak, folk without the will to steer a more moralistic course through life's waters. But, in that moment, she understood completely how one could be carried away in a storm of licentious action. Seeing Alan stroking his length, knowing she was intruding on such an intimate act had her libido revving in top gear. The very sordidness of what she was doing made her hot to rub her excited clit. It was wrong, immoral, dirty and disgusting… And she loved it.

Occasionally she managed to drag her eyes from Alan's big bell-end poking through his busy fist. From time-to-time Sarah's attention flicked to the screen, the debauchery she saw enacted there stoking the raging fires of her yearning. That girl really did enjoy what she did. She had men at her from all angles, two or three simultaneously, Sarah was never sure exactly. The raven-haired, willowy-limbed youngster offered herself up completely. She took one in her mouth, the girth of it stretching her lips – Sarah boggled and surprised herself by wondering what Alan would taste like. She imagined his cock head all gooey and salty with pre-cum. She thought about the mass of him filling her mouth, rubbing herself harder while her fantasy grew wilder.

What about his dick filling her pussy? Oh God, what would he do if she just walked to him, yanked her knickers aside and clambered onto his lap?

The groan threatened again. Sarah just managed to catch it in time, stifling the deep moan with a hand over her mouth, images of herself bouncing up and down on Alan's lap flitting across her mind's eye in a lewd slideshow.

She could fuck the young man, just abandon it all and leave her marriage and morals suspended like knickers from a bedpost.

Sarah came close to succumbing. She imagined herself sinking down onto Alan's fat cock, her body taking him all while she worked at her sex, orgasm looming, her body's need for release giving her fingers urgency between her legs. It was pleasure she hadn't experienced for years. It was hot and so close to irresistible, this dark need to satisfy her carnal desires. Surely one little fuck wouldn't mean much?

She took another pace into the room sure he'd turn and see her. Alan was bound to sense something amiss or catch a movement out of the corner of his eye, and if that happened, Sarah would be confronted with the decision of whether to flee or take action. If Alan turned she would have a few seconds in which to act. While the man gaped, stunned by her presence, Sarah would be forced to climb aboard and jam his meat into her body, or run away.

Her mind whirled when Alan grunted. "Yeah!" he cried. "Oh fuck…"

The realisation of what was about to occur froze Sarah in place. She gaped in wide-eyed and slack-jawed fascination, insides curdling while lust slid out of her opening.

"You dirty fucking bitch," Alan sobbed, the words striking a sharp point of fear between Sarah's breasts.

At first she thought he meant her. Sarah's first impression was Alan had noticed she was there and blurted the comment. A thrilling cocktail of emotions thrummed through her: dread, panic, absolute delight that she could set aside responsibility for once in her life.

Then the reason for Alan's outburst became obvious. With his concentration remaining fixed on the screen, his sole focus was the dark-haired model as she accepted a deluge of ejaculate from two men, their aim apparently to cover as much of her with semen as they could manage.

He'd spoken to the television, directed his comments to the girl a moment before a thick string of jizm flicked from his cock. Spunk arced in a high, steep parabola, the first spurt spattering onto Alan's tee-shirt while a second vehement liquid burst squirted forth. More cum poured out of Alan as he moaned and grunted and continued to yank briskly at his cock.

Alan came hard. He snorted and gasped, tiny mewls of absolute delight escaping while his climax rocked him.

Sarah soaked up the details and, with Alan's at his zenith, knowing the time for action was past, used the cover of the young man's orgasm to sneak out of the room.

She tugged the hem of her skirt to a modest level and hurried to the back door. Sarah took a risky route along the path and out of the gate, concerned about Alan observing her hasty exit, her heart racing more from being seen by Alan than the lewdness she'd witnessed inside.

Sarah reached her own front door and scrabbled in her bag for her keys, thankful she'd had the presence of mind to retrieve her handbag from the kitchen counter in the neighbours' house.

A nervous giggle came out of her when Sarah imagined herself explaining it to Alan. She pictured herself knocking at the door and meekly asking for her bag. *Oh, yes, hello, Alan. Uhm… could I have my bag back, please? I came in to check the boiler but found you wanking off to filthy porn. I watched you masturbate and come and then I left in such a rush I left it behind. I did think about climbing on your cock, but--*

"Oh God," Sarah whined, fingers like pork fillets as she fumbled with the keys.

Finally, she shut the door behind her, resting her back against the uPVC while attempting to steady her breathing and bring her heart rate down to a less apoplectic level.

"Bloody hell, Sarah," said Ray when he arrived home a short time later. "What's got into you?"

"I've been reading a dirty novel," she lied, agitated and squirming. "It's quite racy and I'm all worked up."

Ray stood in the bedroom doorway and surveyed the sight of his wife with her skirt around her hips, work blouse unbuttoned and her bra pulled down around her brisket. "Fucking hell," Ray breathed, agog at his wife in her dishabille. "You look like a right slut laid there like that."

"Then come and fuck me," Sarah gasped, her uncharacteristic outburst sending her husband's eyebrows shooting towards the ceiling. "It's what I want, Ray. Come and fuck me, darling."

Ray's throat worked. He gulped and stared at his wife, the image unprecedented in his experience with her. Sarah's eyes flashed with lust, big breasts rolling while she rubbed her fingers through the dense pubic bush, the dark hair between her legs matted with desire. It was a stranger mouthing those obscenities at him. Ray barely recognised his staid, slightly boring wife in the potty-mouthed slut he'd come home to.

A moment later he was at his belt buckle.

"Come and get me," Sarah purred.

Ten years later

It was summer, a warm day in mid-July. Sarah left the house late on Saturday morning. She had a few things to pick up from the supermarket. Her plan that day was shopping at Marks and Spencer in town who was doing the dinner for two for £10 deal: starter, main, dessert, and a bottle of wine. She quite fancied their curry, despite not having anyone to share the food with since Ray had gone two years before. Sarah didn't have to cook the lot in one go – and at that price it was worth it just for the wine. Sarah thought she could do the shopping, indulge in a long, hot bath, read a bit and then eat her dinner while watching one of the mindless reality programmes on telly. Nothing too demanding; it had been a heavy week at work and she just wanted to relax.

Sarah had nothing much on her mind as she walked down the path towards the gate, mind in neutral. As usual, she winced at the skreek of neglected hinges at the front gate. Sarah always meant to oil the damned thing, but always seemed to forget about it as soon as she set foot indoors.

She had just promised herself she'd do the job the next day when she then almost walked smack into a man who'd been walking past.

"Oh, sorry!" she blurted, apologising even though the near collision wasn't necessarily her fault.

His reply caught Sarah by surprise. "My fault, Mrs Jacobs," he said.

When she recognised him, Sarah felt herself colouring, the heat rising rapidly in her face.

"Are you okay, Mrs Jacobs?" Alan asked.

She knew she must be fire-engine red: *Oh God, stop looking at me.*

"Yes, yes, absolutely," Sarah replied, her eyes sliding away from his concern.

Ever since that day Sarah had never been able to look Alan in the eye. Over the years there hadn't been much contact, but whenever happenstance had chosen to put them in close proximity – his mother's fiftieth birthday, the occasional meeting at Christmas – Sarah had always found Alan extremely awkward to be around.

"Sure?" he persisted. "You've gone awful red, Mrs Jacobs."

"No-no," Sarah twittered: *Really, please, just bugger off.* "I don't know why... Maybe just a bit of a scare?"

Alan's features twisted. He pouted, expression pained. It looked to Sarah as though he was on the verge of saying something, like Alan had a bone to pick.

"Mrs Jacobs..." he began, hesitating before adding an ominous, "Can I ask you something?"

Panic gripped her. Sarah blinked, suddenly short of breath, horrified by what he might say.

"It's just--" Alan went on.

"Oh, Alan, I'm sorry, I really haven't time to stop just now." Sarah could hear the wobble in her voice. She knew she was about to babble but couldn't help herself – she had to get away. "I'm on my way out you see. I'm already late."

His expression struck Sarah as disappointed when she chanced a glance at his face. "Are you on a date, Mrs Jacobs?" he asked. "Uh...

Mum told me about you and Ray. Sorry to hear and all that." His gaze lingered, thrilling Sarah with its intensity. "But you look great, you must be meeting someone."

It was preposterous, the idea she would be out meeting a man...

The sheer ridiculousness of it caught Sarah off guard. "A date? Me?" she blurted, anxious to be away from Alan and his disconcerting stare. She could already feel her body responding to the reminder of what she'd seen a decade before. "No, nothing like that. I was just going to town. I've just got a little shopping to do."

As soon as she said it, she saw Alan had registered her overreaction. She had oodles of shopping time left. It was only just noon and the shopping mall would be open for business for nine more hours at least.

"Must be important shopping, Mrs Jacobs," Alan quipped, his comment reheating Sarah's cheeks.

Flustered, she kept silent. Sarah just wanted to be away from the humiliating situation she found herself suddenly embroiled in.

"Before you go, Mrs Jacobs," Alan was saying. "I just wondered if I've ever done anything to... To offend you?"

Sarah gulped, guilt and suppressed desires, mixing inside her.

"It seems like one day you changed. You started to act all weird whenever I was around. I can't think of anything," continued Alan, perturbed. "But if I've ever said or done anything to upset you – I'm sorry. I just wondered what it might be?" He shrugged and finished with, "I've thought about it a lot over the years and..."

Well, it's like this, Alan. Your mum asked me to check something in the house while she was away. I went in and caught you staring at porn. I stayed and watched you tug your lovely cock – and it's a fine specimen, by-the-way. I watched you until you shot gallons of cum all over yourself. Oh, and I have to tell you I was masturbating while I watched. I rubbed my cunt and creamed my knickers when I saw all the spunk gushing out.

A couple more things you should know, Alan. I was just about to sit on your cock when you came. I'd been imagining riding you, you and me just fucking. Forget I was married at the time. I was so fucking horny...

Well, my nerve failed; and when you came, I ran away. I ran home and frigged myself until my cheating, faithless, wanker of a husband came home.

Finally, Alan, I've used that little scene in countless masturbatory fantasies since. I fucked my wanker of a hubby, but thought about bending over to take your long dick. I've used a dildo on my clitty and imagined you spurting cum over my face, just like that harlot in the film you were watching.

Of course, none of it came out. Sarah kept those thoughts to herself, gaping at Alan like a landed fish until she finally stammered, "I… It… Well… No, Uh-Alan, there's nothing."

Then, out of the blue Alan asked, "Would you like to go for a drink with me?" He paused and gave Sarah a rueful smile. "When you've done your… uh… shopping," Alan added "Maybe later this afternoon?"

It took a few seconds for Sarah to register the invitation, then the heat rose in her face again, embarrassment, incredulity and a kind of delicious anxiety competing for attention.

A drink?

Spend time alone with him?

What a lovely idea!

How terrifying!

It all went on inside Sarah's mind. She thought about the younger Alan, the one from a decade earlier, the nineteen year old who'd stroked his cock and come with such vehemence.

Arousal flared, but Sarah was too much of a chicken. "Oh, Alan, I…" she began, confused and overwhelmed.

It was Alan's turn to stutter and look awkward. "Please, Mrs Jacobs," he wheedled. "I think you're…" He hesitated, mortified by what he was saying and the neediness in his tone. Nevertheless, despite the risk of total humiliation in a flat-out rejection he gamely soldiered on. "Well, I just think you're lovely and I'd like to take you out for a drink… Or a meal, if you prefer. I don't mind either. Come on, Mrs Jacobs," he insisted. "Please say yes."

"But I'm so *old*, Alan," Sarah replied – which was the only excuse she could summon at short notice. Thoughts tumbled. She was staggered yet jubilant to be asked. "Compared to you," Sarah continued. "I'm forty-five, you know."

Was that a sudden look of hunger that flitted across Alan's face? Sarah couldn't be sure. The moment was past and she might be mistaken, but Sarah's insides clenched at the possibilities she divined in that fleeting expression. She experienced a surge of primal yearning, the same emotion she thought she'd seen in Alan's look, and, as she stared at him agog, she saw Alan's throat working.

Then his croaky reply reached her. "You're perfect, Mrs Jacobs."

Her legs trembled when the impossible implication brought her blood to the boil. Sarah hoped she wouldn't stagger and fall as she walked to her car, her mind whirling in response to her reckless acceptance of a drink with Alan.

She drove to town and parked in the concrete monstrosity of the multi-storey car park, distractedly going about her business. All afternoon she vacillated, wavering between meeting Alan or blowing him out with some excuse.

In the end she decided it was a non-starter. There was no way she could stand to be near him with the intimate knowledge in her head.

But, at four-thirty, with the sun on the downward arc, the heat of the day tapering into a cool, benign afternoon, Sarah left her house and saw Alan approaching her gate.

"Perfect timing," he said, beaming a bright smile.

***

They found the perfect spot: a table right at the big patio doors. A soft cooling breeze wafted in from the beer garden beyond when Sarah slid along the banquette, Alan stands solicitously alongside until she was seated.

The pub was in hiatus between the midday rush and serious evening drinkers, a few people clustered around picnic tables outdoors enjoying the sun while some regulars held council on sport and politics and the sorry state of the world at the ninety degree bend at the end of the bar. In the dining area proper, two couples sat with meals in front of them as a lone youngster moved around offering the diners condiments before busying himself with collecting used glasses, plates and other detritus left behind on the tables.

"What will you have, Mrs Jacobs?" Alan asked, eyes wide in enquiry, head canted.

"White wine and soda, please," Sarah replied. She dared herself to meet his eyes. "And please, call me Sarah."

"I'll try." Alan said, pausing before adding, "Sarah. But I've known you as Mrs Jacobs for as long as I remember." He shrugged, a shy smile playing on his lips. "It'll feel weird, but I'll try. White wine and soda?" he confirmed before moving away towards the bar.

"Not Chardonnay!" Sarah called. "I can't stand the stuff. A nice sauvignon would be perfect."

Alan, looked over one shoulder, nodded, and raised a thumb.

Sarah used the time to examine her feelings, analysing her motivation for being where she was.

It's nothing – a *drink, that's all.*

It came back to her, the flash of desire across Alan's face earlier in the day: feral, *hungry…*

Then the vivid recollection of him ten years before burst into her mind: full colour, surround sound. Sarah saw him as he'd been. Alan was in that chair, the girl was muttering filth while he gazed entranced, his fist working.

And when he came!

Sarah longed for her drink as she wriggled against the cloth-upholstered seat, her pussy warm and itchy while her clitoris added to the tumult, tingling, her nipples stiffening against her bra.

"Oh God," Sarah wondered aloud. "Does he *really* fancy me?

Yes, no, Oh God…

Self-doubt surfaced. He couldn't possibly be interested. Alan was twenty-nine, Sarah was sixteen years older. Alan had been six when she married Ray!

However, she couldn't deny was good-looking, attractive, an interesting man with a great career as a chemical engineer for an oil company. He was all around the world working in countries where exotic women would surely catch his eye. What possible interest could he have in a divorced, slightly repressed suburban Englishwoman of middle-age?

It was a ridiculous notion, Sarah decided. His mother had probably put him up to it anyway. She could hear Jean's voice: *Be nice to Sa-*

rah next door, dear. Her husband's gone, you know. It might be sweet of you to take her out for a drink.

Jean meant well, but *was* prone to interfering in Sarah's life to an infuriating degree. Jean's voice sounded inside Sarah's head again: *It'd be kind of you, Alan. Get her out and about so she can find herself a man. She isn't getting any younger. If she isn't careful,* etc., *ad infinitum.*

But Alan had seemed so enthusiastic. And what had he said? He thought she was lovely? He'd almost *begged* her to accept, or at least it had seemed that way to her. Then there'd been the other thing, well, the thing besides his look. It was all a little vague, Sarah had been struggling with the mix of emotions at the time and couldn't be certain – but hadn't he said he thought she was perfect?

Was that the word he'd used?

"You silly cow," Sarah muttered to herself. "You're just confused... and randy."

Her thoughts turned to her dildo and her intention for its robust use later on. When Alan returned, she was squirmy and juicy.

"Here we go," he said, placing Sarah's glass on the cardboard coaster. Apparently oblivious to Sarah's discomfit he raised his glass. "Cheers," he smiled.

Sarah raised her own delicate glass. "Cheers," she responded, suppressing her need as their glasses chinked. She sipped the wine and said, "So, Alan, tell me about all the places you've been." As calmly as she could manage she continued with, "I'd love to hear more."

***

Sarah was giddy after three drinks.

"I'll get them," she insisted, rising. "It's my round."

Alan eyed her, dubious. "Are you sure, Mrs Jacobs... *Sarah*," he corrected himself. "I'm all right as I am. I don't drink much." He threw Sarah an apologetic look. "This month-on, month-off thing with work... We can't drink on the rigs... I'm okay with three beers in me – if that's all the same to you?" he hastily added.

Sarah couldn't believe she'd downed three glasses. It was hardly binge-drinking, but she could certainly feel the effects.

Alan had been a delight, his stories are funny and interesting. He'd kept away from any technical elements, drawing instead on a stock of anecdotes that had her laughing and goggle-eyed with disbelief at the antics of men let loose in places like Bangkok and Perth and Bogota, cities Sarah had never seen and couldn't afford to visit given her post-divorce financial meltdown. The first wine had evaporated and Sarah insisted on buying her round, with Alan getting the third.

Their glasses were empty and Sarah had made the offer, keen to extend the time with Alan, near euphoric in his company and the wine-induced buzz.

"I've had a wonderful time, Alan," Sarah breathed. "You're such good fun." When the words came out it dawned on her the awkwardness had gone. She was no longer ill at ease in Alan's company.

He nodded, obviously pleased. "Me too, Mrs Jacobs..."

"*Sarah*," the pair intoned simultaneously, the synchronicity setting them both laughing.

"Would you like to eat?" asked Alan when they'd both settled. He cast about for a menu.

"Well," Sarah began, the offer coming out before her brain realised what her mouth was doing. "I've got one of those M&S meals at home. Just one of those microwave things; you know, a three-course ready-meal." Sarah grimaced, but continued with, "I know, lazy, but they're really quite good. Of course, there's only me to eat it, but--"

Sarah's voice trailed off. She looked at the table and shrugged, face warming.

"Dinner at your place?" asked Alan.

Self-doubt seeped back in. "Oh, sorry," Sarah responded. "I didn't mean to put you on the spot. It's just I've had such fun and--" Sarah castigated herself internally for being so stupid. Of course he was busy. It was his month off work and it was a Saturday evening. Alan hadn't mentioned a girlfriend, and she hadn't asked, but there was bound to be someone in his life.

Sarah was cringing inside when Alan surprised her. "I'd love it," he said. "I've had fun, too." His eyes bored into Sarah's when she looked up to find him staring. "To be honest, I didn't expect you to come out with me in the first place." Alan paused and picked at a beer mat. "Sorry to bring it up again, but I really did think I'd done something to upset you in the past." He spread his hands and grimaced. You did seem... *off* around me. It's been on my mind for years. I've wracked my brains and I just can't think why."

He shut up and rolled his eyes, hands going up in apology, palms facing Sarah.

Alan smiled and nodded. "Okay, I'll stop. It isn't important and I probably imagined it. Yes, Mrs Jacobs... Sarah... I'd love to have dinner with you."

They left the pub to stroll the mile or so home. At some points it felt like Alan was about to take her hand, especially as they skirted the lake. It was an evening set for lovers, a RomCom ideal. Sarah really did think Alan would make some sort of move.

As it was, he didn't.

They walked, chatting about trivialities and marvelling at the beauty of the scene Sarah's mind also worried over the recurring issue of the distance she'd put between her and Alan in the past. The heady effects of the wine faded and she was growing increasingly concerned, he would continue to press her on the subject.

Suddenly the dinner didn't seem like such a good idea.

Shit – why does it have to be so bloody complicated? Why can't I just forget...?

It seemed the dinner was inevitable. Sarah would just have to push through. She vowed to stop over-analysing every aspect of her life from then on in. Sarah reconciled herself to a meal and some more of Alan's company. Perhaps they'd drink the bottle of wine that came as part of the deal and then, when Alan went home, she could go up to bed and use the dildo to fuck some sense into herself. Sarah would masturbate to a groaning orgasm and purge herself of all the nonsense.

***

The food in the silver trays was in the oven. Sarah brought the wine through to the living room and handed Alan a glass.

"Screw cap bottle," she remarked. "Classy, eh?"

"If the bottle isn't, then you *are*, Sarah."

His remark fired her off all over again. Sarah's hand shook as she poured. So much so that Alan noticed.

"Are you all right, Mrs Jacobs?" he asked, slipping back into the old formality.

"Yes, yes," Sarah trilled, but, after pouring her drink, she slumped defeated into the sofa. "Oh God, Alan," she breathed, emotions swelling inside her. "You're probably going to think I'm a silly old boot, but--"

Sarah balked, slurping wine while a tempest raged within. She wanted to ask him outright if he fancied her. Sarah's body vibrated with yearning. Her pussy oiled and her insides clenched. Loneliness, the sheer physical need to be held, to be kissed, and yes, to be royally fucked by a big cock fought a battle with Sarah's inherent reticence to share her innermost thoughts. She had always been that way; it was how she'd been moulded. Sarah's upbringing was one where she was coached to hold herself in check, told never to lean towards the dramatic or be thought over-emotional. Outward displays of emotion had been frowned upon, public displays of affection scoffed at. But this thing with Alan, the potential of what he might have in mind set against what she'd seen and how she felt towards him wound her tight.

If she didn't do something – *say something* – and soon, she was going to explode. Sarah was certain she would suffer an embolism and drop stone dead if she didn't find some release.

"An old boot? I don't think that about you, Mrs Jacobs" Alan said, smiling kindly. "I would never think that." He sighed and shook his head. "I told you... I think you're lovely."

"Why!?" Sarah wailed, her outburst vehement enough to have Alan rearing back in his seat. "Why do you say that? What are you thinking?

"Oh bloody hell, Alan," hissed Sarah, jaw clenched as the words came through a portcullis of teeth. "Do you fancy me, or what? I'm going insane wondering what's going on."

He stared at her for what felt like hours, but was only seconds in reality.

"Isn't it obvious, Mrs Jacobs?"

"No! Yes!... Oh, bloody hell, I don't know!"

Silence fell like a guillotine after Alan murmured, "I do, Mrs Jacobs. I do fancy you. I have for years."

Following a lengthy pause, Alan continued with, "I wanted to tell you, but you were married." He sucked in air and winced before draining the glass, then went for the bottle again. "When I heard about you and... Well, when I heard what happened with you and Ray I thought I'd be able to tell you how I felt." He implored Sarah with his eyes and went on. "But I thought you didn't like me. You always seemed to avoid me. You wouldn't even look at my face. It felt like I'd done something terrible. It was like I'd kicked your dog or made some inappropriate remark.

"But I can't think of a thing I've done wrong, Mrs Jacobs."

"Oh," groaned Sarah, the sound low and long. "Alan, I--"

"Then I saw you coming out of your house today," Alan interrupted. "I hoped I'd see you and there you were. You looked lovely, Mrs Jacobs. Gorgeous. Your hair--" He gestured towards her with one flat hand. "Like it is now, all loose and shiny and thick--" Alan sighed, a heartfelt judder of emotion in his chest. "I couldn't help myself, Mrs Jacobs. When I saw you it was the perfect moment. I was so happy to see you, to talk to you." Alan paused, hesitating before he murmured, "I just wanted to *look* at you, Mrs Jacobs. That dress you had on shows you off perfectly. I couldn't stop myself looking at your legs and your... your...

"Well, I couldn't stop looking."

The wine, the outpouring of Alan's true feelings and his heartfelt delivery thrilled Sarah, but it was his mention of wanting to look at her which was the catalyst.

"You wanted to *look* at me, Alan?" she drawled, lust a white hot flare between Sarah's legs. Desire swelled inside her, her vulva flooding with warmth. Sarah's breasts ached for Alan's touch. Emboldened with the heat of her carnal urges, reckless with the sudden euphoria set loose, Sarah mumbled a croaky-voiced, "You can look at me whenever you want, Alan. God, how I want you to look."

And then, just as Sarah thought he was about to leap from his seat and ravish her on the living room carpet, Alan brought it up again.

"What was it I did wrong, Mrs Jacobs?"

***

She told him. Sarah stumbled through it, her face burning while she stuttered it all out.

Adam's initial reaction was puzzlement, his expression shifting from brow-furrowed uncertainty to gape-mouthed horror.

"I can't recall," Alan said when Sarah described the early circumstances. "They went to Egypt a couple of times."

"Well," Sarah continued, eyes sliding from Alan's face. "They were away and your mum phoned one morning. She asked me to check the boiler, said something about your dad being concerned about the timer."

Alan snorted and lifted his eyes towards the ceiling in a sign of exasperation. "He was obsessed by that timer. I remember him always going on about gas bills."

Sarah nodded, expression pained – she really did need to get it finished. "Right, anyway, I went round after work and got the key from that false stone in the back garden." Alan snorted again but Sarah ploughed on before he could interrupt. "I let myself in the back door and… Oh God, Alan--"

His eyes were wide with anticipation. "What, Mrs Jacobs?" Alan breathed, blinking.

"You were at home," she croaked, unable to look at him.

"I can't remember it." Alan's head shook side-to-side while he frowned and wracked his brains for the recollection.

Sarah's response was little more than a whisper: "No, you wouldn't remember me being there. You didn't see me. You were… uhm… distracted, Alan."

Alan pouted and shrugged, obviously bewildered. "Distracted?"

Sarah gulped, swallowing heavily before she galloped through to the end. "You were in the front room. You were looking at something on television. It was a film, one you'd had running in the DVD player. I was walking past the living room door and I saw you watching a film where this pretty girl was… She was…"

He shook his head in denial when he realised where Sarah was leading him.

Sarah could tell the enormity of it had hit Alan when she flicked a look at his face, she saw him gaping back at her, his mouth open, eyes wide and his expression shifting with the horror of it.

"You--" Alan croaked. "No. Mrs Jacobs, you didn't--"

"I was there, Alan. I didn't mean to but I caught you in the middle of--" Sarah's face burned with it. She could feel the awful humiliation coming off Alan like a physical wave. The shock was plain to see on his face. Alan sat there, spine rigid, the knuckles of one hand white as his fingers squeezed the butt of the chair arm.

"Ah shit, no," Alan groaned. He slumped in his seat, stunned.

"That's why I couldn't look at you, Alan," Sarah said, her voice rising. It was important he understood she hadn't been offended. Sarah was desperate for Alan to realise her reaction was more to do with her own responses. She needed him to know she'd been embarrassed for him by walking in on his intimate moment. So what if he masturbated – didn't everyone? Alan had done nothing wrong. In Sarah's view, it was all to do with her. She was in the wrong.

"I... I better go," he stammered, dumping the glass onto the floor before rising.

Sarah was on her feet a moment later. "No! Don't go!" she yelped. "Don't leave like this, Alan. You have to understand. You don't have to feel bad because I saw you... Because I saw you doing that."

Bloody hell, why can't I say it? Why can't I just say masturbate or wank? What the hell is wrong with me?

"I was shocked, of course, but I wasn't offended. The reason I couldn't act normally around you is because I stood there and watched, Alan. I *watched*." Sarah's throat worked, her fingernails dug into her palms. "I watched you because I bloody loved seeing it," she gasped, the sudden resurgence of lust curdling the words. "Your cock, Alan... God your lovely big penis was hard. You were staring at that dirty little slut and pulling at it--"

Her vulva suffused with warmth. Sarah could *feel* her labia swell.

Sarah gazed into Alan's face and moaned her way through, "I wanted to sit right on it. I was thinking about how good it would be to just walk up and climb onto your cock, Alan. I think I might have done it, too... But you climaxed."

"Jesus, Mrs Jacobs," gasped Alan, pole-axed by the woman's revelations. He gaped at Sarah for a few rapid beats. "Shit, you mean to say--?"

"All that stuff just squirted out, Alan," Sarah blurted, arousal bringing the words out of her like machine gun bullets. "It was so *sexy* seeing it. I had my hand in my knickers. I was... I was rubbing myself as I watched you. I thought you'd turn round and catch me. I don't know how you didn't notice I was there. I watched you and I rubbed myself and I wanted to sit on your cock. I wanted to fuck you."

Then, with the tale told, Sarah sobbed, "I've played with myself and thought about it, Alan. I've come and come just imagining all of your semen flooding me."

Alan boggled some more, mute with it.

"God," he gasped eventually, lunging for his wine. Alan bent and grabbed the glass from the floor, draining the contents.

They stared at each other, silence around them both while Alan's thoughts raced and Sarah waited anxiously for a response.

Then the smell from the kitchen permeated through to the living room.

"Oh my God!" Sarah cried. "The kitchen will be on fire!" She hurried towards the door, pausing to throw a look at Alan. "Please don't go," she said. "I'll be right back. We have to talk about this."

A minute or two later, after some banging and clattering, Sarah returned to the lounge.

"I got to it just in time," she said, relieved at the useful emergency for breaking the stand-off. "If you can still eat, the dinner is about perfect, she was saying when she saw him. She stopped, a hand going to her mouth while staring at Alan. "Oh my God," she gasped.

"Is this what you saw, Mrs Jacobs," Alan smirked, his fist working slowly back and forth over his very large, very firm erection.

***

"Oh," Sarah whined. "Oh my."

"Show me what you did when you saw me," growled Alan, expression lupine. His eyes sparked fire while he held the woman entranced. He caressed his length and smirked at her. "Watch me wank, Mrs Jacobs," Alan purred, "and show me how you played with yourself, too. I want to see you do that."

"The dinner," Sarah moaned, her world muddled by events.

"Later," Alan crooned. He thrust his chin towards Sarah, who stood there rooted to the floor. "Right now, Mrs. Jacobs, I want to see you with your hand inside your knickers. Or," he added, his grin predatory, "you could take them off."

Desire exploded with such vehemence Sarah gasped and sobbed. She lifted her dress and hauled her underwear to her knees, the fabric tearing in her haste to be free. Sarah yanked her knickers down and mewled with excitement before boldly ruching the dress higher at her waist.

The insanity took her. Sarah felt a sudden, heady sense of liberation, released from her own attitudes and hang-ups about body propriety and body image. Gripped by thrilling euphoria, Sarah thrust her pelvis towards the smirking man. She splayed her labia with the tips of her fingers and challenged him with her stare.

Go on. Look at me. Go on, Alan; stroke that lovely cock and look *at how hot and wet I am for you.*

Sarah was instantly rewarded by an expression of intense hunger on Alan's face. She moaned and slowly moved closer when the speed of his stroke increased.

As she approached, Alan's words thrilled her. The urge to flaunt herself ballooning when, bug-eyed and dry-lipped, his jaw dangling, Alan croaked, "Fucking gorgeous. You're fucking lovely, Mrs Jacobs."

She recalled the potty-mouthed young woman in the film and surprised herself by muttering, "Wank that thing, wank that big cock."

"Well, well," Alan smirked, "listen to you."

"Take your clothes off," Sarah demanded. She fingered her clit and winced, following up with a snapped, "I want to see you bare. Take your clothes off and then sit back down. Wank that cock for me, Alan. Let me watch."

Alan released his erection, the meaty thwack of it springing back against his tee-shirt reaching Sarah's ears. He toed off his shoes and jack-knifed over to tear off his socks. Next, he rose and pushed his jeans down to his shins, boxers going with them. He kicked both garments free and then peeled his tee-shirt over his head.

"What about you, Mrs Jacobs?" Alan asked, pointing a finger at Sarah. "I want to see you, too. I *really* want to see."

"Let me look at you first," Sarah replied, her eyes roving over the long, lean muscles of Alan's thighs. She took in the plates of his pectorals and the bunched biceps, soaked up the jib of his hard-on and wondered how it was going to be when she accommodated the thing inside her body. "You're quite the hunk, aren't you, Alan," Sarah purred, her fingers working at her sex, inhibitions melting in the heat.

The man's head canted. He took hold of his dick and tugged it again. "There's a gym on the rigs, usually. I make time during the off shift."

Doubt abruptly dampened Sarah's ardour. Her hands hung by her sides as she warbled, "I hope I don't disappoint you, Alan. You must have had some beautiful women on your travels."

"Look at me, Mrs Jacobs," Alan replied, holding his erect penis in both hands. "Does this look like you're a disappointment? I've thought about fucking you for years," he added, "just like you've thought about me. I've wanked off thousands of time thinking about you. You're so fucking sexy and you don't even realise."

"But I'm so much older."

Alan sighed. "You're *perfect*." He tugged himself some more. "Now, please, Mrs Jacobs, *please* show me your boobs. I'm fucking choking to see."

Sarah gulped, but hands trembling, slid the straps of her cotton summer dress over her shoulders. The uncharacteristic obscenity coming from Alan fired her again. She let the bodice fall and gathered the whole lot protectively around her waist.

"Ah fuck," he breathed. "Lovely big tits." His fist jacked away as he licked his lips. "The bra," croaked Alan, expression feral.

"Oh God," Sarah whined, unable to believe she was actually doing it even as she scooped one breast free. "There," she breathed, face warm after releasing a second weighty orb. "Satisfied?"

The look on his face told Sarah all she needed to know. Alan hardly needed to add a creaking "Fucking perfect" to tell Sarah he was very satisfied.

"Now," Alan said, pointing to the sofa. "Sit down, spread your legs and finger yourself. Let *me* watch *you* this time."

***

It took a little time, but Sarah's confidence came rushing, her libido surging. She slumped into the sofa, hesitant and unsure while spreading her legs to flaunt her sex with far less assurance. However, after a minute or two of Alan's gaze fixed between her thighs, while he slowly caressed his thick tumescence, Sarah found herself warming down there, her pussy sluicing.

"I love your bush, Mrs Jacobs," Alan growled. "I love everything. You're really sexy. I didn't think this was ever going to happen."

Sarah's fingers slid over her clit, a digit probing her opening. "Do you really feel that way, Alan?" She stared at him, face slackening as a low whine came from her.

Sarah wriggled and shifted her rump along the seat cushion. In a moment of daring she wanted him to *see* her, to really gaze in awe, his eyes filled with need and hunger. Sarah shunted back and hooked her legs over the chair arms, pausing to assess Alan's response before splaying her labia with her fingertips and exposing her scarlet core.

Alan groaned and jacked at his cock. "I mean it, Mrs Jacobs," he grunted, nodding. "I'm glad your husband is gone. The bloke must be a tosser to cheat on you. Jesus, just LOOK at you, Mrs Jacobs. Aw man, I really want to fuck you."

With two fingers inside her body, upper arms squeezing her breasts together, the sight of which had Alan groaning and tugging furiously, Sarah mumbled, "It hurt me when I found out about Ray and his fancy piece, Alan. And the pain lasted a long time." Sarah squeaked and whined and wriggled, fingers of one hand at her clit while the other two found that place inside her that felt so good to rub. "But for this," Sarah gasped, "for being free to do this with you... Oh, Alan, it's divine."

Alan was on his feet, cock waggling. "Can I lick you, Mrs Jacobs?"

In response to the urgent, breathless request, Sarah chewed her bottom lip and nodded. "Yes, please," she gasped. "God yes, Alan. I'd love for you to do it."

He crossed the gap between them, dropping to his knees and forcing Sarah's thighs to a contortionist's limit while gazing at her hairy vulva.

When his mouth touched her, Sarah squeaked and moaned, chin on her chest as she looked down to see Alan's tongue lap at her clit.

"I don't believe I'm doing this," she breathed, astounded how her anticipated evening of a meal alone and reality television had turned out.

Alan pulled away from Sarah's body. He looked into her eyes and nodded. "I didn't imagine it would ever happen between us, Mrs Jacobs. I thought you had something against me. I hoped, but…"

Sarah smiled and stroked a hand gently over Alan's short hair. "But it's happening now. It really is."

Another nod from Alan: "Yes, Mrs Jacobs, it is."

"You have to stop calling me that," Sarah chuckled. "You can't lick me between my legs and *still* call me Mrs Jacobs."

Alan grinned and then ducked in to lap at Sarah's sex. He held her eyes with his own as he did so, smirking up a second later to say, "Why not… *Mrs Jacobs?*" Alan swiped at her with his tongue again. "We could pretend you're the strict teacher." He licked her for a third time, with Sarah squirming and gasping. "I could be the naughty student. Would you punish me?" Alan asked, going at Sarah with several slurps. He wriggled his tongue into her opening, diddling her clit with his fingers at the same time. "We could play all sorts of games during my month at home, Mrs Jacobs."

Appalled yet thrilled by the kinkiness Sarah whined, "Stop it, you dirty bugger," adding a gasping, wide-eyed, "Do you want to spend your time off with me?"

Abruptly serious, Alan leaned back. He held Sarah's stare with his own intense look. "Can I, Mrs Jacobs?"

"If… If you want to," stammered Sarah. "It wuh-would be lovely."

With a crooked smile on his face, Alan said quietly, "Then I will."

A moment later he was concentrating his efforts on Sarah's pussy. Alan licked at her and had her squirming and gasping, her hands on his head as she forced herself against his face. He used his fingers, working them inside Sarah while she grunted instructions as to where and how she wanted his digits curled and rubbing.

Alan eased up, his hand still between Sarah's legs as he suckled at each breast, testing their weight with his free hand before then moving up to kiss Sarah for the first time.

"I can taste myself," the woman breathed when their kiss broke. "Oh my God, Alan, the things I want to do with you."

"I want to do it all with you, too, Mrs Jacobs." He went at Sarah with vigour, the woman's hips thrusting, her body squelching around Alan's fingers.

"Ooh-ooh-ooh," Sarah yelped, glaring at Alan through eyes fired with lust, her climax bubbling on a low heat, the flame strengthening with each second. "Kiss me again, Alan," she hissed, scrabbling at him with one hand, desperate to have him inside her. Sarah wanted Alan in her mouth and her cunt. She was desperate to come while kissing him. It had been so long since she'd been so physically active. Having a man kissing her was divine. She craved the intimacy of his kisses more than his fingers moving inside her. "Kiss me," Sarah squealed, pelvis jerking.

"You're gonna come?" Alan gasped, gaping at the bucking woman as she grunted and begged. "Fucking hell, Mrs Jacobs," he breathed. "That's it, babe. God, look at your tits move."

Alan squeezed Sarah's breasts, one hand mauling tit-flesh while the other continued to work its magic between the woman's legs. Then he kissed her, his tongue sliding into Sarah's mouth, their breaths mingling, with Sarah grunting her pleasure as their tongues slid together in a slippery, serpentine dance.

Finally, Sarah broke away. "I'm coming," she gurgled, glazed-eyed, jaw dangling. She winced and jerked in violent spasms, lifting her buttocks off the seat by pressing her hands against the chair arms. She thrust her chest forward, large breasts swaying, great sobs of delight erupting from her. "Oh, Alan!" she cried. "It's so good... So bloody *good* to have you do this to me. Don't let it stop, darling."

"Fucking hell," Alan gasped, awed at the vehemence of Sarah's climax. "And I thought you were so prim and proper. Jesus," he spat, "just look at you. You're fucking amazing."

He kept going, fingers inside Sarah until, with one huge sob and a gasp she slumped into the chair's embrace.

Sarah sucked in great draughts of air. "Oh God," she panted, expression shocked, her gaze set on Alan as he eased his fingers from her body. "I've never--" she moaned, awed.

Still reeling from the force of her orgasm, the next thing Sarah knew was her hips were being pulled forward, her buttocks sliding over the seat cover. Alan was between her legs, arranging her to his liking, his intention obvious. The man rose up from kneeling, his cock in his fist, the big dome aimed at Sarah's opening. Alan rested his weight on one arm, a hand against the upright back of the chair. Precariously poised, his cock nudged Sarah's body.

"Oh!" the woman yipped. "You're going to fuck me," she gasped, oddly surprised.

He slid into her, the blunt knob-head splitting her open, the thick shaft filling Sarah.

"Ah shit," Alan moaned, his hands moving to find purchase so he didn't collapse on top of her.

"That's big," Sarah groaned, hips moving in an instinctive response. "It's lovely. Oh, Alan, I'm full of you."

Alan winced and clenched his teeth while looking down at Sarah. He grimaced while grunting, "I have to fuck you, Mrs Jacobs. I have to. Seeing you playing with yourself," he added, groaning as he moved in and out. "Watching you watching me… Your big tits… Your bush... Ah fuck, Mrs Jacobs, I have to fuck you. I'm gonna go mental if I don't."

Sarah couldn't help herself. He felt so good inside her. She thrust up, meeting Alan's instroke, buttocks coming up as he fucked into her. She knew the danger, was well aware of the consequences if it all got out of control. And it could, it would be all too easy to throw it all away and allow her galloping libido free rein.

"We shouldn't," Sarah gasped. "Not without a condom. I'm not on the pill, Alan."

He gaped down at his lover following her babbling outburst. "But I can't take it out. I… Oh shit, Mrs Jacobs, fucking you feels so bloody good."

She looked at him and threw it all away. "Then fuck me," Sarah whined, pelvis working back and forth while she placed her hands on Alan's bulky shoulders. "Give me that cock, but please, please don't come inside me."

Their first coupling was a short-lived rutting of two people in desperate need of release. Sarah felt another climax stampeding towards her. Feeling Alan's cock moving inside her body, the sheer mass of him filling her, his length probing while his girth stuffed her brought her second orgasm snarling like a beast.

For Alan it was years of masturbatory fantasy come to life. He was inside Mrs Jacobs. He was fucking her and she was loving it.

"Please don't come inside me," Sarah squeaked, her face twisted into a mask of terror and paradoxical pleasure. "It feels so good, Alan. Oh god, it's divine. I don't want you to pull it out, but you can't come inside me. I'm not protected, Alan. Please! Oh, Alan, please!"

Alan grunted and snarled and leaned in low to kiss Sarah's mouth. "But I want to, Mrs Jacobs," he whined. "I want to squirt you full of cum."

Sarah's hips kept on jerking. Her legs were folded at the knees and she had a tight grip on her lover's pelvis while she fucked herself up onto his cock. It was madness, she was courting danger. Alan could let it go at any moment. She knew if the eruption began there was no way she could hold him off. If Alan's climax hit him, Sarah would find herself flooded with semen, her body vulnerable to the consequences.

It was insane, but such a thrill, the thought of letting Alan bathe her insides with cum sending perverse jolts of delight through Sarah.

"I'd love to feel you pumping it into me, Alan," Sarah grunted, her body maintaining the rhythm of their coupling. Later on, when it was done and their combined ardour had cooled, Sarah would be embarrassed by what she squealed in that moment of heady bliss. She had no idea where the thought or expression came from, it was just there, bubbling out of her on a low moan as she glared up at Alan and dared him to come. "But you'd be fucking a baby into me. If you come inside me, you'll put a baby there."

At that, while Sarah's fingers moved over her clit and her climax thundered in, Alan withdrew, tugging his cock as he stared at Sarah, his teeth gritted.

"Mrs Jacobs!" he bellowed. "I'm coming!"

***

When it was over she couldn't believe the mess. Alan had yanked his cock and flicked semen all over her. She saw strands of jizm in her hair when she surveyed the damage in the bathroom mirror, thick snotty ropes clinging tenaciously while more spunk slid down her cheek. Alan's ejaculate lay smeared across her breasts, dark patches of it staining her dress Gloop glistened in her pubic bush, her own desire leaving the hair between her legs all matted and sodden.

"Look at the state of me," Sarah said, grinning into the mirror when Alan came into the bathroom behind her.

Sheepishly, apparently shy with the heat of the moment cooling rapidly, Alan offered an apologetic smile and ran the palm of a hand over his head. "Sorry," he mumbled.

Sarah wiped between her legs with a wet flannel.

"Don't be," she purred, turning to look at him. "I really loved it, Alan." Sarah sighed and rolled her eyes. "It's the most free I've ever been with a man."

With a jolt, Sarah realised just what it was she'd just said. Her inhibitions were gone. She felt carefree, joyous at what she and Alan had shared.

Buzzing with the intimacy, Sarah asked, "When can we do it again?"

He went to her, taking Sarah in his arms. "Any time, Mrs Jacobs. Whenever I'm home," Alan breathed, planting a kiss against Sarah's lips. "I want to spend time with you. You could meet me somewhere, too," he added, excitement in his tone as the possibility struck. "You know, if you can take a holiday, you could meet me somewhere and we could see some sights."

Sarah blinked when hot tears threatened. "Oh, Alan, really?" she murmured.

Alan grinned and kissed her again. "Absolutely," he said, nodding enthusiastically. "Now, how about we eat that dinner? We can talk about it and then…" Alan's eyes sparkled "Maybe you'd like to watch me wank again? I'm dying to get you into bed, Mrs Jacobs."

Sarah returned the grin. "And you can go and buy some condoms, too."

Their kiss was deep and lingering and full of emotion. Then, naked and blissful, Sarah led Alan out of the bathroom, a new chapter of their lives is just beginning.

End of the 8th Story

BEN E. DORM

HAPPY BIRTHDAY
DARLING

Prologue

It must have been the expression on my face when she caught me looking.

Fiona glanced up from her book and clocked my undoubtedly dopey expression. "What?" she asked. "You want a picture or something?"

I gave my wife what I hoped was a rueful smile, embarrassed she'd caught me studying her so intently. "If it's one of you naked," I quipped. "Or in lingerie…"

Fiona's eyes rolled as she grimaced in mock disgust; then she leaned across to poke me in the ribs with a finger. "You've got enough already," she shot back.

The reminder made my cock twitch. I could feel the thing thickening, growing, getting stiff.

Impulsively, on a sudden burst of emotion I reached for Fiona's hand. Her face softened when I squeezed and said, "I love you, Fi. I really, really love you."

My wife's fingers returned the pressure. "I know. I love you, too."

With Fiona's birthday only two days away, as always, even though I got an immense thrill out of what had become a traditional celebration, I was beginning to feel anxious. It was always a risk, dangerous to put temptation Fiona's way. It's a scenario that's hovered at the back of my mind for a decade, ripples of doubt which swell into waves of uncertainty as the date got closer: what if Fiona decides she wants it more than once a year? What if she tells me this birthday thing isn't enough anymore?

"You look lovely," I said. "Really gorgeous."

It's true, at forty-nine, with her fiftieth looming – hence the flight we were taking – my wife still got more than her fair share of admiring glances. I noticed it at the airport when we checked-in, men taking a second look, surreptitious or openly admiring glances at her legs and bosom. For the occasion of her birthday trip, as usual, Fiona had her hair coloured platinum blonde and, in addition to her striking new colour, in the month before the flight to Barbados she also increased her rigorous gym regime and picked up a light sun-bed tan. She also cut back on food, and reigned in on the alcohol.

The result took my breath away.

"It helps with my confidence," she'd once told me, "the hair colour and being all toned and tanned and slimmer. Somehow I can pretend it isn't the real *me* when we go on those trips. I can pretend to be someone else. Like an actor, Simon. I wouldn't *dare* do those things at home. But when we go away, I can be that wild blonde woman. I can go a little crazy."

I'd seen the blush creep up my wife's throat when she revealed this to me, Fiona blinking and shyly grinning as she said it. A *little* crazy? I'd thought to myself. *Woman, you're a demon when we're away. Out of control.*

On the plane, in Business Class – an expense I was happy about as part of Fiona's special birthday treat – my wife gave me a gentle smile. "Thank you, Simon," she murmured, eyelids dropping to her cheeks, suddenly shy in the face of my compliments. Then, perhaps sensing my disquiet, Fiona added, "Thank you for making it happen. I can't imagine how it feels for you to see it…"

It was a conversation we'd had seriously half-a-dozen times in ten years: how does it feel for me?

Well, truth be told, I can't really answer, it's too complex. The anticipation beforehand is an exquisite agony. I feel jealous; my insides curdle when I think about it. The first time was the easiest and also the most difficult. Ten years earlier I had no real clue what I was doing, but the cuprous jealousy I'd experienced back then still rises like bile inside me from time-to-time. I replay the scenes over and over in my head the closer it comes to Fiona's birthday. I *see* her with that black cock in her mouth; *hear* her moans and gasps and all the other sounds of my wife's pleasure as she slurps and sucks and then fucks another man while I look on. My guts feel heavy, a leaden weight of God-knows-what emotion dragging at me.

But, as much as it disturbs me to see my wife's scarlet cunt stuffed full of black meat, no matter how much she babbles on about the size and how good it is to feel such a *man* inside her, regardless of Fiona begging – fucking *begging* – for him to fill her with cum, despite how inadequate and insignificant it makes me feel, I'm always rock hard as I watch her enjoying herself.

As I sat in the plane and looked at Fiona, I croaked, "It turns me on, Fi. You know it does. I love to see you so... free." Then, craving her reassurances I repeat, "I love you. I really do."

Again, it seemed my wife could gauge my mood. Apparently sensing my unease, Fiona squeezed my hand once more. "And I *really* love you, Simon. Don't worry," she added, "I'm not going to run away with him. I've told you often enough: it's fun, it's *exciting*... so bloody *filthy*...

"The sex—" my wife's eyes rolled "—is bloody amazing; but that's all it is. It's just sex, no love, no real intimacy. It isn't really *me* who does it, darling; or if it is I don't love Emmet." Fiona gave me that soft smile, one that touched her eyes so her love shone through. "I love you for trusting me enough to let me do it." Those eyes widened as Fiona murmured, "How many men love their wives enough to do that, Simon? How many couples *trust* each other that way?"

I pondered what Fiona had said, mulled it over again. I wondered how my acquaintances or friends might react if they knew about Fiona's birthday treat. What would their response be if I casually informed them I let my wife loose with a black lover when we went away? How about if I told them I was there to see it all, I was there to witness bareback fucking and my wife's pussy filled with jizm?

I catch some of them eyeing Fiona from time-to-time. I see them looking at her, hungry-eyed and predatory. I know some of my friends would go behind my back for a chance at my wife. But I take that as a compliment to Fiona. She's a good-looking woman who takes exceptional care of her body and appearance; I know they'd love a ride with her. But such is the complexity of male ego, if they knew I was complicit, if they knew I'd set it up from the first...

Why I'd be seen as weak and spineless.

Howls of derision, I'm sure. A cock who wants to see his wife fucking a black cock? God, how pathetic...

In response to Fiona's question I rolled my eyes and pulled a face. "None that I know of, Fi." I leered at her and added, "You know what? I've got a hard-on." I glanced around the cabin and, knowing she'd refuse, cheekily asked, "How about tugging me off?"

"Thinking about me fucking a thick black cock?" Fiona purred, leaning right across for a kiss. Our tongues slid and writhed for a few seconds, desire flaring. It was intense, it was hot, my cock seeped pre-cum. When she pulled back, eyes shining with whatever delight my wife was experiencing at the time, Fiona murmured, "Are you hard because I'm going to kneel on the bed with my arse in the air so I can get fucked by a lovely black dick? Is that it, Simon? My wet cunt stuffed full of dark meat? Is that what's got you horny."

"Bitch," I moaned. Despite the curdling jealousy her words evoked the lurid, filthy image she put into my head affected me exactly as she wanted it to. I'd seen it before, in real-life. I knew the reality. "Jesus, Fi," I groaned, "stop it."

She chuckled and gave me a lopsided grin; then slumped back into her seat. "I'll make it up to you when we get there, Simon. I promise. I'll put on some of the fancy stuff I've bought. I'll do a little modelling for you. See which you like best. You can decide what I'll be wearing when…"

She left it unsaid and I grinned back at her, the promise of what was to come making my dick pulse. "You're on," I replied, nodding with enthusiasm, wondering if I could knock one out in the tiny lavatory to relieve the pressure. I could already feel the ache in my balls.

Fiona eased the big seat backwards, reclining as she tucked the blanket around herself.

"I'll just have a snooze," she informed me. "Entertain yourself, Simon. Watch a film or something." She eyed me and smirked, "But no wanking in your seat. You'll get us arrested."

I watched my wife as she settled down to catch some sleep, marvelling at her ability to drift away so quickly. Despite the comfort of Business Class, I can't sleep on planes. I'm the same on trains and buses and in cars, constantly alert, unable to let myself go, anxious at the rush of forward momentum.

Nor was I in the mood for a movie, I had too much on my mind. So, with the 747 on-route to the Caribbean I settled back in my own seat and let my thoughts glide back to when it all started.

Chapter One

A bout of depression sets her off. Nothing too deep, nothing that needed a doctor or pills, just the realisation her next birthday would see her hit forty. Fiona dipped for a time but then rallied, gripping the reins and steering her life towards where she wanted to be.

"I want a boob job."

She caught me by surprise, but I made all the right noises: told her she was lovely, gorgeous, desirable and sexy. I said there was no need. I said all the things a husband is supposed to say – and I meant it. I couldn't understand why it was so important to her.

But Fiona's mind was set. She wasn't to be dissuaded.

"What if it goes wrong?" I argued, concerned. There are so many horror stories.

"What if, what if, what if!" Fiona had thrown back at me, strident. "It's what I want, Simon. We can afford it. Why are you so *bloody* set against it?"

I wasn't set against her doing it, *per se*; I was simply worried. I was concerned about the risks and had deeper concerns about the why.

However, in the end she had her way, and I had to admit – *ooh-la-la, c'est magnifique!*

After that Fiona threw herself into a fitness regimen: gym, yoga, swimming. She shed pounds and, lightening her hair colour over time – first it was highlights and then a soft and honeyed blonde – Fiona re-invented herself.

I suppose I didn't notice how dramatic the transformation was because I saw her every day. It was only a chance remark from one of my friends that opened my eyes to the fact that Fiona was so altered. To me she was just the same, although I don't mean physically. In herself, Fiona was just as she'd always been. The brief period of melancholy had lifted, was nine months in the past and my wife was her old self; but that comment about how good she looked made me pause and properly appraise my wife's physical attributes.

And what I saw when I opened my eyes and *looked,* had my jaw dangling.

"Oh, so you finally noticed," Fiona said when I complimented her. She grinned and winked to let me know she was amused rather than pissed off by my failure to register the gradual change.

What I did notice, one difference I could hardly fail to spot was Fiona's new look down below. She stripped off one night for bed, nothing unusual other than I was still getting used to her breasts. But when she slipped her underwear down to her knees, I was boggling.

Then the cheeky minx blatantly thrust her pelvis at me, fists on her hips.

The words came out of me on a gasp. *"Fucking hell,"* I breathed, staring at my wife's smooth vulva.

"You wanna lick me?" Fiona asked in an exaggerated drawl.

The lewd invitation and her depilated state down there had me hard in an instant. Fiona's belligerent stare and provocative stance brought out the beast in me.

"I've been horny all afternoon, Simon," my wife whined. "Since I had it done. It feels so *weird.*"

I went mad for her, slurping her pussy, lapping Fiona's clit, fingering her opening until her desire slid from her and dribbled along the crease of her backside, the damp spot testament to my wife's need.

Sliding into her, my cock engulfed in Fiona's molten embrace, I moaned and gasped and almost squirted all I had straight away. Somehow I held it together. It was a hot and uninhibited fuck. There was no tenderness in it, with no love or emotion at all. What Fiona and I enjoyed that evening was a purely physical encounter. It was robust, vehement, bestial, with us going at one another with breathless urgency, her body squelching around my shaft, my cock like a steel rod. I felt immortal, godlike as I gave my wife her pleasure. It was all-consuming passion, explosive lust burning white hot. Yet, even in the midst of my own supreme delight I felt a curious detachment. I was able to watch Fiona as she writhed and clawed and grunted she was coming. I saw her face twisted into a mask of agonised ecstasy, tendons in her neck taut as she grimaced and spat out obscenities, urging me to fill her with cum.

"I'm coming," Fiona grunted, eyes all furious points of light while her hips worked quickly and she thrust herself against my cock.

"Fuck that pussy, Simon," she squealed at me. "Do you like it like that, babe? Is it turning you on? Do you like my smooth pussy? Is my nasty cunt wet enough for you?"

And right there, there it was, yet another recent addition to Fiona's emergent persona. When she got going something shifted and she turned into a sewer-mouthed slut, a real slide into depraved outburst when Fiona was close to her peak.

Never a prude in the past, her vocabulary usually fell short of the C-word, and to hear her snarling it up at me while so obviously caught up in the maelstrom of her climax took me to the brink.

"You love it, don't you?" I grunted, thrusting hard, probing deeper, ensnared up in the fervour of fucking into the gorgeous woman beneath me. I'd also caught the smutty bug. "Look at you with your big tits and bald pussy," I gasped, lunging and groaning when I felt my wife's insides clench around me. "How fucking wet are you, huh?

"You said you were horny all day – did you play with your clit and finger yourself at work? Did you?" I gulped, the surge rising. Thoughts of my wife diddling her clit brought it out of me. "Did you lock yourself into the toilet?" I groaned. "Did you finger this tight cunt and come?"

And then I juddered, tensed, and poured it all into her.

After that we were a little shy with each other, both of us shocked by what had been said and the near violence of our coupling. Still, it didn't last long, and while the exchanges of obscenities didn't become a regular facet of our love-making, there were occasions when we were both in such a state we turned the taps and let loose with a torrent of filth.

The fateful night came on the night of the staff party, an evening where admin staff and teachers alike went out for drinks and a meal. Fiona came in at just after 1 a.m., tipsy but not sozzled, with just enough booze inside her to loosen her inhibitions.

The sex we enjoyed was intense. It was also the precursor to what followed.

***

The staff party came three months before Fiona's fortieth birthday. It was strictly 'no partners', a caveat that meant Fiona went alone. It wasn't a big issue with me; I had no real interest in socialising with anyone from the school.

My wife looked doubtful. Even at the last minute, standing there near the front door, stunning in a flattering halter neck dress, a string of fake pearls nestled in the crevasse of her newly acquired cleavage, she was making noises about not going.

I resisted the urge to pull down the scooped neck of the dress to free her big boobs, saying instead that she should go and have a good time. "But no flirting," I playfully admonished, with an accompanying wave of a forefinger. I was mock stern, half-joking, the jealousy bubbling inside me at the thought of some snake trying to smooth in on my wife.

"Not even just a little?" Fiona lisped, pouting like a petulant child to match her tone.

I forced a laugh and then gulped when the door snicked shut. She was gone, off into the night, her perfume lingering as I touched my cheek where her lips had kissed me in parting. "I'll be good, I promise," Fiona said in the moment before the door closed behind her.

All I could do was hope so as I spent the next few hours in torment. In my head, I was conjuring up all manner of scenarios, all featuring my wife in some lewd combinations of carnality.

It was a relief to hear the key sliding into the lock at just over an hour past midnight.

I could tell she was flying when I saw her face. Fiona's eyes glittered when she leaned against the living room door jamb and crossed her arms.

"I'm home," Fiona drawled, nodding. She chewed on her bottom lip, her eyes flicking to my crotch. "Have you been looking at porn?"

She was teasing me. It was in her tone and twitching at the corners of her mouth.

"What if I was?" I retorted, relieved to have her home and apparently unmolested.

Fiona detached herself from the door jamb, but remained in the frame, eyeing me with a mischievous sparkle in her eyes. "Oh, nothing," replied my wife, all casual and indifferent. "If you were, I hope you didn't come."

I rose from the armchair after flicking off the television with the remote. "I wasn't watching porn." The remote dropped into the seat I'd been in. "And I haven't come."

Fiona giggled and said, "You wanna?"

"What?" I asked, playing the game. "Watch porn?"

I saw the shutters go down behind Fiona's eyes and felt a quick surge of *Oh shit*.

The impression Fiona had taken umbrage at the question was mistaken. "Well," she said, nose crinkling as she paused with her bottom lip between her teeth. "I *was* meaning more like would you like to come – as in do you want to fuck me?" Then my wife had me blinking in astonishment when she said, "Although I suppose we could do it and watch porn at the same time."

She was quite specific: Fiona wanted a scene with a black cock. "A *big* black cock," she murmured, hugging herself with delicious anticipation.

Another surprise from my new-model wife: not only did she want to look at porn, it had to be black porn.

"Can I look at something where a hunky black guy fucks a white woman? Can you find me something like that, Simon? Something where the woman is… say… in her forties?"

By then my wife was looking for the laptop while I felt a slide of disquiet. Why this sudden interest in black men? Why the fervour over a big cock? I was also burning to ask my wife why the woman had to be white and in her forties. Those details were a touch too close to home.

But Fiona was insistent, not quite manic but close to it. The best thing for me to do, I reasoned, was to let her have her way and try to find out what had triggered this new found interest. The best time to question Fiona about her activities was while she still had wine or vodka inside her.

So I set the laptop up, linking its output to the television.

A quick search on the internet opened a treasure chest of pornographic delights.

While I was busy with mouse clicks and wracking my brains over Fiona's demeanour, the woman herself was in the kitchen pouring a wine for her and popping the tab on a can of beer for me.

"Is it ready?" my wife asked as she sashayed into the room.

I noticed a definite eagerness in her tone before I replied with, "Almost."

Kneeling on the carpet I set it all in motion; then rose to turn and face my wife.

The beer and wine were on the low coffee table in front of the sofa. Fiona was on the settee, on her side in a mermaid pose, elbow against the arm of the seat, her head resting on one fist. Her eyes shone when she looked at me. I could see the devilment in her look. She was still in the dress and her breasts were covered, but what had me boggling was the sight of the dress hiked up to her waist, Fiona's legs spread wide while her underwear lay discarded on the carpet.

"Come here," my wife purred, confronting me with her depilated vulva. "Get on here with me. I want to watch this," she nodded at the television, "and play with myself. I'm a bit horny, Simon."

No shit? I thought. Horny didn't cover it. I could see her labia glistening with her desire as I stood and gaped at the unexpected image of my wife sprawled there, a hand mushing at her sex.

"What brought this on, Fi?" I asked, largely ignoring the action developing on the television screen.

I went to the sofa and plonked down alongside her. She shifted to make room for me, leaving her sloshing cunt alone while she closed her legs and reached for the wine.

Fiona sipped and placed the glass back on the table with the careful deliberation of the slightly inebriated.

When I looked at the screen I saw a decidedly attractive blonde talking to a leering black man. The scene appeared set in a hotel, with the woman acting as a manager of some sort, the dialogue leading us to understand that there had been a problem with the keycard mechanism. Was the card working okay, the woman had asked. The man had nodded and said it all seemed fine and thanked her. Then, improbably yet predictably, the woman recognised the black man as a porn actor. She hesitantly told him she'd seen him in films – was that right? He nodded and told her she was correct.

It looked like the action was set on a foreseeable course: groping, kissing, unzipping and undressing...

"Fi?" I said. My wife flicked a glance at me, apparently entranced. I pointed to the television. "Why this sudden interest in porn?"

With the action still in the opening stages there was no sign of the black cock Fiona was intent on seeing, so she looked at me and said, "Well, I've always wondered about... about fucking a black guy." She rolled her eyes and added, "Of course I know it's a ridiculous stereotype, and I realise it's this kind of thing that perpetuates the nonsense; not *all* black men have enormous dicks, just like they're not all lecherous predators like this bloke here..."

While Fiona pointed at the porn I was mildly amused by her slight stumble over "stereotype" and "perpetuates". She might be a school librarian with a wide vocabulary, but her pronunciation was challenged by alcohol.

"But it's a little fantasy I indulge in from time-to-time, Simon. You know, just a "what if" kind of thing."

That revelation was news to me and I was taken aback. "Wuh-what do you imagine yourself doing?" I asked, picking at the scab. Did I *really* want to know?

"That," Fiona said.

I looked at the television and saw the man was leaning his arse against the shelf fitted to the wall while the blonde fisted a cock of eye-watering dimensions. The woman looked up in adoration, worshiping the incredible length and girth of that black cock before she stretched her lips around the knob-end.

"Oh God," my wife groaned, legs going wide, fingers working at her sex. The sound came out of her and stirred me. It was a primal noise, an expression of some deep, dark yearning inside my wife. She squirmed and rubbed at her clit, another low moan bubbling forth. "Suck that big thing," my wife mumbled, engrossed by the woman's distorted face as she gamely went it.

To my surprise, I was hard, my cock big and stiff – although, admittedly, I was in the lower divisions when it came to the premier league proportions as the man on television.

Then, when Fiona turned her face to me, when I saw her eyes glazed with lust, her expression slack, almost idiotic, an arterial burst of desire exploded inside me.

And what got me really revved up was when Fiona, her voice curdled with apparent desire, said, "Look at her sucking that big cock, Simon. *God*," she breathed, "I wish I was doing that."

"You can suck this one," I growled, lifting my buttocks from the cushion so I could get my jeans down.

My wife scooped her breasts from her dress and sucked me. To my shame I squirted semen over Fiona's face in less than a minute. Seeing her as she got me there quickly and I grunted out I was coming, the first burst splashing across my wife's cheek, spunk pumping from me. She tried to catch the outflow with her mouth, and succeeded in swallowing most of the ejaculate spitting from me, but a good load of the stuff had caught her across the chin and cheek and the bridge of her nose, a couple of dollops glistening on the vast expanse of Fiona's décolletage.

Her calm response surprised me. "You dirty bastard," my wife purred. Normally Fiona would be all concerned about the furniture or her dress, but she didn't seem to be bothered at all. "Look at the state of me," she gasped, tone ebullient. "You covered me in cum."

Then, in an unprecedented and most uncharacteristic move, my wife settled onto her back, opened her legs wider, focussed her attention on the porn, and eased two fingers into her opening. She fucked those two stiff fingers into her cunt, her tongue searching for any splashes of jizm around her mouth.

"Oh God, you lucky bitch," she sighed towards the blonde. "Jesus, just look at that thing going into her!"

I turned to look at what had Fiona so turned on. What I saw was the blonde perched on the counter, next to the electric jug and sachets of instant coffee, her legs folded at her knees, thighs wide in a contortionist pose which afforded the man easy access to her gape-lipped sex. She looked down at where he penetrated her, his length moving in and out in a slow, deliberate slide. The blonde's jaw dangled, her expression one of disbelief, the impression being that the whole situation was entirely uncontrived. It was as though she really was an employee of the hotel chain, that it was all accidental, pure chance she recognised the man from porn.

What hit me in that few seconds was that the man was a professional, and of course it was all set up, but what struck me was the woman's reaction – she really did seem to be enjoying the moment. She came across as nervous and rather amateur and was all the more enthusiastic for it. This was no jaded model-slash-actress going through the mechanics, the blonde was *loving* it. Her pussy actually creamed with lust, the man's shaft was slick with her, dollops of buttery essence clinging to him. That's when it occurred to me that the woman might be a true amateur, a lady with a certain kink who had contacted the professional. She was an ordinary girl who had asked to be in one of the man's films. They'd set a meeting and arranged it all and here was the result.

All of that was going through my mind when Fiona's cry brought me back to the present.

"Simon!" my wife yelped. "I need to come, babe." I looked at her and saw her all scrunched up on the sofa. She looked back at me, eyes pleading, face twisted with desperation. She'd shifted position, reclining against the seat back, buttocks over the precipice with her shoes on the floor while her legs were spread wide and she frigged herself hard. "I can't come," she wailed. "Oh, fuck, I'm so fucking close, but I just can't get myself there."

I gaped at Fiona for a few more grunts and moans before then I grabbed for the beer and chugged a few swallows.

Wiping the back of a hand across my mouth and then I dropped to my knees between my wife's thighs.

She got there after I lapped and fingered her to it. I slurped at Fiona's meaty labia, sucking those flaps between my teeth as I probed at her with two fingers. My wife's hips bucked; she squeaked and yelped and frantically fucked up against my fingers, my lips then tight against one nipple.

"I'm coming," Fiona groaned. "Oh yes, Simon... God, I'm there."

And I was up alongside her, fingers rubbing her insides while her body squelched around them. "You want to suck that black cock?" I growled, the words snapping Fiona's eyes wide open. "You want to get fucked by that thing?" I continued, going at her so she winced and grunted and juddered. "Black cock," I hissed. "You dirty white slut... You want a black dick to fuck you?"

"Oh," Fiona mewled. "Oh... Oh fuck... Don't stop, Simon." She grabbed at my wrist to hold my hand where it was. "Keep rubbing me. I'm still coming." Fiona's back arched, her body almost doubled over, her neck against the seat cushion as she writhed in her bliss. "Keep telling me things," she snorted. "All those dirty things about black dick..."

It got to the point where I was about hard enough again to fuck my wife. The strangeness, the sheer sordidness of it all reviving my tumescence.

"Can you come in me?" Fiona gasped when I slid into her. She enclosed me with arms and legs and pulled me in. "Do what you can, Simon. Fuck me, give me more spunk. I'm so fucking mad for you, darling."

I gave it my best. I went up on straight arms and fucked into my wife's sluicing cunt. It was a combination of hearing her babble on as I watched her face. Fiona jabbered about black cock and white women, her face a mask of desire, her big tits rolling, dress bunched up around her hips. She rubbed at her clit and bucked against me, her body coming up to meet the robust downstroke.

It seemed like she would never stop with riding her orgasm. It hit her and subsided, rolling back in again like a tide. I pumped and plunged and probed, corkscrewing my hips to mix it up and find some friction.

Finally, I got there, the surge just as exquisite as earlier. I don't know if I had much left to pump into Fiona but the sensations were glorious when I juddered and gasped and slumped down on top of her.

"Oh Jesus. Oh God," my wife gasped. "Simon... Oh God, Simon." I could hear the shock in her voice. "That was... That was just so..."

It seemed to me as though Fiona was suddenly sober. Maybe all that robust fucking cleansed her of the alcohol?

"Bloody hell, Fi," I grunted as I lifted myself off her. "God, my back..."

Fiona giggled, sitting upright to cup a hand between her legs. "What happened?" she asked, looking at me as I lay sprawled on the carpet.

I shook my head and reached for the beer. "I have no idea, Fi." Gulping half the contents of the can I then looked at my wife. "You tell me, Fi. What the hell did you do tonight?"

It was fixed in my mind that my wife had experienced some kind of encounter during the course of the evening. What other explanation could there be?

"Pass me the wine," Fiona said, reaching. "And can I have your tee-shirt, please?"

Realising why she wanted the shirt, I peeled it over my head.

Fiona wedged it between her legs and sipped wine. "Thank God it's Sunday tomorrow," she said, grinning at me sheepishly.

"Today, you mean." I grabbed for the remote and cut off the distraction of the black man with his huge dick involved in yet another scene. "It's getting on for half-one."

I stood and yanked up my jeans and settled onto the sofa with my wife. She cuddled in close, an arm going around my waist as she rested her head against my bare chest.

"So, tell me," I insisted. "What brought that on?"

To my relief it turned out to be nothing much at all. One of Fiona's colleagues in the library had found herself a new boyfriend. "He's fit and black and apparently," my wife told me with some enthusiasm, "he's got a huge cock."

"And Jenny telling you this got you all wound up?" I was incredulous, there *had* to be more.

I felt Fiona's face move and heard the grin in her tone. "Well, like I said, it's a terrible cliché, a stereotype, but I've always had this… thing about fit black guys and a big cock." My wife shifted so she could look at me. She held herself on one arm, legs tucked up in another mermaid pose, her big breasts swaying when she moved. "It isn't a big deal, Simon, just a little fantasy thing, but I asked Jenny for a bit of detail and… well, she was a bit squiffy and told me all sorts." Then Fiona looked sheepish. She hesitated, sipping her wine and emptying the glass.

"What else?" I asked, reading between the lines.

Fiona's eyes went wide. "Nothing," she said, and I knew she was lying. "Can I have another glass?" she asked.

I took the glass from her and eased up off the couch – God, my back!

Stretching, I asked, "What else, Fi? Come on…"

My wife's eyes rolled. "Oh God," she sighed.

I stood there, unmoving. "No wine until you tell me."

"Pig," Fiona responded, smiling to show she didn't mean it. "Okay, all right, she showed me some photos she has on her phone." Fiona's next words came on a gasp of incredulity: "*Intimate* photos." She was wide-eyed and scandalised. "Jenny showed me pictures of his dick. She even had some of her sucking it. Fuck, Simon," croaked Fiona, "I can't tell you how hot it got me."

I laughed and said, "I know how bloody hot it got you, Fi. Look at the state of you."

With that I left to get her wine and another beer for myself. We didn't say anything more about it that night. I unhooked the laptop and we watched some late night crap on the television, stumbling up to bed at just after three in the morning.

In the weeks that followed, as Fiona's birthday approached, sometimes when we made love, when we got a bit more fired up than usual and things drifted into the dirty zone, that's when I'd mutter about black cocks and white women. I'd goad my wife with obscene murmurs about her getting fucked by a good-sized portion of dark meat. I get her squealing and grunting, her climax boiling after pouring out a long list of filthy depravity involving her and a black lover. Of course, he always had an enormous cock. Stereotype or not, that's what Fiona's fantasy demanded.

And then the idea just came to me: why not make it happen for her?

***

"*Barbados?*" my wife gasped.

We were having dinner at our favourite pub-restaurant when I gave Fiona the news. It was ten days before the flight was due out, twelve days before Fiona's birthday. I had considered keeping it a secret until the day before we needed to get to the airport but logistics denied me that option.

"Really?" Fiona added, "I don't believe it." She boggled at me for a few seconds and then her face fell. My wife's shoulders slumped and she said, "For my birthday?"

"Yes," I replied, confident. I'd been expecting the exact response and I knew what was coming.

"Oh, Simon, I can't." Fiona looked horrified. "I can't get time off. It isn't school holidays. Oh God!" she blurted. "You haven't paid for anything, have you…?"

"Flights are booked, the hotel, the lot."

She almost exploded at the news and, perverse and cruel it may have been, I was enjoying myself so I let her rant.

"What! Are you mad? Didn't you think? How much has it cost?" Without letting me answer, Fiona was off on one. "Do you think they'll refund? Can you try to change the dates? Oh God," she gasped again, exasperated at my idiocy. "Simon, you know the school's policy. I don't believe you didn't think this through…"

It had gone on long enough. I attempted to interject. "Fi--"

"Honestly, Simon, sometimes…" And then she relented a little by saying, "I know you were being kind and thoughtful. And I *know* it was for my birthday, but--"

I cut her off. "Fiona!" I snapped, reaching for the hand she'd been waving about like a bat-shit orchestra conductor. I gently squeezed her fingers. "Fi," listen, it's all done. It's sorted."

She blinked at me. "Sorted? What do you mean, 'Sorted?'"

"What do you think it means, Fi? I've been on to the school – it's all arranged. Special circumstances, what, with it being your fortieth and that. Like I said, flights are booked, so's the hotel – top-end, by the way."

I didn't mention the special circumstances regarding the hotel, nor did I care to reveal my plan for a the birthday surprise. All that could come when we arrived, when the time was right. Besides, I wasn't completely sure I'd be able to go through with it. It had taken a great deal of soul-searching and introspection on my part to get this far, and I still wasn't one hundred percent sure I could countenance seeing Fiona with… with...

I wouldn't be completely sure about what to do until the day itself?

Across the table, my wife's face was the picture of incredulity. Fiona was wide-eyed and slack-jawed with disbelief. It lasted for a few seconds and then a huge grin split her face.

"Oh my God... Barbados?"

"You've got until the 13th. That's when we're off to Gatwick. You better buy what you have to buy, do what you have to do. What do you need?" I asked. "Hair doing? Nails? Waxing? New bikinis?" Then I leered and added, "Some lingerie?"

Fiona nodded when I listed the necessities. "Currency," she said, my stomach lurching following my quip about lingerie. After all, my wife in sexy undies wouldn't be entirely for my benefit. "We'll need whatever money they use in Barbados," Fiona added.

And so we went on. Preparations were made, with Fiona excited and busy up until the day of the flight. In the background, with Fiona oblivious, emails went back-and-forth, the plan, as simple as it was, took shape.

Chapter Two

Emmet checked us in. He played it cool, acted as the consummate professional, smiling and giving us all the patter he must use ten or twenty times a day. I didn't catch him blatantly checking out Fiona, he just processed us through the computer and then acted as the guide to our room, which actually turned out to be a suite.

"Upgrade," he beamed, showing perfect white teeth in his coal-dark face. "Because it's your birthday vacation, I understand," added Emmet. He directed the words to my wife, but eyed me steadily. "Or so your husband tells me, Mrs Roberts."

"Oh, Emmet," my wife gushed – she was always easy using people's first names. Fiona threw me a look of boundless joy and love and then, to Emmet's surprise, moved to him and planted a kiss on his cheek. It was a nothing gesture, simply overwhelming gratitude, no carnal intent behind it at all. My wife was obviously thrilled – Barbados, a swanky hotel *and* an upgrade to a sumptuous suite, the exciting beginning to an unexpected ten night holiday. "It's my fortieth in a couple of days," Fiona said, and then actually clapped her hands with glee. I thought she might hug herself.

"Forty?" the man responded, casting a conspiratorial look my way. "I don't believe it, Mrs Roberts," Emmet went on, flattering my wife in his sing-song patois lilt. "You're lookin' good on it, let me say."

That remark would be useful to me very soon. It was the perfect thing for him to say.

"Thank you, Emmet" Fiona replied before moving away to the window.

My stomach curdled and slid greasily when I caught Emmet appraising Fiona from behind. The mask of civility slipped for a moment. For a second or two he was no longer the cool, polished under-manager – the man with the power to issue upgrades to guests. What I saw on Emmet's face in those moments was an atavistic hunger. He wanted my wife, Emmet was hungry for her.

"Oh, Simon, come here!"

Fiona's jubilant cry made Emmet blink and I realised I had a burgeoning hard-on in response to his lustful appraisal of my wife.

"Look at the view. It's marvelous."

I glanced at Emmet and caught his eye. He nodded at me, a conspiratorial gesture of approval to my enquiring expression.

"Well, Mister and Mrs Roberts," Emmet said as I went to the huge window to appreciate the view. "I'll leave you to settle in. If you have any reason to do so, you can contact me via reception. I'll be happy to accommodate any needs you may have."

He was looking straight at me when he said the last. I knew exactly what he meant, too.

"Thank you, Emmet," my wife trilled, excited as a six-year-old on Christmas morning. "It's all so wonderful."

He ducked his head and closed his eyes in a gracious gesture. "Thank you, ma'am," Emmet said. He flashed his smile, looked at my wife for perhaps a beat or two too long, threw me another look, and was gone.

***

I was in the shower when the luggage arrived. My wife had waited for our bags to be brought up to the room before she joined me inside the massive cubicle, the rainforest shower head cascading water onto us both.

"I don't bloody believe it," Fiona squeaked. "An upgrade! What a fantastic birthday this is going to be." She pressed her naked body against me and tilted her face for a kiss.

"I hope so, Fi," I murmured above the hiss of the shower.

Taking my wife's hand as we started that first kiss of the holiday, I guided her fingers to my cock.

"Stiff!" she yelped. "Already?"

"I want to fuck you," I growled, a need to dominate her coming at me hard.

I experienced a deep, primal urge to dictate the terms of the sex. I'd seen Emmet in the flesh. It was all becoming real. During all the email traffic, even after seeing the picture of his cock it had been an amorphous entity, a plan I could bat away like smoke. There was no substance to it before arriving and meeting Emmet. But, each second in the plane had brought us closer to the reality. The miles counting down during the transfer from airport to hotel meant I would have to confront my feelings and emotions soon enough. And, eventually, *finally*, there he was.

Meeting Emmet, shaking his hand, hearing him speaking – all of it brought on a surge of territorial primacy within me. If... and it was *still* if... *If* I was going to set it in motion, I wanted my wife to be able to compare me favourably with her virile, young, good-looking and extremely well-endowed lover.

"I want to fuck your tight cunt with this thing," I added, deliberately crude as I thrust into Fiona's clenched fist.

"Simon," my wife croaked in response. "Babe, what's brought this on? Jesus, that's hard!"

I didn't reply. I simply lunged in to kiss her, my hands going to her breasts, her buttocks, and then to her sex in search of her clit.

We stayed under the spray for several minutes, with Fiona fisting my cock while I ran my hands all over her body, desperate in my need. I caressed and squeezed and downright mauled at her. I dropped down in an attempt to lick Fiona's pussy, to lap at her clit and get her as excited as I was. It was awkward in the cubicle. Nothing to do with space, the shower was bigger than some people's homes, my issue was one of comfort, hard tiles against forty-year-old knees and the fact Fiona had to squat slightly with her legs wide for me to be able to get at her.

I gave it up, rising to kiss my wife with frantic urgency, both of us gasping and panting and muttering.

Frustrated, I turned off the water and we both tumbled out, towelling quickly, and largely inefficiently before stumbling into the bedroom from the ensuite.

I threw Fiona onto a bed the size of a tennis court, my wife yelping and giggling as she bounced.

Then I fell on her, forcing her legs wide, gazing at her vulva before stretching out on my front between her smooth legs.

"Yes," she hissed when my tongue found her. "Happy birthday to me."

I paused and looked up. "A couple of days to go, Fi..."

"Well lick me until then," the minx retorted, bringing a snort and a grin from me before I went back to it.

It was one of our heated fucks. Fiona knew right away that it was going to be intense and dirty. My earlier use of the C-word would have given my wife all the clue she needed.

"You horny bastard," Fiona purred while I worked at her clit. "We're not even unpacked yet. Not that I'm complaining," my wife gasped, fingers clawing at the bed. "Oh fuck... Simon, is this how it's going to be for ten nights?"

I went up onto my knees and used my fingers to arouse my wife, sliding two digits in and curling them to rub at her. Leaning in, I sucked at each of her nipples, teasing the aroused flesh with my teeth and lips before moving up to force my tongue into Fiona's mouth.

"This and more," I breathed when the kiss broke.

Fiona couldn't have read the hidden meaning in that statement; she probably thought I meant I would be as ardent as I was at that moment for the duration of the holiday. Not that I was about to elaborate, but I did think it might be a good time to introduce the idea to her – just to test the water, so to speak.

"You look good, babe," I muttered, jacking my cock while I slid a finger around my wife's clit. "I mean, you really do look fucking gorgeous."

Fiona groaned and pushed herself onto my fingers when I probed her insides.

"Fuck Fiona, you're so wet."

"I know," my wife grunted, levering up onto elbows and forearms so she could watch. "Here," she gasped, fingers clutching. "Let me wank you. I want to feel your cock. I love it when it gets so hard."

Fiona's fist tugged at me while I struggled to focus on my original track. "You've come a long way in the last year," I moaned. "The boobs, the yoga..." I gulped and gasped, head lolling, speech impossible for a few moments.

Recovering, I then went on with, "I love the new look, Fi. You're a stunner. You're absolutely fucking lovely."

Unable to take much more of my wife's manual manipulations, I pulled away from her and moved between her legs.

"You gunna fuck me?" she smirked, throwing her thighs wider, splaying the folds of her sex at the same time. "I'm hot for your cock," Fiona added, lewd in her own desire. "You gunna fuck my hot little pussy, Simon?" She shifted against the bed in short, jerky scoots of her buttocks to bring herself closer. "Right there." Dabbing a finger at her core, Fiona's voice croaked the obscenities. "That's where I want your hard cock, Simon. Right here in my hungry cunt."

I fell on her, entering her, my hard-on penetrating my wife while we both groaned and muttered about love.

Then I was up, moving against her as Fiona thrust up to meet me. I hooked her legs around my arms and, with her uptilted and at my mercy, plunged in deep.

"Did you hear what that man said?" I growled.

"Fuck me," my wife gabbled. "Fuck that pussy. Please, Simon, use me."

"Did you hear what he said?" I insisted, trying to batter my way through to Fiona's consciousness while battering her cunt as well.

Fiona's eyes cleared. She blinked up at me. "What? Who?"

We slowed, the tempo easing down several gears, the vehement lunges cooling back, a deliberate action on my part. It was difficult to slow down because every instinct urged me to pound at my wife's body. Inside me, I felt the need to bruise her, to make her tender so she wouldn't be physically able to take another man's cock – especially one the girth and length I knew Emmet could boast of.

I was conscious of what my emotional brain was urging me to do, but, perversely, there was another place inside me that *wanted* Emmet to plunder my gorgeous, intelligent, witty and very loving wife.

"That man," I breathed, gazing into Fiona's blue eyes. "Emmet, he said you were looking good."

"He was just being kind," my wife replied, hips moving as she tried to spur me on. "Now fuck me, Simon. I was getting close."

"I think he was serious," I persisted. "I think he meant it."

"Simon, please, just *fuck me*." Fiona grabbed at me, lunging up as she tried to pull me deeper.

"Would you say that to him?" I asked, my eyes still locked on Fiona's face. "Would you ask that black man to fuck you? He might have a big cock, Fi... Think about *that*. A big black cock, just like you've wanted."

"Shut up," moaned Fiona, eyes like boiled eggs as she gaped up at me. "Don't say that..."

I began to move quicker, rhythm cranking up a notch or two as it went on.

"He's young and fit and good-looking, isn't he?"

"Simon," my wife mewled. "Don't..."

"I bet he's hung, Fiona. I bet he's got a big dick... I bet he'd love to show it to you... I bet he'd love you to suck it."

The heat was on me. In my mind's eye I saw Fiona with her face distorted by Emmet's dick.

"Would you like that, Fi? Would you like to suck a black cock? For real? We could call him now and get him to come up. You could suck his cock and fuck him."

Then, as we were moving together, with Fiona's body giving me the indications I needed, as her moans and gasps and the look on her face all conspired against her to let me know what I was saying was working, I let it out through gritted teeth. "I wouldn't mind, Fiona--"

Only a bit of a lie.

"--If you wanted to fuck him."

My wife grunted and gnawed her bottom lip with her eyes fixed on my face.

"For your birthday," I added. "As a special thing. We're miles away from home. Nobody would know. It would be us and him..."

I was going at her by then. Our bodies thwacked together as I bounced my wife off the mattress. Her tits rolled and quivered, worth every penny she'd spent. Fiona squeaked and groaned and gasped, head rolling side-to-side, fingers clawing at the bed and quite often my arms as well. She came up at me, hissing and spitting, eyes wild, stomach tense as an arm curled around my neck and she pulled me in for a deep, lingering kiss.

"Black cock," I snarled when my wife eventually fell back against the bed. "That young bloke fucking into you, Fi. You could dress up and tease him and then give him what he wanted."

"That's so fucking dirty," Fiona moaned. "Oh fuck, Simon. Keep telling me. Keep fucking me. I'm going to bloody come."

It ended with Fiona wailing and gasping while I pumped semen into her. I don't know if she heard me or not. Fiona was juddering and grunting her way through an apparently never-ending orgasm as my cum flooded her insides.

"I don't mind if you want to fuck him, darling... I don't mind if you fuck black cock... He can fuck you and, oh shit, Fiona, I'm coming, too... Agh... Jesus, that's so fucking good..."

"I don't mind, Fi," I managed to gasp when my surge had tapered. "In fact, I'd love to watch it all."

I slumped down onto Fiona, her lovely body cushioning me, my wife's big breasts squeezed between us. That was the moment I capitulated and admitted to myself I actually did want it to happen.

I *wanted* to watch my beautiful wife taking Emmet's long dark cock.

***

I carried the secret inside me while Fiona and I ate, drank, swam, and made love. Once I'd succumbed to my own base desires, I savoured the freedom without too much more self-analysis. It was a fact: my wife and a black lover turned me on.

It was strangely liberating. I'd let go, relinquished control.

Anyway, when it came to it, Fiona would have the final say. It would be up to her when it came to the crunch. After all, I had no idea she would actually do it. So far it had been her fantasy, lewd frisson between us during our murkier intimacies.

I might have a plan, with Emmet as a willing accomplice, but Fiona would be the one to decide.

Finally the evening was upon us. It was Fiona's fortieth birthday and we were going to enjoy a romantic meal in the hotel restaurant. My wife had been pampered all day. I made a fuss of her, making sure she had a wonderful time. There was breakfast in bed, cocktails by the pool at an irresponsibly early 1 p.m. She had a massage and hot stone therapy. We made soft and tender love in the afternoon, once again with me attending to Fiona's every whim and wish. Our time together was especially poignant for me. It would be the last time we were together "before Emmet". If it went according to plan our lives would be forever altered.

That is, of course, if Fiona went for it.

I was split in two all day: half of me focussed on Fiona and her day, the other half thrumming with anticipation, fear, and a goodly amount of excitement.

Fiona was sitting at the dressing table in the bedroom applying the delicate finishing touches to light make-up, her reflection eyeing me quizzically. "Are you all right, Simon?" she asked.

When I looked at her I felt a surge of emotion. My wife looked delicious, gorgeous, absolutely cock-stirring and sexy enough in her dishabille for me to consider throwing her onto the bed where I could ravish her. She was made-up, pearl earrings dangling from her lobes, honey-blonde bob immaculate.

Fiona surveyed me with a hint of concern in her expression, with me gawking back at her as my cock thickened and grew.

"You look bloody lovely, Fi," I croaked, gazing.

My wife smiled at me, head canting sideways. "Thank you," she replied, a smirk twitching her lips. "But I'm not even dressed yet."

And she wasn't – hence my desire. Fiona sat on the little stool, legs crossed, dark hold-up stockings on her legs. The toned shape of Fiona's calves and thighs stirred me, as did the sight of her all bare from the waist up, big breasts swaying as she moved. With no underwear to mar the outline, I could also appreciate her buttocks, the enticing curve flattened against her seat, with my attention lingering on where the feminine sweep of her hips curved into the cinch of her waist.

"You don't need to get dressed, Fi," I growled. "To cover you up is a crime."

A laugh tinkled out of her. Fiona's earrings swung when she swivelled to look at me straight on. "Simon, are you sure you're all right? You've been anxious all day. What is it? Is something the matter?"

"No-no," I replied, hastily. "I just want you to have a great birthday. One to remember."

God, if only she knew...

Standing, my wife presented me with a gentle smile, the sight of her rising, forcing my throat to work against what felt like a bird's nest suddenly lodged there.

She stepped towards me, moving closer. "It's been perfect, Simon." Fiona grinned at me, eyes twinkling when she added, "You think I should go to dinner in just my shoes and stockings?"

I was hard as iron when she draped her arms loosely around my neck. My hands went to her breasts of their own accord.

"Would you eat anything if I went downstairs like this?" she purred. "Or would you just fuck me over the table?"

I swallowed again, a house brick, not a bird's nest. Then the words came out of me all strained and strangled. "I could fuck you now."

And I wanted to. God, did I ever want to. Doing so would mean the plan would be shot to shit, but I didn't care. I was hot for my sexy wife. My cock was hard and my blood was up. Lust roared through me.

"Could you?" said Fiona, her eyebrows arched as she waited for my next move.

It hung in the balance. I had a mental image of Emmet waiting and wondering. Fiona gazed at me. Her arms were still looped around my neck. My hands were on her waist, fingers around her while my thumbs rested on her jut of her pelvis. It felt like we were going to kiss, tenderly at first before passion flared between us and we began to devour one another.

"I could lick you 'til you come," I growled, willing Fiona to place a palm against the bulge in my trousers. If she squeezed my ardour I would break. "I want you to suck my cock, Fi. I want to fuck you, babe. You look so fucking *good*."

Fiona nodded, eyes twinkling.

Then she ducked in to peck a quick kiss against my lips, dancing away in her high heels, laughing in delight. "Save it for later," she said, mock admonishment in her tone as she waved an index finger at me. "I want to get tipsy and then we can fuck… all night if you can manage it."

Fiona stalked towards the wardrobe and pulled her dress from its hanger. She carefully stepped into the thing, mindful of those killer heels. A shimmy and a couple of tugs and her modesty was restored.

It was a daring choice, an LBD that fell to mid-thigh, a dress that hugged Fiona's bosom, covering her front completely to where it culminated in a priest's collar affair which fastened at the nape of her neck. Fiona's shoulders, arms and acres of skin at her back remained uncovered, the scoop reaching almost as low as the crease of her buttocks.

The effect was eye-popping. It was obvious that Fiona was bra-less, with the next logical deduction being she was going commando as well.

Which, of course, was exactly right, Fiona had nothing on under the dress except stockings and perfume.

Seeing the dress moulded to my wife's round tits only got me hotter. She might have been forty but… *fucking hell, what a body.*

My eyes bulged while I took in the vision. I breathed an epithet and my wife laughed.

"Not mutton dressed as lamb, is it?" she asked, pouting.

I boggled some more, mouth working. "Jesus, Fi," I managed to gasp eventually. "Not at all. It's stunning… I mean it, that's exactly the effect – stunning."

My wife shrugged and said, "You can say that because you know me. I'm your wife and it's my birthday – you *have* to say nice things. Oh well," she continued before I could interject, "at least nobody knows me." Then her eyes flashed with wickedness to match her chuckle when she added, "Men will look and women will hate me." Fiona flashed a grin, checked her hair and make-up quickly and then trilled, "Let's go! Take me to dinner, darling. Get me tipsy on wine and then fuck the arse off me!"

***

It was a heady mix of emotions when I saw Emmet. I felt a rush of *something*, but wasn't sure just what it was in the insane chemical mix: lust; jealousy; fear – even a little possessive anger?

I could taste them all when I looked at Fiona and saw again how desirable she was. Physical yearning nearly overwhelmed me, and then I happened to glance away for further reactions from other diners. I saw men giving my wife the once over, with several taking a second and third look, too. I was proud to be seen with such a gorgeous woman, my ego soaring because she chose to be with me. I was her husband, her lover and partner.

Yeah, look at her, she's fucking *gorgeous. I know. And I'm the one she's with. Look and drool all you want, but you aren't going to fuck her.*

Then Emmet caught my attention again.

My stomach lurched and ice-water dashed over my senses when I heard him say, "Good evening, Mrs Roberts. Happy birthday." He was close by Fiona, smiling at her, those white teeth flashing. "Mister Roberts," the man said, grinning at me, his expression knowing. We shook hands after Emmet released Fiona's fingers, after he'd pressed his lips to her cheek in a perfunctory kiss of congratulations. "Your table," he added, leading the way.

That dinner is a blur, the details vague. It must have been delicious, but I can't recall anything about the food. My mind was set on my wife and the slowly developing scene between her and Emmet. I watched as he charmed Fiona. It was nothing overt, nothing obsequious, and to a casual observer, which I most definitely wasn't – there was nothing casual about my feelings – Emmet was the consummate professional, the perfect host taking care of a guest at a special time. Nobody looking would guess what sordid plan, we had between us, a plan that was rolling along, gaining momentum. It was getting near to the point of no return. Following the starter, by the end of the first course, a bottle of wine down already, I decided I would have to push to the conclusion – whatever Fiona may say or do in response.

Emmet was away dealing with a hotel matter. My wife was lazy-eyed and relaxed, with half a bottle of red doing its work while I was buzzing and on edge.

I gulped down on that familiar house brick, leaned in across the table, took Fiona's hands in mine, and said, "Do you fancy Emmet at all, Fi?"

She blinked slowly, twice, then a third time. "What an odd question," she drawled, head tilting, eyes clearing. The vague expression vanished. "Do you mean seriously or are we playing one of our games?" Fiona grinned at me and pulled her fingers from mine. She eased back in her seat, legs crossing, as she swivelled and presented her magnificent frontage to me in profile.

It was the brick *and* the bird's nest I had to contend with next. Gulping, I managed a strangled, "Seriously. Do you fancy Emmet?"

Fiona's bottom lip jutted, her nose crinkled as she considered the question. It occurred to me that she might be formulating her answer in a form palatable to a husband.

"Be totally honest," I added.

"*Totally* honest?"

I nodded. "Yeah."

It was agony. I wanted to know and at the same time, in equal measure, I didn't want to know. I squirmed in my seat, suddenly desperate to pee.

When Fiona answered, her voice seemed to come at me from a long way away. Travelling along this tunnel, distant and unreal, Fiona's voice said, "I fancy him, sure." My wife chuckled and dropped her tone to a conspiratorial level between us, the atmosphere suddenly clandestine. "I mean you *know* about my little quirk. How many times have you told me dirty stuff when we're at it? I'd be lying if I said I haven't thought about Emmet, Simon. Isn't he just perfect? He's cute, young..." Fiona winced and blew out her cheeks in appreciation. "He's got an incredible bod. I love his muscly arms... And the colour of him..."

"So... so you'd fuck him?" I asked, my own voice a strangled croak.

Fiona's eyes went wide, eyebrows incredulous arches. "Don't be silly, Simon. For a start he's too young. He wouldn't look at me, not really. He's schmoozing me up 'cause it's my birthday, and that's his job. Anyway," Fiona went on, waving a dismissive hand, "I'd be too scared. We're married, Simon. It's you and me. Together. A fantasy is all well and good, a bit of a thrill and that, but I couldn't--"

"Remember," I cut in, "when we first arrived? Do you remember when we were in the shower together... and then in bed... Do you remember what I said, Fi?"

She looked and me and shifted in her seat, eyes flicking away from mine, legs uncrossing. Fiona fiddled with her wine glass. "Not really," she murmured, and then quickly added, "Is there any more wine?"

"You do," I insisted, "you *do* remember."

"Wine, please," Fiona said, lifting her glass to drain it completely before thrusting it at me.

I looked around, frustrated by my wife's obdurate mind-set. A waiter caught my eye and, perhaps briefed by Emmet to take special interest in our table, hurried over.

I ordered the wine and then murmured, "Fiona, you know what I'm talking about. The first day here. After the shower. When we were… were…

"Jesus, Fi. Stop fucking about," I said, exasperated, snapping with frustration and nerves. "We were at it and I said I wouldn't mind if you got fucked by a black bloke. I said I didn't mind if you wanted to fuck Emmet. Nobody would know. It's just us and him.

"I said I wanted to see it."

The silence coincided with the arrival of a fresh bottle. The waiter placed it on the table with no formalities about tasting. Maybe he sensed the strained atmosphere between Fiona and me?

My wife grabbed the bottle as the waiter left. She poured several glugs into her glass and then proffered the bottle towards me, eyebrows raised in enquiry.

I nodded, she poured, and then: "I remember, Simon." A long pause, anticipation ballooning inside me the longer it carried on. Finally, lifting her eyes from the tablecloth my wife murmured, "You know what you're saying, Simon? Do you actually realise what it is you're suggesting?"

I gulped my the wine – Dutch courage at what I was about to reveal. "I know what I'm saying, Fi. That's why I chose Barbados."

Fiona stared at me, puzzled. "What?" she asked, a frown creasing her brow.

"I've been thinking about you and someone else since the night of your staff party. It's been growing, Fi. I had the idea you might like to live it out, on your birthday. That's why I chose Barbados." I gestured with an expansive sweep of an arm. "It's perfect, babe. *He's* perfect. If you want him," I said, my tone low and clear and calm. I kept my demeanour as cool as I could manage, outwardly unfazed while inside was whirling tempest of thoughts, emotions and impressions. "You can have him. I know Emmet would do it, Fiona."

As far as I was concerned the world didn't exist, it was just my wife and I in that place as I waited for a reaction.

Her voice came back barely above a whisper. "How? How do you know?"

Thinking the absolute truth might be a little much to cope with at such an early and fragile stage I bluffed it and said, "I've talked to him, Fi. He's made it clear he's interested."

She was aghast at this snippet. "*Talked* to him?" Fiona gasped. "Oh my God! Really?" My wife blinked and gazed at me, obviously shocked. "What the bloody hell did you talk about? What did you say about me? Jesus, Simon... I can't believe it!"

"Calm down," I urged, worried she might kick off. The last thing I wanted was Fiona, who has a temper on her when riled enough, to jump up and start with the arm-waving and shouting. "Think about it, Fi. Just sit there, take a deep breath, have a drink, and *think*. This could be it. I'm telling you I don't mind. I'm telling you I want you to do it; I want you to fulfil your fantasies. We're away from home. It's just us. Nobody else ever has to know. I love you. I *trust* you. I want you to have it all."

I got through to her somehow. Fiona slumped, hands in her lap, attention intently focussed on my face. She lunged forward, reached for her glass, and took two hefty swigs.

My wife stared at me for several long seconds more and then sighed.

Her eyes shone, they glittered with tears when she whispered, "You trust me enough to let me sleep with someone else?"

I was unsure just what she meant. Fiona's unshed tears and the flat delivery of that statement confused me. Was it burgeoning delight or an accusation? I didn't know.

Ploughing on and hoping for the former, I nodded. "Yes, Fiona, I trust you."

It seemed trust was the key. "Oh God, Simon, I love you, too." Fiona dabbed a napkin at her eyes. "You'd do this for me? Really? You'd let me... Well, you know..."

Keeping silent I nodded again.

I saw Fiona's throat work and my stomach gave that old familiar lurch when, her tone curdling with her own desires and emotions, she said, "Invite him up to the suite. I'll go up first. I need to fix my make-up." Fiona rose to her feet. "Tell him to come up and... and... well, we'll see what happens next."

"Fi... Jesus, you mean...?" I began, the maelstrom of emotions surging inside me again.

My wife cocked her head and pouted. "I'm not saying I'm going to do anything, Simon. It's all such a shock, I just don't…"

She closed her eyes and sighed again. "Invite him up," Fiona continued softly. "That's all I'm saying. A drink and a chat and…" She shrugged and, after chugging the rest of her wine, turned to walk away. "I'll be upstairs," she said, moving from the table.

I watched my wife go, with several other pairs of male eyes appraising her swaying bottom as she went.

***

Emmet's face fell when he returned to find me alone.

"Is everything okay, Mister Roberts?" he asked as he approached.

It took me a few moments to get it out. I realised we were well and truly on our way. If I had any doubts, now was the time to put the brakes on, before the train really started to run away.

"My wife," I said, with my tone and attitude oddly stiff and formal considering the agreement between us. I couldn't believe I was actually brokering the use of my wife to this stranger. I cleared my throat of the bird's nest and house brick, and started again. "My wife has gone upstairs, Emmet." My eyes slid away from his concerned face for a few seconds. "Then, after gathering myself, I continued with, "She… uh… she said she'd like you to come upstairs."

Emmet looked at me with his expression blank for a moment or two; then he grinned and nodded. "Yeah?" he asked, his professional façade slipping, the patois lilt showing through. "She said that?" The man quickly glanced around, grimacing at his slip. He nodded at me, allowing himself a smirk. "Really, Mister Roberts?" Emmet continued, recovering admirably. "Is she… uhm… happy with the arrangement?"

"I'm not sure exactly what she's thinking at the moment," I replied. And I wasn't too sure about my own feelings either. "Fiona said to invite you up for a drink. After that," I shrugged, "I don't know."

The man looked down at where I was sitting. "What about you? You okay?"

I gulped and nodded again, muttering a shaky, "I think so."

Emmet was checking his watch when I lifted my eyes from the tablecloth. "I can be there in ten... fifteen minutes," he said. "I've just got to check that everything is cool." He flashed me a smile that almost ripped my guts out when she said, "I can be with her the whole night if there's no emergency."

The walk from the restaurant, through the bar and past reception is a blur. I felt drugged, as though I was walking on air, reality slewed and distorted. The lift whisked me to the top of the hotel. The doors slid open, inviting me to step out into the hallway beyond but I found I couldn't move. I stood there, reeling.

Oh God, it's going to happen. My wife... My wife and another man. My wife is going to suck a black cock. She's going to spread her legs and take it into her body. I'm going to hear her moan and groan and sigh and murmur about how big he is...

The ding as the doors began to slide shut brought me back to life. I wedged the closing doors open with an arm, forcing them to telescope aside again before I almost jumped out of the box.

Fiona's anxious stare latched onto me when I walked into the sitting room. She was in one of the two easy chairs, legs crossed, fingers gripping the arms while her foot bounced up and down in a signal of agitation.

"Well?" she gasped, with wide eyes, like a rabbit in the headlights.

"Ten or fifteen minutes," I croaked in reply, shrugging while I gazed at her, the wine bottle heavy in my hand.

A hand went to Fiona's mouth. "No!" she squeaked, gnawing at a finger.

"Yes," I insisted. A pause while I watched my wife fidget, then I asked, "How do you feel?"

"Bloody terrified, but excited, too," Fiona answered. Then, coarse with anxiety she blurted, "I'm shitting myself, Simon. But I'm soaking already."

My wife pulled a face to indicate her confusion – didn't I know *that* feeling well.

"One minute I decide here's no way I can do it," babbled Fiona. "Especially if you're here, too. I'm a married woman; I'm a school librarian, for God's sake! I'm not supposed to take a lover; I'm not supposed to let some young guy fuck me.

"But then, in the next moment I'm so fucking horny I could rub myself off. My pussy is sluicing, Simon. If I stand up I think there's going to be a wet patch at the back of this dress; I've probably made a mess on this chair as well!"

Fiona shut up and gazed at me.

After a few beats she whispered, "What are we doing?"

"Living your fantasy?" I suggested. The weight of the bottle reminding me it was there in my hand. I raised it, my eyes asking the question.

"Too right," Fiona responded. "Make it a big one." Next thing I knew she was chuckling and smirking. "A big one," she repeated, the giggles taking her.

I stood there dumbfounded, wondering what the hell was wrong with her. Was she getting hysterical? Was it all too much? Had she gone nuts?

I think the gormless expression I wore made it worse. Fiona looked up at me and let loose a huge guffaw. "Don't... Don't you geh-get it?" Fiona gasped. "A *big* one... A large drink or a buh-big cock..." And she was off again while I poured the wine and thought of it as a puerile joke.

But at least Fiona's outburst went some way to calming her down. She let out a couple of little snorts and then thanked me, soberly, for the wine when I passed her the glass.

"Oh God," my wife gasped after a hefty swig of the wine. "I don't believe this is happening."

Taking my own glass, I perched on the arm of her chair. "It's up to you, Fi," I said, strangely calm. "If you do, you do; if you don't, you don't."

Her hand, wedding ring glinting, caressed my thigh. "Are you *sure*?" she asked, murmuring the question. "Absolutely sure?" my wife added when I nodded my head.

Then, abruptly, shockingly, the time for talking was over when we both jumped at the sound of a knock at the door.

"It's him!" Fiona yipped, wine almost sloshing over the rim of the glass. "That was a fast ten minutes. Oh shit. Oh fuck."

My guts felt like a washing machine on spin cycle as I crossed the room. I opened the door and found Emmet standing there.

"I got us some Mount Gay," he said, holding up a bottle. "There should be some mixers in the mini-bar."

Emmet handed the rum to me and eased into the room.

When I turned and pushed the door closed I saw Fiona on her feet, her face a mask of terror.

"Evening, Mrs Roberts," the man said as they stared at one another. "Happy birthday, ma'am."

***

When they finally got to it, I was fizzy on rum and wine. I sat and watched, transfixed by the developing scene as Emmet and my wife bantered back-and-forth, verbally dancing around one another, neither – it seemed – prepared to make the first decisive move. My emotions oscillated wildly as I observed this mating ritual. I was in the lounge chair that matched Fiona's seat while Emmet occupied the sofa, the young black man cool as you like as he lay semi-upright, sprawled with apparent nonchalance across a piece of furniture the size of a yacht. I held a rum and Coke, ice cubes diminished, drink forgotten for the moment while Fiona reclined in her seat, legs crossed, body angled in three-quarter profile.

And didn't she just ooze carnal appeal sitting there the way she was? My wife looked gorgeous, nipples clearly outlined as they pressed against the snug-fitting dress, a dead giveaway indicator of her arousal.

Fiona swirled what was left of the ice in her own drink. She canted her head to one side, expression vulpine as the vixen drawled a smoky-voiced, "So, Emmet… Have you got a big cock?"

Bird's nests, house bricks and other stuff clogged my throat. Cuprous jealousy rose in direct proportion to the stiffening of my cock. I was appalled yet fascinated. This was a slow motion car crash.

Emmet smirked and flicked a look in my direction. If he was wondering how much Fiona knew about our pre-trip correspondence he kept it to himself. The man necked his drink and placed the heavy tumbler onto a spindle-legged table at the side of the settee.

Then he stood up, still grinning. "Why don't you come check it out?" he invited, a heavy-lidded gaze directed towards Fiona.

She returned his stare for a few moments before draining her glass. "Okay," said my wife. "Don't mind if I do."

I sat there, silent, immobile, not daring to utter a sound lest I intrude. I felt a near irresistible urge to squirm around and release the pressure of my cock straining at my trousers. The need to free my erection and yank at it nearly had me groaning out loud, but I held it in, willed myself to keep still and just watch what was going on.

My wife, the teasing minx, rose. She posed for a time, fists on hips, deliberately taunting Emmet with her stare and her body. Slowly, she walked to him, smirking, without once looking towards me or even acknowledging my presence.

Fiona halted less than an arm's length from Emmet. She paused again and then pulled the hem of her dress a little higher on her thighs before easing to her knees.

The man stood there, his attention fixed on my wife. He didn't say a word, just watched Fiona with an intense expression, fully focussed.

Time stopped, compressing and stretching simultaneously, a weird sensation as I gaped at the slow motion detail of Fiona reaching for the leather belt looped through the hoops of Emmet's fawn-coloured shorts.

I watched her fingers pull the tongue of leather through the buckle. I heard the chink of metal on metal when she pulled the strap free. She went for the button next, deftly flicking the fastening undone before she tugged at the zip.

The waistband gaped.

Fiona took hold and pulled down, a length of what looked to be a section of fire hose hanging there when Emmet's shorts reached his shins.

"Oh!" I heard my wife cry. "Oh wow," she gasped, beaming up into the man's face. "That's big all right. It's the biggest I've ever seen."

Those words cut me to the quick. My wife's enthusiasm and praise for the great appendage dangling in front of Emmet sent a spike of jealousy into my chest. But, paradoxically, as much as I hated to hear Fiona's excited cry, I was growing more and more desperate to see her touch it. I wanted my wife to hold that big mass of black cock and stroke it. I also wanted to see her sucking on it, to have the big bell-end of it stretching her lips.

I didn't have long to wait.

"It's so *heavy*," Fiona cooed when she used two fingers beneath the keel of that monster cock, lifting it while she examined it from close up. My wife gazed at it, assessing the quality of Emmet's penis from the side. "God, it's fucking *huge!*" she squeaked, another stab of emotion piercing my side.

"Happy birthday, Mrs Roberts," Emmet grinned, his smirk melting to slack-faced pleasure when Fiona curled her fingers around his girth.

"This is the best present," Fiona trilled, shifting her knees as she jacked the length of man-meat in her fist. "I can't believe how thick it is... And so long... Jesus," my wife purred, "I'll never be able to get this in my mouth."

Fiona tried, though. Oh, how she tried.

She cranked at Emmet's dick, the man sighing as he muttered about how sexy my wife was. Then, as I sat there, my status reduced to almost non-existent, Fiona flicked her tongue on the underside of the bulging, dark-purple glans.

"Yeah," Emmet sighed. "Yeah, baby."

"Unf," Fiona responded, her lips tight around the cock-head. "Fuck," she gasped, pulling back. "It's big... So bloody *thick*."

She wanked Emmet close to his root as she went at him again. My wife's head bobbed back and forth, cheeks concave as she gommed his cock, the contrast between her white skin and the near mahogany colour of Emmet's penis sending a surge of yearning through me.

"Yeah, baby," Emmet purred, his fingers pushing through Fiona's honey-blonde hair. "Suck that thing. Go on. Yeah, that's gooood. Work it, honey."

Fiona eased away again, smiling up at Emmet before she held him still and wrapped her lips around him once more. The man groaned and nodded, beaming in admiration, muttering encouragement when my wife swirled her tongue around his knob-end.

It went on for a few minutes, with Fiona licking Emmet from tip to balls, pursing her lips to smack kisses off the mushroom helmet from time-to-time. My wife slobbered and slurped and sucked, her fist working the length of Emmet's pole before the man murmured, "Hey, how about we get you outta dat dress? I wanna check those big ninnies. Let me see what you got, Mrs Roberts."

He helped Fiona to her feet as she staggered upright on the high heels.

"Keep the shoes on," Emmet growled when Fiona stepped back and reached for the clasp at the nape of her neck.

"Dirty bugger," my wife quipped. She snapped the catch and then held the dress against her bosom, teasing Emmet with her eyes. "Don't forget," Fiona said with her fingers splayed over her generous chest. "I'm an old woman, Emmet. I'm forty today."

Emmet shrugged and jutted his chin at her. He fisted his cock slowly, staring at Fiona's front. "Show me, baby," he gurgled. "I just wan' ta see."

The man breathed a sigh when Fiona released the dress.

"Well?" she asked, her tone challenging, nearly belligerent when her big breasts swung into view.

"Oh my," Emmet responded, his tongue sliding over his lips in lupine appreciation. "Oh, yeah, that's fine," the man added, his eyes raking Fiona's body when the dress fell to the floor. He worked at his cock with vigorous tugs. "Sexy," the man breathed, eyes roving over Fiona's sublime contours. "Babe, you're a real fuckin' treat for a man's eyes." He gulped and shook his head slowly, taking all of her in. Caressing his length, Emmet groaned, "Forty? F*uuu*ck! You're sexier than a lotta gals in their twenties, Mrs Roberts. Shit," he enthused, "what a fuckin' *rack*, babe."

"Your turn," Fiona returned as she took a pace backwards. With her fists on her hips, my wife added, "Clothes. Off. I want to look at you naked."

Emmet grinned and toed the heels of his deck shoes off. Next were the shorts, with Emmet kicking his clothing away while also peeling the polo shirt over his head.

I heard the catch in my wife's voice when she gurgled a very appreciative, "Oh my dear lord. What a lovely man you are." Fiona moved in and ran her hands over Emmet's chest. She squeezed the bulging muscles in his arms, eyes flicking over every exposed inch of his body. "You're all man, aren't you, Emmet, darling," she purred.

Fiona's rapt countenance and the complimentary tone in her voice had the jealousy curdling my guts yet again. I don't think her words were intended to wound me, but the implication that Emmet was more virile and desirable than me hurt deeply. It was a knife-cut to hear my wife praising Emmet's youth, his physique and that bludgeon of a cock.

But if I'd been hurt by Fiona's statement, it was nothing to how I felt when I saw them kiss. Oddly, Fiona kissing Emmet with such uninhibited enthusiasm cut deeper than anything she'd said. Weirdly, it struck me as more intimate than her sucking Emmet's cock. I think it was the way they devoured one another, Fiona groaning and gasping, sighing occasionally while the man moved his hands over her body.

"Oh God," I whined from my chair. I wanted it to stop. I'd changed my mind. That was my wife – what was she doing letting another man touch her? His hands caressed parts of Fiona he had no right to touch. Emmet's palms cupped my wife's breasts. He held Fiona's tits and nuzzled in, drawing her nipples between his lips, the elongated pink flesh stretching when he sucked. "Fiona…" I murmured, my wife's name coming out as a plea for her to stop.

They didn't stop, however. It went on, with the pair apparently oblivious to my presence. For all the notice they took of me, I might as well not have been there. It was just the two of them lost while they explored and discovered one another.

"Ooh, yes please!" my wife chirruped, moving gracefully to the settee on her high-heels. Emmet had just breathlessly suggested he lick her pussy, an idea that saw Fiona slumped on the sofa, legs wide, labia splayed with her fingertips. "Quickly," she urged, the tip of a forefinger slipping over a decidedly greasy clit. The nub shone with Fiona's desire; her opening glistened when she dabbed at herself with her finger. "I'm so fucking turned on," the woman squeaked as Emmet got to his knees.

Then I had to endure the sound of it, the noises my wife made, the groans, the sighs, the lewd exhortations to suck her cunt.

Emmet went at my wife with enthusiasm. He forced her knees to her shoulders, with Fiona all scrunched up, her pussy vulnerable to the sustained oral attack while Emmet held her wide open and pressed his face to my wife's sex.

I stood up and went to them, dropping down next to Fiona on the couch. Emmet ignored me, his attention fixed on Fiona's vulva while his tongue slurped at her opening, probing so that my wife gasped and jerked like she'd been wired to the electricity supply and someone had flicked the switch.

"Oh," Fiona yelped. "Oh yes! Lick me there. Suck my clitty between your teeth. That's good... That's so *fucking* good. Please, baby... Please lick me, use your fingers, too. Ooh," she squeaked, levering up onto her elbows so she could look along her front and watch Emmet's tongue working on her. "Lick it, finger it." Bent double as she was, Fiona clawed at the fabric, eyes flashing flame as she spat, "Fucking use me! Soon... Use your big cock and fuck me. I want it," gasped my wife, hips jerking while she forced herself against Emmet's face.

It went on in much the same way for several minutes while I sat there and endured, my emotions in turmoil.

But, despite the agony I was also very conscious of the state of my cock. Even in the midst of my emotional pain I was hard.

Then, turning her face towards me, my wife's eyes flicked open. Her face, which had been loose and baggy with gape-mouthed lust, tightened. Her eyes cleared, losing the heavy-lidded distant look when she registered I was there.

"He's going to fuck me," Fiona moaned. The way she said it and the way in which she regarded me gave me the impression my wife was surprised by her own statement. She looked at me like it was a shock the young black man was going to use his big cock against her pink pussy. "Can you stand to watch?" asked Fiona. "Me and him together, Simon... is it okay for me to fuck him?"

I could have stopped it then, I suppose. Even at that late stage, even as far as things had gone I could still have stopped it. What I'd seen and heard so far were serious transgressions. After all, I'd watched my wife sucking another man's erect penis. I'd heard her groan and sigh and squeal in delight. I'd listened to her urging the man to lick her, profanity coming from Fiona that would stay with me forever. In fact, Emmet was still there between Fiona's legs. He licked and lapped and used his fingers *inside* my wife...

I'd sat there and watched them kiss...

I could have stopped them, but I didn't. I was back in the absurd, illogical mind-set where I actively hated what I was seeing and hearing, but where I was also thrilled by the debauchery. It was self-flagellation, seeing my wife with another man was masochism on an Olympic scale. It was torture, sheer, undiluted agony, and I can't fully explain my reasons for saying what I did.

"Duh-do you want to fuck him?" I croaked, staring into my wife's eyes.

Yes, stupid question, absolutely bloody idiotic. Did she *want* to get stuffed by a thick black cock? Did my wife *want* to take the monster thing into her body and have it fucked in and out by an extremely energetic, very fit young man? Did Fiona *want* to have her cunt battered by Emmet's hefty length of man-meat?

Fiona reached out a hand as best she could in her contorted position. Her fingers groped for me. I held her hand and we gazed at each other. I looked into my wife's face and glanced at her shivering breasts. Time condensed. We might have only been like that for a second or two, but it felt like an age. Every detail is imprinted on my memory. I can see Fiona's expression – fearful yet expectant. I can see her big tits rolling as she moved; the crease in her stomach from where Emmet had her bent double; my wife's thighs splayed; Emmet's lips right up against Fiona's labia.

"Can I fuck him?" Fiona moaned, eyes pleading. "I want him so much, Simon. Please..."

My throat worked, I swallowed heavily and, guts wrenching at what I was about to condone, breathed, "God, Fiona, you're my *wife*. I love you, you shouldn't be doing this. I shouldn't have brought you to this."

Fiona wriggled and squirmed, her fingers squeezing my hand. "But, Simon--" she began.

"But," I interjected. "I did bring you here. I engineered this." I had to suck in a huge breath before I could bring myself to say it. "If you want to do it, Fi... Well, I suppose... I suppose I have to let you. If you want to do it, then I won't object. I'm your husband, Fi, you're my wife. As long as you remember we're together..."

And I couldn't say any more at that time. My throat swelled with emotion and I was losing track of what it was I was trying to say anyway.

"Oh, Simon, I love you," my wife sighed. Fiona had pressed a hand to Emmet's forehead and eased him away from her body. The man rolled away and sat with his arms around his knees while my wife thrashed, limbs flailing before she finally managed to sit upright. "We'll stay together, darling," Fiona assured me, holding both my hands in her lap. Her thumb slid back and forth over my wrist. "It'll still be me and you. We'll still be married, babe."

Then Fiona threw a quick look towards Emmet and sighed, continuing with, "It's just sex, Simon. And," she admonished, a gentle rebuke in her tone, "you did make it all happen. It was you who started it."

I nodded, sighing heavily at the truth of it.

Mumbling, I said, "I know, Fi. I know."

"It'll just be here," my wife continued. "When we get home I'll be the same as I've always, been. I don't plan on fucking other men when we go back, Simon." She released my hands and gestured to Emmet with one hand, palm up. "Just this one, while we're here."

Fiona scooted closer, the skin of her hip touching my leg. I could feel the heat of her through my trousers. "Kiss me," my wife whispered. "And remember, I love you, Simon."

I kissed my wife, pouring love into it. My hands went up and I caressed her body, palms smoothing over her breasts and her flanks and down to her thighs.

We broke apart, with Fiona smiling into my face.

"Okay?" my wife asked.

I found myself nodding, somewhat reassured by Fiona's perspicacity, comforted because she'd somehow divined my pain and then gone on to tell me it would just be here, while we were on Barbados that she would let herself go.

I grimaced and shrugged and tried to make light of it all. "Yea, I'm all right, Fi." Then it was my turn to throw a glance at Emmet, the man silent and immobile as he awaited an outcome. "Just sex, no love?" I asked Fiona.

She grinned and replied with, "I love you, darling. After all, you're the gorgeous man who trusts me enough to give me such a yummy birthday present. Remember what you said at dinner?"

"Trust," I breathed. "Yes, Fiona."

Scooping up my hands again, Fiona stared into my eyes, really fixing me with her look. "You can trust me, darling."

She kissed me again, a near chaste pressing of her lips to mine, no tongues.

My wife slid along the couch away from me. "You," she said, curling a finger to beckon Emmet to her. "Get back here and lick me again." Fiona gave me a look, smirking as she winked at me. I grinned back at her, tacit encouragement while Fiona lewdly added, "This time I want to come. It's my birthday, Emmet, and you *have* to get me off with your face.

"Lick my pussy. Give me a nice little orgasm...

"And then I want to fuck your gorgeous big cock."

Fiona dropped an eyelid against her cheek in another lascivious wink. *Thank you, babe,* she mouthed; then groaned when Emmet's tongue found her core.

***

Fiona came.

My wife grunted and lifted her shoes from the carpet, folding her legs at the knees. Her face twisted into a mask of absolute delight before she snarled gruffly at Emmet to keep on going.

"I'm coming," she announced. "Don't stop, Emmet. Lick my cunny. Go at me with your fingers, babe. Oh... Oh, I'm fucking *there.*"

Her climax exploded. Fiona sobbed and wailed, her cries of pleasure so vehement I was sure hotel security would come knocking.

Emmet kept at her, his expression a study in intense concentration, fingers working their magic inside my wife. He went up to suck at her breasts before kissing Fiona deeply, their tongues writhing all slick and serpentine.

Fiona grunted obscenities into Emmet's mouth. She juddered and writhed and lurched forward, jack-knifing at the waist while pushing Emmet away from her. "Sit down," my wife gasped, eyes shining, breathless with the force of her orgasm. "Sit and hold that big fucker upright."

Emmet complied, clambering onto the couch. In his eagerness he sat and tugged his length for a few strokes, holding himself perpendicular as my wife quickly straddled his strong thighs.

"Oh my God, we're going to fuck," squeaked Fiona. "Oh yes, we're going to fuck." She settled herself on her knees, head bowed while splaying herself with her fingers. "Hold it steady," she grunted, easing lower until the big cock-head nudged her opening. "Black cock," my wife groaned at me, her eyes glazed, face slack.

The words came out clotted with Fiona's yearning. I'd never seen such desire in her expression before. It was a different woman astride Emmet's thighs.

My wife gulped and winced, nose crinkling before her eyes flew open and she sobbed a huge blurt of delight. "This is it, Simon," she whined staring at me. "This is it, darling. I'm going to fuck him. I love you... Thank you."

I was on my feet by then, mouth opening to beg her to stop. I'd changed my mind. I couldn't stand to see it after all.

My attention went to ebony cock my wife was so desperate for. It looked huge, the intimidating length of Emmet's dick topped by the blunt glans.

I reached out a hand, the "No" behind my teeth

My wife groaned and dipped her head in to kiss Emmet's mouth. She hovered over him, her scarlet cunt glistening with desire.

"Oh fuck," mewled Fiona, her body accepting Emmet's cock head.

"Ung," I gasped – too late to prevent it. "Oh God. Oh shit..."

When Fiona sank down I I saw her pussy resist the initial penetration. My wife clawed at the sofa, forcing herself lower until the thing popped the final resistance and just disappeared inside her.

Steady," she groaned, hands going to Emmet's shoulders while I gaped at the sweep of her spine, transfixed by the sight of my wife's lovely shape from behind. "Jesus, it's splitting me in two," added Fiona, half the length inside her by then. "I'm so full... It's so big... Fuck, it's *gorgeous*." Craning round, Fiona fixed me with a look that I'll never forget. "Oh God, Simon," she gulped, face split by a huge grin. "This is good, darling." She shook her head and went wall-eyed for a moment, wincing as she sobbed out her feelings. "It's big... It's so thick. I'm stuffed with cock... A black cock..."

The knife twisted inside me when I saw Emmet's hands come round to squeeze my wife's buttocks. Then he held her wide open, showing me her body all tight around his dick, the smudge of her anus visible he had her spread so wide. Fiona's sphincter glistened, the puckered ring greasy with lust that had slipped from her during the foreplay.

I moved slightly to one side, my new position giving me a view of Emmet's mouth packed with breast-flesh. My wife cupped her tits in her palms and offered them to her lover. She crooned at him to suck her teats, to hold her and maul her tits.

"Slow," Fiona cooed, rising until she had just the end of his cock inside her. "Nice and easy, babe," she croaked. "Let me get used to it."

Down she went again, her buttocks flattening against Emmet's thighs, his balls bouncing between the spread of his thighs. Slowly Fiona rose once more, the cock-shaft glistening with her desire, shiny black like a seal's skin when my wife eased up again.

Down she went, bleating a little squeak before a low groan came from her throat, obviously ecstatic at what she was experiencing. On that downstroke, my wife paused, all of Emmet's mass inside her, her hips never quite still.

They kissed again, with Fiona finally coming up so she could gaze down at her black lover. "It's better than I hoped," she said in a whisky-voiced drawl. "Bigger, too. It's lovely to look at, Emmet – your big dick. But it's so much better feeling you inside me."

Emmet chuckled and mumbled, "You're hot, Mrs Roberts. I got to hand it to you, lady, you're fine. I love your titties, ma'am." He blurted a laugh and slapped my wife's rump, with Fiona squealing while her flesh rippled. "Dat ass is good, too. All of you... Damn, if you're not the sexiest..."

"Let me fuck you now," Fiona said, interrupting. "Sit there and squeeze my tits while I ride you." My wife rose and slipped back down again. I could see her body distending, her flesh bulging when she lifted up, her cunt tight around Emmet's girth. Their bodies collided with a meaty thwack, buttocks against thighs as Fiona let herself get carried away.

Before long it was a steady beat, slap-slap-thwack, the rhythm punctuated by my wife's grunts and moans and occasional obscenity. Fiona worked hard, riding Emmet, bracing herself against the back of the sofa, arms straight, pelvis always moving.

I stood and gaped, defeated. It was too late to do anything. My wife had gone to the other side. What we had before, our lives before Barbados, everything was altered.

We couldn't go back, so I conceded.

They kissed some more, with Emmet muttering on about Fiona's body: about how he loved her tits; how tight and wet she was around him; how he loved kissing her and sucking her nipples. The young man raved while Fiona sobbed and grunted, with the flat beating of flesh on flesh a constant in the background.

How long did they go for? I have no idea, but it can't have been more than four or five minutes before my wife eased off Emmet's length.

I watched and heard Emmet's long glistening schlong slapping against his ribbed stomach as Fiona climbed off.

"From behind," the woman squealed, already kneeling on a chair. She looked back over one shoulder, buttocks outthrust in invitation. "Quickly, Emmet. Fuck me doggy, babe. Really give it to me. I want it deep and hard. Batter me senseless with that thing."

Emmet chuckled as he advanced, a fist cranking his length. He gazed at my wife, head shaking in wonder as he purred, "You are one hot-assed bitch, Mrs Roberts. I've never heard that one before," he grinned. "But if you want me to batter you with this…"

He slapped the bludgeon against Fiona's buttocks. Emmet was behind her, one hand on her hip while he aimed his cock-end at her.

My wife gurgled with pleasure when Emmet guided his dick into her.

"But," the man grunted, slipping in with his whole length to make Fiona moan "If you want it that way, baby, well, that's what I'll give you."

And didn't he just. Emmet went at my wife hard. He crouched low and encircled her brisket with both arms, grabbing Fiona's tits in his hands while he deep-fucked her, all of his cock inside her as he dug in hard.

"Oh shit, oh fuck," Fiona moaned, mouth falling wide open. "Yes, that's it, fuck me. God, I love it. Go on, *fuck* me."

She was up on all fours next, with her hips forced back while Emmet held my wife's pelvis and gave her the good news with long, robust strokes.

Emmet leaned back, dark fingers digging into pale skin. His buttocks flexed while he went at Fiona, almost the whole length of him coming out before he went into her again.

"Uh-uh-uh," Fiona grunted, chewing on her bottom lip, head lolling. She swivelled round to look behind her, eyes flaring with fires of lust as she snarled, "Fuck it into me. Use that big cock, babe. Go on... use that gorgeous black dick."

It went on in the same vein for a few more minutes, both of them locked in combat, the pair spitting lewd encouragement before Fiona disengaged again.

***

Emmet emptied himself into my wife's body. When it happened they'd returned to the sofa, with Fiona on her back, the cheeks of Emmet's arse bunching furiously while he held Fiona's legs hooked behind his arms, her body at his mercy.

They'd been like that for some time, with Emmet tormenting my wife with his cock. Sometimes he went in deep and hard, other times slow and easy, feeding himself into Fiona and the obscenities passed back-and-forth.

I looked on, appalled yet deeply fascinated at the awful sight of Fiona's scarlet flesh tight around Emmet's truck of a cock, their sordid vocal exchange interrupted by my wife's urgent demands to be kissed.

The first warning I heard was the man gasping, he was close. At the time I thought Fiona would object, that she'd squeal at him to pull out and perhaps splash his cum over her stomach or her breasts.

But my wife did no such thing, she heard Emmet's warning and just kept on fucking herself up to meet him.

"Mrs Roberts, I--" Emmet groaned.

"Yes," Fiona yelped. "I know. It's okay." Between gasps, while her hips worked furiously, as the blade of jealousy twisted yet again in my core I heard my wife say, "You can come, babe. I want to – Oh God, that's so fucking good...

"I want to... uh... I want to feel you let it go inside me. Come, Emmet... Yes, do it... Come for me."

The man groaned and muttered something incomprehensible. He plunged in deep, savage for three of four deep lunges before finally bellowing out he was coming. I swear I could see the big muscle at the base of Emmet's cock pumping away, each pulse synchronised with a gush of ejaculate into my wife. His cock throbbed and Fiona wailed loudly, her body stuffed full of black meat, her insides undoubtedly flooded with jizm.

Emmet grunted and gasped and groaned, eventually easing back, his length slowly sliding out of Fiona.

A thick ooze of cum rushed out of my wife's gaping opening when he withdrew completely.

"Dear God," I moaned, horrified at what I was seeing. "Fiona, you've let him come inside you."

"Shit, yes, I know," my wife panted, breasts heaving as she sucked in air. "I had to, Simon. I had to feel him coming. I can't tell you why, it just seemed so... so right. He's gorgeous, he fucks so well... I just had to have his seed."

Fiona laid there, slumped, legs wide, creamy spunk sliding from her body where it then slid down the crease of her backside.

"Wooh!" Emmet yodelled from the couch. He sat upright and gazed at Fiona. "Mrs Roberts," he began, mouth working, apparently speechless. "Wow," he breathed eventually, shaking his head in wonder. Then it seemed to register. "Uh, Mrs Roberts... Uhm... You're safe, aren't you?" He eyed my wife with some concern, glancing at me a couple of times, too. "I mean..." Emmet waved a hand vaguely in Fiona's direction.

"It's okay, Emmet," Fiona said, grinning with amusement. "I'm not going to fall pregnant. Don't worry, babe." She rolled her eyes and the grin broadened. "I just had to feel you letting go inside me. It was the hottest..." Fiona looked at me, saw my face and finished with a lame, "Well, I just wanted you to do it."

And, with impeccable timing, Emmet's pager beeped twice.

Abashed by his need for a sudden departure, Emmet apologised, dressing quickly.

"I'm sorry," the man said, tucking his flaccid, yet still large dick back into his shorts. "I hate to cut and run on you like this…"

My wife replied on both our behalfs She waved a hand in an airy gesture of total unconcern, grinning as she purred, "Oh, don't worry, darling. At least I got a lovely orgasm out of it." Fiona's expression shifted to a look of feline smugness. "And you came, too, eh?" She slid a finger into her opening and winced. "Oh God," Fiona crooned. "Didn't you just come so much. I'm full of the stuff!"

"Well, I'm really sorry," Emmet replied. He opened his mouth to add something, but seemed reluctant to do so.

It seemed to me – as I recovered from the shock of seeing Emmet pumping jizm into my wife – that he wanted assurance that everything was all right between us. I noticed him glancing at me several times, like he wanted to know I was okay with everything.

The truth is, I was glad he was forced to leave. I had to talk to my wife. There were things I desperately needed to discuss. I needed Fiona's reassurances that no emotions had been sparked as a result of what looked to have been tremendous sex between the pair.

Fiona shook her head. "It's all right, Emmet. Truly. Do what you have to do." Then Fiona cast a look in my direction. She paused and then added, "If we want to, Emmet… Can… can we call you? Will you be able to come back again?"

Emmet's eyes widened, but he hesitated in replying, looking at me askance.

"Uh," he responded with a shrug. "Okay… If that's what you both want." Unable to suppress his delight at the implication, Emmet grinned and nodded with enthusiasm. "I'd really like that, Mrs Roberts. If Mister Roberts is okay with it…?"

"Hadn't you better go," my wife reminded him. "Isn't there some kind of domestic emergency?"

Emmet's pleased-as-punch look evaporated. "Oh shit," he blurted, adding a quick, apologetic, "Sorry, I shouldn't curse in front of the guests."

My wife laughed at the absurdity. There he was concerned about a minor swear word. Hadn't she just sucked his dick? Hadn't he licked my wife's pussy and fucked her? Wasn't his semen sliding from Fiona?

"Go," Fiona said, her attention fixed on me. "We need a little private time anyway."

Emmet went to leave, but a cry from Fiona stopped him at the door.

"Thank you," my wife breathed, throwing me an apologetic look before she rushed to him. "You've made me very happy, Emmet. You're very kind to make it a special birthday for me." Fiona kissed Emmet again, a languid, post-coital slide of tongues as the man's hand came round to squeeze Fiona's buttocks. "It was wonderful, babe." Next, after stepping back, smirking again, my wife finished with, "I had such a good time. You're a horny bastard, aren't you? I love your big cock."

Emmet grinned sheepishly and sucked in a deep breath. "Damn, Mrs Roberts…" he breathed, obviously reluctant to leave.

"Go," Fiona chuckled.

With a final nod and a sweep of Fiona's curves with his eyes, after a rueful grin in my direction, Emmet eventually left me alone with my wife.

Fiona was almost shy when she turned to regard me standing by the sofa. She offered me a conciliatory grin and murmured, "Shall we pour another drink and have a talk, Simon?"

***

We talked. My wife covered herself in a huge bath sheet after sluicing Emmet's ejaculate from her body. I poured the rum and dashed in the Coke over ice, sipping in a less agitated more reflective mode while waiting for her.

"So," Fiona said, taking a glass from me. She joined me on the settee, curling her legs beneath her. I watched her sip, eyes closed as she savoured the bite of spirits. When my wife opened her eyes again, she asked, "How do you feel?"

Wasn't *that* just *the* question! I pulled a face and shrugged, sighing as I analysed my feelings and emotions and realised I hadn't a clue.

I told her, "Fi, I have no idea just now."

She nodded, lips twisting in a look of, *Well, I suppose that's understandable.* "Do you hate me?" she asked, her tone tremulous.

I was quick to reassure her. "God no, Fi." Pausing, I took stock and tried to make sense of it all. "How can I?" I waved my glass and added, "After all, I brought it on. If I have to blame someone, I should blame myself."

"But it was *my* fantasy," Fiona puts in.

I held up a hand in objection. "Ah, but I was the one who arranged all this." I grimaced again, wincing as I confessed it all.

"You devious bugger," Fiona said after a long time looking at me. "You *planned* it? Between you? You and Emmet?"

"A few emails. I got him to send me a photo of his... erm... credentials. I sent him a picture of you in your bikini. One from that weekend in Brighton..."

Fiona's jaw dropped. "A bloody conspiracy," she murmured, shaking her head. "I should slap the pair of you – Hard!"

"I couldn't *tell* you, could I?" I said, petulant as a two-year-old denied sweets. Defensively, I added, "It seemed safest to just let you make up your own mind." I gave a half shrug. "If you wanted to, you would; if you didn't...

"I didn't want to put any pressure on you. I didn't want to spoil the surprise." I wondered with some trepidation where this would take us while I sucked in a deep breath. Was I going to get a slap from my wife? Would she go on a mad one of ranting and raving? "Wuh-what do you think, Fi? Huh-how do you feel?"

My wife's smirk told me I was in the clear. Relief flooded through me, that glorious sense usurping all of the conflict inside me.

"I think you're lucky I don't smack your face," Fiona grinned. Her eyes sparkled. "But it was bloody amazing, Simon. And all that stuff I said about trust...?

"I meant it. I'm not looking for someone permanent; I don't want to replace *you*."

"God, Fi," I cut in. "I was so jealous seeing you with him. When you told him to come inside you..." My cheeks ballooned. I couldn't articulate my feelings. It was all too new and complicated.

I saw my wife's face drop. Eyes downcast, she murmured, "Oh... Oh bloody hell, Simon. I'm so sorry."

I rushed on, babbling in my efforts to make it clear to Fiona. "No-no-no! No, Fi. That was just part of it. It's difficult to explain…"

Sucking in a deep breath and willing my wife to understand I hurried on.

"Seeing you with him, when you kissed Emmet and when you first… when his cock went into you." My throat worked, it was bird's nest time again, a dozen of them. "I hated seeing it, darling." Fiona's mouth opened. I could tell she was going to speak, but I held up a hand to quiet her. "I hated it, Fi, but in this really strange way it just made it hotter. It was weird. I mean, you're my wife – my *wife*. But there you were fucking this bloke right in front of me." My cheeks ballooned again, my cock swelling at the recollection of Fiona's body accepting Emmet's long cock. "You kissed him and he touched you…

"My God, Fi," I croaked, her gaze set on my face. "I was so stiff seeing you fucking."

Fiona stared at me, rapt. Her mouth hung open, her gaze bored into my face. "Did it really turn you on, Simon? Watching me and him?"

A snort came out of me. "I was so fired up, Fiona… Jesus!" Gasping, I ran my fingers through my hair. "I wanted to pull him off you and stick my cock into you instead. I wanted to give it to you so you could suck me at the same time as he fucked you, Fi."

"What about now?" Fiona asked.

Nodding, I quickly replied. "I'm stiff just remembering, babe."

My wife's words came out half-choked. "Show me."

Next thing I knew I was in front of her, trousers at my shins while she sat up and jacked my cock with one hand.

"I got fucked by a big black cock," my wife crooned, smirking up at me. "He stretched my cunt and pumped me full of cum."

"Fucking hell, Fi, don't. I can't take that."

"Oh, sorry," Fiona replied, completely misunderstanding. "I didn't mean it. I love you, Simon."

"No," I grunted, fucking into my wife's suddenly immobile fist. "I mean I can't take it because I'll come. You can tell me slutty stuff, but I'll come."

"Oh," Fiona said, nodding as she began to jack at me again. "You dirty fucker. You're going to get off because I fucked a lovely young stud?"

I whined and gulped and my wife smirked some more.

"Here," breathed Fiona, pulling the towel away from her torso. "Let me suck you. Let me wank you and just come when you want to. Come on my tits," my wife invited, thrusting her bosom forward. Spunk on my face, in my mouth or spray it all over my hair." Fiona's fist worked at me as she exhorted me to debauch her flesh. "I've been wicked," she smirked. "You should teach me a lesson."

It was heady stuff, it wasn't often Fiona let me loose over her face with a fountain of cum. It's happened but she's usually got to be drunk or in a very expansive mood. But there she was, actively encouraging me to do it, to sully her face or tits with ejaculate.

"You going to come?" my wife squeaked when I began to grunt and moan, fucking into her hand as she cranked at me. "Yeah, babe? You going to do it?"

"Ah fuck," I sobbed. "Fi… Babe… Oh fuck, Fiona…"

When it was over, I gaped down at the sight of my wife's face spattered with jizm. I'd poured a bucketful of semen over her. It was everywhere: on her forehead, sliding down her cheek, dollops of the stuff all over her while a shivering strand dangled from her chin, clinging tenaciously, a trembling strand of silver thread that refused to fall. A rope of cum glistened in Fiona's hair, her tits were smeared and there were dark stains on her hold-ups where cum had spattered down in a heavy rain.

"Oh. My. God!" my wife yelped, carefully wiping spunk away from her eyes. "I'm plastered. I'm fucking *covered* in the stuff."

I looked down, heart filled with love for my cum-spattered wife.

"I love you, too," Fiona replied when I told her how I felt. She even took hold of my cock and sucked the head between her lips, kissing the tip before slumping back, a huge sigh coming from her chest.

"Wow," Fiona said, eyes wide with wonderment. "What a birthday. I can't believe it. Jesus, Simon," she gasped, the realisation hitting her. "The things I said! And you were watching and listening. Oh God, I'm a slut!"

I sat down next to her, my trousers still bunched at my feet. Bare-arsed but still in shirt and tie, I took my drink and gulped.

"Fi?" I said.

My wife replied with a dreamy, "Hmm, what?"

"I know it isn't your birthday anymore in a couple of hours…"

Fiona looked at me. "Yeah. So?"

"Well, would you like to invite Emmet up to the room again? We've got a week or so left of the holiday and I just wondered."

Chapter Three

It became a regular thing. Each year we would fly out to Barbados and celebrate Fiona's birthday in Emmet's company. He cut corners for us every time, providing us with sumptuous accommodation for the price of a less salubrious room. In return, he got to ride the arse off my wife.

The second year, Fiona's forty-first birthday, saw us picking up from where we left off. During those early years I was mainly an observer, a voyeur, watching Fiona and her lover while the same exquisite turmoil raged away inside me. Some nights Fiona took Emmet's cock, others she got the good news from me – and wasn't I ardent!? Wasn't I especially concerned with putting in a damn fine performance because of the competition?

Fiona loved it all. She adored the male attention, both me and Emmet working hard to give her as much pleasure as she wanted. She told me her anticipation heightened in the weeks leading up to the lewd rendezvous. By the time we arrived in Barbados my wife was a quivering wreck, indecently enthusiastic to take her lover.

In the fourth year, I began to join in. Fiona called me over so she could suck me, with Emmet filling her pussy with black cock while my wife slurped at me.

It went like that from then on, the next stage progressing to pictures of Fiona in action. Video followed. My wife enjoys occasionally looking back at her times with Emmet. We watch the films together, Fiona squealing with delighted embarrassment when she first sees herself going for it. The sex is awesome during those evenings at home in front of the television, the laptop plugged in, a private porn-fest on the screen for Fiona's delectation. Winter nights fly by.

And, yes, I get a kick out of seeing it, too.

Then Fiona's fiftieth appeared: a smudge on the horizon. It was Emmet who made the suggestion. An idea formed from a chance blurt from Fiona during one of their trysts.

So, as the big plane touched down and our private transfer whisked us to the hotel, Fiona had no idea what we had in mind for a most sordid celebration of her birthday.

As usual, Emmet met us at the door. "I can't believe it's been ten years," Fiona said, kissing his cheek.

"Mrs Roberts," he replied, grinning, outwardly professional as ever. "A pleasure to see you again, ma'am." He offered me his large hand to shake. "Mister Roberts, sir... Welcome back."

I shook the man's hand and played the game, fully aware he would be fucking his big dick into my wife's cunt very soon.

I shivered when the image popped into my head.

By then Emmet was the second highest manager in the place, with his eye on further progression. Over the previous decade, as he climbed the ladder, Emmet had taken on a more cultured façade, polishing his act. He still had the engaging Caribbean lilt but wore impeccable suits as a mark of increased status, the uniform of the tailored shorts and polo shirts a thing of the past for him.

Seeing him presented as he was Emmet appeared every inch the calm, unflappable hotel manager – although a good number of those inches were reserved for my wife.

"Top suite this year, Mrs Roberts," Emmet went on. "Private pool right up there." He pointed towards the sky. Then, in a break from his usual public propriety Emmet leaned in and whispered, "You can walk around naked up there, Mrs Roberts..."

He chuckled when Fiona quipped back with a murmured, "And I thought you loved me in a bikini and high heels, Emmet darling."

Not long after their quick exchange, we were upstairs, with both Fiona and I blinking at the sheer acreage of our suite.

"Oh my," Fiona enthused when she clocked the pool. "And this is just for us?"

"Exclusive, Mrs Roberts," Emmet confirmed. He joined Fiona at the big sliding doors and looked out at the patio beyond. "Completely private." He checked his watch and gave my wife a grin before turning to look at me. "If you like," suggested Emmet, eyes twinkling, "you could try it now?"

Fiona gave me a look of enquiry, questioning me with her eyebrows arched.

"It isn't your birthday for two more days," I returned, teasing her. I threw a smile at Emmet. "But if you want to test the water, Fi..."

Giggling, Fiona stripped and was quickly naked. She posed for Emmet while watching him remove his suit jacket. Emmet hung it on a rail to avoid unsightly creases – he had a reputation to maintain after all.

"You too, Simon," my wife trilled. "I want both my gorgeous men."

Emmet paused, half his shirt buttons undone as he admired Fiona's toned body and sunbed tan. "Looking good, Mrs Roberts," he commented favourably, a moue of appreciation pursing his lips while he ogled Fiona's breasts. "You got a nice colour there. I like it, baby; I like it *a lot*. You've got it *all* happening, woman. I can't believe you're fifty. You're hot, Mrs Roberts. I've been waiting for you, baby."

My wife chuckled, fingers at her pelvis, head canted and one hip cocked. "I've been working out hard this year, Emmet. I wanted to look good for you." Then she burst out laughing as she said, "You getting excited, babe? Your accent's slipped."

Emmet was down to his socks, big cock waggling. He pulled the socks off his feet and said, "I can relax with you two. We're friends, yeah?"

"The three of us," Fiona purred moving in to take hold of her lover's thick root. "Come here, Simon," my wife purred. "Kiss me, darling." I went to the pair and gave my wife the most fervent of kisses. "My two gorgeous boys," Fiona whispered, her hands ski-poling two cocks, one dark and enormous, the other pale and less substantial.

Emmet slid open the glass doors and padded out onto the patio. Fiona followed.

I watched them at it. I was hard and horny, the usual feelings welling up while my wife lay on a sunbed, legs wide while Emmet stuffed his big dick into her. The pair fucked and kissed, with me in the perfect position to film it all when his cock pulsed and the man flooded Fiona with semen. I went in close when Emmet eased back, his long cock taking an age to slide out, my wife's cunt gaping, a slide of cum dribbling out.

That was the first time I went in after Emmet. I couldn't help myself. I was so worked up, so desperate to come.

"Mix it up, darling," Fiona moaned, her eyes shining. "Stir it up. Fuck me. Fuck into his cum."

I kissed my wife and pumped jizm into her not long after I slid my dick into the gloopy mess

"I'm coming, Fi," I moaned, leaning in to slip my tongue into her mouth. "I love you. God, babe, I love you…"

A couple of days later we revealed Fiona's birthday surprise.

***

"What?" my wife gulped, boggling at me. "No… No way, Simon…"

"It's up to you, Fi," I shrugged. "You've talked about it…" I eyed my wife, eyebrows arched. "…now you've got the chance."

"You're *serious*?" gasped Fiona.

It was my turn to gulp. It was the same mix of confused emotions as when I'd first set it up between Emmet and Fiona. I didn't know how I felt, not properly. I knew I wanted it to happen, but the consequences worried me, the old jealousy percolating away.

"Yeah," I replied, deliberately nonchalant. "Emmet won't be involved. He doesn't want to risk his job." Shrugging again, I gave Fiona a look that I hoped suggested she could take it or leave it. "But they can come up to the suite. It's all set. They're just waiting for me to call."

"Simon… a gangbang? That's what you're suggesting. *Four* of them? Dear God."

Oddly torn by the prospect, appalled at it and drawn simultaneously I felt a flutter of alarm and a rush of relief. Alarm because I thought it was going to sip away, relief because I wasn't sure I could bear to see four men with my wife.

"But you've said before--"

My wife's eyes rolled as she sighed. She was standing in front of me while I sat in one of the easy chairs. It was Fiona's birthday and she was all dressed up, platinum blonde hair immaculate, make-up subtle and understated. For the occasion my wife had squeezed her impressive frontage into the tight bodice of a long evening gown, a six drop suspender belt underneath the dress, the straps attached to black stockings. She wore a triple strand of pearls, real ones that nestled in the deep crease of her cleavage, the round inner flanks of her breasts squeezed together, visible through the keyhole.

"Jesus, Simon," interrupted Fiona, "is there no fantasy of mine you won't fulfil?"

I was confused by that. I couldn't decide if she was pleased or not. Looking up at her, I gulped out, "What? Eh?"

"First it was Emmet... And that's been going on for ten years, babe. Now you're suggesting *four*?"

I pulled a face and nodded warily as I drawled, "Ye-e-s..."

"Four, Simon." Fiona studied my face intently. "You think I'll let four strangers come up here and shag me?"

A leaden sinker plummeted into the pit of my stomach. "Shit," I groaned, head in my hands. "Fi... Oh shit, I'm sorry."

I heard my wife chuckle. "I didn't say no, Simon..."

My head snapped up.

"But I'd like to know what the score is. I mean, they *are* strangers. I might not fancy them, for God's sake."

"Emmet knows one of them," I babbled. "He reckons his mate's a solid enough bloke. He's not dodgy – you now, not into anything illegal."

"But he'll fuck a white woman with three of his friends? No," my wife added, voice heavy with the irony. "He's not dodgy at all, Simon."

I heard the amusement in Fiona's tone. I could see by her face she was only teasing me with that comment.

"You know what I mean, Fi," I replied. "It's the same for us. We're not dodgy and we've been involved in sexy stuff for years."

My wife nodded and murmured a soft, "Darling, I know. I just want to know a little bit about them. I'd feel like a... a... a real slut. My God," she added on a gasp, "it's a bloody gangbang, Simon. You expect me to be all calm and like 'Sure, come on up and fuck me, boys. The more the merrier!'"

"All right, well, like I said, one of them is Emmet's friend. He can vouch for the bloke. And let's face it, Fi, Emmet's been solid with us for all this time. Plus," I held up a forefinger to emphasise my point, "he's got a lot to lose if it goes out of control. If he trusts them enough to let them come up here, I reckon they'll be okay."

Fiona's head tilted. She looked at me with her bottom lip curled, hands on her pelvis, expression contemplative. "If I say yes, Simon," my wife said in a firm tone. "I'll have to take a look at them first. If I don't like the look or if I don't feel comfortable, then it's not on."

I spread my hands. "It was always going to be that way, Fi. I'm thinking more about this being fun for you. It's a birthday special, for your fiftieth. I'm not doing it for me, love; I thought it was something you sort of wanted to do."

Shaking her head in apparent wonder, my wife said, "You never fail to surprise me, Simon." She chuckled and gave me a rueful smile. "I don't know of any woman whose husband would let her have a lovely black cock each year – for ten years, and *then* calmly drop it into the conversation that he's arranged a group fuck."

Fiona stared at me in a way that brought emotion into my throat. My chest swelled with love for her as she added, "You love me enough to give me a run of my fantasies, babe. You really do love me, don't you?"

"It's just sex, Fi," I managed to croak. "We go back to normal when we're at home."

My wife's smile softened even more. "I've never been unfaithful, Simon," she murmured. I saw Fiona's eyes shimmer as she went on with, "I've never gone behind your back, darling. The thing with Emmet has been enough. And before that, I never once fucked around on you."

"You didn't have to tell me that, Fiona. I trust you, babe."

Fiona sucked in a deep breath, a long sigh coming out of her while we gazed at each other. "Oh God," she groaned. "I suppose you should call."

I gulped, the reality of it twisting my guts.

My hand trembled when I lifted the phone to call Emmet.

***

It was more of a party at first. We had beer and spirits, ice and mixers. I called for pizza via room service and we ate it on the deck outside, inevitable reggae coming from the Bose system installed in the suite. It was incongruous, with Fiona formally attired in her dress while I was in a suit, the four local men wearing casual tailored shorts and button-fronted, loose-fitting shirts.

At first it was all a bit stilted, Fiona still in mild shock at the surprise I'd engineered while the men were subdued, all of it understandable given the peculiar circumstances. I was in that state of high agitation after the enormity of the situation hit me full-on. The memory of the initial scene with Emmet had faded. The intensity of my emotional turmoil was diluted by a decade of seeing my wife with him. But there it was again, renewed, this time fourfold. It wasn't a single encounter my wife was about to enjoy, there were four of them.

Eventually, as we sat on the edges of the deck chairs arranged around the pool, the terrace lit by the lights inside the suit rather than the outside light above the sliding doors, my wife looked and me and asked if I was all right with everything.

I nodded while anticipation and arousal sloshed around in cocktail mix – the arousal laced with jealousy. "What about you, Fi?"

I wanted to ask her if she was game to take them all on but dreaded she would say yes.

"Fine," she responded, studying me.

I felt my throat work as I swallowed heavily. At last it came out of me. "Do you," I croaked, pausing to clear the usual blockage. "Do you want to do it?"

Angst spiked inside me when my wife murmured, "Oh yes, Simon. Yes please. I do. Very much."

Fiona drained her rum and coke and held the glass to me. Then she stood up, heels thunking on the deck.

"You want a refill?" I mewled while Fiona eyed the rapt audience around her.

"Yes," she replied, not looking at me. "What do you say, boys? Shall we get this party started?"

The oldest of the group threw a look at me. I didn't know if it was contempt or pity in his expression. To Fiona, he said, "You wanna take that dress off?"

Oh God the agony that cut through me when my wife purred out, "Oh yes," her eyes gleaming like the light reflected from the pool. "But you boys have to strip, too. I'll feel so awkward if I'm the only one."

The man smirked and looked at his friends. "You first, baby," he crooned, his voice deep and melodic.

"Can I get that drink, Simon?" my wife insisted. "And could you help with the zip?" The last was directed to the man with the deep voice.

All of the men had been introduced to me by name, but I was so on edge I couldn't retain the information.

Mesmerised by what was happening, I stayed put, my attention focussed on the man easing the zip down over the curve of Fiona's spine. With her back to the group, she let the dress fall to her waist, shimmying to send it pooling at her feet.

There were some mutterings and a gasp or two when the exquisite shape of her was revealed, ribald chuckling and finger-snapping coming from the boys when they saw Fiona's six-drop and stockings.

Next, with her hands splayed over her breasts, my wife turned, palms covering her big tits and fleshy nipples.

I heard them commenting favourably on Fiona's physique, her stockings and shoes getting some attention, too. Then there were more when Fiona took her hands away, a few wolf whistles amid the collective buzz of admiration.

"Will I do, lads?" my wife gurgled, posing with her hands on her hips as she grinned at them. She knew too well that she looked good. Fiona had worked hard to maintain her figure. I could tell by her face she was thrumming with desire, her dimpled cheeks and bright eyes told me as much. The timbre of Fiona's voice, the slight warble to her tone was another give-away.

"Ooh, yeah," the main man crooned, head bobbing.

"Simon, babe, a drink, please," Fiona reminded me.

I scuttled away and poured. When I returned the men were naked and grouped around my wife. The oldest was kissing her, his hands on her breasts while the other three grabbed at whatever exposed skin they could get their hands on, one of them with his fingers between Fiona's legs.

After that, with me operating the video and stills camera in turn, I endured over four hours of debauchery while Fiona sucked cock after cock, her pussy getting well and truly fucked.

The man with the deep voice insisted on condoms. "Nothin' personal, Fiona," he said before he fucked into my wife's pussy for the first time. "But I don't wanna risk nuthin, man. Yeah, I know Emmet says it's jus' him and your husband…" He offered a rueful, somewhat apologetic smile to my wife before adding, "But, baby, you like to fuck… And you *are* hot… I jus' don' want to take chances with my dick."

It could have been an insult, and I'm surprised Fiona accepted the comments with such good grace.

"I swear it's just been my husband and Emmet. I'm not usually such a slut." Then Fiona shrugged and, as she cranked at two hard cocks with both hands, the fourth man sucking at her breasts, she finished with, "But I understand. It makes sense." My wife glanced at me. "I'd feel safer that way as well."

Hours later, used condoms littered the decking. I counted fourteen in all. Some of the men had fucked Fiona and not come, pulling the johnny-bag off in between goes as they sank their beers and drank their rum. Some of the condoms were heavy with cum, others lay there like shed snakeskins, loose and baggy and shrivelled.

By then my formerly immaculate wife was a bedraggled mess. Her hair was a rat's nest from where their fingers had grabbed at her, the men eager to get Fiona's mouth around their cocks' as she knelt and they encircled her early on in the proceedings. She had spunk on her face and over her breasts; her stockings were torn and stained with silvery snail-trails of spunk.

They'd each come twice, sometimes into the condom as they fucked Fiona, other times making obscene comments about slutty white bitches as they fired right at Fiona's face or over her tits or even splashed spunk across her buttocks.

My wife, for her part, loved it all. She groaned and moaned and begged them to give her the good news. Whatever position they demanded, she was there. I saw Fiona on her hands and knees being spit-roasted, her attention going from cock to cock as the three not in her pussy offered her their dicks.

She rode on long black pole, tits swaying, usually as someone fucked into her mouth, my wife's muffled cries of pleasure coming from around a mouth full of male gristle.

It was truly terrible to see. I could barely stand to watch my lovely wife being used that way. I was in agony, but, as it always had been, I was so bloody aroused by it all as well.

In the end, after the men left and it was just the two of us in the suite, I fucked into her, my mouth locked against hers. I was mindless to the state of her. I didn't care she'd been sucking cock for hours. All I wanted to do was reclaim her. I used my dick and pummelled her scarlet cunt, pouring my seed into her, groaning out how much I loved her as my ejaculate spurted forth.

"Happy birthday, darling," I groaned.

The End

Here is a sample from another story you may enjoy:

* * *

He was ten minutes late. He stood on the doorstep, mortified.

Luis apologised profusely. "I am so sorry, Jan," he said, almost wringing his hands with sincerity. "I hate being late for my clients. I *hate* it," he hissed with Latin fervour.

Jan waved his protestations away. "Don't worry, Luis. It isn't as though I've signed up yet, is it. I'm not a proper client."

"Even more reason I should not be late, Jan." He shrugged and pulled a face, finally taking in the incongruity. "I ... uhm..." Luis began, blinking in surprise. He pointed to Jan's feet. "I don't think you should wear those for training, Jan."

Luis's late arrival gave Jan the excuse she needed. "Oh, the Jimmy Choos?" she said, then lifted one foot. Jan examined the decorative tassels adorning suede straps, the shoes featuring a metal and suede chain that fastened around the ankle. "A shimmering leopard print at the back of the shoe," she informed a clueless Luis. "4.7 inch heels *might* be a little dangerous," Jan conceded with a smirk. "But I was just trying them on. I thought I'd have a little time. They were a gift from my husband. What do you think?"

Still standing at the front door, Luis glanced over Jan's shoulder. "Your husband is home?"

Shaking her head, Jan replied with, "Oh, no, Luis. No-no-no. He's away overseas on business." She offered the man a smile. "Won't you come in?"

Blinking again, Luis followed Jan into the house, his eyes taking in the odd yet extremely pleasing sight of a shapely woman in a tight leotard cut high on her hips who was also wearing high heels.

"I, uh, think those shoes are very nice, Jan," he said as Jan led him along the corridor.

"Thank you, Luis," the woman replied. "This is my little gym," she introduced with a flourish when she opened the door. "I hope you can show me how all the..." Jan paused on a sigh and non-too-subtly added, "...*equipment* works."

It took some effort for Luis to drag his eyes away from that lascivious smirk. But he eventually managed it, somehow contriving to appear interested in the fitness apparatus.

"What--" he gurgled, clearing his throat of the bird's nest lodged there before continuing. "What do you hope to achieve, Jan?"

Luis desperately tried to avoid the woman's intense and very disturbing gaze.

This wasn't a first for the trainer. He'd experienced the come-on before, and – so far – resisted the seductive advances of horny females.

But this one ... *this* one, with her big round tits, fantastic legs, sly smile and those fucking shoes...

She had the edge on the others, and Luis was so tempted to relinquish his proud professionalism and succumb to her obvious desire.

He stepped further into the room, following Jan, her heels giving off a hollow thunk-thunk against the parquet flooring when she moved.

Jan sat astride the rowing machine, back straight, impressive frontage thrust forward.

"I think I'm in good shape already," she said, throwing a meaningful look at Luis. "But I'd like to tone up a bit. My arms, my tummy and legs…

"I want to look good when I go out, Luis. I want men … *young* men to look at me."

Jan's voice dropped to a husky murmur that settled a blanket of anticipation over them both.

"I want gorgeous young men to look at me, and I want them to want me."

Luis gulped, boggling at Jan. His mouth opened and closed a few time until he finally blurted, "But, what about your husband?"

"What about him?" Jan replied, shrugging one shoulder. Then she just came out with it. "How about I suck your cock?"

Luis succumbed, with the straightforward question so abruptly delivered robbing him of the capacity to think. He couldn't formulate a response in time, and before he knew it, Jan had yanked at the elastic waist of his tracksuit bottoms and brought his cock bouncing out, the thing already halfway to an erection.

His penis stiffened considerably when Jan's fist cranked at it, her gasp and subsequent murmur of appreciation aiding its swift growth.

"Oh, God," Jan breathed, her habitual breathless response during sex. She was doing it. This was it; her first adventure planned and executed; her first deliberate cuckolding of Charles.

Jan didn't count Paul as deliberate. In Jan's mind their sexual liaison was a residual effect of what had happened in the workshop, the result of her carnal epiphany.

"I hope I've got condoms big enough for you," the woman breathed, eyes fixed on the tumescent length.

She eased Luis closer by squeezing his cock and gently pulling him round as she swivelled at the waist. Next, Jan jacked Luis's erection several times, threw a glance up to register the shocked expression on his face, and then took him between her lips.

Luis moaned, fingers pushing into Jan's short hair as he tried to take a handful in his grip.

"Jan…" the man mumbled, the sounds of her slurping coming up to taunt him. "Ah, fuck…"

"Mmm," Jan responded, cheeks concave.

She held Luis's cock fast with her mouth while easing the lycra skin of the leotard around the outer flanks of her breasts. Then Jan massaged her boobs and allowed the thick erection to spring from her lips, the thing disengaging with a distinctly juicy plop.

Then she rose to her feet to offer her tits to her lover.

The sight of the distended nipples, Jan's teats long and thick in the coins of their areolae, inflamed the young man, and any doubts about giving Jan what she wanted evaporated along with concerns about her marital status.

Luis grabbed breast-flesh, squeezing against pliant resistance while simultaneously moaning and bending to suck a nipple.

Jan lifted the man's head from her breast…

If you enjoyed this sample then look for **Making Him Watch**.

Also by this Author:

From the Author

If you enjoyed any of my books then please share the love and promote my books in Amazon.

If you write me a review and send me an email I will send you a free book, or many.
(Just know that these emails are filtered by my publisher.)

Good news is always welcome.

One Last Thing, For Kindle Readers...

When you turn the page, Kindle will give you the opportunity to rate this book and share your thoughts on Facebook and Twitter. If you enjoyed my writings, would you please take a few seconds to let your friends know about it? Because... when they enjoy they will be grateful to you and so will I.

Thank You!

Ben E. Dorm
ben_e_dorm@awesomeauthors.org

About the Author

Ben E. Dorm is a former soldier. Having spent 22 years in the British army, Ben now spends his time travelling, most recently through Central America and South East Asia.

He writes every day unless he's sitting on a bus or a train, working on scenes he hopes readers will enjoy.

You may also like the books by these authors:

* * *

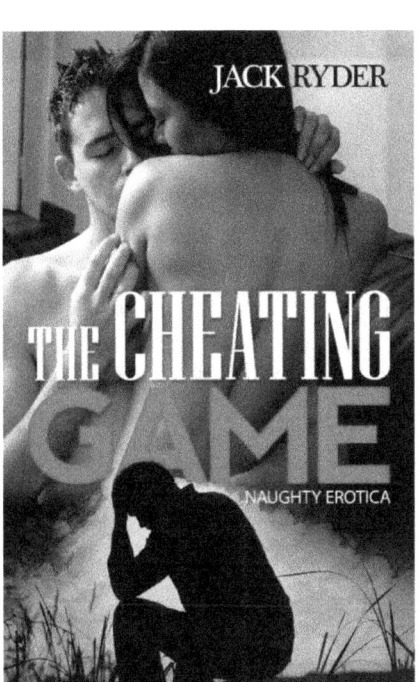

I can't really remember exactly how I came up with the idea. The WHY is as clear as day, even after all these years. The entire motivation behind my sly little plan was driven by a deep rage fueled lust to get even with a malicious infidelity and to fulfill a childhood fantasy. I had fantasized about my sexy MILF mother-in-law ever since I started dating her daughter way back in high school. I had been leery of my best friend Peter's lust for my wife almost nearly as long. It would ultimately be those two things thrown together by circumstance, that would drive me to make the plan and take the actions that I have.

But I am getting way ahead of myself here. I should start at the beginning, so you may understand why this happened and maybe you won't hate me in the end. It's not like I ruined anyone's life or physically hurt anyone. Although I manipulated some situations, I did not force anyone to do the things they did all by themselves willingly. Although I started some wheels in motion, the results found a momentum of their own. The bottom line is that cheaters cheat and I took full advantage of that.

I would have to say that the event that started the ball rolling, happened the night of my bachelor party. It wasn't a surprise to anyone that Nikki and I were gonna tie the knot. We have been inseparable since we first met on the first day of high school. My best friend Pete has been the only other significant person that has been part of the last three years of our lives, along with Nikki's mom Krysta.

Nikki and I wanted to get married right after graduation, so we would have some time together before she travelled across the state to attend college. We knew the distance would keep us apart for certain amounts of time, but we were both determined to continue our plans so we could build a successful life together. I would stay home and continue working, so I could take over my father's company someday. Nikki would complete her education and someday become my accountant. We had a plan and we were certain that we could make it work.

Pete insisted on throwing a big bachelor party. It was sort of embarrassing that most of the fellows that attended that night were really Pete's friends. Although I knew most of the fellows, they were just mostly acquaintances from various school functions. I had asked Pete to keep the party a low key event, but he went all out anyway. It was my initial feeling that Pete just wanted to seem like a big shot to all his other buddies. It wouldn't be till some time later, that he had an entirely different motive.

It was really your average rented bar sort of bachelor party. Complete with strippers, lap dancers, and a lot of liquor consumption. I was pleased that he had at least thought ahead enough to contact a shuttle bus taxi service to get everyone home safely. I made it a point to not get nearly as drunk as the rest of the fellows. But it seemed like Pete was trying his best to force more drinks on my way even if I left them untouched.

Throughout the evening, each of the strippers made their way over to kiss and rub their mostly nude bodies all over the groom to be. It was very unsettling to me as the fellows took cell phone photos each time they did it. But I didn't make a big deal about it, since they were taking photos of all the girls rubbing all over the other fellows as well. I did notice that Pete seemed to get quite excited each time he took photos of the girls humping on me. He seemed to have a huge grin as he snapped his shots. Just before midnight, shortly after I told Pete I was about ready to go home, one of the strippers pushed me down onto my chair and proceeded to sit on my lap for a lap dance.

The fellows were all whooping and hollering, as she ripped off her top and shoved her big hooters in my face. When I saw the flashes from Pete's camera, I knew how this could look if Nikki ever saw them. As I grasped her hips to lift her off, her unfastened bikini bottom fell off and Pete snapped a photo with her nude body pressed against mine.

To purchase the book, look for **The Cheating Game.**

* * *

My name is Dan and this is the story of how I became my wife's slave. I know that sounds strange, and believe me, when you learn the whole story, you'll *know* it's strange. Even to this day, when I think about everything that's happened in the last 10 years, I don't believe it. But then again, reality has a way of rearing its ugly head and reminding you of what's real and what's not.

I guess a little background is in order. I was born into a very wealthy east-coast family. And they were very conservative. My grandfather had been a senator and my father a two-term governor. My mother was a Mayflower descendant and a power in the highest of the social orders in which our lives revolved. I went to the best prep schools, then Yale and finally the Wharton School of Economics.

When I was young, I was always the biggest guy in my class. Today, I stand 6'5" and 240 pounds. I played all sports and usually ended up being the team captain. I won so many letters in sports that they wouldn't fit on my sweaters. I had many offers of scholarships to college, both academic and athletic. I was an All-American athlete in college football and basketball.

I had literally won the lucky sperm club lottery. I was incredibly blessed in all ways. I never got less than an A in all of my schooling. That's straight A's right through my Master's degree in economics. I'm not bragging, just trying to let you realize that I am not some weirdo from a disadvantaged background, some sort of a physical or psychological weakling that was easily led astray.

I also managed to be myself, making it a point to avoid discussing family and things of that nature, always keeping my responses vague. I had learned early on that people were usually far too impressed by who my family was and that led them to overlook who I actually was. So the few people who actually knew who I was gave me the space to be myself and kept the secret so that I could have as normal a college life as possible.

As I was growing up, girls just seemed to be a part of everything. Being the big sports hero made it possible for a parade of girls to be always available. But I had one problem that was sort of two-edged. My cock is just over 10 inches, and most girls, while very eager to see it and play with it, were just unable to handle all of it. I never saw more than two or three inches of it disappear into a mouth, and never had a girl who would let me bury the whole thing in her pussy. Usually they'd try, some of them several times, but eventually it was just too big and they'd move on.

But word spread and there was never any lack of girls willing to try. Most guys thought I was the luckiest person in the world, but they just didn't know how incredibly frustrating it actually was.

Then I met Lucy just as I was finishing up my Master's degree. Of all places to meet, I met her in a bar I had never been in, just happened to stop in for a beer one day when I was thirsty and had noticed their sign.

Lucy was a waitress. She had very short black hair, sparkling green eyes, a very full set of tits filling her bra, and all in a package just a bit over 5 feet tall. Her personality was so engaging and friendly, a smile seemed to be permanently plastered on her face. She seemed to know everyone by name and obviously liked her job. She was so friendly and seemingly flirty that I actually stammeringly asked her if she'd like to go out sometime. I remember her stopping and really giving me a look-over, slowly, from top to bottom. She had a hand on her chin and was chewing her lower lip as she appraised me before finally nodding and agreeing to go out.

Our first date was one of the best times I ever had with a woman up until then. She turned out to be very well-read and interested in just about everything under the sun. When the day finally ended and I took her home, she shocked me by asking if I'd be interested in spending the night.

She laughed at the astonished look on my face as I stood there with my mouth hanging open. Our date had been purely platonic. There had been no sexual tension at all. Her company had been so stimulating and enjoyable, the usual stuff had just never cropped up.

"It's just that I'm really horny and I thought you might enjoy getting laid," she had said.

"Well, yeah," I stammered. "I just wasn't thinking... I just wasn't expecting..."

To purchase the book, look for **Green-Eyed Lucy**.

* * *

John Peters didn't know what his first birth was like, but his second one was agonizing. He remembered the pain, the drowsy driver crossing lanes, the sounds of crushing and crumpling metal and glass, the fire, and the screaming of his lungs out as they were seared by the very air he breathed. This passed and he felt a new sensation of someone using his/her hands to move his legs. Then came the hot kiss of a lash, and he felt as if he were being flogged forever when he tried to open his eyes to scream. Then the pain turned to pleasure and as it continued till the lash fell.

The scream came out as a gurgle, a whisper. His eyes opened to see light blue walls all around him and that he was in a bed. A woman in surgical scrubs was moving his legs and feet, stretching them, moving them back and forth at the ankles and knees. The woman was pleasant, not pretty in the formless clothes she wore, but with her red hair back in a short ponytail. Expressive green eyes is now wide and watching him.

She had stopped what she was doing and was watching a machine beside him. The steady *beep beep* was replaced by something wilder and erratic.

As soon as the woman lets go of his foot, the sensation of being flogged stopped. The combined sensation of pain and pleasure stopped and the machine keeps beeping at a faster pace. She had rushed to his side, and was watching him struggle to form words with his mouth that no longer seemed to work. The noises coming from his mouth were just gargles and hisses.

She left in a hurry and somehow the presence of the fast beeping machine beside him was not an acceptable trade. Still trying to form words, he croaked for help. Where the heck was he and what was happening?

He managed to move his head a little, and look towards left and right. He was in a hospital ward of some kind and bodies on beds were to the left and right of him. Still with IV bags on stands and tubes everywhere, he was sure that he was unmoved. He tried to move his arms and found his arms free and couldn't move a little, since he was so weak.

Minutes passed, the silence was incredible except for the steady drone of the machines and the low beeping noises from all around him. The silence was replaced by the sound of footfalls. He heard hard soled shoes and squeaky rubber ones on tiled floors, walking in a hurry. A nurse in a white uniform and a man in a lab coat flapping behind were at his side. He was older, judging by the wrinkles and gray hair.

"You are awake?" the man in a lab coat asked.

He tried to say "Yes I am and where am I?" but all that came out was a series of croaks and guttural sounds. He did see a name embroidered on the lab coat stating that his name was D. Burns M.D.

He looked at John a few moments, then told the nurse to get some water and straw. He waited till she returned. He poured some room temperature water in a glass, added the straw, and held it to John's lips.

John sucked in the fluid and his mouth seemed to absorb it before the liquid got to his cheeks. The second pull on the straw was better and it got into his throat with the same effect. The third pull went down his throat and soon the dryness and tickling was gone. He pushed the straw away with his tongue and tried to speak again. This time, it came out in a whisper, but intelligible for his ears, it sounded weak and pitiful. "Where am I and how long have I been here?"

The Doctor had to lean closer to hear him. "We will get to that soon, but do you remember your name?"

John whispered his full name to the doctor, then sighed, this was going to be a memory test. Then, while he could, he rattled off his address and anything else that came to mind including his high school and college. The doctor pulled back to look at him. "And what's the last thing you remember?"

"Car, a big white SUV crossing the center line, I couldn't avoid it. I tried running my car onto the sidewalk, it happened fast, the fire, and me screaming." John managed to whisper. "What about my car?"

To purchase the book, look for **The Flog Zone**.

* * *

I am a professional masseuse, and have been for many years. When I say professional, I mean that I do massage strictly with no funny business, or hanky panky. My husband is a successful businessman, so I don't have to work as hard as some of my other LMT friends, but I take my work very seriously. My kids are old enough so that my not being at home when they get home from school is not an issue anymore either. This allows me the freedom to set a pretty flexible schedule.

I have a pair of clients, a husband and wife couple, that I have been massaging for quite a number of years. Doug and Diane are a very active couple with two kids in junior high school. Doug designs websites and Diane owns a floral shop. They do very nicely. Their house is up in the hills on about 10 acres of land, with a spectacular view. We have gotten very friendly over the years, like old friends. When I go to massage them, we usually sit and talk for awhile and have a glass of wine on the deck. They are such regular clients that I leave one of my massage tables at their house; they dedicated a room to it. Our relationship has always been totally professional.

Until recently.

A couple of weeks ago, I got a call from Doug, on the morning of one of our appointments, asking if he could meet me for lunch. This was a bit of an irregular request but we had become close enough client/friends that I agreed and we met at a nice restaurant near his office. We chatted for awhile, about family stuff, some business chit chat until he got around to the point and mentioned their upcoming 17th anniversary; coming up the following weekend. They had both agreed that they wanted to do something really special. Doug seemed very nervous. I asked him what was wrong.

"This is really tough to say," he stammered. "And I don't want to make you feel weird." He paused a while before continuing. "Diane and I both really enjoy your company. We think of you as a good friend, as well as our health professional." I told him that I considered them more than simply clients. "Well, we wanted to,...well, ask you if..." He trailed off again.

"I'm not following." I told him.

"We really don't want to risk our friendship with you." He said slowly. "We wanted to know if...you would consider...getting closer."

"Closer?" I asked, unsure what he meant.

"Well, at the risk of offending you, ..." He was starting to hem and haw about our earlier discussion about professionalism with my work, keeping it totally professional. "We were wondering if you would consider indulging us in a more,... sensual,... kind of massage."

"More sensual?" I asked. "You mean sexual?"

"No, no." He stumbled. "Well, unless..." There was a long look between us, wherein I said nothing.

"This is not going, ... you know, forget it. I'm sorry if, ..." We shared a long fairly awkward silence. I think I know what he was saying, and with any other person, I would be up and out of there already. I knew these people, though. This was not something that would drive me out of my chair as I thought it might. I really liked them and Doug was really embarrassed now.

"Hey. It's okay." I told him, trying to prevent him having the heart attack he appeared to be having. I admit that I was intrigued as to what they might be considering, as a couple. It was their anniversary after all. "Just tell me what's on your mind."

"Diane was in a panic over being the one to ask, but now I wish she was here, ..." I simply waited, trying not to look as flustered as I felt. I had only had to deal with these kinds of come-ons a couple of times, and had simply packed my shit and walked out; perhaps a bit stern a response but I wasn't having this discussion with strangers, men.

"Diane and I both really like you. We both think that you're awesome at what you do. And ... honestly ... we both find you very attractive, and we have both been considering ... you know ... a ... something different." Doug's hands were fluttering as if trying to not say something too outlandish. "Not that you ...", he stammered. I smiled at him.

"When I started in this line of work, I swore that I would never get involved in anything sexual with my clients." He looked a bit sad and ashamed for asking. "Don't get me wrong, I'm very flattered that you are asking. I think that you are both very attractive. Very! I suppose if I was ever to consider something like that, it would probably be with people like you two."

"But, ..." he trailed off. "I hope that you're not offended."

"No. Truly."

"I'm sorry. I really am. I hate to make you feel uncomfortable." I assured him that it was fine; that I wasn't, though secretly I was. My mind was suddenly filled with thoughts of what they might be thinking. I caught myself flashing on both their bodies. I had been their massage therapist for a while and had seen most of them already. Diane's bottom flashed into my mind, unbidden. I had to shake my head to clear it. "Will you still make our appointment tonight?"

I patted his hand. "Of course. Believe me. It's okay." He remained uncomfortable through the rest of lunch and seemed ready as hell to get out of there. The conversation was perfunctory at best; the kids' schooling, the weather; it was agony. I tried to think of something to ease his mind. I didn't want them to be embarrassed for their appointments tonight. He shook my hand rather mechanically when we stepped out onto the street, and he walked away rather briskly. I felt so bad for him. Why I didn't feel worse for myself, I don't know.

I didn't mention my lunch to my husband when I got home, as there wasn't enough time to really get into it. The kids needed feeding and then homework had to be done. I left them in front of the TV as I headed out. Later that evening when I got to their house, I felt like Diane in particular was really embarrassed. It remained that way until we were alone and I was massaging her.

I worked on her in silence until I asked, "Are you okay?"

"Yeah, I'm fine. Why?"

"You seem so quiet."

"Oh, I'm sorry. It's just that … well, I'm a little embarrassed." I asked her about what.

"Well, having Doug ask you to help us with our little … fantasy."

"Oh, please. Don't be embarrassed. Besides, we didn't really get into that much detail."

"I'm sorry for putting you on the spot like that."

"Please don't be." I told her quietly. "Besides, I'm flattered." There was a very long silence for a while, then I asked her, "I was just caught a bit… off guard." She apologized again. I just… keep my business, well… like a business." She said that she totally understood and that she hoped I wouldn't think them weird or anything. "Oh, not at all. What people do behind closed doors…" I was sounding like I was discussing it like I knew their private life. I dropped it.

There was a very long period of silence, while I continued her shoulders and back. "I just don't want you to have the wrong idea about us." She said finally.

"I don't have any idea… It's between you guys."

"It's just a stupid fantasy kind of thing." I didn't ask what.

"Perhaps they are better as fantasies anyway." She said at last. I hummed that maybe so. I finished her legs and then held the sheet for her as she rolled over.

"What is your fantasy?" I suddenly blurted, not meaning to. We remained silent for awhile. She then quietly and haltingly told me how they had discussed getting a sensual massage. She was nervous about the details, so I continued to press her gently. She described a scene with soft sexy music, dim lights and lots of candles, and a sexy scene wherein a female masseuse would be topless or nude, and there would be a lot of intimate touching, between all of them. I admitted to myself that it sounded kind of cool and that my husband Josh would probably love such a thing.

She continued that Doug would help massage Diane and then vice versa. She even admitted to being curious about being with another woman. She must have talked for half an hour about what she would like to try and watch her husband try.

I told her that that sounded like a magical anniversary. She admitted that maybe they should keep it as just a fantasy. I asked her if they did want to fulfill this fantasy what they would do about making it happen. She thought they might call an escort service. We left it at that.

Throughout the rest of her massage and Doug's, I kept thinking about them and the way they looked nude. Doug was silent the entire time.

I was becoming intrigued with the idea of them wanting to try something new and erotic; do it together and share the experience. Even after I left their house, I couldn't get it out of my head.

When I got home, the kids were asleep and Josh was reading in bed. I mentioned it to my husband, who was already half-asleep. He told me that it sounded like fun to him, and that I might enjoy it. He rolled over and turned out the light, but that comment kept me up half the night. It sounded like fun to him. And what did he mean I might enjoy it?

To purchase the book, look for **And Masseuse Makes Three.**

* * *

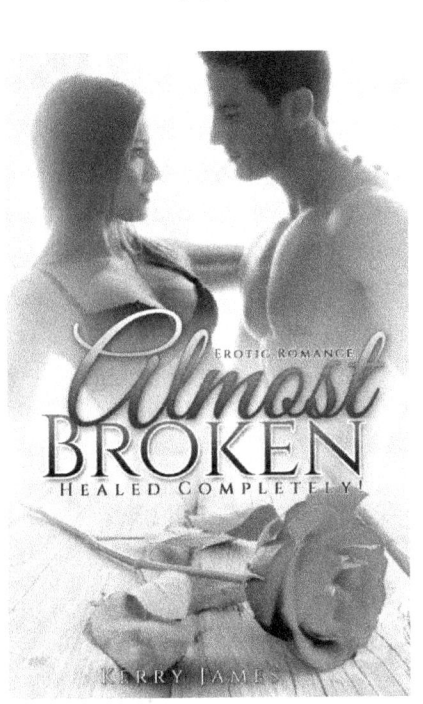

Where does life take us? Why is it that when you have settled on one course, fate comes knocking at your door and takes you off on a tangent? That's what happened to me, it seems to keep happening to me. I get used to my life, and then fate throws a surprise my way. Sometimes it is a little tap-tap on the door, at others it's a loud knock. Sometimes it blows the door open, and when it is really serious fate just takes the thing off with its hinges.

I am Jack Hunter. My life to date had been particularly uneventful, although that would depend on your point of view. I had a wife, and a daughter. I also had an affair which while it didn't become the reason for my divorce, soured me sufficiently to seek to split with my wife. I will hold my hand up and acknowledge that I cheated on my wife. Not a good thing to do, but I will say in my defence that because my wife was in love with the bottle; Vodka and Tonic was her favourite so no one could be actually sure whether she was tippling or not; our love life was virtually zero. It's no easy task to make love to someone who reeks of alcohol. Brenda, my wife didn't appear to be bothered by our lack of intimacy, her next drink was far more important. I tried to get her to admit the problem, her Doctor tried, her mother tried, even our daughter, Libby, only three years old but she understood that something was wrong with mummy. Nothing worked. Despair and frustration were taking my self-esteem to new depths so when I had met a rather lovely lady called Deborah it quickly went from acquaintance to friendship to lovers.

Our affair went on for three years. But when I called quits on my marriage, and as you would expect got taken to the cleaners in the resulting divorce, Deborah made it plain that we were not going to be an item. She came round for the sex but nothing else. Sounds like any man's dream, doesn't it? I had sex on tap and no emotional baggage to go with it. But I was one of those men who wanted emotion in a relationship, so eventually I told her it was over.

The legal process in the UK was slow but exacting. It had however problems in making its judgments effective. I had visiting rights with my daughter, which were denied or delayed for spurious reasons. My solicitor would petition the court again and again to enforce the judgment. The court would confirm the judgment but never took action to ensure it was complied with. So slowly I lost touch with my daughter.

I met Jasmine in a supermarket; I actually helped her with the heavy bags. We had coffee, then dinner and eventually we started sleeping together on occasional nights. We went on like this for five years, until one day I got a fixed penalty speeding fine in the post. The location was not one I had driven through for months, so I queried the penalty. The bloody camera was right, it was my car, but at the time I had been away at a trade show, and I had travelled to the show by train. There was only one person who had access to my house, and the keys to the company car. Jasmine! After a lot of heated arguments she admitted she had 'borrowed' the car. Problem was that she was not insured to drive it, a criminal offence in the UK. If she admitted the offence to the police, chances were that she would certainly be banned from driving, and get a hefty fine. There was also an outside chance of a prison sentence. I paid the fine, took the points on my licence, and Jasmine became history.

A few months after that lesson, I was invited to a party at a friend's house, which was where I met Bridget. We were under no illusions that we had been invited by well-meaning friends who thought that being single was an offence against nature. Well we did hit it off. Remaining friends for nearly ten years, but the tingle was just not there.

To purchase the book, look for **Almost Broken.**